INCINERATOR

A SIMEON GRIST MYSTERY

TIMOTHY HALLINAN

WILLIAM MORROW AND COMPANY, INC.
NEW YORK

Library of Congress Cataloging-in-Publication Data

Hallinan, Timothy.
    Incinerator: a Simeon Grist mystery / by Timothy Hallinan.
        p.   cm.
    ISBN 0-688-10343-X
    I. Title.
PS3558.A3923I5 1992
813'.54--dc20   91-28645
                                                                        CIP

Printed in the United States of America

First Edition

1 2 3 4 5 6 7 8 9 10

BOOK DESIGN BY M. C. DE MAIO

For Pat and Mike,
brothers and friends,
and, still, for Munyin

Acknowledgments

Thanks are overdue for the contributions made to this and previous books by Alex. G. Shulman, M.D., and William Wanamaker, M.D., whose hard-earned medical knowledge I've put to such appalling uses. It wasn't their fault. And acknowledgment, both prior and current, is also due to the person who should certainly hold the Guinness record for the world's briefest phone calls, my ever-understanding agent, Joan Brandt.

PART ONE
IGNITION

In the first moment all was fire, and all shall return to fire.

—Vedic Scripture

When we dream that we are dreaming, the moment of awakening is at hand.

—Novalis

1

First Spark

This is what it said:

You only get to squeeze the bottle four times.
The first two are business. You aim for the clothes.
The third is for fun. Does he have long hair?
You squeeze the bottle the fourth time after you wake him
up, to let him in on the joke. Then you throw the match.
As the flame rises from the offering, the gods of carrion
gather like flies to wheel and circle in the smoke. But they
do not come for the flame. They come for the smoke and the
dirt of the offering, and the offering is carrion. The Flame
purifies it.
The only clean gods are the gods of Fire.
Flame licks the heels of the corrupt gods and consumes their
wings, and they spiral like bats into the Flame. Flame turns
corruption into heat and Light. When the Earth is cleaned of
its corruption, what a Light there will be. It will dim the sun.
There is so much corruption.

The words were written in metallic gold ink on the back of
a brown square of paper cut from a supermarket shopping bag.

The first letter, a capital *Y*, was much larger than the others, set up straight to form a twisted cross in a tiny landscape of flaming hills. At the bottom of the paper, in the same shiny gold, was a very skillful drawing of flames. Arms and legs, inked in vivid colors, protruded from the flames like bits of human barbecue in a demonic illuminated manuscript.

The lines the words formed were painstakingly and precisely parallel. He'd kept both margins plumb-line straight. The text of the letter formed a square that could have been framed with a ruler. The paper had been folded sharply, once in each direction, and the folds intersected in the absolute heart of the square. Once folded, the letter had fitted exactly into the envelope, so tightly that I'd had to tug at it to pull it out.

The paper smelled of gasoline.

Three days earlier, I was relatively certain, the person who wrote the letter had poured gasoline over a sleeping drunk in a doorway somewhere in downtown L.A., and then struck a match.

The letter was addressed to me. At home.

Even though I'm a private detective, I did what anybody else would have done. I called the cops.

"Why you?" Lieutenant Al Hammond asked. Actually, "asked" is a euphemism. Hammond was demanding an answer, not asking for one. He was literally bristling at me. It was a Sunday, and nowadays Hammond didn't shave on weekends. He said it was because he didn't have to, but I figured he'd read a men's cosmetics ad that said that shaving was hard on the skin, and Hammond, recently separated from his wife and reluctantly on the loose in his middle forties, was trying to save his face for anyone who might conceivably be interested in it. Hammond was supposed to be my friend, so he was the cop I'd called. Now he glared at me over a thick, unlit cigar while the other cop in the room downtown, the fat young cop, kept his eyes demurely on the steno pad and took notes. The young cop's name was Willick.

"Hell, Al," I said, yet again, "I suppose it's because of the girl."

Willick scribbled to show how busy he was. His hair, pale and already thinning, framed a face that could have been sculpted from margarine. It melted downward, dripping a tiny, pinched nose that almost touched the upper lip of a mouth made of rubbery fat and as uneven as a discount-store gift bow. The bow had been tied over a dimpled chin that looked as if it puckered easily and a thick, soft neck. It was hot in the room, just as it was everywhere else in L.A., and sweat gleamed on Willick's forehead like congealed cholesterol.

It wasn't hot enough, though, to melt the sliver of chill that had bisected the center of my back ever since I'd opened the letter.

"What girl?" Hammond's eyes, on this hung-over afternoon, were an interesting two-tone scheme, brown and red.

"We're all over the news," I said. "Al, that's why the lunatic wrote me, if it really is the lunatic. Because of who the press is pleased to call the beautiful heiress. The newly orphaned Miss Winston."

The name registered, as it should have. The lady in question was no slouch at breaking print.

"Her father," Hammond said grudgingly, "or something like that."

"Something exactly like that."

Hammond grunted. He had a vast repertoire of grunts, an Esperanto of grunts that was equally understandable in Los Angeles, on Red Square, and in Djakarta, Indonesia. Willick unwisely attempted a matching grunt, part of his cop training. Nettled, Hammond impaled him with a red-rimmed glance and repeated, "Winston." He was circling in on it, in his own fashion.

"*Annabelle* Winston," I said. "Her father got burned like a pile of autumn leaves right here in L.A. early Thursday morning."

"Hey," Willick said, looking up from his notes as the penny dropped. "The Crisper." At least someone on the force was interested.

"Just write," Hammond said shortly.

"The Crisper," I agreed. "The guy who's spent the last couple of months torching the folks who make Skid Row so colorful."

"Three months," Hammond corrected me, to show that he was on the ball.

"This note was from *him*?" Willick asked, alertly if unwisely. His raised eyebrows were engaged in a battle for territory with his hairline. They'd have won if his hairline hadn't been in such hasty retreat.

"Is your pen out of ink?" said Hammond, curling his upper lip nastily. Hammond's upper lip got a lot of use. "Want a pencil?"

"Sorry, Loot," Willick said, redirecting his attention to his pad and pretending to write something.

"Lieu*tenant*," Hammond corrected him.

"Look, Loot," I said, "this is Sunday."

"Jesus," Hammond said, slamming a hand over his heart with a thump that sounded like Dumbo landing. "Glad I'm sitting down. Look, work out a signal, willya? Wave a hand or something next time you're gonna drop a bombshell."

"He had to deliver it himself," I said. Hammond's expression didn't change. He still looked sour. "He had to put it into my mailbox."

Hammond gave me a heavy nod. "Must be why she hired you," he said. "Brains like that. Wish we had that kind of intellect on the force."

"You've been to my house, Al." Willick's eyes widened. He started to take a note, but Hammond grabbed his hand. Hammond didn't want our personal relationship on the record. "How many houses are there on my street? Five," I answered myself, since Hammond didn't look like he wanted to play. "And it's a dead end."

"Yeah, yeah, yeah," Hammond said, anticipating me.

"What I'm suggesting," I began.

"I said yeah," Hammond said gruffly.

I wanted the idea to find its way into Willick's notebook, so I plowed on. "I just thought maybe it would have occurred to the LAPD to check with my neighbors, see if they saw a car they didn't recognize. One of them might even have seen the driver. Of course, this suggestion is made in all humility, from one with no experience of the inside workings of a great police force."

Hammond gave me a silent-movie squint that said, *Don't push it*. He hated it when I got ahead of him. Add that to a hangover that would have felled a twenty-mule team, and he was operating under a lot of disadvantages.

"We're doing it," he said, accompanying the words with a curt little gesture that told Willick to write. If they weren't doing it already, they soon would be.

"I figured you were," I said to pacify him.

"Winston," Hammond growled, giving me what was for him a gentle prompt. "I'm not exactly at my best, you know."

Indeed he wasn't. He'd been royally blistered the night before, which was the last time I'd seen him, and I hadn't been notably abstemious myself.

"Abraham Winston," I said charitably, even though Hammond's headache was no worse than mine. It couldn't have been.

"Ex-something," Hammond prodded me. As always, he looked as though he'd been sewn into a very large suit and then inflated like a balloon in the Macy's parade.

"Ex-a lot of things," I said. Hammond's sheer size always cowed me slightly. "Ex-Weinstein, for example. Also ex-financier, ex-entrepreneur, ex–charitable donor, ex–big deal Chicago businessman. And, until the Crisper picked him out of ten or twenty bums lining various doorways, he was a present-tense alcoholic transient, and maybe someone with an advanced case of Alzheimer's disease. What do you think, Al? *Is* this note from the Crisper?"

"And Baby hired you," he said, ignoring my question in practiced cop style and giving the lady the name the tabloids had saddled her with since she was fifteen. He already knew she had; he was just keeping the conversation going while he waited for some of his brain cells to come back from vacation.

"Baby did," I said. "Baby Winston, Annabelle Winston."

"And that was a big flash here in L.A.," Hammond said. "Hold the presses."

"Slow news day," I said, "plus big money. Baby Winston paid a lot of money, a *whole* lot of money, Al, to some PR man who called a press conference to announce that the L.A. cops couldn't do the job and so she'd hired the guy who just broke up the big, mean kiddie prostitution ring. Meaning me. And the TV stations ran the story, and the papers printed my name, and that's why the Crisper wrote me the letter. If it really was the Crisper. It wasn't my idea that she should go to the press, and you damn well know it. I had no idea she was going to do it."

Hammond rested his heavy head in his hands, breaking his cigar on the point of his chin, and burped. Blanching, Willick watched one of his idols hike his cuffs to reveal clay, cop-sized feet. "Okay," Hammond said without looking up, "let's take it from the beginning."

2

Annabelle

"My father was a great man," Annabelle Winston had said on the preceding day.

There's not much you can say when someone tells you her father was a great man. For one thing, she's almost always wrong. Baby Winston being Baby Winston, though, I'd tried to look interested.

It wasn't just that Baby was the best-dressed woman I'd ever seen, which she probably was, or the best-looking, which she wasn't. My ex-girlfriend, Eleanor Chan, was better looking. But combine the second-best-looking woman I'd ever seen with the best-dressed, and you had, as a friend of mine named Dexter Smif might have said, powerful juju. And so I sat there and wondered what the point was.

She was wearing a hand-sewn silk suit that was greener than the Sargasso Sea. The combination of the suit plus her reddish hair and perfectly white skin was what the people who designed the Italian flag had been trying for. Under the reddish hair was a broad, unlined forehead and a pair of eyebrows that tilted up at the ends. The eyebrows set the stage for wide-spaced gray eyes as reflective and as communicative as a cop's sunglasses. There was a nice little accidental bump, like a glitch in an otherwise perfect blueprint, on the bridge of her nose, and she wore one superfluous layer of dark lipstick. The lipstick decorated a mouth that was about as yielding as the Maginot Line. In all, she was the most tightly wrapped human being I'd ever met. Including cops. Male cops. If I'd had to guess an age, I'd have said thirty-two.

"So this is about your father," I said at last, sounding to myself like a shrink who was in the wrong line of work.

She took a breath and then blew it out without putting words in front of it. The suite in which she'd set up camp was one of the Bel Air Hotel's best, full of hand-carved rosewood furniture, Chinese antiques, and a baby grand, perched on a carpet deep enough to lose your keys in. It had a name on the door rather than a number.

"Drink?" she offered, backing away from whatever she had been going to say. It was about noon.

"I'll wait. What about your father?"

She gave me the gray eyes. "He was set on fire here," she said in a matter-of-fact voice. "Day before yesterday."

"Love a drink," I said. "What have you got?"

"Absinthe to Sambucco," she said. There was no feminine litter in the suite, no open suitcases, no little silver picture frames, nothing personal at all: just two open lizard-skin briefcases full of tidy, sharp-edged manila folders. Unruly papers were not permitted to peep out of the folders. One of the cases was on the table in front of me. The other was on the piano.

"How about a beer?" She followed my gaze and closed the briefcase protectively to prevent me from exercising my X-ray vision on the manila. Her nail polish looked like Chinese lacquer, and it matched her lipstick. Like the lipstick, it was too dark, and the nails were a quarter-inch too long. Whatever she did, she didn't do her own plumbing.

"Sure," I said. "Whatever's on hand." Singha, from Thailand, was too much to hope for.

"Would you like a Singha?" she asked, snapping the latch on the briefcase closed like someone arming a land mine. "From Thailand?" She didn't even smile.

She had my attention. "You have no idea how much I know about you," she said in the same even voice. "You're easy."

There were two things I wanted to do: get up and leave. I did neither. "And you've been spending money. What's my inseam?"

She measured me with her eyes. There was nothing personal in it. "Thirty-three. And you like a break in the trouser leg."

"I'd like a break at this very moment. For example, where's the beer?"

"On ice," she said, "like my father." The sentence couldn't have been flatter if a grammarian had ironed it. No untidy emotion threatened the symmetry of her face.

"If you don't mind, I think I'd like the beer before we get to your father."

She got up from the couch, a green steel bouquet on the move, and crossed the beige suite to the discreet rosewood wet bar in the fewest possible number of steps. A straight line from point to point. She was the kind of trim that you don't get for free. Air-conditioning thrummed a muted bass chord, filtering out the blistering October heat and the acrid stench of smoke from the burning hills. They call October in L.A. "the fire season." It's a euphemism. A bad October, and this was a very bad one, is a month of fearsome, random firefall: Black ashes flutter down from the sky, to paraphrase Dickens, like snowflakes gone into mourning for the death of the sun.

Except that in L.A., we get the sun, too, drying the air and driving the winds, fierce Santa Ana winds that clear the smog and then fan the flames to spread dark streaks of smudge across the skies like finger marks on a wall. In October the pool cleaners of Beverly Hills work overtime, straining ashes from the surface of placid blue water.

Annabelle Winston pressed a cold bottle of Singha into my hand and sat down beside me. "Drink it," she said in a voice that brooked no objection, "and then we'll talk."

"You're not having anything?"

"No," she said. "I don't need it." She used the tip of one of those nails to remove an imaginary fleck of something from the corner of her mouth. The mouth was her problem, from an aesthetic perspective. With a little less lipstick and a little more smile, it would have been quite a mouth.

"I'm not exactly sure I need it, either," I said. "I *want* it, since you offered, but when I need it, I'll probably quit."

"What I need," she said, all focus, "is a detective. I've chosen you."

I sighed. "Set on fire," I said.

She gave a tiny nod. Nothing changed in her eyes. She kept all her movements small, as though she were conserving her energy for whatever was going on inside.

"Still alive?"

Annabelle Winston twirled a ring on her right hand. The stone was an emerald. "In a manner of speaking," she said, looking down at the ring. Emeralds are basically corundum, same as sapphires and rubies, but even more expensive. She regarded it as though she were trying to figure out why it was green, rather than blue or red.

"What does that mean?"

She turned the stone inward and closed her hand over it protectively. "It means his vital signs are being monitored and, to whatever extent it's possible, maintained. It means they're pumping fluids into him to keep him peeing because that means his life isn't evaporating faster than he can replenish it. That's what happens when our skin is gone, you know. We evaporate. I don't suppose that's common knowledge, is it? They've put a plastic shell above him, like the spatter shield over a salad bar, to slow the evaporation." She looked at the stone folded into her palm as though she could see through her fingers, using the other hand to pick at the corner of her mouth again, although she knew nothing was there. "It means that one or two days and a few hundred thousand dollars from now, he'll be dead." Except for the nervous finger at her lips, there was still no sign of emotion.

"Where did it happen?"

Now she looked at me. "Skid Row."

"Miss Winston," I said, "if you can afford this suite, why was your father on Skid Row?"

"Why was he in Los Angeles, you mean," she said. She picked up a black lacquered box and took out a cigarette, then lit it with a filigreed gold lighter. The hand was as steady as a dial tone. Belatedly, she offered me one. I shook my head. I wanted one, but I'd quit again.

She turned the ring back around and addressed the emerald. "He was here because he got lost, Mr. Grist. He got lost on his daily walk in Chicago when his male nurse stepped into a bar for a couple of quick ones. Isn't that what they call it, 'a couple of quick ones'? The nurse didn't stop knocking back his quick ones until he realized Daddy was gone. Then, according to the police in Chicago, he went to the station and got on a train going somewhere."

"Where?"

She gave me an economical shrug. "They've narrowed it down to east, west, north, and south." The coal on her cigarette glowed, and she blew smoke professionally out through her nostrils.

"Why'd he do that? Why didn't he report your father missing?"

"Because he knew I'd kill him." There was no attempt at drama in her voice. She might have been reading the farm report.

She tapped the cigarette into the ashtray at precisely the right moment. Another second, and ash would have tumbled into her lap. "My father was Abraham Winston, once." A minor chord sounded in her voice, and I recognized it as fierceness. "When he was still Abraham Winston, he built a dirty little grocery store in the poorest, blackest part of Chicago into a chain of sixty-two supermarkets. Then he decided to make some *real* money. He bought up the ranches that supplied the meat and the farms that supplied the produce. He bought canning factories and dairies. He owned the companies that made the paper for the shopping bags that women put his vegetables and meat and milk into. He was a man who liked to own things."

"When did he stop being Abraham Winston?"

"Not all at once," she said. Then she closed the gray eyes for a second. When she opened them, they were clear and dry. "Drink your beer. And I've changed my mind, which was supposed to be a woman's prerogative, back when women still had them." She gave me the wisp of a smile.

She got up and went again to the bar, where she poured a finger of bourbon into a heavy cut-glass tumbler. She lifted the glass in a mock toast and drank all the whiskey at once. Her throat hardly moved. Even Hammond would have been impressed.

"He went into commodities after my mother died," she said, pouring another. "That was three years ago. He'd done most of what he did for her, my analyst says, and she wasn't around anymore. I guess the satisfaction of it died when she did. And there wasn't a son, of course."

"I wouldn't know." I swallowed some beer, just to be polite. Okay, that's a lie. I needed it.

"Well, there wasn't. There was only me. Only Baby." She pronounced her nickname with the kind of venom one associates with the more effective Islamic curses. "Not that any of this matters now. I was enough, as it turned out. But after she, meaning Mommy, was gone, it wasn't enough for him to own everything in the present tense. He had to have a piece of the future, too. That way, you see, he could own time. Time was his enemy. It had given him almost everything he ever wanted, thought he wanted, anyway, and then it took away his reason for having wanted it in the first place. Mommy, I mean. Leaving only a few hundred million dollars and me." She emitted a short, ugly laugh and took a swallow, a sip this time, from her glass.

"And?"

"And what?" She arched an eyebrow. A single eyebrow; more economy. Whatever it was that was going on inside, it needed most of her energy. "There are a million ways I could answer that."

"So choose the one that appeals to you."

She lifted the green silk shoulders a quarter of an inch and let them fall again. "Do you know much about commodities?"

"I don't even know what they are." I pulled at the beer again.

She was leaning against the bar with both elbows. It was supposed to look relaxed. "They're futures, bets against the future. Choose an item, pork bellies or platinum or September wheat, and bet which way the prices are going to go x number of months from now. Rise or fall, it doesn't make any difference, as long as you bet right. Bet right, you make a million dollars."

"Bet wrong and you eat the big patootie," I ventured, drinking again.

"This is a small part of the story," she said, straightening up. "I hope you're not in a hurry."

"You said a hundred an hour to talk," I said. "I'm not getting fidgety."

"Good. I want you to understand." She took another judicious sip. "You don't like me."

It was my turn to shrug. "Your father apparently got burned pretty badly two days ago. Without any attempt to be offensive, you don't seem exactly desolate."

"I haven't the time to be desolate," she said. "I told you there wasn't a son. I'm it. I'm Winston Enterprises." She tossed a hand toward the briefcases as though several thousand tiny employees were slaving busily away inside them. "I've got too much to do to be desolate, or to waste the day trying to make you like me. All I want to do is sell you on helping me."

"Sell me?"

"You're stubborn, they told me," she continued. "They told me that you worked on that case with the little kids even after you lost your client. 'He has to be interested,' they said." She tapped out a military drumroll on her glass with the formidable fingernails.

"Who are *they*?" I asked. "And why not hire them?"

She put the glass against her cheek as though it cooled her, although she looked cool enough already. "Who says I haven't?"

I looked at my watch. "Call it an hour," I said, putting down the beer and getting up. "You can mail the check."

"Sit down." She pointed to the couch with the hand holding the glass. The glass was heavy, but it was a truly imperial gesture, a gesture that belonged to the days of the Holy Roman Empire.

I stayed on my feet. "Skip it. I have a policy. It's called staying alive. And it means that I don't get involved if anyone else is."

"And why not?"

"Fuckups," I said. "If anyone's going to fuck up, it's going to be me. At least that way I know there's been a fuckup."

What she did with her face wasn't exactly a smile, but it was the closest thing I'd seen in a few minutes. "That's a good answer," she said. "A good business answer."

"Thanks. Call me after you fire them."

"I haven't hired them. I didn't say I'd hired them. I said, Who says I haven't."

"Eleven hundred and thirty-two," I said. I was still standing.

"What?"

"That's how many angels can dance on the head of a pin. Medieval theological mystery. 'How many angels can dance on the head of a pin?' The answer is eleven hundred and thirty-two. Exactly. Anyone gives you a different number, he's wrong. Or, on the other hand, maybe he's lying. Or maybe *I'm* wrong. Trouble is, who can tell the difference?"

"There isn't anybody else." The imperial gesture had been a dud, so she reversed tactics. She went to the couch herself and sat down, going for submissive instead. She was surprisingly good at it. She gazed up at me, looking like the Little Match Girl with only one match left.

"Is there going to be?"

A minute shake of the head. "Not as long as you're on the job." She stretched out a green silk arm and patted the couch next to her, and I sat back down. How often do you get a chance to say yes to silk?

"I'm insulated," she said, putting a hand on my wrist. "It's the nature of money. I can't help it." This time both eyebrows went up to show me how insulated she was and how much she couldn't help it. "Everybody pretends he wants something different, except that it always comes down to the same thing. Money. Please. Please, Mr. Grist. What was I supposed to do?"

I sighed. "Nobody else is on the job."

"Nobody." Her fingers tightened on my wrist as though she were afraid I was going to run. I couldn't tell whether the gesture was a real impulse or just the next card off the top of the deck. She seemed to have the fullest deck this side of Las Vegas.

"Nobody except the entire LAPD," I said.

"Them," she said dismissively. "How long has this been going on? Five people are already dead. Burned to death on the sidewalk, for God's sake. If it hadn't been for an old lady, my father would be dead now, too. What does it take to get their attention? If somebody set up Auschwitz on Sixth Street, it would be a year before they noticed, as long as nobody respectable got burned. When you talk to them, if you have to, they won't know what you're talking about. The case doesn't matter to them. The homeless don't pay taxes."

She released my wrist and gave me a full-bore twelve-gauge gaze.

"Will you do it?" she said.

My wrist felt cool now that her hand was gone. I rubbed it once and then reached over and picked up the beer. I hadn't decided, but I was open to persuasion. Fire is an awful way to die.

"Tell me what happened to him," I said. "Not how he got burned, but—"

"Commodities," she said promptly. "I suppose that was the first thing. He ate enough of the—what did you call it?"

"The big patootie."

"Enough of the big patootie to make him feel mortal. Financially mortal, at any rate. He'd been feeling personally mortal ever since my mother died, but that was the first time he'd been wrong in a business sense. He dropped about seven million pretax dollars."

I probably winced.

"He didn't say anything at the time—he never said much about anything that was bothering him," she said, settling herself further into the cushions and clinking her glass against mine in a neighborly fashion.

Obediently, I drank. I felt like a good puppy. "My father believed in good news or no news where his family was concerned," she said. Around the next mouthful of whiskey, she added, "He was the wall around us. The Great Wall of the Winstons." She put the glass down, and I swallowed some beer. "But he began to drink more than his usual one or two cognacs after dinner, and he started putting in fourteen-hour days instead of his usual twelve, and about a month later he had a stroke. Such a calm word, stroke. It sounds like something you do to a cat."

The best thing I could think of was to take another sip of beer. She did the same with her whiskey and then poured more. She'd brought the bottle to the table.

"Nothing serious," she continued. "Completely reversible. That's what the doctors said, reversible." Her voice could have grated Mozzarella. "But what does *reversible* mean? He got back his speech and the use of his legs, but he was *older*. He started to dodder. Do you know what I mean?"

I nodded and drank.

Annabelle Winston gave me the agate-gray eyes, full-on. "So that was when I began to get involved, not that I wanted to. I had to. I wasn't the son he'd been supposed to have, and he wasn't the kind of man who could hide his disappointment that I wasn't, but there wasn't anything else he could do. It was me or some accountant. He chose me." She sounded like an abandoned child. I took refuge in my glass.

"And I did what I could," she added, ignoring my reaction. "It was a big business, about three hundred million a year at the time, and I set out to learn it the same way I'd learned my *ABC*s. First you memorize, and then you try to use what you've learned. I was up to about *D* when he had the second stroke, and he had the third one six hours later. He hadn't even left the hospital."

She stretched out long, thin, elegantly articulated fingers and used them to rub her eyes. "This is *his* story," she said, "not mine. Winston Enterprises was—is—a conglomerate, and it was more complicated than world-class Parcheesi. Still, you have to understand something about me. I sat next to him, on a chair next to his bed with a dopey schoolgirl's pad and a cheap ballpoint pen in my hand, locking my ankles together for months, bleeding him dry. He couldn't see my ankles. I couldn't let him see them. If he'd seen them, they would have been a dead giveaway. If he'd seen them, he would have stopped talking. I was too anxious, and my ankles gave it away. So I kept them under the bed. I couldn't let him stop talking, I had to understand what was what and what was where. There's no dramatic punch line here. The ankles were my problem."

She took another belt of whiskey, and I snuck a look at her ankles. They weren't locked together. "He got more and more vague," she said over the rim of her glass. "He stopped caring if they shaved him in the morning. He began to call me by my mother's name." She paused again, looking at the pattern cut into the glass. "Then he began to call me Joshua."

"Who's Joshua?" The sun was doing a depressive slant through the windows, and I'd stopped counting the hours, even at a hundred dollars per. She hadn't gotten up to turn on the lights, and the tasteful rosewood furniture was beginning to disappear into the walls. From my perspective, it looked better that way.

"There wasn't any Joshua," she said in a muffled voice. "Joshua was the name he and my mother had chosen for me if I'd been a boy."

I waited for another piece of upholstery to fade and listened to my watch ticking. "He invented a son," I said to animate the silence.

"He reeled in the past," she said, "and cast it out again, and when his hook came back to him, it had an imaginary son at the end of it."

"You."

"You can't imagine how I hated it. 'Joshua this, Joshua that,' he'd say. 'Joshua, guard the money.' I mean, I answered to the name anyway, but I went to bed every night and before I fell asleep, I killed the brother I'd never had, over and over again. God, if you could be punished for imaginary murder." She drained the whiskey.

"You can't. Except in your imagination." I held out my empty glass, and she took it.

"If you could, my father would have outlived me," she said. She seemed to have forgotten that she was about to make the economical trip to the bar. "There I sat at his bed, me, Joshua Winston, learning the business."

"I'm sorry," I said.

She gazed at me, gray-eyed, through the gloom for so long that it made me feel uncomfortable. "Are you," she finally said, almost grudgingly. "Yes, maybe you are." She got up at last.

"Miss Winston. I may not be rich, but I've got parents."

"You're an actual person," she said, halfway to the bar. "Aren't you?"

"On my better days."

Stopping, she treated me to another mininod. "So he got worse," she said. The bar gave her a silent hello, and she ignored it. "The ludicrous thing was that he got stronger physically as he got weaker mentally," she said, both glasses, hers and mine, in hand. "After the second series of strokes he could barely lift an arm, but his mind was sharp. Later, when his mind was going, his body came back to him. Toward the end, he could have qualified for the Olympic hurdles, but he couldn't have found the starting line." She covered the rest of the distance to the bar in the same straight, economical course; Columbus had sailed that straight for the Indies, steering dead-on for China. Of course, he hadn't known that a continent had drifted into his way. Something very large had obviously drifted into Annabelle Winston's way.

"Therefore, the male nurse," I said as she poured.

"Harvey Melnick," she said, "may his soul roast."

"Who was he?"

"Who knows? Somebody with a résumé. Big, which was important because, like I said, Daddy was strong. One gold earring. The earring should have told me." She hoisted both glasses to show me they were full, navigated the room, and sat on the couch.

"There's nothing you can do about it now." I took the beer away from her.

"I need your skills," Annabelle Winston said in a brittle voice. Her body had gone rigid, and she sat back. "I don't need your comfort."

"Hey," I said, "we're both real people."

She stood up suddenly and turned away from me. She didn't go anywhere. She just stood there with her back to me while the light waned and the Bel Air's highly paid birds twittered and whistled outside. "Excuse me," she finally said.

"Excused. Take your time."

"There isn't time," she said. "I want the shithead nailed." Her back was as rigid as rigor mortis.

"Despite the gold earring, you hired Harvey," I said to her back. Then I reached out and tugged at her arm.

She swiveled as though her arm were a rope and she were a floating boat at its other end. There was moisture on her face. "Daddy needed someone twenty-four hours a day," she said defensively. "At night, we could use women. In the daytime, we needed a man."

"Why?"

"He wanted to go to the store." Slowly, grudgingly, she sat down beside me.

I listened to the words again, sifting them for sense. "What store?"

"The first one." She gave her cheeks a proprietary little wipe. "The little grocery store. We'd sold it years ago, of course. He'd wake up in the morning saying he'd forgotten to take inventory. Inventory, inventory. He had to count the cans, he said. Every can of soup was twelve cents. By then he was worth maybe four hundred million dollars. He'd lost all that. Mentally, I mean. He was back in the time when every twelve cents could be squirreled away for little Joshua's education. He kept talking about the day he'd be able to buy my mother a fur coat. 'She should be wrapped in fur,' he said. When my mother died, we had an apartment with a walk-in freezer that was used for nothing but to store her fur coats. My mother had more fur coats than the Russian imperial family."

"So Harvey took him to the store every day," I said. "But there wasn't any store."

"I bought one."

"I beg your pardon?"

She took another cigarette from the box and lit it. "I bought a store. The one he'd started in was gone, but I bought one near it. In a black area, just like the first one. It opened at nine, about half an hour before my father arrived. It closed half an hour after he finished taking inventory, the minute we knew he was around the corner. We never sold anything, of course. I wrote it off as a business loss. The IRS never asked a question. Anyway, the costs were nothing. All we ever really needed was someone to dust the cans and replace the meat and vegetables once in a while. After we gave them away."

"Why didn't you leave it open? Sell stuff?"

"His inventory would have been off," she said. "He had an inventory from some day in the past, a Tuesday or whatever, stuck in his head like Moses' tablets. At first we operated it like a real store. We bought and sold. But he got so upset because the numbers didn't work out that one day he knocked everything off the shelves and sat in one of the aisles, crying. That night I made him write the whole inventory down. It took hours, but I didn't mind because it was like being with my father again, before . . . well, before. He remembered *everything*, every tiny detail. After he went to sleep, we worked all night to stock that store. By the time he arrived the next morning, the inventory matched. I'd made goddamn sure it matched. We kept it that way for more than a year."

"A museum."

"The world's first grocery museum. The last, too, I suppose. And I was the curator."

"You must have loved him very much."

She stubbed out the unsmoked cigarette. "Don't make me get up again," she said. "He's still alive, for the moment, at least. I still love him. How could I not love him? This was a man who bought a hundred Christmas trees every year, *and* all the presents under them, and had them delivered to poor families in Chicago. And he was a Jew, for Christ's sake."

"How did he know what to buy?" I asked, fascinated in spite of myself.

"He hired Santas and put them into the worst neighborhoods. The Santas had big bellies with little tape recorders hidden in them. After they talked to a particularly sweet little kid, the Santas were supposed to ask them their full names and where they lived. On Christmas Eve, Daddy or one of his Christmas crews would show up, all dressed like Santa, with the whole shebang. The tree, all the presents the kid had asked for, something practical for the parents. He made a ceremony of telling Mommy and me about it the next morning. Christmas morning. He'd drink his eggnog with cognac and tell us about Christmas Eve. That was our Christmas. Hearing Daddy talk about what happened after they knocked on the doors in their red suits and their white beards, and what the people said and how the kids acted. It was the kids who got to him. Sometimes he cried like a baby. They really killed him. Oh, Lord," she said, getting up again. "Oh, Lord. Just sit there and don't say anything."

She had her back turned to me, her shoulders stiff and high. I tried not to say anything and failed. "You never got anything for Christmas?"

"My whole life was Christmas," she said without turning around. "I was Santa's daughter. I was one of the elves." She lowered her head, and her shoulders began to shake.

She needed something to do. "I'd like another beer," I said.

Annabelle caught her breath with a rasping sound. "Easily arranged," she said. She was herself again, or close enough to fool someone who wasn't paying attention. "This is the last, I think. Shall I call down for more?" She went to the bar and opened the door of the refrigerator.

"This is it. I've got an evening in front of me."

"Lucky you," she said. "I've got a sleeping pill." I would have traded my evening for her sleeping pill. It was nothing I looked forward to. She uncapped the beer, reached for a glass, dropped the cap into the wastebasket with a metallic ping of precision, blinked, and said, "So we got Harvey, and Harvey took him to the store every morning. That was Harvey's whole job. Not such a hard job, would you think? And one day Harvey didn't come back, and neither did Daddy. We hired the world to find him. Hundreds of people. Then I got the call from L.A. saying some bum has been burned half to death and he's got a MedicAlert bracelet, the bracelet Daddy wore because of the Alzheimer's, identifying him as Abraham Winston. Do I think the bracelet might have been stolen? Well, I don't know where Daddy is, so my first impulse was to believe that the bracelet was wherever he was. And I came here, and it took me an hour to recognize him. He didn't look like Santa Claus any more."

She sat down on the couch, and both she and the upholstery sighed. The bottle trembled in her hand. "Will you help me?"

"I thought we'd settled that," I said. "I'm going to try."

"Oh," she said, and she leaned forward until her forehead touched her knees. "Oh."

I didn't want to ask, but I had to. "Was his face burned?"

"No," Baby Winston said, without straightening. "Only the lower two thirds of his body. But they were third-degree burns." She was talking to her lap.

"Then why did it take you an hour to recognize him?"

She remained folded forward, tighter than a jackknife. "Let's hope you never have to find out," she said.

3

Al the Red

That evening I had a prearranged date with Hammond. The bar called the Red Dog glares out onto a block of Hollywood Boulevard that only the most foolhardy walk at night—the most foolhardy and cops. Not that the two categories are mutually exclusive.

The Red Dog has a corny sawdust floor and a sixties jukebox, recycling hits from the Summer of Love at numbing volume. The latest hits reach cops last, and it's probably a good thing. Otherwise they'd be able to figure out what the rest of us are up to.

Hammond had a red kerchief tied crookedly around his head when I walked in. It wasn't a good sign. His broad face, shadowed with a day's worth of whiskers, gleamed with sweat and malice, and he had a drink in each of his ham-sized hands.

"God damn," he said. He darted a glance at me and missed by about a yard. "I was afraid I'd have to drink both of these."

"What a fate," I said, taking the nearer of the two. It was sweating more heavily than Hammond. After all the beer I didn't want it, but it seemed like good policy to slow Hammond down. "Nice hat, Al."

"I'm a pirate," he announced vehemently. "Al the Red." He looked around for someone to contradict him.

"Shiver me timbers. Where's your parrot?" The whiskey tasted like recycled perspiration: flat, malodorous, and for some reason slightly salty.

"Don't need no fucking parrot. Parrots got lice."

"That a fact?"

"Every parrot I ever knew. Al the Red is a bad guy, but he doesn't have lice. Lice, they'll eat your peg leg right out from under you."

"I thought that was termites."

"Termites eat *houses*," Hammond said with leaden patience. "Lice eat peg legs. Termites I got. They ate my whole fucking house already."

"Al," I said as gently as possible. "You've still got your house."

"Who said anything about houses?" Hammond asked belligerently. "Al the Red lives on a ship." He tugged the kerchief to a more rakish angle. "What the fuck good is a house? Can you take it anywhere? Huh? Can you sail your house into a harbor and fire cannons at the civilians?" He drained his drink, leaned toward me, and tapped the back of my hand meaningfully. It felt like a hammer. His eyes narrowed. "Can a house do twenty knots?"

It was going to be a long night.

"Where's your crew?" I asked, and instantly kicked myself under the table. It was the wrong thing to ask.

"Deserted," Red Al said. "Every man jack of them. Every woman jack, too. Desertion. That's the trouble with houses. They're too easy to leave." His eyes closed heavily, and he rested his big forehead on the rim of his glass. I glanced around for help and didn't find any. Cops avoided my eyes. Our table reminded me of the drop of penicillin in the center of a petri dish: The area around it was a vacuum, vacated by the swarms who had withdrawn to the walls, cops and cop groupies carrying on earnest conversations over the din of the music—by now it was Sly & the Family Stone. I searched for the black cop who might have dropped that particular quarter and didn't find him. He was hiding. Like everybody else.

Hammond lifted his head. The circular impression of the glass was printed on his forehead, like a target. He squeezed his eyes shut, opened his mouth, and bellowed, *"PEPPI!"*

Peppi, the barmaid, was as butch as Hammond but a lot smaller. I'd never been sure which of the two I'd rather fight. She materialized at a safe distance from the table and said, "Yeah?" She'd traded in her trademark black net stockings for a pair of silvery Spandex tights under six inches of black cloth. It hadn't been a wise fashion decision. From the waist down, she looked like two fish trapped in a miniskirt.

"Al the Red is thirsty," Hammond said in an eminently reasonable tone of voice. "So is his first mate."

"Comin' up." Peppi wheeled to go, and Hammond leaned forward and grabbed a fistful of her short skirt. Peppi stopped shorter than a fishing weight at the end of a snarled line. "Hey," she snarled.

"Peppi," Hammond said. "Tell you what. Make a woman of you."

"I've already taken that course," Peppi said. "I changed majors."

"Try a real man," Hammond said. He gave her a lopsided leer.

"Find one," Peppi said, tugging her skirt free with red-knuckled hands. "Just find one."

Hammond directed his gaze toward her silver knees and winked appreciatively. He was even drunker than I'd thought. "Great gams," he said inaccurately.

"You," Peppi said, looking at me. "You. First mate."

I looked up.

"Take care of him," she said.

"*Me?*" Hammond said, pounding the table with a fist slightly smaller than West Virginia. "Take care of Al the Red? Nobody born can take care of Al the Red."

"Yeah," said Peppi, who had never liked me. "That's why I picked him."

Hammond gave up. "Grog," he said. "Posthaste." Peppi marched off, and he looked up at me balefully, "Am I making an asshole of myself?"

"Yes," I said.

"Well, fuck it," he said. "And fuck you, too, while I'm at it. I won't remember in the morning. Funny what you remember and what you forget."

I agreed that it was funny and then tried to do some business.

"Listen," I shouted over Gary Lewis and the Playboys or someone like that, "what do you know about this guy who's setting fire—"

"The paper plates," Hammond said. "Did I tell you about the paper plates?"

I shelved my question and shook my head. The paper plates were a new wrinkle.

"I get home," Hammond said, taking the glass from my hand and draining it in a single gulp, "and the door's open." He looked down at the two empty glasses in front of him. "Where's the goddamn grog?"

"Coming."

"That's what's wrong with grog. It takes too long. I don't know how Francis Drake did it, waiting all day for his fucking grog. Do you think Francis Drake ever got home and found the door open?"

"No," I said. "His boat would have sunk."

Hammond licked a finger and made an imaginary mark in the air. "One for you," he said. "Problem was, I was living in a house, not a boat. I mean, what's it supposed to sink into, the lawn? Nothing ever sank into a lawn."

"Newspapers do. Every morning. They sink completely out of sight."

"So I get home," he said, ignoring me, "maybe eleven o'clock, maybe later. I mean, I'd been out drinking, but nothing new. Did it every night. Same as you. Everybody does."

So far, except for the paper plates, we were on familiar territory. Everybody didn't, of course, but most cops did. They had to. Whiskey was the anesthetic that made it possible for them to get home and pretend for their children's sake that the world was sane.

"And the door's open." Hammond belched. "There's light pouring through the door. Hazel never left the lights on. She's the original Scrooge McDuck. She thinks every time she turns off a light it's a hundred in the bank. All for little Al's college."

I thought about Annabelle Winston and the twelve cents per can and kept my mouth shut.

"But that night it's like she's watering the lawn with light," he said. "So I did what anybody would do. I grabbed a .45 and headed for the front door. Have I told you this before?"

"No," I lied.

"Good. I may be an asshole, but I don't want to be boring. So I hold my breath and kick the front door the rest of the way open. God only knows what I expected to find. A bunch of fundamentalist towel-heads maybe, or the Mansonoids who got away." Like most cops, Hammond believed that the majority of the Manson Family, or, for that matter, Butch Cassidy's gang, were still on the loose. "And there's nothing inside, and I mean nothing. It looked like a surgery room. Where's that goddamn grog?"

"Behind you," Peppi said. She plunked down a couple of glasses that held, conservatively, triples.

"About time, too," Hammond said. "Next time I'll have my parrot make it." Peppi gave me a concerned look and headed for the relative security of the bar.

Hammond hoisted his drink and knocked back half of it. I drank most of mine and put the rest closer to him. He'd drink it eventually. The whiskey sang off-key in my veins. He hunched his massive shoulders up around his ears, making his neck disappear completely, and said, "A moving van. She hired a fucking moving van. All that was left was my chair, the stuff in my den, and a couple guns. Hazel never liked the guns. Also my bed. Did I tell you we slept in twin beds?"

"Better that way," I said. "Women have cold feet."

"Hazel has feet like the polar ice cap. It was like sleeping with Greenland." He finished his drink and stared at what was left of mine. I put it into his hand.

"Not drinking?" he said. He didn't really care.

"I already had a few."

"Who was buying?"

"Client."

"Anything for the cops?"

"Yeah. About this pyromaniac who's torching the homeless."

I might as well have been Demosthenes at the seaside, waiting for applause from the waves. Hammond's kerchief had slipped down over his left eye, and he tugged it upward. "Where'd this come from?" he asked, looking up at it.

"Al the Red," I said, abandoning the topic. "Scourge of the Caribbean."

"Bet your ass," he said. "There's not a palm tree safe."

"Well, what are they good for anyway?"

"Target practice." He made a pistol out of his hand, sighted over it, and said, *"KABOOOM!"* People gave us nervous looks. It takes a lot to make a roomful of drunk cops nervous, but whatever it takes, Hammond had it.

He blew on his fingers to disperse the smoke. "She took the kids, of course," he said.

"She would," I said. "She's their mother."

"Yeah?" he said. "What'm I, an unindicted coconspirator?" He drained the drink and signaled for two more.

We'd had this discussion before. "You said something about paper plates," I said.

"Wrapped in cellophane." He closed his eyes for a long time, and I hoped he'd gone to sleep. "With little blue flowers on them," he added, eyes still shut. "On the sink, right where the real plates would have been if she hadn't taken them. My mother gave us those plates. Did I tell you my mother's on Hazel's side?"

Peppi clunked a couple of drinks onto the table, and Hammond opened his eyes and put four ounces of whiskey into the realm of memory. I took a whack off the other one. I was getting drunk.

"So what was I supposed to think?" he asked me.

I'm not a guesser. I wouldn't guess my own weight if I were standing on a scale. So I just said, "What?"

"I figured it was like she was tipping me a wink," he said, sighting me through the bottom of the whiskey tumbler and looking like a middle-aged pirate with a truncated spyglass. "It was like she was saying, Hey, I've taken the kids and the furniture, but I'm still worried about what you're going to eat and what you're going to eat it off of. You can still get us back. I was alone in the house, it was the middle of the night and the house was empty, but there were these paper plates, and I looked at them like they were the fucking Holy Grail and figured she's pissed off but we can straighten it out. We always did before."

"Good for her," I said. It was my turn to wave for Peppi. Peppi shook her head meaningfully and looked away. "That's a woman for you," I added, flagging Peppi again. "Sentimental."

Peppi poured and trudged grudgingly toward us. She didn't look sentimental. She looked like a woman with a rattlesnake in her hip pocket.

"Except it wasn't," Hammond said as the drinks landed loudly on the table.

"What wasn't?" I asked. To Peppi, I said, "Two more." I was tired of waving.

"You're driving," Peppi said unpleasantly. Peppi had unpleasant down cold.

"Aren't you listening?" Hammond said to me. "Plates. We're talking about paper plates. I sit around for eight days going out of my mind. I'm trying to pick the tattoos off my arms. There's no note, no phone number, no nothing. I go to the assholes in Missing Persons and they laugh in my face. Guys I *know*, for Christ's sake. Every morning I wait for the mailman, catch hell because I'm coming in late. No letter. No birthday card, even."

"Happy Birthday" didn't seem like the right thing to say. I drank instead.

"And then her sister calls me," he said as Peppi plunked the full glasses on the table. For once, Hammond didn't give them a glance. He still had half a belt in his hand. "Her sister. Zora, for Christ's sake. I've only called the bitch forty or fifty times since Hazel left, and it's always 'Oh, I don't know anything about it. How terrible for you.' So Hazel finally lets go of her sister's leash, and the bitch calls me and says everybody's okay.

"'Everybody who?' I say. 'I'm not okay. I seen DOAs who are more okay than I am.' And she laughs this pissy little laugh and says, honest to Christ, Simeon, she says, 'Oh, you men. You don't know when you're well off.'

"'Well off,' I say. 'What the fuck are you talking about?'

"'Hazel told me how you swore,' she says. 'I must say, it's not very becoming. Not in a grown man, anyway.'" Hammond finally registered the new drinks. He finished the one in his hand.

"Drink, me hearty," said Al the Red, hoisting the fuller of the two new ones.

I drank. The room was beginning to waver as though I were seeing it over an active radiator.

"Well off?" I asked.

"Sure," Hammond said in a voice that would have straightened the hair on a sheep. "After I apologized for my French and asked her real polite and genteel where they all were and she said she couldn't tell me, then she said, and listening to it would have given Liberace diabetes, she said, 'Wasn't it sweet of little Al to go out and buy you those paper plates? He wouldn't leave until he'd done it.'" He lowered his head onto his bulging forearms. "Little Al," he repeated. "Holy Jesus, little Al."

Without thinking, I reached over and put my hand on top of his head. Sober, he'd have killed me. "Hey, Al the Red," I said, "let's go home."

He straightened up and looked at me as though he'd never seen me before. I yanked my hand back. Three feet from my nose, it smelled of hair oil.

"Fuckin' A," he said. He threw the half-full glass to the floor. It splintered and splashed. Still no one looked at us. We were invisible.

Hammond lurched to his feet. "To the ship," he said, adjusting his kerchief. "And damn the torpedoes. Full fucking speed ahead. Whatever way ahead is."

After I drained my glass, I guided him unsteadily to the street, my arm around his Mount Rushmore shoulders, and steered him into Alice, my car. He snored all the way to his empty house and then refused help getting inside. I watched Al the Red go, and waited until the door was slammed shut and locked. A hot wind blew, and the air smelled of smoke. I had to make a detour on the way back to Topanga to avoid a fire area, a long-familiar profile of mountains now enveloped in flame.

Between the beer and the whiskey, it took me only a few minutes to fall asleep. When I woke up the next morning, I was famous.

4

Fame

The phone started in at eight o'clock. It rang several times, penetrating a rather large region of murky pain that turned out to be the inside of my head. When it became apparent that the phone had more stamina than I did, I rolled over and picked the damn thing up.

"Hang up and call me tomorrow," were my first words of the bright new day. I'd sweated into the sheets, and they were damp and wadded. They stank of whiskey and smoke and the Red Dog and something even ranker, something I couldn't place.

"This is Channel Five," said the female voice on the other end, as though that explained everything.

"I don't care if it's the Channel Islands," I said. "Get the hell out of my ear." I hung up, hard enough to crack the handset. Then I rolled over, clutched the dank pillow to me, and pretended that the pillow was my ex-girlfriend, Eleanor Chan. Eleanor smelled better, but she wasn't there. My eyelids scratched closed over shards of broken glass, and I dozed instantly.

I hadn't even had time to work up an erotic dream when the phone screamed again. "What time is it?" I demanded.

"Eight-twelve by my unreliable, mass-produced watch," said a supernaturally cheerful voice. "Seventeen jewels, and all of them fakes. How you doing, Simeon?"

"What a goddamn stupid question," I said.

"This is Pat."

In the whole world, I couldn't think of a soul named Pat. Pat Nixon came belatedly to mind. This, however, was a male.

"Patrick Henry, at the *Times*."

I rubbed my eyes with a hand that smelled like a rubber glove full of wet cigars. It had to be important for Pat to call himself Patrick. He'd been my student once, when I was still teaching English at UCLA.

"You're up early," I said. Good. I congratulated myself. A civil sentence.

"And you're on the front page," Pat said.

"Slowly, Patrick," I said. "Of what?"

"The *Times*."

It took both hands to make my head feel smaller. "Pat," I said, pressing the phone between ear and shoulder and working on my temples with fingers that felt like Smithfield hams, "it's Sunday."

"That means you're reaching our biggest circulation," he said proudly. He'd always been a smart-ass.

"Sunday," I said, "is a day of rest. Go rest somewhere." He sputtered at me, but I hung up. Then, at long last, I yanked the cord out of the back of the phone, rolled over onto my left side, and grabbed my other pillow. It smelled terrible in a familiar fashion. It growled at me.

"God damn it, Bravo," I said, shoving at the foul-smelling pillow, "where did you come from?"

Bravo Corrigan, Topanga's itinerant generic dog, exhaled a bagful of dead fish at me, got to all four feet, and shambled to the foot of the bed, pausing just long enough to shake himself. With a fine snowfall of long dog hairs settling over me, I shut my scratchy eyes and aimed myself toward the Land of Nod.

Bravo's stomach rumbled. I forced my eyes to remain closed. I thought about getting a drink of water. I thought about it for so long that I finally fell back asleep and dreamed of helicopters dumping tons of cool water over acres of fire. It didn't do any good. The water exploded like gasoline.

When a hand touched my shoulder, I jumped all the way to the foot of the bed, clawing at the air for a weapon. Instead, my foot found Bravo, and then my other foot found nothing at all, and I collapsed on the floor, shoulder first.

"For heaven's *sakes*, Simeon," Eleanor Chan said.

I got my eyes open and focused with an effort that seemed to involve even my stomach muscles. Eleanor stood there, looking cool and unruffled and amused, wearing a loose wrinkled white shirt—one of mine, from the years when we'd lived together—and tight, ragged bleached jeans with a rip exposing one creamy knee. She'd had her black, perfectly straight hair cut short and spiky on top. On her it looked good.

"You're green," Eleanor said. She'd always been observant.

"Hammond," I said by way of explanation. I tried to unknot my legs. "Dawn patrol."

"Poor baby," she said. She liked Hammond. I liked him, too, but I'd never have called him baby. "And speaking of Baby," she said, holding out a newspaper.

"I can't read," I said desperately. "I can barely talk." I became aware of the fact that I was naked and plucked up a corner of the dank sheet. Eleanor laughed.

"The media should see you now," she said. "Hello, Bravo." Bravo's tail thumped.

"Eleanor," I said, getting experimentally to my feet. The room swam. "Can I go dynamite my teeth or something before you start telling me about the media?"

"You're a star," she said, waving the paper at me in an aggressive fashion.

I shrugged it off for the moment and slipped laboriously into a pair of drawstring pants. Standing on my left leg took most of my day's meager allotment of equilibrium. "Make coffee," I said, barely avoiding dropping to my knees in supplication. "Please?" I went into the bathroom and tried to scrub off the residue of the night. Hot, cold, hot cold. Then some more cold. Wash the hair twice. Slap both sides of the face sharply under the stream of icy water. It was a routine I'd practiced frequently in the weeks since Hammond's wife had left. Hammond was doing fine, I reflected, pulling on a T-shirt. I was the one who was turning into an alcoholic.

I heard Eleanor puttering familiarly around in the kitchen of the house she'd found and rented for us all those years ago as I combed my hair with trembling fingers and checked the mirror for signs of permanent damage. My parents' durable genes had survived another fusillade of abuse. I still looked like someone to whom you might conceivably lend a quarter.

Two cups of Eleanor's bitter, highly stimulating coffee later, I was wired enough to look at the *Times*. "How do you do it?" I asked. "Have you got a corner on the caffeine they take out of decaf?"

"You'll need it," she said, handing me the paper. Bravo, sitting directly on Eleanor's feet, watched it suspiciously. Whoever his original owner had been before Bravo gave him a final high-five and went out to play the field, he'd apparently been a member of the rolled-up newspaper school of training. "This is going to make you really popular with the cops."

I glanced down and read. My eyes closed of their own accord. "Mother of God," I said. And that was just the headline.

MILLIONAIRE IMMOLATED ON SKID ROW, it said. Under that, in type the size of John Hancock's signature: HEIRESS ACCUSES POLICE OF INCOMPETENCE.

"It gets better," Eleanor said over the rim of her cup.

Taking another sip of coffee, I accidentally cracked the heavy mug against my front teeth. It helped me to focus.

> *Police spokespersons last night positively identified a transient who was doused with gasoline and set on fire Thursday night on Skid Row as Chicago multimillionaire and philanthropist Abraham Winston. Winston, 68, is in critical condition at the Blumberg Burn Treatment Center in Sherman Oaks.*
>
> *Police have tentatively linked the assault to five others committed over the past three months, all in the same area. In each case, the victim was a transient, and all incidents have occurred between three and five A.M., when the victims were asleep on city sidewalks. All five of the previous victims died of their injuries.*
>
> *Winston, who reportedly suffers from Alzheimer's disease, disappeared from his Chicago home more than a month ago. It is not known how he got to Los Angeles.*
>
> *"We can't say for sure it's the Crisper," said LAPD spokesperson Lieutenant Alfred Brown, using the name police have given to the assailant. "All we can state at this time is that the method and the choice of victim are consistent with the Crisper's past attacks. We're pursuing our leads with all due alacrity."*

"'Alacrity'?" I asked Eleanor.

"Keep reading," she said.

> *At a press conference called immediately following the
> LAPD announcement, Abraham Winston's daughter, Anna-
> belle, denounced police action on the case to date. "The victims
> are dispossessed persons," Miss Winston said, reading from a
> prepared statement. "That does not lessen the agony they experi-
> enced. If these people had lived in Bel Air or in Beverly Hills,
> rather than on the streets, someone would be in jail by now.
> Instead, five people are dead and my father will probably die
> within a matter of hours. I have no faith in the ability of the
> Los Angeles Police Department to bring the murderer to justice.
> Therefore, I have hired a private investigator who will report
> to me, and I have put the resources of Winston Enterprises at
> his disposal. At the least, I hope my action will goad the police
> into a renewed effort. At the most, I believe that the man I
> have hired will bring this monster to justice."*

"Where are you?" Eleanor asked.

"Something about monsters and justice. I wonder who wrote
this stuff for her."

"A PR man," Eleanor said. "You don't just call a press conference, you know. Somebody has to know which press to call."

"Sweet bleeding Jesus," I said, reading ahead.

"I was waiting for that," Eleanor said. "Read it out loud."

> *"In response to reporters' questions, Miss Winston, who
> was nicknamed Baby by the media during her reign as one of
> America's most prominent debutantes, identified the investigator
> she had retained as Simeon Grist of Topanga. Mr. Grist, thir-
> ty-seven, came to prominence several months ago in the breakup
> of an interstate ring that was trafficking in children for im-
> moral purposes. Several suspects are now in custody, awaiting
> arraignment in that case. One of them is a former LAPD ser-
> geant."*

"See what I mean?" Eleanor said. "Double whammy."

"'Attempts to reach Mr. Grist for comment were unsuccess-
ful,'" I read. "That's because I was out getting poisoned with
Hammond. They called again this morning, though."

"Don't talk to them until you know what to say," Eleanor
said. "What about your answering machine?"

"I didn't check it."

"If you had," Eleanor said, "you'd have known that I called to tell you that your name was on the radio last night."

"Radio?"

"And television. And now print. Home run."

"I haven't got a friend in the world," I said.

"You've got Baby." Eleanor's tone wasn't pleasant.

"Swell. An ex-debutante with a checkbook. I feel like the last candle before the ice age."

Eleanor sat back and regarded me as though I were a new and unpromising life-form. Jealousy hadn't been a factor in the early stages of our relationship, but it had found its way in when I began cheating on her, for reasons I still didn't understand. Now that we were no longer together, the jealousy remained, vestigial, like the knee-jerk reflex in an amputated leg.

Balancing my cup unsteadily in my hand, I checked the machine. I had urgent messages from channels Two, Four (twice), Five, Seven, Nine, Eleven, and Thirteen. Also CBS News in New York and six local radio stations.

"Just what every private detective wants to be," I said. "Public." I changed chairs and sat on a large, uncompromising lump.

"If I might suggest a policy," Eleanor said, softening enough to lean forward. She looked good enough to spread on toast.

"Suggest until you're blue in the face," I said, fishing the lump out from under me. It was Dreiser's *Sister Carrie*, one of the challenges I'd promised myself I'd get through in what had looked like a nice, slow summer. "I haven't got a clue."

"It's a two-point policy," she said. "First, plug your phone back in and say something boring to everyone who calls. That was Henry Kissinger's policy. Whenever he was asked a question he didn't want to answer, he began his reply with the words, 'As I said yesterday,' and everyone stopped taking notes. Just tell whoever calls that you've given an exclusive statement to someone else. At least it'll get them off your tail."

"And the second point?" I realized I was still holding *Sister Carrie*. It felt heavier than a broken promise, and I dropped it to the floor. It landed with the substantial thump of serious literature.

"Quit the case." She put down her cup. Bravo's ears went up, as they always did, at the clink of crockery.

"That's not so easy," I said.

"And why not? This guy could wind up burning you."

"Abraham Winston was a good man. He didn't deserve to be cooked on the sidewalk. And she's right, the cops *haven't* been doing all they could, or even half of all they could. It's just a bunch of bums as far as they're concerned. Remember the Skid Row Ripper? They never worked that one out, either."

Eleanor gave me an eloquent Chinese shrug, a shrug with thousands of years of equivocation behind it. "So hang yourself out to dry," she said. "There's still point one. Plug in the phone."

I did, and it rang. I looked at her questioningly, but she'd already gotten up to get more coffee. "Boring," she said, over her shoulder. "Just be boring."

I picked it up.

"Mr. Grist?" said a voice I almost recognized. "Please hold for Mr. Stillman."

I covered the mouthpiece. "Norman *Stillman*," I said in agony.

"He could be interesting," Eleanor said without looking around. She was pouring.

I doubted that, but I hung on. I had met Stillman before. In fact, I'd worked for him, and not very happily, when one of the stars he employed had gotten himself into trouble. His company, imaginatively named Norman Stillman Productions, gave the television audience what it wanted, which is to say blood and guts and sex and sensationalism and depravity, all under the banner of family entertainment. And maybe it was, for the Manson Family. Stillman's virtue, in my eyes, was that he actually *liked* the shows he produced.

There was a muffled *click*, and Stillman came on the line. "So, Mr. Grist, you're famous at last," he said unctuously. It wasn't hard to picture him in his big, fat office with nautical charts all over the walls and a big brass-and-wood wheel from a nineteenth-century sloop mounted above the desk.

"You can't imagine how I've hungered for it, Norman," I said. "It's a dream come true." I shrugged helplessly at Eleanor.

Stillman judiciously measured out a laugh. "Well, when I saw your name this morning, the old penny dropped." He sounded paternal and jocular. When Norman Stillman sounded paternal and jocular, it was time to button your wallet and count your change.

"Was I in *Variety*?"

There was a moment of silence, during which Stillman decided to take it lightly. "I read the *Times*, too, Mr. Grist," he said. "I must say, I had hoped time would have mellowed you."

Eleanor handed me a fresh cup of coffee. "You were saying something about a penny," I reminded him.

"A penny? Oh. Oh, yes, the famous dropping penny. Only figurative, of course. I had something considerably more substantial in mind."

Eleanor sat down opposite me, her eyebrows raised. I waited. Stillman didn't say anything. After a moment, I started to whistle. I've found it irritates the hell out of the person on the other end of the phone.

Stillman said, "A few minutes, Dierdre." I was willing to bet that Dierdre, his long-suffering secretary, wasn't even in the room. Then he said: "Do you know Velez Caputo?"

"Personally?" I mouthed at Eleanor, "Velez Caputo." Eleanor made a sign in the air that looked like a backward *S* with two vertical strokes drawn through it.

"I wouldn't expect you to know her personally," Stillman said avuncularly.

"And your expectations would be correct," I said.

"But you know who she is."

Indeed I did. Velez Caputo was a svelte, acutely intelligent middle-thirties Chicana who helped 20 or 30 million Americans waste their afternoons five days a week. Into her viewers' living rooms, with chronological predictability, Caputo brought an unending parade of rapists, batterers, batterees, bigamists, trigamists, transvestites, and people who enjoyed dressing as members of other species, who spent ninety minutes happily calling national attention to what should have been their deepest secrets. And Americans tuned in by the millions to see the country's newest subculture: the proudly weird.

"I never miss Velez's show," I said, "unless I can help it."

Eleanor laughed, but Stillman was beyond listening. "Velez has a concept, a brilliant concept, one that will make television history. What are the two most popular kinds of shows on the air today?"

"Norman," I said, sipping my coffee, "how the hell would I know? The last time I watched television, Raymond Burr could still see his feet."

"True-life crime shows and game shows," he said promptly. "That's depressing."

"So what do you think Velez's concept is?" He liked to ask questions.

"A true-life crime show," I said. Eleanor held her nose. Bravo looked at her expectantly, waiting for the next move in the game.

"A true-life crime game show," Stillman said triumphantly. "What do you think?"

"I'm speechless."

"So do you see where I'm going?"

"To the bank, probably." I drained the rest of my coffee and held the cup out. Eleanor poured part of hers into it.

"The format's already in the can. Three contestants, Velez as hostess, of course, footage from some true-life crime with clues planted here and there, three suspects. One of them is the real-life crook."

I drank the coffee and grimaced. Eleanor, despite her New Age convictions, put enough sugar in her coffee to rot a tyrannosaurus's teeth.

"The home audience sees one or two clues the contestants don't see, just to make them feel smart," Stillman said rhapsodically. "The audience always has to feel smarter than the contestants," he added, reciting the time-honored dictum of game-show producers all over the world. "The jerks should always be sitting at home slapping their foreheads and swearing over how much money they'd be winning if they were in the studio."

"And the winner gets a date with the crook."

"That's what's so brilliant," Stillman said. "The winner gets a reward that's posted at the beginning of the show. Remember Wanted posters?"

I looked at my watch. If I was going to quit the case, now was the time to do it. "Look," I said, "you can't imagine how exciting this is, being on the inside like this. It's almost as good as having a subscription to *Broadcasting*. But what's it got to do with me?"

"Advisers," he said, a bit petulantly. "We'll need advisers. Somebody to help us reconstruct the crime scenes, plant the clues, guide Velez in her prompts to the contestants. So whaddya say?"

"I'd say it's a lot of work for a penny."

"Twenty-five hundred a week," he said.

I began to whistle again. Eleanor winced. I can't whistle on key.

"Three if you work out," Stillman said, a bit too hastily. "Maybe thirty-five if the show goes."

"*If* the show goes? Norman, have you got a show or not?"

"I told you," he said, sounding huffy, "the format's in the can, plus we've got Velez. Come on, it's a certified check. There's just a few little wrinkles to work out."

"Like selling it?" I asked.

"Well, yeah," he said. "We still have to sell it, of course."

I waited. He waited, too. While I was waiting, I polished the phone with my shirt. I was working on the earpiece when I realized he was talking, so I put it back to my ear.

". . . only exploratory, of course, just to see if you're interested. You're at the top of my list."

"Norman," I said. "The sun is approaching its zenith. I have a beautiful woman with me. It's Sunday, for Christ's sake. Why in God's name are you calling?"

He put a lot of work into a manly chuckle. "That's why I thought of you," he said. "'Sharp,' I said, 'the boy's sharp.'"

"Well, now that we've settled that I'm sharp," I said, "what do you really want?"

There was the kind of silence that liars loathe.

"Ah," Stillman said reluctantly, "there was one other thing."

"I thought there might be."

"First," he said.

"What do you mean, first? If there's only one other thing, how can what you're about to say be first?"

"See?" he said. "See why I called you? 'Sharp,' I said. 'The boy's sharp.'"

"See?" I echoed. "See how sharp I am? See why I'm going to hang up?"

"Okay, there's two things. About this dinkus with the lighter fluid."

"Ah. As a great man once said—Jesus, I think it might have been you, Norman—'The old penny drops.'"

"You'll be great on the air. Will you do Velez's show tomorrow? It's about the people who track serial murderers. The title is 'In Death's Footsteps.' Or maybe it's 'Footprints.' Whaddya think? A thousand, cash."

"No. I'm not going on Velez's show."

"I knew you'd say that," Stillman said promptly. "I told Velez you'd say that. What about two thousand?"

"No. And second?"

"Um," he said. I visualized him shining the buttons on his nautical blazer. Norman owned a yacht solely as an excuse for his taste in clothes and interior decorators. "Has any other producer called you?"

"Norman," I said unctuously, "*is* there any other producer?"

"Not who's worth talking to."

"So talk."

"If you get this dinkus," he said, lowering his voice conspiratorially, "you hold back a couple of things for me. There's nobody who can handle this kind of thing like Norman Stillman Productions. You play ball, we'll do ninety minutes live on network the night after the dinkus gets jugged. We already got the title."

"I don't want to hear it."

"'The Fire Within,'" he said obliviously. "Or something like that. Bring me the right stuff, we're talking six figures."

"As in three figures comma three figures?" Eleanor arched her eyebrows.

"You got it."

"What's the first figure?" I asked, just out of curiosity.

"Ahhh," Norman Stillman said, "that's a detail. That's for the bookkeepers."

"Have your bookkeeper call me," I said.

"Hey," Stillman said apprehensively. He was working up to something better, but I didn't hear it because I hung up.

"Who would have thought it?" I asked. "I get hired to find someone who's torching the homeless, and people start throwing money at me. Come on, I've had cases that began and ended in Beverly Hills, and no one's ever mentioned six figures before."

"Six figures sounds good to me," she said. "You've never had this kind of media attention before, either."

"Public television hasn't gotten to us yet," I said, feeling momentarily optimistic.

"It's their pledge week," she said. "They're on documentaries about baby pandas and the giant sea slug. They're concentrating on endangered species."

"I'm an endangered species," I said, taking an emotional nosedive. "I'm in danger of being put out of business."

"You can still carry out point two. You can quit. I don't care about the nice man who got set on fire, I care about you. That Baby or whatever her name is had no right to call a press conference without telling you she was going to do it. How do you know this crazy won't come after you?"

"I'm not his type," I said, with more conviction than I felt.

"It even says where you live. In Topanga. Suppose—"

"He's been burning the homeless."

She looked around the shack, much the worse for wear since she'd left. "You almost qualify."

"I'll be okay," I said, watching her. We hadn't been talking much lately, since she'd begun to date someone else. Jealousy worked two ways.

"Well, she shouldn't," Eleanor began, then stopped, catching my eyes. "She shouldn't have held that press conference, even if she does have all the money in the world. That guy . . ." She trailed off. "This is complicated, you know?" she asked, looking at Bravo. "I mean, I still love you. In a way."

"I'll be careful," I said. I didn't have the courage to say anything else.

Hand in hand, something we did out of habit, we went down the driveway, on the way to the Bel Air Hotel to tender my resignation. Bravo Corrigan trotted along next to us, sniffing professionally at the bushes, a big, long-haired, raffish canine bum. At the bottom of the driveway, I noticed something unusual for a Sunday: The red flag on the mailbox was vertical, and there was a piece of paper wedged between the hinged door of the mailbox and the mailbox proper. And with Eleanor standing behind me and looking nosily over my shoulder, I opened and read the letter from the Crisper.

"Darling," I said, calling Eleanor something I hadn't called her in more than a year, "all the rules just got changed."

5

The Brotherhood of the Pumpkin

The first thing I did was get rid of Eleanor. She protested that I'd promised her lunch, but I sold her on a raincheck and watched her coast her little Acura down the hill. After she left, I waded through the heat and back up the rutted, unpaved driveway and put in the call to Hammond.

Then came the hangover-fueled discussion at Parker Center. When it was over and Willick had retired to some upstairs cubicle to type his notes, Hammond walked with me to the underground garage.

"So now what?" he asked, lighting one of the vicious cigars he smoked to enhance his image.

"So now I quit, Loot," I said, fanning at the smoke. I opened the iridescent blue door of my car, Alice, and got in. Hammond propped a size-twelve double-E shoe against the door to keep me from closing it.

"You're the only one he's written to," he said.

"And let's not keep it that way," I said. I used my own foot to shove Hammond's away and slammed the door. "What do you think, Al, that I want to be on that lunatic's Christmas card list?"

"We're going to check the cars on your street," he said. "I mean, we're already checking them." He leaned a beefy forearm on the open window on the driver's side. "We could be looking at a lead."

"Look at it by yourself. I'm out. All I have to do is talk to Baby. Then I'm going to go surfing. Phone me at the beach if you need me."

"Could be important," he said.

"I hope it is," I said. "I hope you nail the clown. You, not me."

"The note's for real," he said, telling me something I hadn't learned while Willick was present. "The psychologists say so."

"Well, good for them. Here's hoping he gets one of their addresses next time."

"He won't. The shrinks are invisible."

"Well, then, here's hoping he gets yours." It was a nasty thing to say, but it had been a nasty morning. I twisted the key in Alice's ignition, and she caught.

"Sure," Hammond said. "There's nobody living there anyway." He lifted his arm from the window while I tried to think of anything to say.

"Thanks for last night," Hammond said unexpectedly. "I know I was pushing it."

"Al the Red," I said, leaning out to thump him on the shoulder. It was okay with Hammond if you touched him, but only if you did it with your hand clenched into a fist. "Nobody's going to get Al the Red."

He nodded in a morose way, and I headed Alice out into the sparse Sunday traffic toward Bel Air.

The Bel Air Hotel on a Sunday afternoon, even during the worst week of the worst October in years, looked more like a postcard than it did like a real place. I crossed the bridge over the hotel's private stream, and one of the hotel's private swans hissed a welcome at me. Tall sycamores shaded the grounds, their broad leaves intercepting the steady rain of ash from the latest rash of fires in the Santa Monica Mountains. Even so, there was a short Hispanic man with a wet cloth and a bucket of water cleaning the ferns. He did it slowly, meticulously, with total absorption, one frond at a time, as though there were nothing more important in the world than preventing the sensibilities of the rich from being offended by the sight of ash on the ferns.

The rich themselves were in ample evidence, their sensibilities apparently intact. I'd forgotten which room Baby Winston was in, so I checked the dining room first. It was packed. Sunday is brunch day at the Bel Air. From about eleven until about five, rich people carefully underdress and pay someone to tousle their hair before heading for the Bel Air to compliment each other on their appearance, compare notes on doctors and domestics, talk deals, and get swozzled.

Baby wasn't there. That left what I should have done in the first place. Resigning myself to the possibility that I might never develop her economy of movement, I crossed the little bridge over the moat and headed for the front desk.

"I'm sorry, but she's not here." The desk clerk was a motherly type in her middle forties who had chosen to celebrate Sunday by pinning a large, purple, vaguely vulpine orchid to her left lapel. The desk clerk shook her head sympathetically, and the orchid stuck its purple-specked tongue out at me.

"Perhaps she left a message," I said. "My name is Grist."

"Well, perhaps she did." The desk clerk sounded as though she disapproved of the fact that she hadn't thought of that on her own. "Perhaps, perhaps, perhaps," she sang to herself on a descending scale as she flipped through a stack of envelopes. "Whoopsy-daisy, here we are." She started to hand me an envelope and then pulled back her hand and regarded me suspiciously. She pursed her mouth, working out the protocol. "Mr. *Simeon* Grist?" she asked, the picture of vigilance.

"Yes."

"All right, then. This is for you." She smiled maternally and handed me the envelope.

"Look," I said, "you did that all wrong."

"How do you mean, dearie?" I wondered what I'd done to become "dearie." "Miss Winston said to give it only to *Simeon* Grist, and that's what I did." Her blue eyes were as open as the Canadian border.

"Never mind," I said. "Love the orchid."

Annabelle Winston's note was an address: 13731 Moorpark, Sherman Oaks. Beneath that she'd written, *Ten till six*. There was no phone number.

"Well, shit," I said out loud. Sherman Oaks was a long way to drive just to quit a case.

"Icky, icky," said the desk clerk behind me. "There's no need for such language." The way she was looking at me, I was no longer "dearie."

"You're right," I said. "I'm sorry. I have no breeding at all."

I took Laurel Canyon up over the top of the Hollywood Hills. Rainbirds chopped at the air like machine guns, shooting out long, glittering arcs of water. People were keeping the foliage green just in case, a perfect example of baseless optimism. A really hot fire creates its own winds, and the winds always blow up. Given enough momentum, a brushfire can move up a hill at twenty miles an hour, exploding everything in its path. A nice green lawn offers about as much protection as drawing the venetian blinds.

The San Fernando Valley was 8 to 10 degrees hotter than the other side of the hills, making it around 100. The Santa Anas had shouldered the smog out over the Pacific, and the Valley spread below me like the world's biggest, driest sink.

The Moorpark address was a small hospital, obviously private, a cluster of low white buildings sheltered from the slanting afternoon sunlight by tall eucalyptus trees. There were lots of visitors' spaces, most of them empty. I pulled Alice into one and left her there, a bright blue blemish on the asphalt.

The starched, crinkly white imitation nurse wrapped an expensive smile around the information that Mr. Winston was in 312 and that Miss Winston was with him and that I should follow the yellow line. Sure enough, there was a yellow line on the floor. There were also blue and red lines. Fighting down an obscure desire to find out where the red line went, I followed the yellow one down a long, arctically air-conditioned corridor and around a corner. There, seated on a black leather couch with chromium armrests, was Annabelle Winston.

She wasn't alone. With her was a youngish man who was clearly working at looking youngisher. His dark, wet-looking hair was combed straight back from a high, tanned forehead. His eyes were too close together, but he had fine bones and a broad mouth with a little too much lower lip. It looked as though he'd pouted once too often as a boy and the expression had stuck, just as my mother always predicted my eyes would when I crossed them. He was holding Annabelle's hand in what seemed to be a brotherly fashion.

The two of them got up together as I rounded the corner. Annabelle extracted her hand from the man's grasp and said, "Mr. Grist. Thank you for coming. Have you got anything for me?"

"You bet," I said.

"This is Bobby Grant," she said. Bobby Grant stuck out a tan paw, and I shook it briefly. His white linen safari shirt had enough pockets for a very long safari indeed, and his beige pleated trousers were accented with pencil-thin green and red stripes about two inches apart. He wore lizard-skin loafers with no socks. I've never trusted men who don't wear socks.

"Bobby is the one who arranged the press conference," Annabelle Winston said. "He handles all my West Coast PR."

"Good job yesterday," I said nastily.

"We had a real story," Grant said in a higher voice than I'd expected. He obviously thought he was looking at me, but his eyes were focused about two inches above my head. "It's easy when you've got real news," he added, modestly minimizing his accomplishment. "A lot easier than product." He also, I noted, sported a single gold earring, a modest loop that dangled from his left earlobe. He reached up and tugged on it, and Annabelle Winston looked on obliviously. The lesson of Harvey Melnick hadn't taken.

"Product?" I asked. I didn't have the faintest idea what he was talking about.

"We put Bobby in charge of introducing our new skinless franks a year ago," Annabelle said. She was wearing a silk suit that could have been a twin of the one she'd worn yesterday except that it was gunmetal gray. It complemented the agate eyes very nicely. "There wasn't much space from that one."

"Well, wieners," Bobby said. I wondered if he'd still call himself Bobby when he was sixty, and decided that he probably would.

"Franks," Annabelle Winston said absently.

"Miss Winston," I began.

"Call me Annabelle," she said. She reached up and touched my cheek. "I feel I know you well enough for that." She wasn't making it easy. "You're my main hope," she said, making it even worse.

"I spoke to the cops today," I said, by way of starting out.

"And they didn't know what you were talking about," she said.

"Well," I admitted, "not at first."

"Even after the papers this morning?" Bobby Grant sounded personally affronted. "My God, front page of the *Times*. What are these people, blind?"

"Do you see why I need you, Simeon?" Annabelle said.

This was not going right. By now I should have been back out in the parking lot, sweet-talking Alice into starting. I drew a breath.

"Listen," I said, "I'm quitting."

Annabelle Winston took a step back, and Bobby Grant put out a hand to steady her. Even at that moment, I'd never seen a woman less in need of steadying. Her eyes widened.

"What does that mean?" she asked.

"It means I'm off the job. Finished. Kaput." The word brought Velez Caputo to mind, and I shrugged it away. "You told me I was the only person on the case."

"You are," Annabelle Winston said, her eyes fixed on mine.

"Yeah? What's he?" I asked, nodding toward Bobby Grant. "A skinless wiener?"

Bobby Grant's lower lip protruded even further. I wondered how much of it he was holding in reserve. Maybe he kept it curled up, like a butterfly's tongue.

"He's not a detective," she said, as though that answered everything.

"He held a press conference," I said. "He and you," I amended. "You announced to the whole world that you'd retained me. You didn't even have the courtesy to let me know. I wake up in the morning, and everybody except David Frost is calling me for an interview."

"David Frost is in England," Bobby Grant said professionally. "If he weren't, this is his kind of story."

"I don't want to be part of anybody's story. I'm a detective. I need a certain amount of anonymity in order to be able to do my job. Not to mention the fact that the guy who burned your father wrote me a letter and delivered it to my house."

"He did?" It was the first time I'd seen Annabelle Winston look genuinely surprised.

"Himself," I said. "When I took the job, I acknowledged that I was willing to go looking for him. I'm not willing to have him looking for me. I'm flammable."

"We made a mistake," Annabelle Winston said contritely.

"What are you *talking* about?" Bobby Grant said. "He's writing letters now. That could be a breakthrough," he added, sounding like Hammond Lite.

"Bobby," Annabelle Winston said. It was the vocal equivalent of a one-way ticket to Siberia. "Go away."

"But, but," Bobby sputtered.

"Just scram," Annabelle Winston said. "Down the hall. Anywhere. This instant." She snapped her fingers. Bobby gave her a betrayed look and faded about six feet behind her.

"We made a mistake," she said again. "All I was trying to do was light a fire under the cops."

"Miss Winston," I said. "You succeeded. You also robbed me of whatever advantage I might have had in trying to find the Crisper." She winced at the word. "What's more, and what's probably more serious, you pissed off the police. Before Bobby orchestrated his headlines, I had a chance at getting hold of whatever they have. Now I might as well be wearing a bell around my neck and a sign that says Unclean. They're embarrassed. Cops are macho, you know. They don't like to be embarrassed. It makes them feel impotent."

She lowered her head. "Forgive me," she said.

"I forgive you," I said. "But I'm finished."

"We're finished, Miss Winston," echoed a male voice. "You can go back in now." I hadn't heard the door open.

The owner of the voice was a young doctor wearing an ill-advised pencil-thin mustache. His face was the shade of gray that the relatives of patients don't want to see. He'd been through something for which his training hadn't prepared him.

"Is he . . . ?" Annabelle Winston let the question hang in the air.

"Sedated," the doctor said, touching the mustache with an experimental thumbnail. "This is the part that hurts." He looked at me. "Changing the dressing," he explained. "We have to put him out."

"I thought it all hurt," I said.

"He's got third-degree burns," the doctor said. "That means

total loss of skin. The nerves go with the skin. Where he hurts most are the boundaries between the third- and second-degree burns. Where he's got some skin left."

Annabelle Winston started crying. This was nothing controlled, nothing like the averted face in the suite at the Bel Air. This was tears and snot and screwed-up eyelids and a sound like someone exhaling golf balls.

"Now, now," the young doctor said ineffectually, out of his depth again. The mustache made him look like a kid fancied-up for Halloween. He put a hand on her arm, but she shrugged it off and grabbed my wrist. Her fingers felt like bridge cables. "Come in here," she said fiercely. "Get your ass in here." She dragged me through the open door with a strength that almost dislocated my shoulder. Bobby Grant followed us, hovering like a bad conscience. The doctor, abashed at the reaction he'd provoked, came in and closed the door behind us.

"Take a look," Annabelle Winston said shakily. "The brotherhood of the pumpkin."

Abraham Winston—what had once been Abraham Winston—lay in a bed that looked like one of the roasting racks at the Escorial, the Spanish palace of Philip II, where heretics had been barbecued for the enlightenment of the Saved. The bed was a metal frame hitched up to a complicated series of levers and pulleys. Winston was swathed from feet to nipples in white bandages, and the skin that was exposed was covered with a ghastly, greasy white ointment.

His head was enormous. It was swollen and blistered, all the features concentrated into an area in its center. His hair was gone. His face looked like the crimped end of one of Hammond's cigars, eyes, nose, and mouth pinched into the middle. The eyes, mercifully, were closed.

"Um, pumpkin," the young doctor said. "All serious burn victims look like this." I was looking at what Annabelle had hoped I'd never see, the reason it took her an hour to recognize her father.

"Why not a real bed?" I asked. I just needed to make sure that I could talk.

"We have to be able to turn him," the doctor said. He'd

used the time to recover his equilibrium. "You can't change his bandages, you can't put the ointment on him, without turning him."

"Why is his head swollen?"

"Blistering." The doctor made a small motion that took in Annabelle, asking me not to force him to discuss it further. His tongue snaked out and touched the bottom of the ridiculous mustache.

"The head's only part of it," Annabelle said mercilessly, recovering her power of speech. She drew a gray silk arm across her face. So much for that suit. "Tell him about his lungs."

The doctor looked down at his feet. One shoe went back and forth, grinding out the cigarette he probably wanted. I wanted one, too.

"He inhaled fire," the doctor said. "He got up before the old woman threw the blanket over him. Perfectly natural reflex, of course. Anybody who'd been set on fire would get up. Try to run away from the fire. Try to find water, maybe. I'd do it, too. Even though it's the worst possible thing to do." He exhaled a quart of pent-up air. "But there wasn't any water around. So he breathed fire."

"So he can't talk?" I asked.

"Nothing anybody could understand," said the doctor.

Bobby Grant put an arm around Annabelle's shoulders, and she shrugged it off like an unwanted fall of snow. Her eyes were on her father.

"Isn't there someplace else you can take him?" I asked. "And what old woman?"

"The old woman who kept him from burning to death there and then, may her soul rot in hell," Annabelle Winston said. She was finished with crying; she'd put it behind her as though it had been a social gaffe. "At least then it would have been over quickly. Instead of *this*. And, no, you can't move him. Even if there were anywhere better, which there isn't. We already moved him once, from County USC to here. They didn't even want us to do that."

"Burn victims just get worse," the doctor said apologetically. "Infection. Every burn is infected. The skin, the hair follicles, are teeming with bacteria. Move them and they die. Excuse me, Miss Winston."

"I've heard it before," Annabelle Winston said. "Take a look at Santa Claus, Simeon. Take a good look, and then tell me you're quitting."

Bobby Grant put in his two hundred dollars' worth. "I don't know how you could," he said.

"Well," I said, "you're not me." I turned to go.

There was a sound behind me, like the rasping of a file over iron, and I turned back. The human parody on the metal bed lifted a greasy, ointment-covered arm.

"He should be out," the doctor said worriedly. "A normal human being would be out cold."

"He's not a normal human being," Annabelle said, crossing to the bed. "He's Abraham Winston."

"Schossshuaaa?" said the thing on the metal frame.

"Yes, Daddy," Annabelle Winston said. "I'm here. It's Joshua."

"Surrammatagga," said the thing on the metal frame, its open eyes locked on Annabelle's. "Dhooo shomeshing." With supernatural force, it lifted its shoulders and turned its head. "Dhooo shomeshing," it repeated.

"We're going to do something," Annabelle said in a businesslike tone. She turned and pointed a gray silk arm at me. "We're going to get him. This is the man who's going to do it."

The pumpkin head turned to me. Its red, tiny, swollen eyes bore in on mine and found me lacking. Then, with a clogged cough, Abraham Winston passed out.

"Everybody," the doctor said in a stricken voice. "Everybody out of the room. *Now.*" We all went. Even Bobby Grant had nothing to say.

In the corridor, Annabelle Winston clutched my hand in hers. All the control was gone, washed away by tears and terror. "Say you'll stay with it," she pleaded. She'd gotten a case of hiccups. They made her sound twelve years old.

"I don't know," I said. "Maybe." Bobby Grant was smart enough to shut up and stay shut up.

"You *have* to," she said. "You've seen him."

"Maybe," I said again. I shook the two of them loose and headed for the parking lot. Alice started with ironic ease, and I drove home, full of righteous determination to quit once and for all the next morning. When I got home, I opened a Singha beer and congratulated myself on a narrow escape. Resolving myself that I'd quit for good over the phone in the morning, I drank until dark. Then I went to bed and tried not to dream. I almost succeeded. I only had to get up twice for water.

While I slept, Abraham Winston died, and the Crisper set fire to another bum. When I woke up and went down the driveway on my way to Eleanor, there was a new letter in my mailbox.

PART TWO

COMBUSTION

"What's one less person on the face of the earth, anyway?"

—Serial murderer Ted Bundy

6

Starting Over

This is what it said:

You didn't answer my letter. Is that polite? I want very much to be polite. Etiquette is one of the few things left to us in these times. I'm joking, of course. You couldn't have answered my letter no matter how polite you are.

The people I burn, they have no notion of what it is to be polite.

Who are they, anyway? Biological misfires. Good for fuel but for nothing else.

All right, perhaps the next-to-the-last one, the Winston man, was a mistake. Even if he was past it when we met. Past knowing, past doing. Can't I make the occasional mistake? God knows, whichever god we mean, everyone else makes mistakes. Ahriman has his way more often than we would like to admit. Last night's fire, however, was no mistake.

You and I, though, perhaps you and I are brothers. Or, perhaps not. Perhaps you also are fuel. You would know more about that than I. Surely you can also smell the corruption. If you cannot, if you are also fuel, I will know it before you do. I will know it long before you do.

There was a double space, a breathing space, exactly ruled out on the brown paper of the shopping bag, an ironic choice of stationery given the possessions of Abraham Winston, possessions that included a skinless-wiener factory, a forest, and the paper mill that turned the forest into the paper bags that happy housewives carried home from his supermarkets. After the double space, the gold-lettered, precisely formed message continued.

> *Still as long as we're chatting, I am not the Crisper, of all the ridiculous names. It sounds like the place where you keep the lettuce. I am, respectfully yours, the*
>
> *—Incinerator*

"He's in his forties," Hammond said to the very full room. "No one younger than that remembers incinerators. The law against burning trash passed in 1957."

The comment fell flat. It lay in the center of the big conference table and writhed a while, waiting for someone to come to its assistance.

"Hey," said the cop who was working the slide projector. "We through with this thing or not?"

"Not," said the ranking cop in the room, a white-haired man with a flat stomach, high, narrow shoulders, and an alcoholic's map of veins on his cheeks. "Just leave it on the screen." He also had small, deeply set eyes and a mean pug nose that brought to mind the old joke about Polish bulldogs getting flat noses from chasing parked cars. The magnified version of the Incinerator's letter, illuminated with metallic flames and floating spirits, remained on the wall. As before, the first capital initial was larger than the others, a carefully drawn *Y* arising from a bed of coals. Various people either looked at it or ignored it. There were a lot of people.

"I remember incinerators, too," Annabelle Winston said. "We had them in Chicago." Next to her, nodding agreement, sat Bobby Grant, wearing yet another safari shirt. This one had enough pockets to outfit the expedition that found Dr. Livingstone, with spare room to bring everybody home in. He'd removed the gold earring, a sensible move, in preparation for this meeting. On her other side sat a man whose clothes featured more buttons than a nuclear submarine. He had four buttons on each jacket cuff, buttons holding down the points of his IBM-white collar, a tiepin that was a silver button with a little diamond in its center, and a ring that was round and flat on top like a heavy gold button holding his hand on the table. In front of him was a closed attaché case. He had a mouth like a snapping turtle and a forehead like a Mercator projection, which is to say that it bulged in the middle. He had to be a lawyer.

"So who's Ahriman?" the ranking cop asked.

"The devil," I said, since no one else volunteered. "In Zoroastrianism." People looked blank. "An ancient Persian religion."

"The Crisper's a Persian?" Until he spoke, I hadn't realized that Willick was in the room, but there he sat at the other end of the table, notebook in hand and chins blossoming over his collar. The question was greeted with a flinty silence, and Willick buried his drooping nose in his notes.

"The Zoroastrians worshiped fire," I offered into the silence. "Their good god was the creator of light and fire, and their bad god, whose name was Ahriman, was the creator of darkness. They saw the world as a series of twelve-thousand-year cycles of light and darkness, with first one god ascendant and then the other. They kept perpetual fires burning in their temples."

"They still do," said a very small, balding man in civilian clothes who was sitting next to the man with all the buttons. He gave us all a bland smoker's smile, unsheathing crooked amber-colored teeth. "I'm Dr. Schultz," he said to me. "Dr. as in psychologist."

"Simeon Grist," I said.

"I know who you are," Dr. Schultz said, making the teeth go away. The crinkly smile lines around his eyes stayed put, as though he'd drawn them on with a pencil.

"Just being polite," I said.

Dr. Schultz had forgotten me. "He's an educated man," he said, looking over his shoulder at the projection of the note. "No grammatical errors, no spelling mistakes, good sentence structure, he's got some familiarity with ancient religions. He uses perhaps frequently. Most people would say 'maybe.'" He subsided, pleased with himself.

"What my client would like to know," said the lawyer to the room at large, tapping his briefcase for emphasis, "is what you're going to do to capture this maniac." He put his hand flat on the table again, and the gold ring made a clacking sound that put a large black period at the end of his sentence.

"We're working on it," the captain said shortly.

"With all due respect, Captain," Annabelle Winston said, almost pleasantly, "I'm not sure you are. But maybe—or, rather, *perhaps*—that's because we don't know what it is that you're doing."

"We're doing everything that can be done," the captain said flatly. "What do you suggest we should do?"

Annabelle Winston thought for a second. "I'm not a policeman," she said. "I don't know what you should be doing. But I know what I'm going to do if you don't make me happy. Tell them, Fred."

"We offer a reward of a million dollars," Fred the lawyer said. Large cop feet scuffled nervously beneath the table.

"After taxes," Annabelle Winston said quietly.

"After taxes," the lawyer parroted, although his eyebrows, skyrocketing toward his hairline, revealed that this was clearly a bulletin as far as he was concerned, "to any citizen who conclusively identifies this . . . this Incinerator."

"My God, you're turning it into the lottery," the captain said. Nobody else said anything. Hammond pulled out a cigar.

"Please don't light that," Annabelle Winston said. "I can't stand smoke."

I stared at her. I'd seen her smoke. Hammond's face turned the color of rare roast beef. Captain or no captain, it was clear whose meeting this was.

"We're prepared to post the reward at a press conference at two this afternoon," Fred the lawyer continued. "That will enable the television-news operations to scoop the *Times*, as I understand it." Bobby Grant gave a nod of encouragement.

"It's more their kind of story," he said. "They'll go to town with it. And then, of course, there's the radio news stations."

"Has this press conference been announced?" That was the captain.

"Not yet," Bobby Grant said, "but I can have it on the city news wire in five minutes."

"You're interfering with a police investigation," the captain said. His face was redder than Hammond's.

"What investigation?" Annabelle Winston asked. "We don't know what that means. Forgive me, gentlemen, but my father died last night, and so did Leo Quint, was that his name, Leo Quint? That makes a total of seven, and where are you? Seven human beings."

"Ten," Dr. Schultz said.

The silence that followed was broken by the lawyer unsnapping his briefcase and taking out a pad. He made a note in a lawyer's tiny handwriting. When he was finished, he looked at Dr. Schultz.

"Ten?" he said.

"None of this goes out of this room," the captain interposed.

"Listen," Annabelle Winston said, leaning forward to put her elbows on the table. "It goes wherever we want it to go if we're not satisfied with the course of action you propose."

"Miss Winston," the captain said with leaden geniality. He sounded as though he were talking to a little girl who'd just asked for a pony for Christmas. "Surely some information is privileged."

"If the people the Incinerator is burning were privileged," Annabelle Winston said acidly, "he'd be in jail by now. Let me make our position clear, Lieutenant."

"Captain," the captain said.

"It doesn't make any difference to me if you're a choirboy," Annabelle Winston said without raising her voice. "Shut up and let me finish." The lawyer tried to pat her wrist reassuringly, and she slapped his hand away. "Either you satisfy me, or we're going to make a laughingstock out of the entire Los Angeles Police Department. You don't think we can do it? I'm Baby Winston. I go to the bathroom and it's news. I buy a hat in New York, and designers in Paris change their plans. I've fought that kind of attention since I was fifteen. Well, now I'm going to invite it. How would you like to see me on the cover of *People*? I can arrange it, or Bobby can."

"'Orphaned Heiress on the Hunt,' something like that," Bobby Grant said with relish. It would look good on his résumé.

Annabelle Winston lifted the hand with the emerald, and Grant clamped his lips shut, further eloquence reduced to a bubble of air that pushed his mouth forward like a monkey's. "The offer of a million dollars is on the square," Annabelle said. "I could spend that on eye shadow and not miss it. I may only be a girl, Captain, but I've run a multimillion-dollar corporation on my own for three years. I went to Mr. Grist because I didn't trust your abilities," she said, looking at me while I tried to figure out how to slide under the table without being missed. "The fact is, gentlemen," Annabelle Winston said, "as far as this case is concerned, you don't know jack shit."

I tried to think of something conciliatory to say as Dr. Schultz and one of the lieutenants both pulled out packs of cigarettes and then remembered the ban on smoking. The lieutenant put his pack back, while Dr. Schultz laid his on the table and drummed his nails on it.

"The deal," the captain said grudgingly, trying to sound like someone with an option. "We might as well listen to the deal."

"Give us all the information. Give us a full game plan. If I'm satisfied, *Captain*, I'll be a good girl." Annabelle Winston gave him a winning smile along with his proper rank. "Just persuade me that you've got an idea that will catch the Incinerator, and I'll fade away. Catch him, you get all the credit. Don't catch him, and I'll fry you alive."

She looked around the table. "Sorry about the metaphor," she said. She didn't sound sorry.

Nobody spoke. Then the captain looked at Dr. Schultz and nodded.

"Here's what we know," Schultz said smoothly. He directed the smile, crinkles and all, at Annabelle. "He started last year at about the same time, the beginning of the fire season. September twenty-sixth he burned a bum named Warren Fields. A transient, same as the others. October nineteenth we had another incident. Same *modus operandi*, same results. Two men this time. The victims died of third-degree burns. Then nothing. We hoped that the, um, Incinerator was one of the two, that maybe he'd made a mistake and doused himself with gasoline, too, and that the two of them had gone up in smoke, as it were, together."

"Wishful thinking," Annabelle Winston said, dropping the words onto the table like rocks.

She got a mournful gaze from Schultz in return. "Well, it seemed to be the case, because that was the end of it. Until this year." Schultz gazed around the room, looking more defeated than he wanted to look. "Then it started again." He regarded the note projected on the wall as though he hoped it held hidden clues.

"He waits for the fire season," I said.

"He's *activated* by the fire season," Schultz replied. "The fire season triggers something irresistible in him. Maybe it's the television coverage or the smell of smoke. Who knows why he burns someone one night but not the next? You must understand, Miss Winston, that a serial murderer is the most difficult of all." Annabelle didn't look particularly understanding, but Dr. Schultz plowed on. "Eighty-five, eighty-seven percent of all murders in the United States are committed by someone the victim knew, usually intimately, and that statistic takes into account the people who are killed during violent crimes, robberies, and so forth. Well, that's relatively simple. You sift through the possible suspects and choose the most likely. Most of the time you're right.

"But the serial murderer, like this Incinerator," Schultz said, pronouncing the word with evident distaste, "chooses his victims at random. Stranger to stranger, the new murder fad. They have no relation to him. He can kill anywhere, at any time."

"He doesn't," Annabelle Winston said abruptly.

"Beg pardon?" Schultz asked. He'd picked up his cigarettes again as though he hoped someone would give him permission to light one.

"He doesn't kill just anywhere. He kills in a very specific district, and he kills only one kind of people. Skid Row and bums. Like my father."

"Your father was hardly a bum," Schultz said.

"Dr. Schultz," Annabelle Winston said, stressing the title in a way that would have made a lesser man leave the room, "you think he made my father fill out a financial statement before he struck the match? You think that bums feel like bums? You don't believe that all of them think that they're going to find their way back to, to, I don't know, clean clothes, and friends, and a decent room at some point in the future? You think that all of them secretly want to be a bonfire?"

Schultz shuffled some papers, taking refuge in facts. "He's educated, probably college educated. Probably comes from a broken home, middle class or lower middle class, almost all serial murderers do. At some point in his childhood, he had a traumatic experience with fire. Traumatic, in this case, means—"

"I know what traumatic means," Annabelle Winston said. "'Activated' was a new one to me, but I've been analyzed to the point of death."

Schultz permitted himself a superior smile. "The analysand," he said, "usually knows less about analysis than the doctor."

"I know bullshit when I hear it," Annabelle Winston said, "and I'm listening to it now." She touched her lawyer's shoulder. "Fred," she said, "why don't we leave? They haven't got anything."

"He lives alone," Schultz said, a trifle desperately. "Or with parents, more likely with his mother, someone who doesn't question his actions. His mother is *extremely* important to him. He's manipulative, probably has been since childhood. Good at hiding who he really is, his secret identity. In a way, you could say he's playful."

"Playful?" It was the captain, and it was scornful.

Schultz anxiously pressed his thinning hair down onto his scalp. "He's been fooling the world for as long as he can remember. He enjoys it. He's a trickster and he thinks of himself as more intelligent than anyone else. He loves making all of us sit up or roll over, whichever he wants." He seemed to lose his place and glanced down at his notes. "And he kills men. That's very significant." He paused, waiting for someone to ask him why.

"Why?" I finally asked. I was feeling sorry for him.

"Male serial murderers—they're almost all male—kill women," he said gratefully. "That makes him very unusual. It's also unusual that he kills people at the very bottom of the social ladder, so to speak. Most serial murderers kill up, by which I mean they take revenge on members of a class that's above them."

"How do we know it's not a woman?" Annabelle Winston asked.

"Hermione," Hammond said unexpectedly from the end of the table.

"And who's Hermione?" I asked.

"That's to come," the captain said, glaring furiously at Hammond.

"It's to come right now," Annabelle Winston said. "Otherwise we're walking." To emphasize her point, she stood up.

"The lady with the blanket," Hammond growled.

"She has a name," Annabelle Winston said. "Does she have a location?"

"She's here," the captain said to the table, "in protective custody."

"Mr. Grist will need to talk to her," Annabelle Winston said, sitting. "If you know he's a man, she must have seen him."

"I thought you quit," Hammond said, sounding betrayed.

"I did," I said.

"I didn't accept your resignation," Annabelle Winston said. "And if you quit, what are you doing here?"

It was a good question. "I had to bring the letter down anyway, and I'm nosy. I figured I might as well hang around for the meeting, since you'd invited me. But I'm afraid that I really do quit."

"Actually, I don't think you do," the captain said.

"Um," I said, feeling like a hiker whose compass had just reversed itself. "Captain. Captain, ah . . . I'm afraid I didn't get your name."

"Finch."

"Right, Captain Finch. Nice to meet you." Finch's stare said that he'd just as soon have met me via a head-on collision. "I don't share Miss Winston's opinion of the LAPD. I think you're going to catch him. And I don't really like the kind of exposure I'm getting. I especially don't like the fact that the Incinerator knows where I live, and I'm not crazy about knowing that he's trying to figure out whether I'm friend or fuel. Anyway, as I say, I quit."

Captain Finch gave me a narrow glance as he weighed the consequences of shooting me and then turned for help to Dr. Schultz.

"Well," Schultz said, with some discomfort, "with all due regard for the police officers present, I share Miss Winston's feeling." He gazed at me and worked on his facial muscles until he was smiling. "We may not catch him without your help."

Now everybody in the room was looking at me. I may have been the center of attention, but I wasn't popular. "And why am I so important?"

"Because he's talking to you," Schultz said. "It's exactly what we haven't had until now. It's why we haven't caught him. Look at the tone of that letter. He's joking with you about not answering the first note. 'As long as we're chatting,' he says. 'We might be brothers,' he says. He's having fun, but this man is obviously starved for someone to talk to. You're a link, Mr. Grist, the first human link we've had to him. We can't lose you. It's that simple."

"It's nowhere near that simple," I said. "I'm not a telephone,

and I'm not willing to be your open line to someone who's burned
ten people to death. Not when I might be number eleven. This
is not a line of fire I want to be in. Excuse the metaphor, as Miss
Winston said a few minutes ago."

"Why do you know about Ahriman?" Dr. Schultz asked.

"One of my degrees is in comparative religion."

Dr. Schultz's eyebrows went up. "*One* of your degrees?"

"I have four," I said. "That's what I did before I became an
investigator, I was a professional college student. A teacher, too,
briefly."

"So we should be calling you Dr. Grist," Schultz said frater-
nally. He had a heavy hand with the butter.

"I'll leave the titles to you. Call me anything you want,
but call me at home. I really quit." I pushed back my chair
and stood up.

"You can't go," Finch said.

"Watch me."

"Willick," Captain Finch said.

I laughed. "*Willick?*" I said. "You're threatening me with
Willick?" Willick stood up, looking hapless. "Choose somebody
else," I said. "I never hit a man wearing a notebook."

"Please, Mr. Grist," Annabelle Winston said. I paused, looking down at her. She was wearing less lipstick, and her mouth
wasn't the problem it had been on Saturday.

"He's opened the channel," Dr. Schultz said impatiently.

"What channel?"

"The channel of communication," Schultz said. "He's been
alone with his secret, with his secret *pride*, for more than a year
now. Now he's chosen someone, and the person he's chosen is
perfect. Educated, sympathetic—he hopes—even conversant with
ancient religions. My guess is that this man knows all there is
to know about fire, from a physical, chemical, mythological, and
religious standpoint. And now he's found a kindred soul. At least,
from his perspective, someone he can play with. Please understand, Mr. Grist. You're one end of a thread. The Incinerator is
at the other end."

"The Minotaur was at the other end of Theseus' thread," I
said. "No, thanks."

"He wants to talk, Mr. Grist," Schultz plowed on. "Specifically, he wants to talk to *you*."

"You're grasping at straws," I said. "He'll find someone else to talk to."

"He will *not*," Dr. Schultz said. "He's chosen you. He's *fixated* on you, for God's sake. He's searched the world, and he's found a friend. Read the *letter*, would you?"

"I've read it, thanks. He more or less suggests that he might throw his next match at me."

"He won't, if he thinks you're on his side," Dr. Schultz said. "He won't talk to anybody else. Please. Ten people have died."

"One of them was my father," Annabelle Winston said. "He killed Santa Claus."

Even her lawyer blinked.

"Why won't he?" I demanded. "Why not get some newspaper columnist to write something, an open letter or something?"

Dr. Schultz shook his head. "Newspaper columns have been written. He didn't respond. He hasn't responded to anything so far, and that's unusual, too. The rocket went up when your name appeared in print."

"Why? All it was was a name and the fact that I was a detective. I don't recall anything about a degree in comparative religion."

"Unless I'm wrong, Mr. Grist," Dr. Schultz said, playing his trump, "I think he knows you."

The room didn't exactly whirl, but I put a hand on the back of the chair I'd just vacated. "Do that one again," I said.

"You may not know him," Schultz said, "or you may have forgotten him, but I believe that he knows you. I believe that he read your name and recognized it and wrote that first letter. I think you're going to get more letters in the future. So, you see, you're not just one end of the thread. You're a clue."

I needed a moment to think, and they gave it to me. At the end of the moment, I'd made up my mind, and my decision scared me silly. Since I'd decided, though, I decided to lend Hammond a few points. I knew he'd been slipping since Hazel left.

"What do you think, Al?" I asked him. "I'll do whatever you say."

Finch cleared his throat. Hammond took his time, fighting down a grin. "I think you should stay on it, Simeon," he said at last.

"Can we hear the deal?" I asked, sitting. "Miss Winston's game plan?"

"The deal," Finch said, "is that you appear to remain in Miss Winston's employ."

"Forget it," Annabelle Winston said. "He does not 'appear' to remain in my employ. He *does* remain in my employ."

"A thousand a day," I said, trying to smooth my goose bumps. The son of a bitch *knew* me?

"Done," Annabelle Winston said, without so much as a glance in my direction.

"Wait a minute," Finch said. He didn't make a thousand a week, or anywhere near it.

"Would you prefer the press conference?" the lawyer asked.

"*People* magazine," Bobby Grant chimed in. "Big print."

Finch tugged angrily at his pug nose as though he were trying to make it longer.

"Since I seem to be the key," I said, driving another nail into Finch's coffin, "I positively decline to participate in an investigation I'm not part of. I'll need the benefit of everything you've got, beginning with the strange cars on my street yesterday. Al?"

Hammond looked at Captain Finch. After what seemed like a century, Captain Finch dropped his chin half an inch. I've seen football teams gain fifty yards with less effort than it took Finch to nod that half an inch. Hammond opened his notebook. "It wasn't easy," he said for the benefit of his superiors. "The Sunday edition of the *Times* hit the streets at six-thirty. Figure the guy doesn't live in Topanga—no one does—and figure it takes an hour to drive there from downtown, where the fires have been. Simeon got the letter at about eleven, so that meant we had to find someone who'd been awake and more or less focused on the street between seven-thirty and ten-fifty."

"Spare us the difficulties," Finch said sharply. "Just get to it."

"We found a kid," Hammond said. "William Pinnace, aged fifteen."

It was my turn to grin. Billy Pinnace was the biggest grower in Topanga. He had at least a dozen marijuana patches tucked away in the chaparral. Of all the people on the street, he had the best reason to be looking for unfamiliar cars.

"The Pinnace kid was very cooperative," Hammond said, ignoring me. "There were four cars. A Cadillac, an old pickup—he didn't know the make—a Mazda RX-7, and a Nissan Sentra or something like that."

"Did he get license plates?" Finch asked.

Hammond gave him a street-weary gaze. "Oh, come on," he said.

"It was the Mazda," I said. I had the room's attention. "Why was it the Mazda, Dr. Schultz?"

Schultz winked at me. It took me by surprise. "Zoroastrianism," he said. "The fire religion. Ahriman was the bad god. Ahura Mazda was the good one."

"You pass," I said. "What color was the Mazda?" I asked Hammond.

"Gunmetal gray," Hammond said.

"The driver?"

"Male, blond hair, thirties, the kid said."

"I'll want a full briefing later," I said to Finch, just to rub it in. "For now, let's divide up chores: what I do, what the police do. Let's make it good enough to persuade Miss Winston to call off her press conference. And then let's go talk to Hermione."

7

Aged Ladies

"He was tall," Hermione Something said in the voice of one who's been asked the same question many times. "Tall and thin and black. He looked like a big black cigarette."

"He was black?" I asked, remembering the blond driver of the Mazda.

"Stupid," Hermione Something said to herself. "Cops are stupid."

"I'm not a cop," I said. Behind me, Hammond muttered something that might or might not have been a blanket defense of cops.

"*He* is," Hermione said, scratching a grimy leg. "You're with him, aren't you? What does that make you, a Girl Guide?"

I tried to reconcile Hermione with the vision I'd had of her when I first heard her name. At the time I'd thought of an aged lady, a distinguishedly aged lady whose contemporaries might have been called Ora or Blossom or Mayme. With a Y. Hermione was a name that conjured up screened porches and soft evenings and silk fans fluttering like cabbage moths over white wicker furniture, something from the summertimes of long ago, when the hills didn't catch fire and the eucalyptus trees imported from Australia hadn't taken hold to spike the California horizon. A name with mint juleps in it. All that was left of the vision was the mint juleps. The Hermione I was faced with, in a relatively comfortable cell in Parker Center, was someone whose skin was coated in the kind of dirt you couldn't remove with steel wool, whose hair hadn't been washed in a month, and who would probably choose a mint julep over a pint of turpentine if the choice were at hand. If not, she'd have drunk the turpentine.

"From England, aren't you?" I asked.

"Who are you to say where I'm from?"

"Girl Guides," I said. "Girl Guides are British."

"Well, aren't you the nosy parker," Hermione said. "What difference where I'm from? I saw him, didn't I? Am I going to get my blanket back?"

"You don't want that blanket," I said. "It's all burned. We're going to give you a new one. Was he black?"

"A new blanket?" Hermione asked cannily.

"Brand-new. Plus a hundred dollars." Hammond sneezed discreetly behind me, but I ignored him. "Was he black?"

Hermione rubbed a rope of dirt between her right thumb and forefinger. "You can get me out of here?"

"Are you sure you want to get out? You saw him."

"And he saw me. He couldn't have been less interested. A right poofter, if you ask me." She waved a limp and extremely dirty wrist in the air to indicate that any male who could resist her charms was a right poofter indeed.

"And was he black?"

"He was *wrapped* in black," Hermione said. "He was as white as you and me."

"What else?"

The wrinkles around her eyes deepened into rivulets. "*Can you get me out of here?*" she asked again.

"Al," I said, since nothing else would satisfy her, "can I get her out?"

"Absolutely," Hammond said.

"You're out," I said. "What do you mean, he was wrapped in black?"

"Head to toe," she said. "All black. Wrapped up tight, like I said, like a cigarette. Light hair, he had. The color of good champagne. Do you like champagne?"

"I like beer better."

"Another member of the dreary proletariat." Hermione scratched familiarly at something under her left arm, probably something I'd spent most of my years trying to avoid. "Where's the life these days?" she asked the world at large. "There used to be life."

"It's where it always was," I said. "Hanging out in expensive places. What else can you tell me?"

"Very tall," Hermione said again, running a tongue over her lips before she disclosed her secret, whatever it was she hadn't told the cops.

"What else?" I said again.

"Walked with a tilt." She pronounced "with" as "wiv."

"With a tilt?" I asked.

"Wrapped all in black," she repeated. "Walked wiv a tilt. Crippled. Clubfoot, if you ask me." She got up. "Squeaked, too. Now where's that blanket?"

Hammond said, "Squeaked?"

Hermione was back on the street, and I was nowhere.

I was in the precise section of nowhere where the burnings had taken place, the area Los Angeles calls Skid Row. Skidded Row would be more precise; it's where people wind up at the end of their skid. For a few people, a statistically dismissible few in these years of Republican optimism, the trapdoor beneath their lives drops open one day, and they find themselves on a slide, a slide greased with alcohol or psychedelics or opiates or racial discrimination or just plain rotten luck, and the end of the slide dumps them out on Skidded Row. Some of them bring their children with them. The American postnuclear family.

What the hell did "squeaked" mean?

I'd considered the idea that I knew the Incinerator and dismissed it as useless. I was inclined to agree with Schultz, up to a point: He might know me, but I certainly didn't know him. Our lives are full of people who remember us with love or loathing, and whom we've forgotten entirely. He'd sounded, in Hermione's description, like a fairly memorable figure: tall, blond, walked with a limp. I'd played flash cards with my memory for hours after the meeting without coming up with anyone who fit the bill. Of course, the limp could have been faked. The hair could have been a wig. He could have been a dwarf on stilts, too.

Why hadn't he killed her? She'd seen him. Under the circumstances, chivalry didn't seem like an acceptable reason.

So at four on a hot Monday afternoon, I was walking aimlessly around the outskirts of Little Tokyo in downtown L.A., looking at people with neither money nor hope, feeling guilty about Annabelle Winston's five-thousand-dollar check in my pocket, and—and doing what? Gathering impressions, I told myself. Visiting the scenes of the crimes. This was where they'd happened: This was where the Incinerator had materialized nine times, tall, black, slanting, and squeaking, over his sleeping, wine-sodden victims, poured gasoline on them, and struck a wooden kitchen match. The police had found wooden kitchen matches at all the scenes, broken matches that had failed to strike. I imagined him, frenzied, furious, desperate to light the sacred flame, flinging the defective ones aside. He must have been frantic. But he'd taken the time to stand there and strike match after match, moments that must have seemed like centuries to him.

Gathering impressions, I looked down at two men, two unimaginably filthy men, sleeping as though they were dead in the doorway of an abandoned shop. Their limbs were sprawled loosely, and one of them had thrown his arm heavily over the chest of the other. I could have been John Philip Sousa, marching band in tow, and they wouldn't have known I'd paid them a visit.

Setting people on fire, I thought, is a labor-intensive method of murder. For one thing, it requires that the victim hold still. First you had to squirt the gasoline, four times, according to the first letter, and then you had to strike matches until one finally caught, and the victim had to cooperate by not going anywhere in the meantime, while three or four or five matches broke or sputtered out before you got the one that did the job.

Schultz came unbidden to mind—I certainly wouldn't have consciously summoned him—and said something about it being unusual that the Incinerator struck at people at the bottom of the social ladder, such a smug phrase, and I suddenly dismissed the Incinerator's verbiage about carrion and biological misfires, and imagined myself asking him the question: "Why the homeless?"

"*They hold still*," he answered in my imagination.

Experimentally, silently asking someone for pardon, I nudged one of the sleeping men with my foot. He held still.

I went knocking on doors.

                              *   *   *

I must have knocked on forty doors, concentrating on the dreadful little apartments one story above the abandoned, urine-sodden shops, the apartments that faced the street and whose windows opened only ten or twelve feet above the sidewalk, before I hit Mrs. Gottfried. I'd been rejected in various dialects of English and Spanish before Mrs. Gottfried peered out at me through a door featuring no fewer than three slip-chains on the inside and said, "So? *Nu?*"

It was a new dialect, at any rate. "I'd like to talk to you," I said.

"I paid the water," she said. Her face was so narrow that I could see most of it through the two inches of cracked door, and her bright black eyes regarded me with enough distrust to suggest several lifetimes of unrelieved betrayal.

"It's not about the water," I said, searching through my repertoire of ingenuous facial expressions to find one that would reassure her. I failed.

"So go away," she said, trying to close the door. When she couldn't, she looked down and saw my foot wedged between the doorjamb and the edge of the door.

"Move the foot," she said. "You don't move the foot, I call the cops." The accent might have been Polish.

"Call them," I said. "Call Lieutenant Al Hammond downtown and tell him that Simeon Grist is here. I'll wait. I'll even move my foot and let you close the door if you want, as long as you promise to open it and talk to me after you finish with the cops."

"Cops I don't like," she said. "I seen enough kinds of cops to know they're all the same." Then she squinted up at me. "You're no cop. Cops don't say 'cop.'"

"No, I'm not. I'm a private detective."

"What's it to me?"

"I've been hired by a woman whose father was burned to death on this street."

"Abraham Winston," she said. "All the papers. I can read English."

"Weinstein," I said. "Abraham Weinstein."

She looked down at the gnarled fingers wrapped around the door. "Well, I figured that," she said. "Please. Abraham? My kids changed their name, too. Now it's Godfrey. Fitting in, huh?"

"I saw him before he died."

"Ach, the pain," she said, "I can imagine."

"His daughter saw it, too."

She kicked my shoe with a tiny black-clad foot. "So come in," she said.

The apartment was tiny and dim, crowded with dark, heavy furniture. There were carpets everywhere, and a smell of cooking in the air. Mrs. Gottfried was thinner than a lost hope. She gestured me toward the chunky sofa.

"So sit," she said. "Hungry?"

"No," I said.

"Me, too," she said. "I cook for the smell. Smell is the sense closest to memory, do you know that? That was Freud, hah? I cook to remember. When it's finished cooking, I give it to them." She pointed at the window, in the general direction of the homeless. "I been hungry, I know what it's like."

"Have the cops asked you questions?"

"No." She sat beside me, slowly and experimentally, as though she wasn't sure her body was up to it. "They tried. I looked out through the little hole I had somebody put in the door, I saw the uniforms. I hate uniforms, so I went away and let them knock."

"That was why you wouldn't talk to them? Because of the uniforms?"

She looked at me as though I were the youngest and most innocent human being on earth. Then she stretched out her right arm and showed me the number tattooed on it. There was something formal about the gesture, like a lady at the Viennese Opera demonstrating the quality of her full-length silk gloves.

"371332," she said without looking at it. "It's a big number. They all wore uniforms. How neat their uniforms were, and how dirty we were. That was part of what was so terrible. When I got brought to New York, when it was all over, I couldn't take the bus. The man in the uniform scared me. I couldn't even walk, because how could I ask a cop for directions if I got lost? The uniform, huh? So I stayed home. A car backfiring in the street made me cry. I was crying a lot then." She peered up at me, proving that her eyes were dry.

"Who brought you to New York?"

"My children. A boy and a girl, the boy older. When we saw

how it was at the beginning, my husband and me, may God rest his soul, we packed them up and got them out. We sent them to my sister in New York. But we still didn't believe all of it, so we stayed. There was the business." She smoothed back her graying hair. Her knuckles were swollen, knobby, and arthritic; they looked like the joints at the end of a drumstick. She could have removed her rings only with wire clippers. "The business," she said. "My husband was in fur. We sold to the top monsters. We protected their wives and their fancy women against the cold. 'People will always need fur,' he said to me. We wrapped ourselves in fur against the Holocaust. Are you sure you're not hungry?"

I'd never been less hungry in my life. I shook my head.

"We should have known better," she said. "Fur burns." She closed her eyes. "*Scheiss,*" she added. She wasn't Polish. She was German.

"And your husband?"

"He burned, too," she said dispassionately. She opened her eyes and looked at nothing. For her it was an old story.

"Where are your children now?"

"East. New York. I told you already. The big hepple." She waved the arm with the tattoo to indicate the walls, lined with photographs of heavy men with beards wearing dark suits. Assembled around them were impossibly large families, huge broods of smiling adults and children, now lost, scattered, annihilated, incinerated. "We had to sneak the pictures in their bags after the children slept," she said. "Old pictures don't mean anything except to old people."

"So you sent them out with the children."

"If I hadn't," she said, "I wouldn't have any past. Any happy past, I mean. Nothing left but the fires and the curses. What's my life, huh? These pictures."

"And the soup," I said.

She gave the idea of the soup a one-handed gesture that could have sent it all the way to Latvia. "I do it for the smell," she said again. "It makes the pictures move."

"Sure," I said. "That's the only reason you make the soup."

She tossed a bright, dry, sparrowlike glance at me. "So it's more than that," she said. "That's a federal case? They're hungry, right? Like I said, I been hungry."

"How did your children let you escape from them?" I asked.

"Oh, well," she said, placing her hands in her lap. Her fingers folded over each other like the leaves of a prized manuscript, yellow and faded and hard to read. I thought of Hermione's palm. "I embarrassed them. I couldn't go nowhere. Anywhere, I mean. I couldn't sleep. I was cold all the time. I lost weight in Treblinka, you know? Thirty pounds, no less. I never got it back."

She held up a parchment arm. "Look at me, skin and bones. The New York winters drove spikes through my skin. I felt—what's the word?—impaled, like I was nailed to my bed by icicles. So I woke up in the mornings, on the nights I went to sleep I mean, and I made problems. When I slept, my dreams were all people dead or dying, so I stopped dreaming. Skinny, no English, crying in the middle of parties, scared by loud noises. My grandchildren laughed at me. I embarrassed everybody. It wasn't their fault." She blinked, heavy as a tortoise. "It's a terrible thing to stop dreaming."

"So you came to California," I said for lack of anything else.

"I was brought here," she said. "My children talked about it and brought me out here. I had friends here then. They're all gone now. I got here, it was clean, there were orange trees, you could smell the ocean. Not like now. And it was warm."

"They write you?"

"Oh, sure. Letters every month. They come some, too. My son is very successful now, very busy. When they come, they stay in a hotel."

"No room here," I suggested.

"You," she said, smiling, and I caught a glimpse of the girl she must have been. "More flies with sugar than with vinegar." Unexpectedly, she laughed, a low, rhythmic chortle that summoned up the sound of a tropical lizard on the wall. "You look like my grandson, Eli. That's why you got in the door. You don't need all the sugar."

"You're not a fly," I said.

"No," she said, tapping me on the knee. "But you're not Eli, either. And you didn't come here to pass time making *spiel* with some old lady. You want to know did I see something."

Without realizing what I was doing, I crossed my fingers. "Did you?"

"Yes," she said. She reached down and uncrossed my fingers, laughing again, and then sat back triumphantly and glowed at me.

"Will you tell me about it?"

"What, I'll tell you my whole life story and I wouldn't tell you that? This man, he burns people. I testified," she said proudly. "I testified at Nuremburg. I did that, and I wouldn't testify for you?"

"What did you see?" I asked.

"First was hearing. I was sitting here, right where I am now. I still don't sleep so good. First thing, I heard somebody laugh." She rubbed one forearm as though she'd broken out in goose bumps. "I never heard a laugh like that, and I've heard every noise a human being can make. This laugh wasn't nothing—*any*-thing—human. Then the screaming started, and I went to the window."

The window was four good strides from the couch. "I had to get the shades out of the way," she said. "The screaming kept up the whole time. When I had the shades up, I opened the window and leaned out and looked."

"And," I said.

"And he was on fire, the old man, and the little old lady—I seen her before, I gave her soup a couple of times—she was trying to get the blanket on him. And then I seen—saw—him."

"Saw him? Saw him where?"

"Coming up the street toward me. The streetlights are good here. Not much else, but the streetlights. He had a bottle, some kind of bottle, in his hand, and he tilted to one side like he was broken. 'Hey,' I yelled, '*Schiesskopf.*' And he looked up at me."

"He saw you?" I could barely breathe.

"Saw me? He smiled at me. The old man was on fire, and he was still screaming, and this one smiled at me and waved with the hand that didn't have the bottle in it. It had something else in it, though."

"What?"

"Something square, only not square, you know?"

"Rectangular," I said. "A box of wooden matches."

She nodded. "Could be. And then he said something to me."

"What did he say?"

"He said, 'Hey, Granny, got anything you want to cook?'

And then he waved at me again and ran away. Except he didn't really run, it was like one foot weighed a lot more than the other one."

"Mrs. Gottfried," I said, "what did he look like?"

"Like a Nazi general," she said as though she'd been waiting for the question.

My stomach sank. I had the feeling that a lot of people looked like a Nazi general to Mrs. Gottfried.

"In what way," I asked, "did he look like a Nazi general?"

She lifted her chin and regarded me with the black eyes. "You think I'm making it up," she said accusingly.

"No," I said. "I already know he limps. I believe you saw him. I just want to get a good description."

"I gave you a good description," she said stubbornly. "He looked like a Nazi general, but younger."

"Please, Mrs. Gottfried, I don't know what a Nazi general looked like."

"Blond," she said.

"Why a general?"

"His coat," she said. "How could you not know what a Nazi general looked like? You should know. How could people *forget*?"

"Tell me about his coat."

"It was a, a what do you call it, what Humphrey Bogart always wore."

"A trench coat," I said.

"That's it," she said, "a trench coat. It went all the way from his shoulders to his feet. And it was black."

"Was it canvas?" I asked. She shook her head. "Leather?"

"No," she said. She gave me the sparrow's glance again. "It squeaked."

I thought for a moment. It got me nowhere. It hadn't gotten me anywhere when Hermione said it, either.

"Squeaked?" I asked at last.

"Rubber," Mrs. Gottfried said, sitting back again. She smoothed her skirt with her arthritic hands. "His coat was rubber."

"Mrs. Gottfried," I said, "could I have some soup?"

8

The Radicchio Patrol

"He's a tall, thin blond man with a clubfoot, and he drives a gray Mazda and wears a black rubber trench coat," I said. "He can't be that hard to find."

Pasty beneath the humming fluorescents, Hammond and Dr. Schultz regarded me skeptically. I'd insisted that I report to Hammond, partly to give him something to do and partly because it was nice to be in a position where I could insist on something, and I didn't want to waste it. As a trade, Captain Finch had insisted that Dr. Schultz be present whenever I did. Willick, who was apparently connected to Hammond by an invisible silken cord, sat fatly at the foot of the table, taking notes.

"Who's your source?" Dr. Schultz asked through a cloud of smoke. He was leaning back, his chair tilted on its rear legs, the picture of manicured ease. The cigarette in his hand, his third in fifteen minutes, was a Dunhill. I might have known.

"For what?"

"Rubber," he said to the cigarette. "The supposition that the trench coat is made of rubber. Hermione told you everything else."

Hammond fidgeted.

"Skip it," I said. "She doesn't want to talk to the police. And, by the way, Al," I added nastily, "thanks." I knew that Hermione hadn't told anyone but me about the limp. She'd been saving it to get out of the jug. Was Hammond my friend, or just another cop?

"Procedure," Hammond said automatically. He didn't meet my eyes, though.

Dr. Schultz clenched his teeth together in a way that made his jaw muscles bulge. His eyes were smaller than caviar. I tried not to look too terrified. Hammond looked as reasonable as it was possible for Hammond to look. Willick made scratching noises. "This is a cooperative investigation," Schultz said.

"Who's cooperating with me?" I asked Hammond.

"You've had everything we've got," Dr. Schultz said. "There's no reason to be hostile."

"Then may I have your address and phone number?" I asked him.

"For what?" he asked, streaming smoke, blue under the lights, through his nostrils.

"For the next press conference."

He tilted back a little farther in his chair and then had to catch a foot under the table to keep from going over the rest of the way. The foot made a hollow *thunk* on the underside of the table, and Schultz had a coughing fit. He hunched over, hacking into his cupped hands. "Of course not," he said when he'd finished. "Do you think I'm crazy?" He glanced at Willick as though to reassure himself that there was at least one person in the room who hadn't seen him lose his balance. Willick was staring at him, his mouth open.

"Then don't tell me there's no reason for me to be hostile," I said. "He knows where *I* live, and I doubt very much that you're giving me everything you've got."

"Then how can we verify it?" He gave me the amber smile again. He saw me staring at the pack of Dunhills, positioned on the table like a Chinese household god, and picked it up and extended it to me with the generous confidence of a born skinflint who knows that his offer will be rejected. I reached out and took the pack.

"Thanks," I said. "I can't usually afford these."

He kept the smile in place. He was being very professional, very doctoral. Just one Ph.D. to another. "I ask you," he said, "how can we verify it?"

"You can verify it by your common sense," I said. "It was rubber because rubber isn't permeable. Rubber keeps the gasoline from getting on his clothes. He gets home, he hoses off the coat, and he's as pure as the Madonna. The one in the paintings, not the one who sings songs in a girdle."

"That's no girdle," Hammond said. "That dame don't need no girdle." Willick looked surprised at the fact that Hammond had heard of Madonna. I was surprised, too: So much for my theory about cops and popular songs.

"And who was the source?" Schultz asked again, putting out the filter of his cigarette and stealing another glance at the pack in my hand. He was sitting straight in his chair now. He only lounged when he was working on his emphysema.

"No one you'll ever meet," I said.

"I'm not sure that's wise," Schultz said, making a note.

I got mad. Maybe it was the note. "So tell me how wise it was to sit there dreaming up elaborate theories about why the Incinerator was hitting people at the bottom of the social ladder. I believe that was your phrase?"

"It was," Schultz said. He tried the smile on me, without much success.

"Have you ever burned anyone to death, Dr. Schultz?"

As a man with credentials, he frowned. "Of course not."

"He chooses them because they hold still," I said. "You're a psychologist. Why haven't you asked why he uses wooden matches? Why not switch to a Bic or something so he doesn't have to stand there breaking matches until one finally lights? He lights fire to the homeless because they're anesthetized, because they're dead to the world, because they *give him time*. He needs time partly because he's using wooden matches."

Hammond said something that sounded like "whuff." Dr. Schultz, with the expertise that comes with years of being on the profitable end of psychoanalysis, said, "Interesting," and changed the subject. "Have you figured out where he knows you from?"

"No," I said.

"My guess," Schultz said, closing his eyes to prove how hard he was thinking, "is college."

It sounded like a good guess, and it was one I'd already made myself, but I was still aggravated that Hammond had told him everything that happened in Hermione's cell. "I was in college most of my adult life," I said. "I'll work on that if you'll work on this: Why does he stick with wooden matches?" I twisted the cigarette pack into a crumpled spiral by way of emphasis. "Golly," I said, dropping it. "Oops."

Dr. Schultz finally managed to display his awful teeth. "Maybe you'll eventually tell us," he said. He smiled again, an expression with no more affection behind it than a misdirected Valentine, and reached out to take the crumpled pack. With small, precise gestures, he began to smooth it out. When it was almost rectangular, he opened it and tugged one into the light. It was broken. So was the next. He pulled out a third.

"Willick," Dr. Schultz said, "have you got any Scotch tape?"

Eleanor and I had determined several days earlier that it was time to move Hammond into group therapy. Sitting there, I regretted the decision.

"He didn't quit the case?" Eleanor asked Hammond, sounding disbelieving.

"He couldn't," Hammond said. His beefy growl undercut the silvery clink of silverware against fine china and the discreet Vivaldi piccolo concerto that recycled endlessly through the speakers mounted on the silk-covered walls. We were spending Baby's money in a Brentwood restaurant frequented by people whose faces you usually saw in only two dimensions and four-color printing.

"And why not?" Eleanor asked. She was all in black, and she looked like the whitest woman in the world. She regarded her salad doubtfully, as though it were something that had sprouted on her plate.

"Honey," Hammond said, patting her wrist. He was the only man in the world who could have called Eleanor "honey" and lived. "He's stuck."

"Any word from Hazel, Al?" I asked to change the subject momentarily. I had a lot to say to him, but I wanted to wait for the right moment.

"I heard from her lawyers," he said. "Fifty percent of the world." His tone turned that avenue of conversation into a dead end. He hadn't drunk enough for the therapy to begin. Anyway, I'd just decided there wasn't going to be any therapy tonight.

"Lawyers are the utensils people use to eat each other with," I said, poking through my own salad. "No bandanna tonight, Al?"

"What's a bandanna?" Hammond asked, the picture of innocence.

I skipped the idea of waiting for the right moment. "It's a hat worn by somebody who wants to prove he's stupid," I said, leaning forward so quickly that my plate skidded away from me. Eleanor forgot she was mad and stared at me. "Like you, you bluecoated Kim Philby."

"Who's she?" Hammond asked, looking almost nervous. "Kim Novak I know."

The headwaiter, who had been hovering over us, cleared his throat and looked down at my plate, which was teetering on the edge of the table. "Something is wrong?"

"Radicchio," I said. "Major allergy. It could kill me."

He made a clucking sound. They must teach it at the Culinary Institute of America. I'd heard it all over the map. "I'm so sorry," he said. "Something else, then?"

"This," I said, handing him the plate to get rid of him. "Just pick out the radicchio."

"*Simeon,*" Eleanor said, with a spot of color on each cheek. She hated scenes.

"And chop-chop," I said. The headwaiter gave me a ghastly smile and retreated toward the kitchen. I even had Hammond's attention.

"We have ground rules to get straight," I said. "I'm contagious, and you're not helping, Al."

"You're stuck," Hammond said once more. "Ignore this boor, Eleanor. Eat your salad."

Eleanor looked speculatively at me, consulting her bullshit-detector.

"No fooling," I said to her. "You were the first one to spot it. This could be fatal. And not just for me."

Hammond sat there, his eyes very small, looking like the Hammond I'd first met, back when I was seeking a police contact. If there had been ground to paw, he would have pawed it.

"Your impressive Dr. Schultz," I said to Hammond, "thinks

that the Incinerator knows me, remember? Thinks he's *fixated* on me. Even if he's wrong, which I don't think he is, the nutcase knows where I live. He's delivered letters to me. How hard would it be for him to find out about Eleanor, too? How hard is it to believe that he's out there, right now, watching this restaurant because he followed me here?"

"He's not following you," Hammond said in the tone of a fundamentalist confronted unexpectedly by a fossil. "He couldn't take the chance."

"Al," I said, leaning across the table and grasping his forearm, "this one is crazy. He thinks he's a god. For all we know, he's sitting right out there on the other side of Twenty-sixth Street, waiting to crank up his Mazda and follow one of us home." Hammond and Eleanor looked at each other. "And, Al, he already knows where I live. He's not going to follow me. That leaves two, right?" Hammond sat back very heavily.

"He doesn't burn women." He glanced involuntarily at Eleanor.

"Not yet," I said.

The headwaiter put my salad, much reduced, on the table in front of me with a badly suppressed sniff. "No radicchio, sir," he said.

"Says you," I said. "Take it away." I thought he was going to bite me, but instead he picked up the plate and left, walking like a gymnast on the balance beam.

"Okay, Simeon," Eleanor said when he'd gone, "you've been very impressive. Now what's the point?"

"It's just like you said yesterday," I said, drinking some of the vault-quality Margaux she'd chosen when I'd told them the evening was on Baby. "There are two points. The first point is that I'm off-limits. Either of you wants to meet me, the first thing you do is call. We set something up, something that involves me doing everything I can possibly do to avoid a tail. Nobody comes to my house, not ever. Yesterday was the last time, until this is over." She nodded, although a tiny twitch in her eye said that she was dying to argue with me.

"If anybody at Parker Center needs to talk to me," I told Hammond, "it has to be set up far enough ahead of time so I've got the hours it takes to get from one place to another without this pyromaniac being able to follow me there. Better yet, we never meet at Parker Center. We set a meeting place that he wouldn't suspect, a shopping mall or a motel or some damn thing, and all the cops get there fifteen minutes before I do, so he can't possibly see them arrive if he's following me, and they leave an hour before I do. And someone is positioned to watch my back from the moment I arrive at the location until I'm out of sight. And if it's a motel, the cop should be a woman."

"Why do they leave earlier?" Eleanor asked, ignoring the last remark. "Instead of after?"

"Because if I leave first, he may wait for whoever comes through the door next and follow him instead of me, and if he follows him back to Parker Center, I'm fuel. I've had many ambitions in life, but none of them was to be fuel."

Eleanor wrapped her arms tightly around herself, digesting it.

"What's point two?" Hammond asked.

"Point two," I said, "is that the jerk I've chosen for my contact, since I'm stuck with this suicidal job, keeps his big fat mouth shut."

As Hammond seethed, a new waiter—the headwaiter was keeping a sullen distance—put the main courses onto the tabletop with reproachful thunks, loud enough to make other diners stare at us.

"Al," I said, as the waiter huffed toward the bar, "there is no margin for bullshit here. You're a leak."

Hammond recoiled, knocking over his drink but recovering it before most of it spilled. "A *leak*," he said, outraged, "to the *cops?*"

"Exactly. You don't tell me what you've told them, you're a leak, pure and simple. I'm the end of the thread, remember, Al? I said it to Baby Winston, and I'll say it to you. If there's a fuckup, I want it to be *my* fuckup. I'm dangling out there, and maybe you are and maybe Eleanor is, and Eleanor means more to me than you and I do put together. I have to know who's involved, and I have to know what they're doing. I don't want somebody like Willick, or somebody even remotely like Willick, moving on his own without me knowing everything, and I mean absolutely everything, every detail and every stitch in the pattern, out front. If you're not happy with that, let me know, and Baby and Bobby Grant can hold their press conference and everybody can go home and see what happens. Me, I'll move into a Holiday Inn until it's over."

Hammond gazed regretfully at the tiny splash of spilled wine and calculated the odds in his head. When he'd finished, he looked up at me like the Hammond I'd grown to know, a fundamentally good man whose brutal and brutalizing job had cost him his family. "Just tell me what you want," he said.

I pushed my main course aside, and silverware clattered. Eleanor had already floated hers out into the center of the table. "I want to know that you understand that when I tell you something it's because I need your brains, *not* because I want it passed on to a bunch of strangers. I'm not willing to trust my life, or Eleanor's life, or even your life, to people I don't know. I'll tell you what I want passed on and what I don't. And if you tell me everything your guys get, I'll tell you everything I get. Otherwise, I'm in a Holiday Inn, someplace like Denver or Des Moines, until you catch him."

"You won't like Des Moines," Eleanor said as the headwaiter hovered, looking down at our neglected entrées.

"Then we'll go to Thailand," I said. "I've got five thousand dollars in my pocket. We'll leave on different flights, you first by a couple of days, both of us going someplace else, and after I check every single passenger on my first flight and make sure he's not on my second one, we'll meet up in Seoul, and then we'll check all the passengers again and go to Thailand and wait for Willick to catch the Incinerator. Then we'll come home."

"Not so fast," Eleanor said. She looked up at the head-waiter and said, "Do you *mind*?" He stepped backward suddenly, bumping into the table behind him. "Simeon," she said as the headwaiter apologized to two anorexics who were picking at their salads, possibly seeking the deadly radicchio, "we've got our own problems to work out. Also, I've got a book contract to fulfill."

"It's a lot less pressing than the possibility of burning to death," I said.

"True," she said. "But there's Burt."

Burt was the publisher, an inexhaustible optimist who had pronounced her upcoming book, *Eastern Roots*, based on her recent visit with her own extended family in China, a Really, Really

Important Book. More important even, in the Universal Scheme of Things, than her last, *The Right-Brain Cookbook*, a collection of recipes that were supposed to enhance creativity. I had my own opinion of both the book and its publisher. My opinion of the book was based on the fact that its inspiration had been a sarcastic remark I'd made about the old belief that some foods were supposed to be brain food, and wasn't *that* a pregnant topic for the New Age? She'd taken me up on it. My opinion hadn't been changed by the sales, which were, as they say, brisk.

My opinion about Burt was more complex. "Burt's a nit," I said. "He wears imitation everything. Imitation Gucci, imitation Armani, an imitation Rolex. He's got an imitation smile, and his vocabulary is an imitation of Norman Vincent Peale. Even his hair is an imitation, for Christ's sake. It looks like something that a misguided housewife would put on the lid of a toilet seat."

Eleanor was looking at me with an expression I couldn't read.

"Except that it isn't pink," I added. "I've seen better rugs for sale on the sidewalk. In bad neighborhoods."

"What he thinks about me is real," Eleanor said stubbornly, "which is more than I could say for some."

Hammond looked from her to me and got up. "Pit stop," he said tactfully.

"Have a lube job while you're at it," I said. "This could take a while."

Eleanor regarded me steadily as Hammond headed for the john.

"So much for Thailand," I said.

"You don't have to like him," Eleanor said. "I think we're past the point where you have to like him."

"As someone who's halfway to being a guru, you should know more about male psychology."

She looked out the window, and I wondered who might be looking back in. "It's supposed to be a surprise that you're possessive?"

"Oh, bull's-eye," I said nastily. "And you don't go all white around the mouth every time Baby Winston's name comes up, do you?"

She turned back to look at me. "Are you sleeping with her?"

"It's not just possessiveness," I said. "A large part of my self-esteem is anchored in the fact that you fell in love with me. How am I supposed to feel when you fall in love with this bedbug, a guy who couldn't tell an ounce of iron pyrite from the Lost Dutchman's mine?" I wasn't whispering, and the headwaiter was glaring at us.

"How are you supposed to feel about yourself, or how are you supposed to feel about me?" Eleanor demanded. "Disregarding your insults about Burt, it usually seems to come down to yourself, Simeon."

I took a breath and used it. "About both of us. It works both ways. I guess one of the reasons I love you is that you had the good taste to fall in love with me."

Eleanor laughed, then stopped abruptly. "I can't have you," she said. "Or, at least, you can't seem to have just me. There always have to be a bunch of other females on the fringes. What am I supposed to be, a quasi-widow? Sleeping in a virginal bed and going on alternate Sundays to clip the grass around the gravestone, while you're still alive and kicking everybody in sight? You haven't got any right to ask that."

I pushed my luck. It's a life-long habit. "Are you sleeping with him?"

She looked away. "I just asked you the same question, except for the pronoun at the end of it. You answer me, I'll answer you."

"No," I said, with all the force of the righteous.

She picked up her glass and took a ladylike sip. "Yes," she said.

It was a little bit like being kicked in the stomach, and picking up a glass seemed like a very good idea. I picked up mine and polished it off and then picked up Hammond's. Eleanor put her hand over mine to keep it on the table. Somebody behind me whispered.

"Don't be silly," she said. "He's a very nice man. What good is that?"

"It's better than listening," I said. I shrugged her hand free and knocked back Hammond's drink. I'd been expecting this, but not just yet.

"You never want to listen," she said. "That's why our talks never work out. You never want to listen. You only want to talk."

"I don't get surprises when I'm talking," I said. "I know how it'll come out."

"You know how you *want* it to come out. But what about me? What about how I want it to come out?"

"Well," I said, "that's up to you and Burt now, isn't it?" I hoisted Hammond's empty glass. "Here's to two-way conversations," I said. "May you have many of them." I poured some more wine, feeling the alcohol hit the complicated traffic pattern of my central nervous system and turn it into gridlock.

"He's not like you," Eleanor said earnestly.

"No kidding. Are his teeth real?"

"Get off it," she said. "I'm an adult female with adult needs. These aren't your precious Victorian times. Trollope and Dickens are dead. We're not supposed to turn our heads, grit our teeth, and bear it just to keep the species going. Yikes, Simeon, what am I supposed to *do*? Haven't you heard about Freud?"

"Just today," I said. "Has he found your G-spot?" The head-waiter, six feet away, cringed.

"My G-spot is in Delaware," she said, her jaw tight.

"Buy him a plane ticket," I said.

"He's afraid of flying," she said.

I started to laugh. I always laugh at the wrong time. After a moment, Eleanor laughed, too.

"You kids have made up, huh?" Hammond said, dropping a heavy hand onto each of our shoulders.

"In a manner of speaking," I said. "We've made our beds and decided to lie in them. You been lubed?"

"I've had my fucking tires aligned," he said loudly, sitting down and looking at the table. "Where are the drinks?"

"Coming up," I said, pouring. "Eleanor drank yours."

Hammond made a fist and put it under my chin. "This is for you if you made her need it," he said genially.

"I'm no longer the one who can make Eleanor need anything," I said. "The torch has been passed."

"And you passed it," Eleanor said. "And never, *ever*, say that I wanted you to."

The headwaiter cleared his throat assertively. "The entrées are not acceptable?" he asked. If his life had depended upon it, he couldn't have kept his upper lip down. It had a life of its own, and its life depended on heading north.

"Are the entrées acceptable?" I asked Hammond. "Perhaps we'd like them flambé?"

"We don't do flambé," the headwaiter said, losing control of his upper lip entirely. It flapped upward like a beached flounder. Flambé was yesterday's culinary news.

"No flambé," I said. "Gosh, too bad. You two still hungry?" I asked Hammond and Eleanor. They both shook their heads. "Check, please," I said. The headwaiter, nearing the part of the Dining Experience during which the Tip usually appeared, mastered his upper lip long enough to smile and headed upwind, away from us.

"You two leave," I said. "The drill begins now."

"He's not following you yet," Hammond insisted, putting down his wineglass.

"The odds against getting AIDS in the course of normal heterosexual contact are about four thousand to one," I said, looking not at Hammond but at Eleanor. "Fooling around much?" I asked him.

Eleanor got up. "Good night," she said. She headed for the door.

"That's one down," I said.

"You don't know shit about women," Hammond said, watching her go. "You know that? Piss her off and send her home into the arms of that clown with the bad toupee."

"Better him than the Incinerator," I said. "When are you leaving, Al?"

"Give this fish a good tip," Hammond said, rising. "You put him into a new life-insurance category. Well, 'night."

"'Night yourself," I said. "Half, huh?"

"And the house," he said. "Women don't fight fair. She'll get the kids. Kids aren't community property. They're all that matters, but they're not community property." People were looking at us again. Hammond glared around the room, and people suddenly found something very interesting on their plates.

"Kids need houses," I said.

"They need fathers, too," Hammond said defiantly. "What do they need more, fathers or houses?"

"Al," I said to the room at large, "don't ask me. My former girlfriend is sleeping with a publisher." The few brave ones who had looked up dived back into their plates.

"Yeah," Hammond said. "So we'll all sleep on it." He picked up a knife and made fencing motions in my direction, to the genteel embarrassment of all in sight. "'Bye," he said, dropping the knife onto the table.

"'Bye," I said. He wove his way to the door, heading for the car that would take him to his empty house. People watched him go, an extravagantly overmuscled man in a tight suit.

"Thank you so much," the headwaiter said, dropping the check onto the table as though it were a leper's shirt. "And *please* come back."

"If I do," I said, handing him a hundred and ninety bucks, "you could get a terrific chance to learn about flambé."

9

Mirrors and Hindsight

The rearview mirror was more or less empty.

It had been more or less empty for four days.

It was an old rearview mirror. Alice, my car, was almost thirty, and I had no reason to believe that the mirror wasn't original. That made it almost as old as Eleanor. Some of the silvering had given way to a kind of powdery blackness, and there was a little continent of black, shaped vaguely like Australia, in the upper left-hand corner. The rearview mirror was falling apart. Eleanor, on the other hand, was in great shape.

I'd spent most of the last four days either watching the rearview mirror or thinking about Eleanor. The two activities had been equally productive. I had decided to replace the mirror, and Eleanor, at long last, had decided to replace me.

I pulled into a hot, flat little cul-de-sac in the Valley and waited for nothing.

Eleanor and I had met more than ten years ago, at UCLA. I'd been finishing a master's degree in English lit, and she'd been a visitor from the Department for Asian Studies, looking into early British translators of classic Chinese novels. At the time, *The Dream of the Red Chamber*, probably the best of the bunch, was my favorite book in the world, and I'd had the pleasure of introducing her to David Hawkes's wonderful modern English version, which he calls *The Story of the Stone*. Six months later, we were living together.

Within a year, she had threatened and cajoled me out of smoking a pack and a half a day, and she'd managed somehow to get me out of my armchair and onto the jogging track. In doing it, she taught me a great secret: I had never known it could be pleasant to perspire. I'd never understood that it could feel good to have aching muscles. I hiked. I ran. I surfed. I dropped thirty pounds. I swam happily in the love of a good woman. I also found a vocation, after almost nine years of meandering in the Halls of Academe, seeking initials to string, like magic talismans, after my name.

It began when a cokehead, his dipswitches permanently fused in the manic configuration, dropped a sweet Taiwanese girl named Jennie Chu off the roof of one of the residence halls. Jennie had been a pianist and a gymnast with a shy smile and a wicked sense of humor, and she'd been Eleanor's closest friend. She died by mistake. The cokehead couldn't tell Asians apart. As my contribution to Eleanor's recovery process, I worked out who did it and delivered him to the police with his elbows broken. I later regretted the elbows.

Eleanor discovered the dreadful little shack in Topanga Canyon and fixed it up. We lived happily for a few years, me practicing my new job part-time while I earned a few more useless degrees, and even teaching for a couple of semesters, and she working on her writing and turning out her first book, *Two Fit*, about how couples could help each other to become healthy. It sold like radishes. Then, for reasons I still don't understand, I started fooling around, stupid, pleasureless, meaningless betrayals with people whose names I barely knew. Eleanor put up with it for a while, and then she didn't. She moved to Venice on her royalties, and we entered into a new stage of the relationship. It didn't make either of us particularly happy, but it was better than not seeing each other at all. She remained the most important person in my life.

And now there was Burt.

Time, as everybody says nowadays, is relative. Sitting there in that stifling cul-de-sac, sending mental letter bombs to Burt and watching two Chicano kids squabble over a garden hose, the three minutes I'd promised myself that I would wait for nothing to happen seemed to take a decade. At two minutes and forty seconds, I decided to cheat. I started Alice and pulled out of the little circle of faded houses, making a right onto Sherman Way and cruising in Alice's stately fashion past the hospital in which Abraham Winston had died.

I'd been cheating on the surveillance times quite a lot lately. The four days had passed like sludge. The waiting, as infuriating as it would have been under any circumstances, was made all the more unendurable by the fact that I couldn't pull myself away from watching the bloody pot. As a result, all the nothing that I experienced took a lot longer to happen. I felt like a particle physicist put on permanent standby until the elusive graviton—the Snark of subatomic particles—popped out of the void to explain why his feet remained anchored to the ground. And it didn't.

Even during the brief interludes in which I pursued my own business, it took five times as long to do anything because I had to drag myself through all the double-backs, loop routes, feints, detours, and parking stalls that make up the vocabulary of checking for a tail. With my Thomas Brothers map book open in my lap, I turned into every dead end and cul-de-sac I passed, waited for three minutes—or, lately, two and a half—and then came back out again with my eye on that blemished and blistering rearview mirror. So I drove and fretted and fretted and drove again and consoled myself with the knowledge that at least no one else had been burned to death.

Wallowing through the slog of time, I knocked on more doors to apartments overlooking the various death scenes and got nothing. I'd talked to the homeless, to the extent that anyone can talk to the homeless. I'd distributed fifteen or sixteen of Annabelle Winston's twenties, hoping for information, and purchased nothing more than fifteen or sixteen vicarious drinking binges. I'd talked to Eleanor and Hammond on the phone. More consolation: No one seemed to be following them, either.

By the third day, I was so desperate that I'd let Hammond and Schultz, who had been surgically attached to Hammond, talk me into setting up a phony meet. The idea was to pick someplace relatively conspicuous and let the cops station half a dozen watchers in the neighborhood, three on wheels, three on foot. The meet was set for 7:00 P.M., by which time some anonymous optimist in a uniform had decided that rush hour would have died down. With an unpleasant prickling on the back of my neck, I drove to the location—a motel in Santa Monica, nicely positioned at the end of a dead-end street off Ocean Boulevard—went to room 22, as directed, and knocked.

Willick opened the door. He opened it very wide, as though he wanted to ensure good sight lines from the street.

"I was hoping it would be you," I said, fighting down a sudden desire to burst into tears. "This is very reassuring."

Willick beamed. He was wearing the worst set of plainclothes I'd ever seen. His tie was skinnier than pasta, and it made his face seem even fatter. His sport coat was the precise shade of green that electric eels are supposed to assume just before they give you thirty volts. His jeans were pressed and fresh from the laundry, and they were so short that you could see the white socks above his big black cop shoes. "Nice disguise," I said.

"The jacket's my brother-in-law's," he said proudly.

"I didn't know you had a brother-in-law on the force," I said, waiting for him to close the damn door.

His smile slipped a little. "Whole family's on the force," he said.

I used my foot to close the door for him. "That explains a lot," I said. "Have we got watchers?"

"They're all over the place," Willick said enthusiastically, turning to the window. "See? The guy fixing the Coke machine—"

I slapped his hand away from the blinds, and he yanked it back and flapped it in the air a few times to cool it, looking like a little kid who was deciding whether to cry.

"It's not polite to point," I said, smoothing the blinds down. "How long are we supposed to be here?"

"Until we get the all-clear," Willick said. He blew on the back of his hand, caught me looking at him, and put the hand behind his back.

"And how are we supposed to do that?"

"On this," Willick said, hefting a ten-pound walkie-talkie in his other hand. It said PROPERTY LAPD on the side in enormous yellow stenciled letters. They looked bigger than skywriting. "It's already on the right frequency."

"Good, good," I said, wondering if this were Hammond's little joke. "Be terrible to be on the wrong one. You know, someone could be listening."

"Oh, no," he said, giving me the ultimate reassurance. "I set it myself." I think I smiled at him. At any rate, I felt my cheeks creak.

"What about that?" I pointed to the phone, prominently positioned on the table between the beds. "See that?"

"Oh," Willick said. He didn't say it loudly.

"Might have been easier," I said.

"Well," Willick said. He lowered the hand with the walkietalkie as though it were suddenly too heavy.

"Wouldn't have required you to get up here carrying something that says LAPD on it, either."

"I hid it under my coat," Willick said. He showed me how he'd hidden it under his coat. Only the letters LAPD showed.

"You're doing great," I said.

The thing snapped, crackled, and popped. Willick almost dropped it trying to tug it free of his coat. He'd snagged it on the orange Paisley lining. I helped him get it clear and then took it away from him. He stretched out a white, margarine-coated hand and closed his fingers on air, a good fourteen inches from the walkie-talkie.

"Phoenix One to Phoenix Three," said a gravelly voice.

"Al," I said. "Al, this isn't funny."

"Wrong," Hammond said. "It wouldn't be funny if you weren't clean. But you're clean, so it's hilarious."

"How many cars?" Willick was watching with a wounded expression.

"We got three."

"All plain?"

"What, are you kidding?" Hammond sounded aggrieved. "Sure, they're plain."

"Radios?"

"What do you think this is?"

"I think this is a Triple-E ticket for Disneyland, is what I think it is. Schultz has to be Phoenix Two, right?"

Hammond grunted electronically.

"I want the cars to do a circle. The whole block, then the block beyond. I want them to do it twice. I want the walkers to do the same. And Phoenix," I said. "That's clever. The bird that rises from its own ashes. What if he's got a shortwave, Al?"

"He doesn't know the frequency."

"There's a telephone in this very room," I said. "Right here, not six feet from me. Don't tell me about shortwaves, and don't tell me about Phoenix. And don't use this again. When the cars and the walkers have done a double circle, call me on the room phone. Have you got someone there who knows how to dial?"

"Don't be silly," Hammond said.

"Right," I said. "Sorry. I forgot that Schultz was there."

I turned off the walkie-talkie. Willick murmured in genteel protest. The whole family was on the force, I remembered. Just for insurance, I took the walkie-talkie into the bathroom and dropped it into the toilet.

"Settle down," I said, as he fished it out. He looked at it, streaming water, with an expression of unadulterated terror on his face.

"I checked this out myself," he said. "I signed my name. I'm responsible."

The bathroom towels were white and fluffy, and I tossed him one. "So dry it," I said. "And work on your heart rate. We're here until the phone rings."

The phone rang five minutes later. Willick was sulking on the other bed, and I beat him to it. "You're clean," Dr. Schultz announced smoothly.

"And you're an idiot," I said. "There are twenty things wrong with the way this was handled."

"We were going for broke," Schultz said, unruffled. "If he'd been behind you, we would have had him. If not, no harm done."

"Thanks for the information. It would have been nice to have had it ahead of time."

"We couldn't be sure how you'd behave, could we?" Schultz was working on silky. What he didn't say was, *We decided to make you a target, see if we could draw the son of a bitch out.*

"Is Al on the line?"

"He could be. Would you like him to be?"

"No," I said in a tone of voice that sent Willick's eyebrows skyward with the force of the space shuttle. "I only asked because I wanted to propose to you."

There was a little muffled urgency, and then Hammond said, "Yeah?"

"You're both there?"

"I'm here," Schultz said serenely.

"Al?"

"Sure."

"Okay. I dumped Willick's walkie-talkie into the john. Write it off as a loss, but don't charge him with it." Willick sat upright on the bed, looking ridiculously grateful.

"That it?" Hammond asked.

"No," I said. "Your thread to the Incinerator, to use Dr. Schultz's memorable phrase, is hanging by a thread. You do this to me once more, and you've lost me. I'm in the Des Moines Holiday Inn, Al."

"He'll follow you," Hammond said.

"Interesting time to bring that up," I said.

"Simeon," Al said.

"Your cars, your walkers," I said, cutting him off. "They've done two circles?"

"Like you said."

"Tell them to do another two. Then phone." I hung up.

Willick was watching me as though he expected me to sprout razors from the ends of my fingers and go for his fat throat.

"Alone at last," I said to him, settling back onto my bed. Willick didn't look reassured. He just mopped at his walkie-talkie.

When I finally left, about twenty minutes later, it took me more than three hours to get home. I'd refused to speak to either Hammond or Dr. Schultz. I got partway up the coast and then turned around and headed back to Santa Monica, twice. I bought a pair of running shoes I didn't need, watching the street so closely that I got the wrong size. I took every switchback and cul-de-sac I could find. It was after eleven when, reassured at last, I pulled into the turnaround at the foot of my driveway and climbed out of Alice.

There was a full moon. It was bright enough to show me that the flag on my mailbox was upright.

There was a sprig of some kind of plant in the mailbox. It

smelled sweet. I don't know anything much about plants, but it smelled a familiar kind of sweet. I tossed the sprig onto Alice's front seat and trudged up the driveway to the house. Halfway up, wearing my too-large new shoes, I stumbled over the tripwire that I'd set up myself. I got a nice mouthful of loose dirt.

I had a rotten night, full of dreams that were all fire.

With the burn hospital receding into the rearview mirror, I headed over the Sepulveda Pass toward Bel Air. The only times I felt I could drive safely without one eye epoxied to the rearview mirror was when I went to the Bel Air Hotel to talk to Annabelle Winston. After all, as far as the Incinerator was concerned, that was something I was supposed to be doing. I almost wanted him to be watching.

The meeting was the kind that you have just to have a meeting. Its highlight came when I realized that Bobby Grant now had two earrings. In the same ear.

"Maybe he's given up on you," Bobby Grant said for the second or third time. He'd been agitating to hold his million-dollar press conference. He looked clean enough to wrap around a wound.

"Bobby," Annabelle Winston said, smoking the same kind of cigarette that she'd forbidden Dr. Schultz. She was seated at the table, wearing a russet silk suit and a pair of jade earrings, moving some papers around. She'd had two more phones put into the room. They squatted at the corners of the desk. "Use your head. He hasn't done anything. He's not activated, as that little cockroach of a doctor might say."

"Activated," Bobby Grant pouted. "You sound like an acting teacher I had once, except that he'd have said 'motivated.'"

"I knew you'd been an actor," I said.

"You did?" Bobby asked in his deepest tenor. "How?"

"Just the way you carry yourself," I said. Grant gave me a suspicious look.

"What are we supposed to do?" he asked sarcastically. "Just *sit* here and wait for him to set fire to someone?"

"Yes," I said, sitting down. "That's what you're supposed to do. I'll keep doing what he expects me to do and trying to avoid what the cops want me to do, and maybe he'll communicate with me. If he doesn't, we wait until he burns someone. Then, if he doesn't contact me, you can hold your press conference."

Bobby gave the suggestion 25 percent of his lower lip. It made him look like a fountain. "Maybe we could just do a release," he said. "Something about progress. Picture of the two of you."

"No," Annabelle Winston said without looking up from her papers. Her father had been flown home for his funeral, and she'd accompanied the body, been photographed in a veil at the cemetery, chaired an emergency stockholders' meeting, and flown back to Los Angeles, and she looked as if it had been a week since she'd walked around the block. In her spare time, she'd been running the business.

"What's this?" I asked her, holding up the sprig that I'd found in my mailbox the night before.

Annabelle turned the page she'd been reading facedown before she reached up and took the small piece of greenery, which was in mid-wilt. She sniffed it, then shrugged her disinterest. "It's some kind of herb."

"What *is* this?" Bobby Grant asked the heavens. "A segment of *The French Chef*?"

"Shut up, Bobby," Annabelle Winston said absently. She rubbed the leaves between her fingers, bruising but not crushing them, and then moved her fingers back and forth beneath her nose. "Fennel," she said. "So?"

"So maybe nothing," I said, retrieving the sprig.

Annabelle Winston inhaled the fragrance on her fingers again and then wiped them on her skirt. The woman was hell on expensive clothes. "Have you talked to anyone at your college yet?" Annabelle Winston said.

"In twenty minutes," I said. "Not that I expect anything."

"Please," Dr. Nathan Blinkins said, rolling his eyes around the room as though he were looking for his headache. "Fire? There's not a religion in the world that doesn't involve fire in one way or another."

Dr. Blinkins was a professionally slim man with too much hair in some places and not enough elsewhere. He grew his silvery sideburns long and curly and combed them back to cover his ears, perhaps hoping to strike an average with the expanse of gleaming dome he called his forehead. He affected suede jackets, black turtleneck sweaters, and pre-faded jeans. If asked to describe himself in a single word, he probably would have suggested "imperial." It was hot in his office, and he wiped his face with a Kleenex, leaving a film of white lint trapped in the postfashionable stubble he was cultivating. Blinkins had been my graduate adviser in comparative religions. Given how profoundly useless the degree had proved to be, I felt he owed me one.

"I'm looking for someone who was here when I was," I said.

"Well, that's fine," Dr. Blinkins said with ponderous irony. "If you want to know about students who specialized in fire religions, I can probably help you narrow it to three or four thousand. As I recall," he said, settling himself back in his chair, "you were here for quite a while." He smiled to demonstrate the impossibility of the task. "In fact," he added, "when you called, I wasn't sure I recalled the name."

I gave him the nicest, which is to say the only, smile I could manage. I'd been at UCLA, in fact, longer than he had. "Let's start with Zoroastrianism," I said.

"Zoroastrianism," Dr. Blinkins said comfortably. He probably had a Parsi temple in his backyard. "Who are we looking for?"

"A male. Tall, blond hair. Walked with a limp." I felt the frailty of the description as I spoke it.

"No blonds," Dr. Blinkins said. "Zoroastrianism is almost exclusively the purview of Iranians now. Has been for some time." He spread his hands. He had very clean hands. "Historical interest, you know. In fact, the stock, so to speak, for Zoroastrianism is down just now. Aboriginal religions, that's the thing. Lots of room for a good paper. Zoroastrianism's pretty much worked out. Unless you want to do a bibliography, of course. Always room for a first-rate bibliography."

"And I can't think of anything I'd rather do," I said. "But I'm looking for a man, not a degree, and the man I'm looking for is familiar with Ahriman and Ahura Mazda."

"Who isn't?" Dr. Blinkins said with the very large and very selective blind spot of the scholar.

"Doctor," I said, just to puncture the envelope of his self-esteem, "this guy is setting fire to people."

Dr. Blinkins blinked. Then he passed long musician's fingers over his chin and looked down at them. They had little threads of Kleenex on them. "Holy moly," he said.

"*Excusez-moi,*" he said, opening a desk drawer. "I've heard something about that." He peered into the drawer, pulled out a round shaving mirror, and examined his face. "Now how did *that* happen?" he asked himself.

"This isn't academic," I said.

Ignoring the comment, he tugged a Kleenex from a box and scrubbed at the lint. It left more lint. "Aha," he said. If he hadn't had both hands full, he might have snapped his fingers. Holding the mirror in his left, he used his right to unfold a linen handkerchief with a large *B* embroidered into one of its corners, and wiped his face clean. He studied the results, fluffed one of his sideburns, and dropped both the mirror and the handkerchief into the drawer. Then he winced and quickly picked up the mirror and checked that he hadn't broken it. "I've heard something about you, too," he added, apparently forgetting that he hadn't remembered my name.

"All too true."

"You mean," he said calmly, opening his blue eyes wide to show me that he was impressed, "that you really *are* some sort of detective, that you're looking for this maniac." He slid the drawer closed with a nice, dramatic *snick*.

"What about the other fire religions?" I felt I was swimming backward.

"Well, really." It was the verbal tic of a man who felt himself frequently imposed upon. He brought one of the hands to his mouth again and gnawed at a nail. A thick steel Rolex Oyster glinted on his wrist. "As I said, all religions are fire religions at heart. What are the candles for in a Catholic church? Don't all Christians believe in hellfire?"

"There are people in Los Angeles," I said, "who are being burned to death."

"I'm not ducking the question," he said, blinking rapidly. "I'm only trying to give you an idea of how complex it is. If there's a common denominator among the world's religions, at least in their earlier and purer forms, it's fire. Fire cleans, it purifies. Gold is refined in fire. The Ten Commandments came to Moses from a burning bush. The Romans carried fire in front of the emperor. Every twenty years the American Plains Indians piled their possessions together in the prairie and set them on fire. Alchemists sought to reduce the universe to its elements through fire. Do you see what I mean?" He laid one long hand on top of the other and looked down at the ragged nail he had gnawed. Quickly, he put the other hand on top.

I looked elsewhere.

"Even during the Renaissance, Botticelli carried his obscene paintings to the Burnings of the Vanities in Florence. Fire equals light, and light is the opposite of darkness. Fire worship dates back to the ice age. The last one, I mean," he added by way of clarification. "Look, we're discussing a major religious theme here. Every religion worth its salt has put faith into purification, and most of them have chosen fire as the purifier. Think about the level of technology available to these people." He grimaced. "They *sat* around fires, for heaven's sake. Fire was an inescapable symbol."

I sat back, waiting for something that made sense. "Go on," I said.

"What do you mean, go on?" Dr. Blinkins looked at his Rolex with some irritation.

"No more than another ten minutes," I said. "Just free-associate."

"An unpleasantly Freudian term," he said. Dr. Blinkins imagined that his loathing for Freud was legendary. "This is impossible."

"Humor me."

"Well, the Stoics," he said. "They envisioned periodic world conflagrations, an intuitive guess at the expanding and contracting universe of modern physics, a world born out of an unimaginable fire and ultimately returning to it." His eyes rolled again, this time out of sheer effort. "Heracleitus of Ephesus, around 500 B.C., said that the world is a never-ending fire, an eternal state of process. Fire is the 'agent of transmutation': All things derive from, and return to, fire." He smiled apologetically. "As I'm sure you know, this was the concept seized upon by the alchemists, whom I've already cited, in their attempts to turn lead into gold through fire. Talk about wasted effort," he said, in his regular-guy tone. I remembered that tone, and not pleasantly. "For Heracleitus, reason and consciousness were manifestations of the element of fire. By inference, brutishness, swinishness, drunkenness, and depravity are impurities and can be burned away only in fire. Fire is elemental; there's nothing personal in it." He was listening to himself with pleasure. "That's interesting," he said to himself, "most fire gods are impersonal." He made a note on a little pad with his name printed on it. It said, NATHAN BLINKINS, PH.D.

"So is my lunatic," I said. "He picks them at random as they sleep in doorways."

"Surely, not at random," Dr. Blinkins said. "Nothing in the universe happens at random."

"I'll hold that thought," I said. "You're certain that you don't recall this guy pursuing a fire religion." Dr. Blinkins shook his spottily well-groomed head. "Okay," I said, "Heracleitus. Let's stick with the Greeks. They're the common denominator, right?

"As far as Western religions are concerned."

"Good, well, let's focus on Western religion."

"It all begins with Prometheus," he said, after a moment's reflection.

"Well," I said, searching my memory, "sure it does."

He settled back in his chair and spread his shining fingers over the tiny paunch blooming beneath his turtleneck. It hadn't been there when I saw him last. "Prometheus is complicated," he said.

"I'll follow you somehow," I responded. He wasn't listening.

"Prometheus was a Titan and a trickster and a traitor, to begin with," he said, enjoying the alliteration. He smiled and then sucked inward on the corners of his mouth, imagining that he had my full attention. Actually, I was trying to figure out why I'd just sat up straight. Most of what Blinkins had said had slid smoothly over me, but something had snagged and caught. For a moment I'd heard another voice. "In the war between the Titans and the gods for control of the universe," Blinkins rolled on, "Prometheus advised guile rather than brute force. When his advice was rejected, when the Titans chose to use force and lost, he changed sides." He gave me a glance that requested understanding, and I recognized a need for sympathy that had been born out of years of treacherous faculty battles, civilized back-stabbings, and learned betrayals. I nodded, one conspirator to another, and tried to look understanding. *What* had he said?

"Well," Blinkins continued comfortably, "Hesiod and Aeschylus turned Prometheus into the creator and salvation of man; he supposedly made the first men from clay, and Athena breathed life into his models. He made the first woman, too, Pandora. And look what became of *that*." Not for the first time, I wondered about Dr. Blinkins's private life. "And Zeus," he added, with a hand gesture that might have been a way of winding a nonwinding wristwatch, "motivated either by jealousy at Prometheus' creation or by the desire to create a race of his own, decided to destroy humanity. Might not have been a bad idea, in retrospect. Zeus looked down from Olympus, and he saw a scattering of campfires in the dark. I think that's an eloquent image, don't you? A scattering," he repeated, "of campfires in the dark."

He didn't wait for me to reply, which was a good thing. "So Zeus began by depriving mankind of fire." He passed a hand over his gleaming forehead, looked at his palm, reached into his drawer for a Kleenex, and thought better of it. With the linen handkerchief in his hand, he glanced across the desk at me, looking vaguely perplexed, like a man who has lost his place in a book. "We're talking about fire, right?"

"Fire and only fire," I said, trying to back up my mental tape recorder.

Pleased with himself, he wiped his face with the handkerchief and studied it suspiciously, as if he expected to find ballpoint-pen ink smeared across it. "Well, then. Prometheus couldn't let *that* happen, not after all his work. So he tiptoed to Hephaestus' forge while Hephaestus was off shagging Aphrodite—now *there* was a match made in hell—and stole fire. He went to earth, carrying the fire in the stalk of a plant, and gave it back. As revenge, Zeus had him chained to the rock and sent the eagle to gnaw on his liver. Of course, you know all about that. Shelley and so forth."

"Of course," I said. "The stalk of a plant." I reached into the pocket of my shirt and pulled out the sprig I'd found in my mailbox. I handed it across the desk to him.

Dr. Blinkins gave it a whiff. He seemed to like the smell, but he had the puzzled, faintly outraged expression of someone who's just had a card trick worked on him. "Why did you let me go on like that if you already knew?" he demanded.

"Fennel," I said.

"Certainly," he snapped. "Prometheus brought fire to earth in a stalk of fennel." He closed the drawer again to indicate that the conversation was over.

That night, when I got home, the flag on the mailbox was up again. Inside it was an envelope that said, DELIVER BY MESSEN-

GER. Within the envelope was an old-fashioned dance card from the late fifties, about Alice's vintage. It had a carnation embossed on the cover and parallel lines ruled inside, each with a time indicated next to it. On the left-hand side of the card, written in metallic gold, were all the things I had done that day, up until I left Blinkins's office, around four. Every single one of them. The times were all indicated precisely, in that infuriating straight-line lettering. At midnight it said SWEET DREAMS!!!

I got the prickles on the back of my neck again.

The right-hand side of the card had a slash drawn through it, dispensing with the first five dances. Under the slash was a double line, followed by the next day's date, and the time 8:00 P.M. Below that was the message SHALL WE DANCE?

A stalk of fennel had been folded into the card.

As I dropped into the kind of sleep even Macbeth would have scorned, I heard Blinkins and Schultz say one word in unison. The word was "trickster."

10

The Doopermart

"It's a phone booth at the corner of Los Angeles Street and Sixth," I said to the second button on my shirt. I turned right through the heavy downtown traffic, feeling all the muscles in my back bunch and jump independently. They made me think of the frog's leg through which we'd passed electricity in high school biology. It had bunched and jumped, too. And it had probably wanted to be on that ceramic tray about as much as I wanted to be driving through downtown L.A. at 8:25 on a Saturday night, on my way to a waltz with the Incinerator.

The wire tucked into the back of my jeans was about the size of an audiocassette. It bulged against the base of my spine, feeling bigger than a Cadillac Eldorado. Something no thicker than sewing thread connected it to the second button in my shirt.

"I'm slowing," I said, trying not to move my lips and feeling like a fifth-rate ventriloquist. "Traffic. I may be late to the phone booth."

No one answered, but, of course, no one could. I had to take it on faith that someone was on the other end. I might be able to meet the Incinerator wearing a concealed microphone, but I certainly couldn't do it with a plug in my ear.

"It's construction," I said. "I'm going to be late." I heard the unsteadiness in my voice. I went on, nevertheless. "Are the ground rules straight?" I asked no one who could answer. "Remember that it could be a trick," I added, thinking about Prometheus. "It could be that he just wants to see if I've got cops with me. You don't move unless I tell you to." Trying not to move my lips, I sounded to myself like Humphrey Bogart. "Anybody moves, Al, I'm in Des Moines. This is the last pass, as far as I'm concerned."

The traffic started to move. I pressed Alice's accelerator in the direction of fate.

We'd started the preparations on the previous evening, three minutes after I got the dance card. I'd called Hammond at home—with certain misgivings—to tell him about it. He'd been awake and morose and drunk, but he sobered up in seconds.

"You'll need a wire," was the first productive thing he said.

"And how are you going to get it to me? Al, I'm being watched, remember?"

"A girl. Have I got a girl for you. Got a great little wire, too, real hi-fi."

"Al," I said, backing up one giant step, "why do you assume that I'm going?"

"You want this geek preserved in amber," Hammond said. "Same as me."

"Well, I'm not going," I said. "Not unless I make the rules."

"Your rules," he said instantly.

"I need to talk to Finch," I said, although I knew it would piss Hammond off. "And Schultz. Why isn't Schultz sleeping in the guest room?"

"You should write for TV," Hammond said. He despised TV. "On the phone at ten, okay?"

"And Schultz," I'd added unwisely.

"I heard you the first time," Hammond said, banging the phone down.

The ten o'clock conference call with Finch, Hammond, and Schultz had been punctual, short, and unsatisfying.

"Goes without saying," Finch said gruffly. "You call the shots."

"No shots," I said. "That's the point. Nobody pulls a gun, nobody moves, nobody shows himself, unless you hear me ask for it."

"Don't worry," Finch said. "You're the boss."

"Al?" I said.

"Yo," Hammond said.

"You're my guarantee."

"Hell," Hammond said, in spite of his injured feelings, "I'm your friend." *There*, his tone told me, *I've said it.*

I looked at my bare feet. They would, I thought, catch fire easily. "Okay," I said. "I'll go, and I'll wear the wire. But nobody moves unless I give the word."

And the wire had arrived at eleven the next morning, carried in the purse of a female police officer who looked no older than sixteen, dressed in a T-shirt and strategically slashed jeans, and the Incinerator had called at seven-fifteen and had said nothing more than "Dumpster at the Fernwood Market." He'd hung up, leaving me looking at the phone. If I'd ever heard the voice before, I couldn't place it.

Taped to the side of the dumpster facing away from the street, I'd found a tightly folded square of paper, no more than an inch on any side. It said SIMEON on the side facing me, in shiny gold lettering. It gave me precise directions to a pepper tree in Reseda Park, in the Valley. On the trunk of the tree in Reseda Park, a monstrous pepper that was methodically killing the grass beneath it, was another note, riven to the bark with a hatpin. It said, YOU'RE A GOOOOD DRIVER, SIMEON. CAREFUL AND COURTE-OUS. PHONE BOOTH, CORNER OF THIRD AND LOS ANGELES, DOWNTOWN. Downtown. At the periphery of Little Tokyo. On his territory.

I'd driven quite a way before I called those directions in. I was having second thoughts about virtually every aspect of my life, and not least about my decision to involve the cops in this meet. I knew no one had me in visual surveillance—Finch had promised that the cars would use parallel streets and remain out of sight until and unless I yelled for help. I could, I reasoned, just stop calling in and meet the Incinerator alone, assuming that he'd actually be there, which I didn't think he would be. I was pretty sure that he'd be positioned very carefully somewhere where he could see me, but I couldn't imagine someone who preyed on the immobile having the recklessness to risk it all on a guess about my character. He just wanted to know whether I was friend or fuel. He would materialize in the flesh at the next con-tact, or the one after that.

On the other hand, what if I were wrong? So I called in when I was most of the way downtown and felt briefly grateful that I wasn't wearing an earpiece and didn't have to listen to the cops swear and scramble for position across the broad L.A. Basin.

The phone booth where I was supposed to wait for a ring and then do anything the Incinerator told me to do was one of those stingy little waist-high spatter shields, standing bravely on a corner that the homeless had claimed for their own. I leaned against it, wishing my legs were steadier, and it rang.

"Hello?" I said, forcing my voice downward from the tenor pitch it seemed determined to assume.

"Hello, Simeon," the Incinerator said. "Remember me?"

"No," I said.

"Aaahh," he said. "That's not polite. Not considering how well I remember you."

"Memory," I said. "It's so selective. In what context should I remember you?"

I heard a chuckle. "Not very flattering," the Incinerator said.

"When I see you," I heard myself saying in the earpiece.

"Well, of course," he said. "That's what this is all about, isn't it? A couple of guys, getting together. Hashing over old times." He laughed.

"So," I said, "where?"

"Let's not rush into this, no matter how eager you are to see me. You're not being followed, are you?" The voice was somehow both light and heavy, insubstantial and menacing at the same time.

"You know I'm not."

"And no wire?"

I leaned my head against the plastic and smelled my own sweat. "No wire," I said.

"Peachy," he said. "Just a couple of guys. Go to the park. Los Angeles and Second. Sit on a bench."

"Los Angeles and Second. A bench," I said into my second button.

"You were quicker in the old days," the Incinerator said forgivingly. "A bench, you know? Something you sit on."

"And do what?" I asked.

"And *sit*," the Incinerator said. "Sit until the gods call for you." He hung up.

The park at Los Angeles and Second was an open-air motel, a local branch of the Motel Zeroes that have opened all over America, patronized by those who can't afford a bed with a roof over it. Most of the benches were full. Some of them were occupied by people who could still sit upright. Alice was parked half a block away.

For credentials, I'd visited the local brown-bag store and bought a gallon jug of Thunderbird. When I swung my bottom aggressively against the woman at the left-hand end of the bench closest to the curb, she said, "Hey." I handed her the jug, which I'd already opened, and said, "Shhhhh."

"You bet," she said, taking the wrinkled bag and its contents. "How you doing, brother?"

"After you, sweetheart," I said. "After you. Then I'll be doing just fine."

She upended the bag and swallowed many times. "Thunderbird," she said appreciatively. "Sweet and awful. What do you want?" She handed the bag back to me.

"Just sitting," I said, looking for cops. "What do you want?"

"A bath," she said promptly. "I'd sell my soul for a bathtub with no drain in it."

"Why no drain?" I said, pretending to drink from the bottle in the bag and then deciding what the hell and drinking quite a lot of it.

"Because I could get clean and die at the same time," she said.

"You don't want to die," I said. It was just a reflex.

"Well," she said, "I don't want to die dirty." She gave me a sidelong glance. She was cleaner than Hermione had been, but her gray hair hung matted at her shoulders. She wore an old man's coat and somebody else's skirt and nylon stockings rolled halfway down her calves. I felt like Beau Brummel. "How long you been out here?" she asked.

"Not so long," I said.

Someone pressed something between my collar and the back of my neck. By the time I could turn around, he or she was gone.

"Man or woman?" I asked the old lady.

"Who?" she said.

"Keep the bottle," I said, getting up.

"You got a tub or a shower?" she called after me.

THE DOOPERMART, the note said, in the glare of Alice's over-head light. SECOND AND ALVARADO. YOU'LL LIKE IT. THE SOUTH-ERN DOOR IS OPEN. IT'LL BE NICE TO SEE YOU.

"It's something called the Doopermart," I said into my but-ton. "I'm supposed to go in through the southern door." My mouth was so dry that I could hear my tongue and upper lip clicking like billiard balls. "Let's remember the rules, okay?"

Second Street took me across a long-disused stretch of rail-road or streetcar tracks, lined with buildings of old, grimy brick, four or five stories tall, with faded signs painted on them and plywood over their windows. Once they had been factories, or vegetable warehouses, or even hotels. They all had the same dis-mal Edward Hopper rectangularity, the blind sadness of buildings with no one in them, buildings that have been given over to the tenancy of spiders and rats and warp and rot.

It was fully dark by the time I reached Alvarado, but it was still hot, and I was soaked in sweat. None of the buildings had lights on inside them, and the only illumination came from Alice's headlamps and two streetlights, one that I was passing on the left, and one that gleamed in front of me. The one in front of me shone down on a big, low barn of a building with picture windows fac-ing onto the street. The windows had been painted black. A mar-ket. Probably the last time it had seen life was in the sixties, when some counterculture entrepreneur had painted THE DOOPERMART across its front and set up business, selling whatever a Dooper-mart sold—organic vegetables, perhaps, incense, and macramé yarn.

A rutted and broken parking lot surrounded the building on three sides, faded paint lines indicating where the pigeons were to leave their vehicles before they went inside to get plucked. One of the sides of the building that faced the parking lot was the south side. There was, as the Incinerator had promised, a door set into the center of the southern wall, the only door or window to interrupt the blankness of the wall. It was ajar. I had to look at it, then close my eyes and look in its general direction without focusing to see that a very thin, pale light fell through it. The light was cold and chalky and not at all reassuring. It looked like the phosphorescence of decay.

Corruption, I thought.

"The door's open," I said softly to the wire. "There's some kind of light inside. Not much, but enough to see." I took five deep breaths. "Going inside," I said.

Feeling like the only man in the world, I climbed out of the car. I caught myself shutting Alice's door very softly, and then pulled it all the way open and slammed it. Let the man know I'm here. The door made a nice, sane sound, and I started across the asphalt toward the other door, the insane door.

The door was solid metal, painted, no window, and it opened in. I pushed it slowly, but even so I pushed too fast to avoid breaking the fine black thread that had been strung across it, about four inches above the floor. I saw it snap as I yanked the door back toward me, and then all the lights inside went out.

No, not all of them.

I banged the door all the way open and went in. One kerosene lantern, mounted high on a black pole, glowed in the center of the space, more or less directly in front of me. The interior was a single room, dark as fate in the corners and only very dimly lighted in the vicinity of the lantern. Rows of empty shelves stretched away from me in parallel. They were supermarket shelves, too high to see over. That's a feature of supermarket design: Don't let the customer see beyond the brand names that are nearest. Each aisle should be a new vista. Each of these aisles was certainly going to be a new vista, and I had a queasy feeling I was meant to explore every one of them.

Like readers of European languages everywhere, I headed left. We're used to starting at the left. Then I realized what I was doing, stopped, and went to the right instead. Walking on the balls of my feet, I stepped into the aisle that was farthest right.

The upper edge of the shelf to my immediate left cut off the pale glow of the lantern. This aisle was almost entirely dark. Each one to my left would be slightly brighter as I worked my way toward the lantern in the center, and then they would get darker as I zigzagged toward the left side of the store, but this was the only one that mattered now, and it was as dark as the inside of my skull.

"Hello," I said. My voice cracked.

Someone tittered.

From *where*? The titter bounced around the room. I couldn't fix its direction. It probably came from the left, but it might have come from directly in front of me.

"Just a couple of guys," I said in what I hoped was a friendly tone. No response. I had to go down the aisle, but I couldn't bear the thought that I might walk right past him and not know it, and then he'd be behind me. The one thing I knew was that the titter hadn't come from behind me. Nothing was behind me but the south wall of the building. I stretched my arms until I could touch the shelves on either side. My fingers encountered grease and dust and cobweb. It took everything I had to keep them out there, but one step at a time I walked the length of the aisle, slowly, arms outstretched, a human scoop hoping it wouldn't scoop up anything that might decide to kill it.

When I got to the end of the aisle, a stroll that seemed to take half an hour, I pulled my arms in and laughed from sheer relief. I couldn't help it. Somebody moved, nearer to the center of the store. Somebody squeaked.

Do all the aisles anyway, I told myself. *Every damn one of them.* As I spread my arms and started up the second aisle, my ankle snagged something, and it broke. Another thread. I had a sudden image of myself in a web. I loathe spiders above almost anything else.

I was a third of the way up the aisle when the pillar of fire bloomed in front of me. It towered six, then eight, feet tall, too bright to look at, and I scuttled backward as fast as I could until I slammed against the wall at the end of the aisle, the end farthest away from the door I'd come in through. As the fire fell, I saw, or thought I saw, someone standing well behind it. He was tall and wrapped in black. The fire died, and I heard the squeaking sound again.

Then I was aware of a wild flapping sound that seemed to come from all over, and in my peripheral vision, which was all that I had left after the brilliance of the pillar of fire, black pieces of paper tore themselves to shreds above me and scattered through the darkness in all directions. Something knocked against the side of my head, and I screamed higher than the girl in a horror movie, and pressed back against the wall as the flapping died away. Something cooed.

The place was full of birds.

It was a bunch of birds and a firework, that's all. One of those stupid cones that look so nice on the Fourth of July.

"Very pretty," I said, wishing I hadn't screamed, wishing I

could keep the quaver out of my voice. "Have we got any more of those?" My direct vision was completely gone, the imprinted image of the fire pillar working my retina overtime, a green and red ghost vision that totally blocked out the tiny amount of real light in the room. I put my arms out again and swept the second aisle in a blind run, moving by touch until I was at the other end and I knew it was empty. I turned with my back to the south wall and panted, waiting for my eyesight to return and bring my courage with it.

Had he been standing at this end when the firework went off? My memory said yes, but I couldn't be completely sure. "Okay," I said out loud, partly for his ears and partly for the wire. "Okay, then." Something squeaked, definitely to my left this time.

My feet didn't want to take the three sideways steps to the left, but I still had control of my feet. I sought reassurance in the fact. "Ready or not," I said, "I'm coming."

I could see almost the entire length of the third aisle. The lantern's light created an edge about three feet down the shelves to my right. It looked empty, but he might be crouched down against the left-hand shelving. I was certain he was to my left, but I knew now that I could hear him move, and I had decided to sweep every aisle. It might not have been much of a plan, but it was the only one I had, and I wasn't going to abandon it. Hands out again. Test for a thread with the foot. Nothing there, but that didn't mean there wouldn't be one part of the way down.

There was, and this time the fire erupted behind me. It cast brilliant light all the way to the wall, and I pulled in my hands and ran for it while the glare lasted. The birds went crazy again, and I looked up and saw them diving and swooping for refuge among the open rafters, and then the glare died down and we were all back in the almost-dark.

"I liked that," I said, turning to press my back against the wall. "Keep them behind me. Will you work on that?" I wondered what Hammond and Finch were making of this monologue. Probably asking Schultz to analyze it. The smell of the firework was sharp and pungent and familiar from the summers when I was a boy, and it tickled my nose. I might even have enjoyed it, except that the air was getting smoky, and that canceled out the increased visibility from the lantern. It was only one aisle over, but the air in the aisle in front of me was milky and hard to see through.

"Well, shoot," I said. "Here we go again." I touched the shelves and moved down the aisle, more slowly this time, putting out a tentative foot to test for threads before committing myself to a step. Nothing. The aisle was clear, and I got to the end, put my back against the wall again, and sidestepped to find myself staring down the next one, the aisle that had the lantern standing in its center. The air was too smoky to see the black pole on which it stood, but the lantern shone seven or eight feet up, in the center of a soft halo. The door through which I had entered was behind me, and it was closed.

I had left it ajar.

"Nobody there?" I called, before I noticed the thread. It was pinned to the shelf to my left and looped through a bent nail on the shelf to my right, and it disappeared down the aisle into the skim milk of the air. He'd taken a lot of time with this.

"Would you like me to break this one, too?" I asked. "Or can we just talk?" There was no answer, so I leaned down and yanked at the thread with my hands.

Music shattered the air, music so loud that it seemed to gather the smoke into balls and roll them at me. Handel. *The Royal Fireworks Music*. I covered my ears, knowing that now I couldn't hear him squeak anyway, and took a step forward.

A cone of fire licked its way toward the roof at the far end of the aisle, and he was standing behind it, tall, wrapped in black, fuzzy, and indistinct though the smoke. Then the cone died.

"Wait," I said, half-blind again, taking another step. The music boomed out again, and another flare erupted, closer to me this time, and he was there again, just behind it, moving in time to the music, and he was taller than I had imagined he could be, and stick-thin in his black coat. He had one hand out.

As the flame guttered and died, I backed up and tried the door behind me. It wasn't locked. That was something.

The air was full of smoke now, the lantern only a firefly floating in front of me, and I had just let go of the door when the next cone blossomed, and he was only eight or ten feet from me, impossibly thin, with scraggly straight blond hair that was wrong somehow, on *crooked*, and a broad grin with very few teeth behind it. He leaned forward, extending the hand toward me. It had something in it. The smile was as crooked as his hair, and the birds cut through the smoke like lunatic confetti in a murderer's parade.

"Stop," I said for some reason, and stepped forward.

The cone went off almost at my feet, and I leapt back, and he was right behind it, four feet away this time, baring red puffy gums in a meaningless smile and showing me ravaged skin and empty blue eyes that were paler than ice. He stepped around the cone, so close that I could hear the rubber coat squeaking over the music, and looked down at me and pressed whatever it was into my hand.

A stalk of fennel.

He leaned down until his mouth was against my ear, and I was scrabbling for the gun in my pocket.

"Ten dollars," he said. He smelled like a dead cow at the side of the road.

The cone died down, and the store and my mind went black simultaneously. *"What?"* I said.

But he was past me then, shaking his head and heading for the door, and I heard him squeaking through the smoke and I turned to watch and then threw up a hand to protect my eyes as he pulled the door open into an impossible blaze of light and squeaked through it and birds exploded through the doorway and into the light, and over the music someone shouted, "Stop or I'll shoot," but he didn't stop, and two loud booms shook the smoke like water in a jar, and he went down.

And I ran through the door into the glare from the headlights of six LAPD black-and-whites and saw him on the broken asphalt, twisted like a scout's knot gone wrong in the center of what seemed to be a pool of black ice, and I looked around and, with an effort that began at my toes, I did my level best to break Al Hammond's jaw.

11

Solo

". . . a transient," Captain Finch was saying. "Acid burnout name of Dennis Thorpe. Thirty-four. From Indiana."

"But not the Incinerator," Annabelle Winston said in a voice that was, at once, soft and awful.

Finch was already red, but he got redder. "Not," he said. He looked around. Nobody came to his assistance.

"And why not?" Annabelle Winston's voice might have been a whisper, except that a whisper would have carried farther.

"Not mentally capable," Dr. Schultz interposed, and Annabelle Winston's head came up. "No long-term cognitive processes left. He was told he could earn ten dollars if he followed the fireworks around and gave the fennel to Mr. Grist here. That's about the limit of his, uh, capability." Schultz obviously wished he could have found another word.

She nodded, gazing at Schultz. She seemed to be very far away.

"And then, of course, there are the others," Finch said, talking like someone who had just had his wisdom teeth extracted.

"Yes, the others," Annabelle Winston said. She turned toward her meticulously buttoned lawyer. "You know, Fred. The ones who got burned last night, after the police shot Mr. Thorpe. The man."

No one said anything. She waited. Thirty seconds later, no one had said anything. Hammond had a bandage on his jaw. I had a puffy right hand.

"And the woman," Annabelle Winston finished, in a voice that would have withered a hedge. "Twelve people," Annabelle Winston said absently to Fred the lawyer, as though it were the last thing on her mind. "Plus one man in critical condition. Of course, we can't blame the Incinerator for Dennis Thorpe. The LAPD shot him."

"That's enough of that," Finch said thickly.

"Is it," Annabelle Winston said without looking at him. "I had understood that Mr. Grist was to give the orders. As opposed to the LAPD, I mean."

Hammond glanced at me and then looked away. We hadn't exchanged a word since I'd knocked him facedown into Dennis Thorpe's blood.

"Correct me if I'm wrong," Annabelle Winston said, to her ring this time, "but it was my understanding that Mr. Grist agreed to risk his life in the belief that the Incinerator would *not* actually meet him, and that he'd been guaranteed that the police would stay out of sight unless he called for help."

"We misunderstood the signal," Finch said. "Grist said 'Wait.' He said 'Stop.' He sounded panicked. We thought his life was in danger."

"Then isn't it interesting," Annabelle Winston said, "that you were able to get all those cars into the parking lot so quickly? I listened to the tapes. Mr. Grist said 'Wait' and 'Stop' only a few seconds before poor Mr. Thorpe opened the door. Your officers must have driven very fast."

"They did—" Finch began.

"And they must have been very close," Annabelle Winston continued in a low alto with an edge like a slap. "Much closer than Mr. Grist had requested that they be, isn't that right, Mr. Grist?"

"I wanted them in Texas," I said, still looking at Hammond.

"His life was in danger," Finch said. I half expected him to spit.

She still didn't look at him. "No one went into the building. If he'd been a police officer, you'd have had ten men in there the moment he said 'Wait.'" She looked around the table, finally including Captain Finch in her gaze. "But that isn't the point, is it?" she asked conversationally. "The point is that Mr. Grist thought, and *told* you that he thought, that the meeting would be a fake. A way for the Incinerator to prove to himself that he could trust Mr. Grist. That Mr. Grist, in short, might be a friend."

"The psychology of the man," Schultz said, trying for momentum.

"Dr. Schultz—is that your name?" Annabelle Winston interrupted.

Schultz nodded. He'd forgotten he was smiling, and it made him look like a man between photographs.

"You're the one with all the degrees in psychology. Mr. Grist is the one who said that the man wouldn't be there. Cutting through all the condescension of modern medicine, Dr. Schultz, who was right? The psychologist who was sitting comfortably on the other end of the transmitter or the untutored private detective who actually walked into that Doopermart or whatever it was called to test his hypothesis with his life?" She raised both eyebrows on my behalf. "*Was* the Incinerator there?"

"No," Schultz said stubbornly, "but he might have been."

"Who was right?" she demanded, drumming the nails—Chinese red today—on the tabletop. It was the first display of emotion.

"Dennis Thorpe could have been the Incinerator," Schultz maintained stoutly.

"He still might be," she said. "Except that the miracle of modern psychology tells us he's not. And then, of course, there's the man. And the woman."

What does she need a lawyer for? I thought.

"You know," she said, "a million dollars isn't much to me. I think maybe Bobby should hold his press conference."

All hell broke loose. Finch slapped his hands on the table, Hammond grunted, Schultz said a sentence that contained many polysyllabic words. Cops conferred.

"Hold it," I said. To my amazement, everybody held it.

"Um," I said into the silence.

"He's being polite," Fred the lawyer cut in. "You'll all go home tonight and tuck in your wives and children," he said into the silence, "and Mr. Grist will go home and wonder where the fire is going to come from. Gentlemen," Fred the lawyer said, leaning forward against the mass of his buttons, "why shouldn't my client offer the reward and also offer Mr. Grist the security of anonymity? Surely he's earned it."

"It's not just me," I said, and Schultz said over me, "He's the thread."

"It's not just me," I said again. I looked at Hammond, who was still avoiding my eyes. "He sent me a timetable of my movements. He knows," I said, "where I've been and who I've seen. It's possible that he knows who I love." Hammond turned his wristwatch down toward his palm with a violent gesture, but he didn't look at me.

"I'm vulnerable," I said to the room at large, "unless she's safe."

"Can you make her safe?" Annabelle Winston said to Finch, giving me a glance I didn't quite understand, "As safe as he was?"

"We'll put five men on her," Finch said. Nobody said anything. "Six," he said, budgeting into the silence.

"Satisfy Mr. Grist," Annabelle Winston said, turning away from me at last, "or it's the press conference and the reward."

"I don't know," I said, "satisfied or not, I don't know. And I may not decide today. Tell me about the messenger who brought the dance card." I felt very old and very tired.

"Zip," Finch said. "A loose call, not a regular account. Paid cash. Told the dispatcher to pick up at Hollywood and Vine."

"Description?" I asked.

"Street person," Finch said. "A woman wearing plastic trash bags. A cutout."

"Did she describe him?" Finch wasn't going to volunteer much of anything.

"Yeah," Finch said grudgingly. "She said he looked like an angel. Said he had wonderful manners."

"That's it?"

"That's it," Finch said. He touched a stubby finger to his temple. "Nothing there," he said.

"The special effects in the building," I said. "In fact, the building."

Schultz stepped in. "It hasn't been used for years," he said smoothly. "No surveillance. The strings touched off timing devices, rather sophisticated, actually. Stopwatches and cute little mercury fuses. Everything timed to the split second."

"Mercury fuses?" I asked.

Schultz spread his hands apologetically. "Boy's had education," he said.

"So have I, but I don't know anything about mercury fuses."

"You said it last time around," Schultz said. "This freak knows everything there is to know about fire." He'd been the one who said it, but he was being a psychologist.

"You know," I said to him, "if you and I could ever wind up on the same side, you might be useful."

"We are on the same side," he said, treating me to a forced version of the amber grin.

"I think we can dispense with etiquette," I said. Schultz fiddled with an unopened pack of Dunhills and looked longingly at Annabelle Winston.

"How long would it have taken him to set it up?" I asked.

"A few hours," Schultz said. "There are holes in the roof, that's how the birds got in. He could have done it during daylight, any day this week."

"The guy you shot," I said, "whatever his name was, he was wearing a rubber trench coat. What about the coat?"

"It's a specialty item," said a new voice. I looked up to see Willick bending over his notes. "Something like that, you have to order special." Willick looked up, feeling the speculative gaze of the entire room, and blushed scarlet to the roots of his receding hair. "I checked this last week," he said. "Just working a hunch." He was redder than Finch.

"Where did it come from?" Captain Finch rapped out.

"Place on Santa Monica," Willick said, going from red to pale green without so much as a transition. "The Pleasure Closet."

"Hammond," Finch said, "it would seem we've underestimated your protégé."

"Who gives a shit?" I said rudely. "Who ordered them?"

"Somebody named Festus," Willick said.

"Great," Finch said. "Festus. Nobody is named Festus."

"There was that guy on *Gunsmoke*," Willick said helpfully.

Finch took a long breath before he said, in a regretful tone, "I knew your dad." He blew the breath out. "Expensive?"

"Three hundred bucks a pop," Willick said, reassured to be on familiar ground at last.

"And they never asked for his last name?" I said. "He ordered a few three-hundred-dollar coats, and they never asked for his address?"

"Oh, no," Willick said. "He paid in full, in cash, in advance."

"How many?" I asked, when the silence made it clear that Willick had been abandoned, rubber-coated, on his desert isle. "How many coats did Festus order?"

"Three," Willick offered humbly. "He ordered three."

"When?"

"Two years ago, the first one. The others he ordered on May twelfth."

"What did he look like?" I asked Willick.

"Like everybody," Willick said. "Middle thirties, short brown hair—not blond—thin, no notable scars or birthmarks."

"Where'd Dennis Thorpe's wig come from?" That was Hammond, so he was awake after all.

"We don't know yet," Finch said, "but it's just a cheap Halloween wig. Sold all over the place."

"Prints in the Doopermart?" Hammond again.

"All over the place," Finch said. "Hundreds of them, from dozens of people. The place has been empty for years."

"Then he probably did the setup yesterday," Hammond said. "If there are people in and out, he couldn't have left it there without someone accidentally triggering it."

"Thank you, Lieutenant," Finch said with some asperity. "And, yes, we're already talking to people in the area to see if anyone saw anything."

"Captain," Hammond said, sounding something like his old self, "would you like me to leave the room? Dr. Schultz just suggested that the clown could have rigged it any time in the past few days. Well, he couldn't, could he?"

"*None* of this," Annabelle Winston said, rapping the table with her knuckles. "I'll have none of this. If you withhold information one more time, we're going public with the reward."

"He wasn't withholding anything," Hammond said, staring at his knuckles. "He just hadn't figured it out." From the look Finch gave him, Hammond's future with the LAPD wasn't going to be a happy one.

"It's going to be hard to find him through UCLA," I said, just to ease the tension. "Especially since he's probably not blond." I summarized the conversation with Dr. Blinkins.

"We'll work that end, then," Schultz said. "Talk to all the teachers, all the graduate students."

"Suppose he's still there?" Fred the lawyer said.

"He already knows we're looking for him," Schultz said calmly. "It may push him into doing something stupid."

"Like burning another woman," Annabelle Winston said. "We've seen what he does when the police give him a push."

A uniformed patrolman came in and handed Finch a note. Finch read it and handed it back. "No calls," he said.

"He didn't know she was a woman," Schultz said as the patrolman left. "She was wearing a man's coat."

The floor rippled and heaved beneath me. "Oh, no," I said.

People stared at me. "Was she wearing a skirt?" I asked. "Nylons rolled down on her calves?"

Schultz looked at Finch, and Annabelle Winston rapped the table again and said, *"Now."*

"Yes," Schultz said, searching for something to look at.

I shook my head. Something sharp and hot had pushed its way up into my throat, and I wasn't sure I could speak.

"He talked to a woman last night," Hammond said. "The one who wanted a bath. Remember?" Schultz didn't reply.

"She wanted to die clean," I finally said.

Schultz exhaled in a thin hiss. "He couldn't have been watching," he said uncertainly. "He was in position by then. That was the last stop."

"Stick it up your nose, Schultz," I said. "When was the last time you were right? I'll bet you've got it marked on your calendar. Not this year's calendar, probably one from some year with a six in front of it." Schultz started to say something, but I found myself standing, holding on to the edge of the table with both hands. "You stupid son of a bitch, you heard me talking to her last night, you heard it all, and this is the first time you've even asked your highly trained self whether he didn't burn his first woman on purpose? Whether she might be a message to me?"

"Sit down," Annabelle Winston said quietly.

"You're right," Schultz said quietly to me.

"I'll sit down when and where I feel like it, and I already know I'm right. I don't need positive reinforcement from some overeducated household appliance with thirty initials after his name. In case I'm not making myself clear, Dr. Schultz, I think you're a brass-plated, steel-riveted asshole."

"You're right," Schultz said again. He was looking at his lap.

"Thank you," I said, "I can't tell you how much that means to me."

"I fucked up," Schultz said, looking squarely at me. "We knew it was the same woman. We just didn't tell you."

"That's it," Annabelle Winston said.

"You should have followed her," I said.

"It's even worse than that," Schultz said, without taking his eyes off me. "We wouldn't have had to follow her."

"You're joking," I said, appalled.

"He burned her on the bench," Schultz said. Then he looked down at his stomach, very quickly, and sat still for a moment. "Right where you talked to her," he said.

Then he put both of his hands, very empty hands, on the table.

"I'm sorry," he said.

"Simeon," Hammond said into the embarrassed silence.

"I don't want to hear from you," I said.

"You're absolutely right," Dr. Schultz said to me. "I should have known. I should have anticipated it. I'll go to my grave—"

"Not soon enough," I said.

"—knowing I should have anticipated it. I ask you to believe that." He raised his head slowly and sat forward. "But look. He's still trying to talk to you."

"Wonderful," I said.

"Even after, after what happened last night. He backtracked to that woman because he wanted to do something that would reach you. He was. . . " Schultz said, looking up at me. He stopped and licked his lips again. "This is only an opinion, okay? Nobody has to take notes or anything. He was making a statement. He felt betrayed, and he was showing Mr. Grist what would happen if he was betrayed again."

"A statement," Annabelle Winston said flatly.

"If he wants to make a statement," I said, "he knows how to make one that would finish me, and I don't mean by lighting fire to me."

Annabelle Winston gave me the look again.

"I have to talk to him," I said.

"The press conference." It was the first thing Bobby Grant had said all morning.

"No fucking way," Captain Finch said.

"You're not exactly in a position to insist, Captain," Fred the lawyer said.

"Shut up," I said. To my surprise, they did. "I need to think.

"I need a way to tell him," I said, feeling my way, "that I had nothing to do with what happened last night. He has to believe that I've cut all ties with the police. At the same time, I need the police. I need them to watch the person I need them to watch. Hammond knows who she is. In fact," I said, gaining a degree of confidence, "I need Hammond assigned to watch her. And he reports to *no one*. No one, is that clear? He knows her and likes her, and I won't have him reporting to anyone who might decide to use the lady as bait the way I was used." Hammond still hadn't looked at me.

"It's not usual," Finch said lamely.

"Would you prefer the press conference?" Annabelle Winston asked.

"No press conference," I said. Bobby Grant groaned. "The print media can get it wrong, and TV will give me a minute, maybe the wrong minute. Also, I don't want him to know that I'm still working for you," I said to Annabelle Winston. "I will be, but I don't want him to know it. I want him to think that I'm out there on my own, solo, scared, sorry as hell, and waiting for him to talk to me."

"You want to go one-on-one with him?" Schultz said. "He'll burn you. Honest to God, he'll burn you. As you said, I could be useful." He spread his hands apologetically. "At least, that's my opinion."

"What's the problem with one-on-one?" I asked. "It hasn't been so great to be on the big team."

"Like me or not," Schultz said very quietly, "and I'll understand if you hate my guts, I know him better than anyone else here."

"And the cops buy your lunch."

"Not necessarily," Schultz said.

"He's on our payroll," Finch said promptly.

"I've got a practice, too," Schultz said, bridling. "Mr. Grist could become a private patient." Finch looked as if he wished the entire room were an antacid.

"Information privileged?" I asked.

"Absolutely." Schultz avoided looking at Captain Finch.

"Maybe," I said. "But Schultz, the first time I think you're shucking me, I'll kill you."

"I'd almost deserve it," Schultz said.

I held his gaze for what felt like an hour and then gave it up. "I'll need everything your guys turn up," I said to Finch, "either on the phone or by regular mail. Call me the day after you send me anything. If I haven't got it by the following day, if I think it might have been snatched out of my mailbox, I'll call. And no surveillance on my street."

"That's dumb," Hammond said without glancing at me.

"He'll spot it," I said, "and then we'll be back to nowhere."

"How are you going to talk to him?" Annabelle Winston said.

"The press conference," Bobby Grant said again, seeing his future written in the skies.

"No," I said. "I need more control. Captain Finch," I said, but Finch was looking up at the same uniformed patrolman. The patrolman looked nervous.

"Captain," he said, "there's this guy on the phone. . . ."

"I said no calls," Finch said curtly, "and I meant it. What do you think, my jaws need exercise?"

"He's called five times this morning," the uniform said, "and he's threatening to call the chief. Needs to talk to someone on the Incinerator investigation. Says he knows the chief personally. Says he's a—"

"Tell him to fold, spindle, and mutilate himself," Finch interrupted.

"—television producer," the uniform plowed along. "Norman something."

I got up again. "I'll talk to him," I said.

PART THREE

CONFLAGRATION

I just wondered how it would feel to shoot
Grandma.

—Serial murderer Emil Kemper

12

Live and in Color

This is what it said:

You made me break a rule.
You don't know how important the rules are.
If I had my way, I'd do five a night, every night of the
week, every week of the year. The rules save lives. And you
made me break one.
You'll be sorry. When I kill the others, you'll be sorry.
When I liberate your phlogiston and leave nothing behind but
calx, you'll be sorry.

This one had been written in a hurry: same gold pen, same
inexorably straight margins, but no picture at the bottom, no
fancy first initial at the top. Like the dance card, it had been mes-
sengered. Same approach, different service, no lead.

We could have been friends. I used to think we were
friends. I hoped we could be friends again.
You didn't recognize my voice. Well, keep an eye over
your shoulder. If you don't recognize me before I throw the
match, you'll be sorry. Of course, you'll be sorry either way.

> *You saw what I did to your girlfriend. She made a lovely*
> *light.*
> *Tell your other girlfriend to be careful too. And, by the*
> *way, I don't think much of the guy she's fooling around with.*
> *Real drop in quality there.*

I'd attempted, but failed, to prevent them from showing that part. As it flashed onto the screen I wanted to perspire, but the makeup they'd caked on my face wouldn't let me. I just tried to penetrate the glare of light pouring down on me to locate a friendly face. No deal there, either.

> *I tried,* the note continued. *I really tried. But you're*
> *an *******, just like all the others.*
> *So you'll burn.*

The note hadn't said *******, of course. It had used a much more descriptive term, which had been covered, for today's purposes only, with asterisks. This was, after all, family entertainment.

"That's a letter from a man who has burned thirteen people to death in Los Angeles," Velez Caputo said, bright as a silver quarter, into the nearest camera. "We're coming to you live today to bring you this amazing story. The show that was scheduled for this hour, 'Transvestites and the Women Who Love Them,' will be shown tomorrow. And we'll talk with the man the killer sent that letter to after this commercial message."

The lights on the set went out, and the television monitors facing the set went dark. The sound track to a commercial for disposable diapers boomed through the speakers, preternaturally loud, as though mothers and babies were universally hard of hearing. "Relax for sixty seconds," Velez Caputo said to me with a smile that had probably sent her dentist's kids through college. "I *love* live TV."

I smiled back, feeling the makeup stiff on my cheeks. I didn't love live TV, but at least I could see again.

It was Tuesday afternoon. Two days had passed, and the Incinerator had burned three people, two of them out in the Valley, in Van Nuys. Another departure from established procedure.

The one in Van Nuys and one of the L.A. victims had been women, which had the effect of making things more urgent. The media were howling.

Stillman had agreed to my insistence on the telephone that we do the show live rather than waiting the usual two weeks between taping and airing, and had even bought full-page ads in both the *Times* and the *Daily News*. Velez Caputo had come into the studio on Sunday afternoon to tape radio and television commercials, and they'd been on the air by Sunday night. Only in the L.A. market, of course. Norman wasn't going to spend any money he didn't absolutely have to spend.

So the Incinerator was probably watching. I'd guessed that he followed the media, if only to see what they were saying about him. Maybe I'd been wrong. Schultz, for whatever it was worth, was positive that he did. Now that he wasn't Captain Omnipotent, Schultz and I were getting along better.

Schultz smiled at me.

He was sitting rigidly in what I'd been told was called the Number Two Seat. I was in the Hot Seat. A couple of people I didn't know filled seats Three and Four. No one had rushed forward to tell me who they were, but Schultz had vouched for the one in Number Three. Behind the cameras and the lights a sort of Peanut Gallery rose in tiers, people packed shoulder to shoulder in narrow, uncomfortable-looking chairs. Their clothes marked most of them as out-of-towners, and the way they gaped at me—those of them who could tear their eyes off Velez Caputo—reminded me of the old adage about fools' faces. Few places were as conspicuously public as this.

"Fifteen seconds," said a man wearing a headset. The man had a nervous tic that effectively deprived him of control over the lids of his left eye. Velez Caputo smoothed her dress and licked her lips. Velez Caputo had wonderful lips, and no tics to speak of.

There were, I'd been told, eighty people sitting out front in the Peanut Gallery. Among them were Eleanor, whom I'd been unable to talk out of attending, Hammond, and three of his boys. They'd followed her in, at a presumably discreet distance, when she absolutely refused to stay home. In exchange for coming, she'd accepted the deal: She had to leave early. In case the Incinerator was waiting outside.

Velez Caputo gave her microphone cord a tug. It was attached to an oversized spool, like the one that lawn maniacs use to keep their garden hoses tidy. An anxious-looking man presided over it as though it were the only responsibility worth shouldering in the entire world.

The lights came on. "Five seconds," said the man with the headset and the tic. His eye was firing off random squints. "Four, three," and then he held up a hand and counted down, two, one. He pointed a discreet index finger in the general direction of Velez Caputo. *No one* pointed directly at Velez Caputo. The little red light on the camera closest to her winked on.

"They call him the Incinerator," Velez Caputo said immediately. "He's the latest and most sensational member of a breed that's become only too common in this decade, the serial killer.

"Where do these people come from?" She stopped smiling and assumed an expression of High Episcopal Seriousness. "What goes through their minds? Why do they walk among us? And what is it like to know that one of them has targeted you?

"When people think about their deaths, what do they dread most? Is it death from a lingering disease? No." She was reading off a transparent TelePrompTer that spooled by in front of the camera she was facing, invisible to the people looking in, the same elite device used by presidents of the United States, and why not? She made a lot more money than the president. "Is it death by drowning? No," she answered herself, just in case the folks at home had gotten it wrong. "According to a Louis Harris poll, it's death by fire. By flame," she said. "And that's how the Incinerator kills his defenseless victims. We have with us today four guests."

The light on her camera went out, and I saw myself, wearing makeup, on the monitors, looking as if I'd wandered in from the show on transvestites by mistake. "First is a Los Angeles private detective named Simeon Grist." The words SIMEON GRIST appeared on the screen beneath my face, which had frozen into a sort of muscular death mask. In print, my name seemed foolish and wrong, like an alias assigned by a substandard intelligence service.

"Mr. Grist," Velez Caputo was saying about the idiotic-looking individual on the monitors, "is the man who broke up a child prostitution ring here in Los Angeles last year. He was retained by the famous heiress Baby Winston when the Incinerator burned her father, and now, as you've seen from the letter we just read, the Incinerator has threatened to burn him alive. It took great courage for him to join us today, ladies and gentlemen. Simeon Grist."

People applauded, and the idiot on the monitors grinned emptily. Hammond clapped, slowly and ironically. Eleanor sat forward, looking concerned. Stillman, behind the cameras in a nautical blazer, made up for my old pal's lack of *joie de vivre* by applauding more enthusiastically than anyone. The light on my camera went off, and none too soon.

"Our other guests," Velez Caputo said, "are a psychologist specializing in serial killers for the Los Angeles Police Department, Dr. Norbert Schultz."

Schultz smiled in a nervous, yellow fashion, and I thought, *Norbert?*

"From VICAP, the Federal Bureau of Investigation's central index, where national information on these maniacs is stored," Velez Caputo continued as the monitors reflected a sallow individual wearing a blue tie with little red fish all over it, "William Stang."

William Stang didn't smile. He probably hadn't smiled since the day his wife fell through the ice.

The man in the farthest chair had gotten up, and a woman took his place. Great, I thought, a surprise.

"And, finally, the woman who's being called the Homeless Heroine, the woman who fought off the Incinerator to save the life—only temporarily, I'm afraid—of Baby Winston's father. Ladies and gentlemen, Hermione X."

Hermione X, not a new hallmark in alias creativity, had been considerably cleaned up. Wearing a mask that made her look like an aged Lone Ranger in drag, she waved at the audience. They applauded. She was a hit. She was also loving it.

I was hating it a lot. "He could kill her," I said over whatever Velez Caputo was reading off the TelePrompTer, a stream of over-written conjecture about what has gone wrong with our society.

"Mr. Grist?" Velez Caputo said, swiveling to face me. It would take a lot to surprise her.

"This isn't smart," I said. "She has to go back to the streets when you've finished with her, and he saw her. So what if she's wearing a mask? He knows who she is."

"We're paying for her security," Velez Caputo said smoothly. I saw Norman wince. "Anyway, we're sending her home."

"The woman doesn't know her last name. Should be an interesting passport."

Caputo frowned at me, but Stillman's face cleared.

"Don't worry about me, Ducks," Hermione said gaily.

"I'd think, Simeon—may I call you Simeon?" Velez Caputo said.

"Call me whatever you want," I said. I'd been warned that there would be surprises, but I hadn't figured on Hermione.

"I'd think, Simeon, that you'd be more worried about yourself." The man with the headset was making frantic signals in the direction of the TelePrompter, his left eye sending out a semaphore of panic. She ignored him.

"Well," I lied, "you'd think wrong."

"And yet this lunatic has told you what he's after. Specifically," she added. "You."

"He's not a lunatic," I said.

"He's not," Schultz said, leaning forward in his chair as he picked up his cue. "Clinically, he's probably as sane as you and I."

"Sane?" Velez Caputo said, arching an eyebrow that probably required its own gardening staff. "He's torching defenseless people!"

"Precisely," Schultz said. "They're defenseless. He's got a plan. He's got rules. We've all got rules. Don't cross on the red, don't cheat on the wife, don't do anything that might make you lose the job. Well, he's got rules, too, and he followed them for a long time. They're not our rules, but they're rules. And insofar as the legal definition of sanity is concerned—whether he can distinguish between right and wrong—well, of course he can. And he's proceeding anyway, in accordance with a program he's created. He's completely in control of himself."

"He's very much in control," Stang said. He'd interrupted a sentence fragment from Velez Caputo, but she looked at him as gratefully as though he'd just offered her the names and addresses of seventy Nielsen families. "Your mass murderer, the guy who shows up at McDonald's with an AK-47 and shoots thirty people, he's maybe crazy. He kisses the wife and kiddies good-bye and slips a clip into the magazine and blows people away until the cops put a couple through his skull. He knows he's going to die, and he doesn't care. *That's* crazy. But your serial murderer, he's careful. He chooses one kind of victim exclusively, and one way to kill them, and he makes sure that no one will catch him. He looks both ways, so to speak, and when the field is clear, he slits the throat. . . ."

"Or throws the match," Schultz said.

"Or throws the match," Stang said crankily. "It doesn't matter."

"Doesn't *matter*?" Velez Caputo said, smelling a fight.

"Well, it matters to the victim, I suppose," Stang said. "But, you know, when you're about to die, there isn't time to decide that you'd prefer a different form of murder."

"Mr. Grist?" Velez Caputo said. Hermione cawed something, but Caputo ignored her.

"He's sane," I said, "whatever sane means."

"He's bloody crackers," Hermione said. "You should have heard him laugh."

"Hermione," I said, "can it."

"Time for a break," Velez Caputo said to the camera, and the lights went down.

"*You,*" she hissed to me, "don't interrupt. We have to get a flow going here."

"Would you prefer that I leave?" I asked. "Want to fill some time?"

"Norman," she said, but she didn't have to. Stillman was already there, standing over me and looking down with fatherly concern.

"Simeon," he said, "you haven't said it yet."

"If I leave," I said, "you've got an awful long time in front of you." The computer behind Velez Caputo's eyes began to click.

"Fifty minutes," she said to Stillman. "I told you live was a mistake."

"Thirty seconds," said the man with the headset.

"This is national?" Velez Caputo said.

"You wanted it to be," Stillman replied, demonstrating an Olympian mastery of the sidestep.

"Can I interrupt?" I said as the man with the headset told us that twenty seconds remained. Velez Caputo looked from Norman to me. "Leave us alone," I said.

Velez Caputo gave me a stare packed with the kind of loathing I usually reserve for the poetry written by characters in novels. "That's not how it works, sonny," she said.

"Five," said the man with the headset, over the strident tones of a commercial for laundry detergent. "Four, three," and he held up the fingers for two, one. He pointed vaguely in Velez Caputo's direction.

"We're back," she said, sounding very glad to be back. Stillman had retreated behind the cameras. "We were talking to Dr. Stang," she said, making her first mistake.

"Mr. Stang," Stang said.

"Of course," Velez Caputo said, coloring beneath her makeup. "Mr. Stang of the FBI. We were talking about why you're so sure that the killer is in control of himself."

"These people," Stang said sourly, "serial killers, I mean, decide consciously to give up their own lives to take the lives of others. They exert enormous control to do so."

"Surely that's insane," Velez Caputo said. Stang shook his head.

"Painters," Schultz interrupted, following the script we'd developed, "give up their lives—normal, secure, middle-class lives, I mean—to paint. Writers decide to write, no matter what. This man is following a kind of creative urge. It's a twisted kind of creativity—"

"I don't believe what I'm hearing," Velez Caputo said.

"—but it's a kind of creativity," Schultz said doggedly. "As in any art form, he's decided to accept the limitations imposed by his materials—in this case, gasoline and matches—and he's trying—"

"You're a *doctor*," Velez Caputo accused him.

"—he's trying to take it to the ultimate, trying to do something that no one else has ever done with those materials, all the while facing the challenge of capture." He sat back, having done that bit. Velez Caputo's face filled the screen, and Schultz gave me the high sign.

"You sound as though you admire him," Velez Caputo said. "What about the deaths? What about the agony of the victims?"

"No one's forgetting about the victims," I said. "All Dr. Schultz is saying is that it's a mistake to imagine him as a drooling maniac, hovering in doorways waiting for someone to fall asleep.

He's got a highly developed set of criteria, and he's almost certainly a very intelligent man. Probably a brilliant man." Point two.

"So what's phlogiston?" Velez Caputo said, retreating to consult the TelePrompter at last. "What's calx?"

"Phlogiston," I said, glad to get to an easy part, "is a bad idea from the early nineteenth century. It was a principle, sort of like an element, and it was proposed by a German chemist named G. E. Stahl as the thing that actually burned when anything caught fire. Calx was whatever was left over."

"So he's saying," Velez Caputo said, cutting through the history of science with a straight razor, "that he intends to burn you to a crisp."

"That's what he's saying," I said.

"Because he thinks you betrayed him. I should explain," she said, turning to the cameras, "some of the background here." The TelePrompter was whirring again, and she explained it in about forty compact seconds. Finishing, she turned to me. "So how do you feel about that, Mr. Grist?"

It wasn't time for that yet.

"Miss Caputo," I said.

"Velez," she said. "Call me Velez." Off camera, nobody called her Velez.

"How would you feel if he were after you? And who knows? He may decide to go after you next," I said. "Surely, he's watching us now."

Caputo said, "Well, I don't—"

"He might like to burn a celebrity," I said maliciously. Schultz was making frantic hand signals. "Think of the media coverage."

"And yet," Velez Caputo said, a trifle grimly as the man with the tic made frantic adjustments in the TelePrompter, "up until a few days ago, this Incinerator specialized, as you say, in men. Then he apparently decided to kill women as well." She paused and licked her lips again, and this time the gesture looked functional rather than cosmetic. "Why?" she asked. "Why do you suppose he changed course?" The man with the tic pointed at Schultz, and Caputo turned toward him. "Dr. Schultz?"

Schultz was sitting taller than a man who suspected the presence of a whoopee cushion. He hadn't wanted to do this part. He'd asked me repeatedly to do it myself, but I'd refused. If he did it, it meant that he hadn't talked to Finch.

"He feels that the rules were broken in the, um"—he looked at me, and I returned his gaze, feeling my heart pound against the walls of my jugular vein—"in the, in the . . ."

"Police action," Velez Caputo said.

"Yes," Schultz said, and his Adam's apple did a little swan dive. "In the police action last Sunday evening." Hammond, in the back of the room, glared first at me and then at Schultz. "He feels that Mr. Grist betrayed his trust by talking to the police, and he broke his own rules in return. So he burned his first woman."

"We have a picture of her," Velez Caputo said, and Schultz sagged back into his chair as a photograph flashed onto the monitors. It might have been the woman I talked to, but the photo had been taken in a different life, a life when she shopped and went home and went to the beauty parlor, and there she was with a matronly smile on her face, a woman living safely within the walls of a world that shut out rain and cold and Thunderbird and bottles of gasoline and Incinerators.

"Helena Troy," Caputo said. The name sounded like a sick joke.

"Mrs. Troy," Schultz acknowledged.

"A woman deserted by her husband in Boston less than a year ago," Velez Caputo said. "Left with nothing, not even the rent for her apartment. Mr. Troy, wherever you are, I hope you're watching. She was the first woman he killed," she said to Schultz.

"Yes," he said, looking like someone whose shoes were wet.

"And you think this is significant."

"We think, that is *I* think," Schultz said, "as a trained psychologist with some experience with this kind of mentality, that he's been *keeping* himself from burning women, that, in fact, women have been his real target all along. He's been denying himself that target—"

"I'm not sure I understand," Velez Caputo said, on behalf of the folks at home.

"Remember the note," Schultz said. The camera had had enough of the note, and it remained on him. "Remember the control in that note. He talks about the rules. The rules protect people, he says. Remember his behavior. Always the homeless, always within a certain area, until after the, um, police and Mr. Grist broke the rules. He could have killed elsewhere, someplace the police weren't looking for him. He didn't, until the, ah, police action Sunday night." Dr. Schultz was sweating like a waterfall. He was a police psychologist, and he'd just suggested police culpability not only in the shooting of Dennis Thorpe, but also in the deaths of three women. I felt sorry for him, but I also felt a small thrill of victory at recognizing an ally. He hadn't consulted with Finch.

"So he felt Mr. Grist had broken the rules," Velez Caputo said. "Why did he react by burning women?"

"Because," Schultz said, advancing the theory we'd spent two days arguing over, "he'd *always* meant to burn women."

"Please," she said. "Can you be more specific?"

"With considerable effort," Schultz said.

"Male serial killers always kill women, unless they're homosexuals who derive sexual pleasure from killing men," Stang broke in. "That's been the problem from the beginning. There didn't seem to be any sexual element. Put him into a whole new category. He was just burning them and going away. What was he getting out of it?"

"He was deriving the same kind of enjoyment," Schultz said, literally shutting his eyes so he could plow ahead with a theory he hadn't shared with the LAPD, "that an artist gets by not putting real wood, say, into his paintings but rather facing the challenge of painting wood. Wood has a very difficult texture. To paint wood in its natural state, wood that's full of whorls and loops and seemingly random patterns, well, that's very difficult indeed. Why not just put a piece of wood into the picture and paint around it?"

"You keep comparing this man to an artist," Velez Caputo said.

"He *is* an artist," Schultz said. "He's an artist of death. Death is his area of creativity," he said, word for word from the script, "and, like all great artists, he set down rules, limitations for himself." Schultz drew a deep breath. "And the primary limitation he established, I believe, was that he would only burn men, even though his hatred, the spark that ignited his rage, was women. When Mr. Grist broke the, um, when the . . ." he faltered. "Oh, hell," he said, settling into his chair at last, "when the LAPD broke the rules he had set down for talking to Mr. Grist, he threw out his own rules and started to burn women instead."

"Women," Velez Caputo said neutrally.

"Women were always his main target," Schultz bravely reiterated, risking his professional reputation. "It's women he hates."

"We'll be back with Mr. Grist's reactions—and a very personal plea to the killer," Velez Caputo said into the camera, "after this."

Things went dark. "And keep it short," Velez Caputo said to me as a squadron of makeup women rushed to repair the damages of whatever real emotions she might have endured while we were on the air. They were finishing when the tic with the headset said, "Fifteen."

Two men were hustling Hermione out of Seat Number Four, and she was cawing protest.

Three, two, one, the man with the tic counted with his fingers. The lights had come on.

"Mr. Grist," Caputo said, and then she looked at Stillman and fought down a rebellious grin. "We've heard from Dr. Schultz that the Incinerator may concentrate on female victims from now on, and yet this note was addressed to you. We promised that we'd get your feelings about all this, but before we do"—she glanced to her right, where a woman was being seated in Hermione's place in Seat Number Four—"we want to focus on that note. In fact, on *all* the notes."

I glanced wildly toward Schultz, who looked like he'd just been hit by a train.

"Hold on," he shouted.

"There have been three," Velez Caputo said, as though Schultz hadn't spoken. He got up, but the first note was already on the screen, pictures and all, in glorious color.

"That's not allowed," Schultz said helplessly, still standing there. People waved him back to his chair. "That hasn't been made public."

"Sit down, Doctor," Caputo said, flicking a finger at the floor director to keep the note on the screen. "It's public now."

I got up, too. "You won't show the other one," I said, "or Dr. Schultz and I are leaving."

The monitors opened up to show a wide shot, Caputo,

Schultz, and me all standing there, the woman in Seat Four looking calmly on. Schultz was jiggling from foot to foot like a prize-fighter.

"And why is that?" Velez Caputo asked, looking happy. She'd finally gotten her fight.

"Because it's privileged information," Schultz said. "In any murder investigation, certain details are kept quiet. Do you know how many people have confessed to these murders?"

"How would I?" Velez Caputo said accusingly. "The police haven't released much of anything."

"More than a dozen," Schultz said.

The first note flashed back onto the screen.

"We'll make a deal," Velez Caputo said. "We won't show the second one."

"You sure as hell won't," Schultz said. "You'll give it back, and you'll tell us where you got your copy."

"We'll talk about that after the show," Caputo said. She came back onto the monitors. Up in the booth, the director must have been tearing his hair out. "For now," Caputo continued, "we believe that the note you're now looking at—where is the *note*?" she demanded. It reappeared. "We believe that the way this note is written tells us something entirely new about the Incinerator, and we have with us an expert who can enlighten us. Joining us," Velez Caputo said, "is Dr. Catherine Cowan of the University of Southern California, an expert on medieval manuscripts."

"Hello," Dr. Cowan said to the cameras. She was an angular woman of forty or forty-five with a determined jaw, a large Victorian garnet brooch, and a beehive hairdo that suggested a hidden fondness for country music. Schultz was studying her as though she were a piranha that had popped up in his bathtub.

"Dr. Cowan," Velez Caputo said, "you've had a chance to review all the Incinerator's letters to date."

"I have," Dr. Cowan said.

"And what is your opinion of them?"

"They're parodies," Dr. Cowan said, "no, that's not the right word because they're not scornful—they're imitations of illuminated manuscripts of the Middle Ages."

"We already know all this," Schultz said.

"Our viewers don't," Velez Caputo said. "And what are illuminated manuscripts, Dr. Cowan?"

"Well, as I say, they're medieval," Dr. Cowan said, settling into her chair for a nice long chat. "Should I establish the dates?"

"Never mind," Velez Caputo said. "The Middle Ages."

"Yes, well, illuminated. Anything illustrated in silver or gold. Usually, although not always, containing religious texts. They're hand-painted, of course, on vellum, which is the stretched skin of a goat. Vellum is very durable."

"Is it?" Velez Caputo said, a bit impatiently.

"Certainly," Dr. Cowan said serenely. "In fact, the most common surviving objects from the Middle Ages are books."

"Isn't that interesting," Velez Caputo said. "Now the notes—"

"It's not just interesting," Dr. Cowan continued, "it's fascinating. Remember, most of the libraries and monasteries that held them have crumbled away into ruins, and they were made of stone. But the books are with us still."

"And looking at this note," Velez Caputo prompted.

"Some illuminated manuscripts survived appalling treatment. In Ireland, they were dipped in cattle troughs because it was thought that their magic would protect livestock." Dr. Cowan permitted herself a well-bred snicker, and Caputo used it as a shoehorn.

"Dr. Cowan," she said in a tone that would have halted an avalanche in midslope.

Dr. Cowan had her mouth open to say something, but she took a little bite out of the air instead. "Sorry?" she said.

"The note from the Incinerator," Velez Caputo said briskly. "The one that will be on the screen as soon as the technical staff gets on the ball." It appeared. "We'll confine our discussion to that note," she said, glancing at Schultz but meaning the words for Dr. Cowan. "Now, in what ways does this note—*this note*, Dr. Cowan—resemble an illuminated manuscript?"

"Well," Dr. Cowan said, her mouth a straight line, "it's written in gold, of course. One of those cheap metallic pens from Japan. An authentic illuminated manuscript, you understand—"

"Please," Velez Caputo said. "It would have been written in real gold. We understand that."

"Not pure gold, of course," Dr. Cowan began.

"Ink with gold in it then," Velez Caputo almost snapped. Schultz was beginning to enjoy himself. I, on the other hand, was feeling distinctly odd. I was hearing echoes.

Dr. Cowan had her mouth zipped tight. "What was the question?" she said, after a moment. Schultz grinned uncharitably. Norman was wilting.

"Other points of resemblance," Velez Caputo said. "Looking at this note and this note only, Doctor."

"The drawing at the bottom," Dr. Cowan said, giving Caputo's attitude back to her, with change. "It resembles a miniature, a painting on an illuminated manuscript. They're not called miniatures because they're small—"

"Minium," I said out loud. I felt as though I were saying it with someone else's voice. Something that might have been a worm seemed to be crawling up my spine.

Velez Caputo shot me a glance, but Dr. Cowan rolled on.

"—but because they're painted with a lead-based paint called minium. That's one reason they lasted so—"

"What do you know about minium, Mr. Grist?" Velez Caputo asked me. I shook my head. The worm, or the tremor, or whatever it was, had just about reached my shoulder blades.

"The big initial at the very beginning," Velez Caputo said, giving up on me and turning back to Dr. Cowan.

"It's an historiated initial," Dr. Cowan said tightly, and the little worm reached the back of my neck and set off a small firework inside my skull, and just for a moment I saw a face, a very young face, and then it broke and shivered apart like a reflection in water that's been disturbed.

". . . They have scenes painted in them," Dr. Cowan said. Schultz was staring at me as though I'd popped out in spots. "Or around them, like this one," she added, apparently unable to stop talking.

"So what does this tell us about the man who wrote this note?" Caputo asked, happy to be back on track.

My ears were humming, but I gathered that it meant that the Incinerator had some training in art history.

"We already knew that," Schultz said, a bucket of cold water in Seat Number Two. He was looking at me, but I barely saw him. I was wondering whether I'd kept any of my notes. My God, it had been thirteen or fourteen years.

". . . After this message," Velez Caputo said. The studio went dark.

"I *must* say," Dr. Cowan began angrily.

"Thank you, Doctor," Velez Caputo said, dismissing her. The powder-puff brigade reassembled and began its repair work. Norman and a helper ushered Dr. Cowan off the set. She sounded a lot like Hermione.

"God damn it," Schultz said to Velez Caputo, "where did you get that note?"

"Sources," Caputo said airily.

"Simeon," Schultz turned to me. "I promise you . . ."

"I know," I said. "Skip it." I was trying to reassemble the face I'd glimpsed.

"You're next, Mr. Grist," Caputo said as the tic started to count down from fifteen. I must have looked vague, because she said, "Mr. Grist?"

"Yeah, yeah," I said.

The lights snapped back on.

"Well," Velez Caputo said, "this *has* been interesting. New information about the nation's most dangerous serial killer." Stang made a scornful sound. "And the man who probably has most to fear from this monster is here in the studio. Mr. Grist," she said as the monitors reflected a two-shot, "let's assume that the Incinerator is watching. Have you got anything to say to him?"

"I do," I said, through the buzzing in my mind. The camera was now on me, as we'd been promised it would be.

"And what is it?" Velez Caputo said, checking her lipstick in a mirror held by one of the makeup girls.

"As you know, I got your letter," I said to the camera. It was very hard to keep my eyes on the camera, as opposed to looking around the room for someone—Eleanor, or even Hammond—to whom I could speak directly. I'd been told, though, that skipping past the camera would look shifty and untrustworthy, so I forced myself to stay locked on the lens that had the red light beneath it, feeling like someone practicing a speech to an ashtray. "We all know what it said. It said I made you break the rules. It said, basically, that I'd betrayed you." I took a deep breath and tried to keep my eyes on the camera lens.

"Well, I did. I betrayed you. I was frightened, and I didn't remember you, and I betrayed you. But, and I ask you to believe me, I told the police to keep their distance. They didn't." Behind the cameras, I saw Hammond bristle. Too bad.

"I had a friend on the force," I said, deviating from the

script. "I trusted him to keep the cops under control. He couldn't, but that wasn't his fault. It was my fault for having involved him, and the LAPD, in the first place. So here's what I'm saying."

I looked over toward Schultz, and he nodded encouragingly.

"I'm saying no more cops," I said between dry lips. "I'm saying that I've stopped working for Annabelle Winston. I'm saying that I'm hanging out there solo, and if you want to write me a letter, or talk to me, or burn me alive, there won't be any cops around. Check out my street, if you've got the nerve." The challenge had been Schultz's idea, and I hadn't been sure I'd use it until that moment. "Or else, wait a week and follow me. You'll see. I'll be clean." I couldn't look at the camera any longer, and I lowered my head.

"Are you finished?" Velez Caputo said.

"No," I said. I encountered the camera's gaze again and drew breath to steady my voice. "When you're certain, come to me. Or make me come to you. But as long as I'm straight with you, no more women."

"A courageous pronouncement," Velez Caputo said, pleased to have it behind her at last. "I'm sure we all sympathize with Mr. Grist." She beamed to demonstrate her sympathy. "But tell me, if you will," she said, and the camera once again switched to a two-shot. "This man is after you. Tall, dressed in black rubber, a cheap fright wig on his head, and a bottle of gasoline in his hand. Tell us, Mr. Grist, aren't you afraid?"

"Miss Caputo."

"Velez," she breathed invitingly.

"Velez," I said to the whole nation on live television, "that's a fucking stupid question."

13

Aftermath

There was more, but it was mainly Schultz and Stang and another expert brought in from God knows where. I reacted like a good monkey whenever I was cued. Eleanor left before it ended, as arranged, accompanied back to whatever hotel she'd been packed away in by her squadron of bodyguards. If the Incinerator decided to turn off his TV set early and show up outside the studio, I didn't want him tagging along after her.

She'd blown me a kiss as she left.

I'd managed to be civilized, but inside I was in a towering rage, and it was all directed toward myself. I'd looked at the content of the letters and not at their form. I'd been so full of comparative religion, so full of *myself*, that I'd been staring into the wrong rearview mirror. He was back there, all right, but he wasn't in the region of the map I'd been staring at.

Try as I would, I couldn't bring the face back.

Whoever it belonged to, he was back there somewhere, buried in volumes of notes, possibly notes I'd long discarded, from years and years of college, years I'd spent wasting time in a system I understood, postponing the day I'd have to step out into a system I didn't understand. Back then, at twenty-five, I hadn't been able to figure out how they, whoever they are, assign you grades in real life. I still hadn't found out.

The show ended with a round of insincere congratulations. I shrugged off Schultz's questions and headed for the parking lot. Breathing in the heady atmosphere of downtown L.A. in the late afternoon, I stood next to Alice for a good ten minutes, thinking and giving the Incinerator, assuming that he was still watching and that he was still interested, time to make sure I was alone. Then, for want of anything better to do, I went to see a movie.

I never see movies, and I didn't see much of this one. I stared up at large guns and screaming tires and myriad violations of Newton's laws, and improbable heroism, and searched the baggage of my memory. Whatever had sent that worm crawling up my spine when Dr. Cowan had said whatever she'd said, when I'd first heard it, it hadn't been important. It had been nothing.

When I realized I was hungry, I left.

The theater, I saw with some surprise as I emerged from it, was on Hollywood Boulevard, not far from the studio where Velez Caputo taped her show, and even closer to the Red Dog. For a long moment, jostled by freaks, tourists, and drug dealers, I thought about going into the Red Dog to see if Al the Red was terrorizing the natives. Too early, I decided, and anyway, he was with Eleanor. And, of course, we weren't speaking.

At the Gold Jug Coffee Shop, once a center of the underage hooker trade, my waitress stared at me until I wondered whether my nose was bleeding. When she refilled my coffee cup, she poured some into my lap.

"Okay," I said, "what is it?"

She was young, no older than eighteen, and uselessly, even harmfully, pretty.

"You're him," she said, brushing the coffee ineffectually off my lap. It felt good, anyway. "Aren't you?"

"I'm certainly him," I said. "But which him?"

"The one on TV," she said. "The one who's going to get burned."

"I'm not," I said, "and could I have the check?"

"You're not?" The coffeepot tilted dangerously in my direction.

"I'm the him on TV," I said. "But I'm not the him who's going to get burned."

No one behind me on the way home. No one behind me as I turned left off the Pacific Coast Highway and headed up Topanga Canyon Boulevard. I pulled over half the way up. Nine cars, headlights beaming merrily into the night, passed me before I departed my patch of chaparral by the side of the road and headed the rest of the way up the long hill.

At the Fernwood Market, I stopped again, partly to check for a tail and partly to fill a more pressing need. I was out of beer. The Fernwood stocked Singha just for me, in recognition of my status as a regular customer and a reliable prealcoholic. The "pre" was my estimate.

Once home, I patted Alice on the rear fender, opened the empty mailbox, and hiked up the driveway toting the beer. Here, away from the glare of L.A., stars fired off sparks above me. "Nice to see you," I said to them halfway up. "I was afraid you'd moved." The beer was heavy, so I took the rest of the driveway at an unaccustomed lope and turned the lock in the one and only door, the one that opens directly into the kitchen.

When I turned on the light, he was standing there.

I jumped back and hauled the door closed. The bag full of beer landed at my feet with the sound of shattering glass.

The cops had taken my gun after I decked Hammond. Holding the door closed with one hand and listening for movement inside the house, I reached down very slowly and fumbled around inside the wet paper bag. I sliced my index finger on something sharp before I managed to grasp a broken bottle by its neck.

I hoisted it in my hand, jagged points forward, and waited. I counted to one hundred. Not a sound.

I let go of the door, kicked it in, and jumped through it, bottle extended.

In the center of the kitchen, my own raincoat, stuffed full of newspapers, dangled from a string. A balloon bloomed above the neck. On top of the balloon, a blond wig squatted. A hot breeze made an entrance through the open door, and the ghostly assemblage did a graceful pirouette on the end of its string.

I was so furious, furious at my fear, that I pushed the shards of the bottle into the face drawn on the balloon. It exploded, and the wig floated to the kitchen floor like a large blond spider. Blood dripped from my finger onto the floor, making bright splashes around the wig like berries on a Christmas wreath.

All four burners on the gas stove were flaring merrily away, little campfires of blue. I kicked my raincoat aside and turned them off. The raincoat was swinging back and forth like a hanged man as I shut down the gas jets.

"You sadistic shithead," I said to the air. I licked my finger. Then I smelled the gasoline.

I turned as though someone had tapped me on the shoulder. Heat rose in waves against my back, and I kicked the oven door shut and felt behind me for the large, greasy knob that turned it off.

"Are you here?" I demanded. "Well, you got me."

No one answered me. A gust of wind made the walls of the shack rattle. The raincoat did a little jig. I grabbed paper towels off the roll and wrapped them around my finger.

"Got me good," I continued, stepping silently forward. "Got me with my own raincoat."

The smell of gasoline was stronger in the living room. "Got your little squirter?" I asked the darkness on the other side of the door leading to my bedroom. "I thought this was supposed to be a conversation." I still had the broken beer bottle in my right hand, the hand festooned with paper towels.

Still nothing.

"You should do something about that B.O.," I said, edging toward the door to the bedroom. "You smell like a diesel." There were only the four rooms upstairs, the kitchen, the living room, the bathroom, and the bedroom. Both the bathroom and the bedroom were on the other side of the door I was facing. The door was ajar. "Downstairs" was a euphemism I used for an empty room that could be reached only by going back outside and clambering down the hill on a suicidal goat path that led to its one and only door. I almost never used it.

Anyway, the smell of gasoline was up here.

"I've got a surprise for you, too," I said, clutching the bottle more tightly as I stepped through the door and flicked on the light.

The fumes of gasoline rose and hovered above my sodden bed. It had been soaked all the way to the mattress.

I had checked the empty bathroom and peeled back the tatty curtain on the shower stall, a place where mildew gathered to plot its way up the food chain, before I realized that I'd seen a rectangle of white placed dead center on the bed. After I'd satisfied myself that the shower contained nothing that I hadn't already regarded, with serious misgivings, on earlier occasions, I went out and down the hill into the breath of a mummifying wind and opened the door to the spare room. A cloud of gasoline fumes struck my nostrils.

Something whimpered.

I hit the light switch and found myself staring at a bearskin rug. A *sodden* bearskin rug. A rush of fury hit me so strongly that it literally blinded me: The room went black. Clutching the doorframe for support, I heard a familiar thumping sound, and as my sight cleared, I saw that the rug was wagging the tip of its tail.

"Bravo," I said in a voice thick with relief.

He lifted his head and looked at me briefly, then looked away. Shame plastered his ears to his wet skull. I went to him and ruffled his soaking fur. He hung his head even lower. Good dogs have a tremendous sense of duty.

"Good boy," I said. "It's okay. He charmed you, didn't he?" Bravo looked up at me again and then shoved his nose under my hand. "Come on," I said. "Let's give you a bath."

Outside, using my best shampoo and the garden hose to wash a maniac's gasoline out of my temporary dog's coat, I suddenly started to laugh. How did I get here? I thought. Bravo took advantage of my lapse in attention to shake himself, covering me in foam and diluted gasoline, and I sat down in the mud puddle I'd created and hugged him to me. "You dope," I said, still laughing. "Next time, you'll rip his legs off and eat them as drumsticks." Enjoying my tone, Bravo hit me in the face with his tail.

When he was clean, I climbed the rest of the way up the hill to open the waxy envelope and study the latest communiqué from the Incinerator.

Sweet dreams!!! it said. I crumpled it up and threw it against the wall.

My college notebooks, at least a hundred of them, were piled on the floor of the smaller of the house's two closets. They were all alike, flat blue hard-covered books filled with lined paper. I picked up as many of them as I could carry and staggered down the driveway to Alice as Bravo watched with the sympathetic expression dogs save for working humans. Then I went back up the hill, got some more, took everything I might need for two or three days—including my five remaining beers—put out food for Bravo, and left.

I needed to see if he'd been to Eleanor's house, too. There was no way to be sure he knew where she lived, but I didn't want her coming home from the hotel to any surprises. Alice purred with uncharacteristic smoothness through Santa Monica, heading south, and then carried me west, onto Windswept Court, toward the little house that Eleanor's royalties funded. I parked Alice half a block down and did the rest of it on foot.

There were lights on in the house. A car I didn't recognize had staked claim to the driveway, a big American gas-guzzler that reflected the boundless optimism of Detroit.

I smelled smoke briefly as I approached the house, an acrid, sharp smoke that was both familiar and unfamiliar. The hot wind blowing toward the ocean dissipated it before I could grab a second breath, but I knew Eleanor wouldn't allow anyone who smoked inside her house.

An overgrown hibiscus crowded up against the picture window in front. The house had been built in the thirties, in an age when no one imagined that people might someday be lurking around in front of picture windows to get a look at the picture inside, and Eleanor had fed and watered that hibiscus religiously, using Billy Pinnace's special ultra-wowie fish-emulsion mixture, to get the hibiscus to mask the window. She had succeeded beyond her wildest dreams, and I cursed Billy Pinnace and all dead fish everywhere as I pushed my way through the sharp, brittle bush to get to the glass.

The first thing I saw was a pair of feet.

They were a man's feet, clad only in argyle socks.

The second thing I saw was Eleanor, coming into the living room with a couple of wineglasses in her hand. She was smiling.

The third thing I saw was Eleanor seeing me. She gasped and dropped a glass, and then she realized who it was, and said, very plainly through the glass although I couldn't hear the words, "Oh, *Lord.*"

The fourth thing I saw, as he leapt out of his seat, was Burt. He goggled at me like a landed fish as Eleanor leaned down to pick up the unbroken wineglass from the carpet. I went to the door and used my key.

"What are you doing here?" I demanded.

"I was about to ask you the same thing." She stood in the hall with the empty glass in her hand, and Burt poked a cautious head around the doorframe behind her.

"You're supposed to be in the hotel," I said, pointing an accusing finger. She looked at it, and I followed her gaze to see the blood-soaked paper towel dangling from it like the flag of a defeated army.

"You've hurt yourself," Eleanor said.

"Thanks for the news."

"Um," Burt said, "hello, Simeon."

"You know each other," Eleanor said, sounding faintly embarrassed.

"I'll admit it," I said. "But just barely."

Eleanor looked at the finger again. "Be nice, please. This wasn't anybody's idea. Do you need a bandage?"

"He was at my house tonight," I said. "I wanted to make sure he hadn't been here, too."

"Were you there?" she asked, her eyes widening.

"The Incinerator?" Burt asked, a gratifying two beats behind.

"No," I said to Eleanor. "Yes," I said to Burt. "The Incinerator. He left me a couple of surprises, and I thought he might have done the same here."

"He didn't," Eleanor said.

"So I see," I said, wondering how far I could throw Burt.

"That means he doesn't know where I live," Eleanor said triumphantly. "I can come home."

"No, you can't," I said. Eleanor set her jaw, and I retreated. "What I mean is, please don't. He's got his own agenda. There's no way for us to know what he'll do next. And yes," I added, "I'd love a bandage."

"Right back," Eleanor said, heading for the bathroom. Burt looked at me, and I looked at Burt.

"Well, well," he said, coloring brightly.

"Go away," I said, moving into the living room. I stumbled on something and looked down at his shoes. They had Velcro flaps in place of laces.

"You've got it wrong," I said nastily. "It's the Japanese who want you to take your shoes off at the door. Chinese couldn't care less."

"This Chinese could," Eleanor said, coming back in with an assortment of tinctures, gauzes, and tapes. "I think it's very nice." I looked down and saw that she was barefoot.

"Is this the little girl," I said, "who used to sleep in a new pair of running shoes to break them in? Is this the freckle-faced little girl who once took a shower—a shower I shared, by the way," I said to Burt, "in her nice new running shoes because she figured the water would mold them to her feet?"

"Sit down," Eleanor commanded, blushing, "and let's see the finger."

"It hasn't been amputated," I said, obeying orders and sitting in what once had been my chair. "You've got more junk than Florence Nightingale had at the Battle of Crimea."

"There's no need to be offensive," Burt ventured. He caught my eye. "On the other hand," he said promptly, "you've been hurt."

"He's not really violent," Eleanor said to Burt, unwrapping my finger. "He just talks that way." She looked at the cut. "It's deep," she said.

"'No, 'tis not so deep as a well nor so wide as a church door,'" I said, "'but 'tis enough, 'twill serve.'"

"That's Shakespeare, Burt," Eleanor said, swabbing at the cut with something red.

"I admire a man with a frame of reference," Burt said gamely.

"Do you know one?" I asked.

"We were about to have some wine," Burt said. "Would you like some?"

"Look," I said, "I'm not going to be all Noël Coward about this. I'm going to be unpleasant." Eleanor gave the bandage she was wrapping around my finger an unnecessary tug. "I know I'll hate myself in the morning," I continued, talking to Burt, "but right now, I hate *you*."

Burt was on his way to the kitchen, but he stopped and turned to face me. "Like Eleanor said, nobody wanted this to happen," he said. "Do you think this makes me comfortable?"

"Who cares?" I asked.

"Well, then," he said, keeping his eyes away from the injured finger. Well, I was keeping my eyes away from it, too. Only women can look at a really deep cut. "Think about Eleanor."

"That's enough, both of you," Eleanor said, finishing with my finger. She gathered up the medications and stood. "Burt was just leaving," she said.

"Now, wait a minute," Burt said.

"And I'm leaving with him," Eleanor said. She was looking at the bandages in her hands. "Burt," Eleanor said, "get the wine, would you? We'll take the rest of it with us."

Burt said something, but he left.

"Simeon," Eleanor said the moment he was out of the room, "are you being careful?" She looked down at the bandages again and then dumped them on the floor.

"Careful? You're back here, in this house, and you're asking me—"

"The police are outside," she said.

I suppose I opened my mouth. Certainly, I felt cool air on my tongue.

"They are?" I asked stupidly.

"You must have walked right past them."

I dismissed it. "Eleanor," I said, "I need you."

She looked past me, at the picture window, and said nothing.

"There's no one I can talk to," I said.

"You can talk to me," Eleanor said, her face down.

"With him around?" I asked. *"Homo imitatiens?"*

"He won't be around tomorrow," she said in a muffled voice.

"I need you tonight."

"Well," she said, lifting her face to me, "I'm sorry. It's a little bit late, isn't it? There's a life going on here even when you're not around, Simeon," she said. "It wasn't my idea that you wouldn't be around. Lord, Simeon, how long did you think—"

"Okay," I said, not knowing whether I wanted to cry or kill someone. "Fine. Skip it."

"Please," she said, "don't—"

"I've recorked the wine," Burt said from the door that led to the kitchen.

"Then we can go," Eleanor said with her back to him, passing a hand over her face.

"Well," I said. "Then let's go."

"Simeon," Eleanor said. "Will you call me?"

"Sure. See you," I said, heading for the front door and feeling no more substantial than my own raincoat, filled with newspapers.

Outside, the hot wind blew, and the moon shone brightly enough to evaporate water, brightly enough for me to see the unmarked police car waiting across the street. I navigated across the smooth black asphalt and looked down at Hammond.

"Al," I said, "you could have spared me that."

Hammond took a puff off the cigar I'd smelled before and leaned forward to twitch the ignition on. He used the power to hit the window button on the driver's side, and the glass slid up. He still hadn't looked at me.

"You forget," he said just before the window sealed him off, "we ain't buddies anymore."

The window closed, and I lifted my arms high above my head and slammed the roof of Hammond's car with both fists, putting a substantial dent in it, before I drove away from my ex-friend and my ex-ex-girlfriend and did what I'd been threatening to do: headed for a Holiday Inn.

After I checked in, I hauled the stack of notebooks out of Alice's trunk and toted them upstairs. It took two trips, just as it had going down the driveway. Then, knowing I wasn't going to be able to sleep anyway, I went out to a convenience store around the corner and bought a jar of instant coffee. It could be mixed with hot water from the tap. Or, what the hell, I could eat it with a spoon.

The notebooks opened up like rooms from the past, furnished with odds and ends—many of them *very* odd and most of them dead ends—that had once seemed important. Names, dates, places, impossibly broad concepts, niggling details, the occasional carpet of plausible language to sweep stubborn facts under. I had spent fifteen years of my life doing this, and I had gotten very good at it.

The instant coffee kept my eyes open and my heart pounding, pounding erratically but pounding, and the frequent trips to the bathroom gave me a little exercise. All in all, I was in pretty good shape at eleven the next morning when I opened the ninth book at random, somewhere toward the middle, and found myself looking down at a preliminary outline for a paper, one of literally hundreds prepared for literally dozens of classes in comparative religion.

The paper was entitled "Faces of God," and beneath the title, signaled by an important-looking Roman numeral, was a list of the visual traditions I'd intended to ransack with the least possible effort and at the last possible moment. And under Roman numeral III was the heading "Illuminated Manuscripts," and below that, in parentheses, was the Incinerator's name.

14

The Empire of the Sun

"Wilton Hoxley," Edna Vercini said promptly. She snapped her gum and took a bite of sugared doughnut that did not, against all the laws of physics, seem to dissolve her gum, then followed the doughnut with a long and apparently satisfying hit off an unfiltered Camel. "'Tiltin' Wilton,' we all called him." She chose the nearest from among a bewildering assortment of styrofoam coffee cups and slurped, making a face. "Not me, of course," she said.

"Of course not," I said, wondering as I had for years whether the desk also held a set of hypodermic works. Either they were hidden in a drawer, or else heroin was the only life-threatening habit to which Edna did not subscribe. Nonetheless, she was as slender as she'd been when I'd first met her, and her forty-five-year-old complexion was flawless.

"Good old Elvis," Edna said, consulting another of her vices, the latest edition of the *National Exposé*, which lay open on her desk. "Now there was a man who knew how to eat. He would have swallowed a tennis racquet if someone could have figured out how to deep-fry it." She advanced into the depths of her doughnut.

"Tiltin' Wilton," I suggested.

"Nice enough boy." She shifted the doughnut to one side so she could work on the gum. "I mean, a specimen to be preserved on the end of a pin if there ever was one, but that wasn't his fault." Edna was second assistant to UCLA's chief librarian.

"Then whose fault was it?" I asked.

"That foot," she said. "Poor kid had a clubfoot, didn't he?"

"Edna," I said, sipping from the coffee cup nearest me. It was sweet enough to gag a primrose, but the caffeine felt good as it did its dubious magic to the ganglia of my nervous centers. It was noon, and I hadn't slept a minute. "*Did* he have a clubfoot?"

"Well, sure," she said. She searched among the flotsam and jetsam atop her desk to find something sufficiently horrible. Finally, she chose the oldest and emptiest of the coffee cups, one rimmed with lipstick above half an inch of black fluid with powdered nondairy creamer bobbing on top of it like a ghost's dandruff. "That's why Tiltin' Wilton." Edna quaffed half of the ghastly liquid in the cup before she said, "And that's why he changed his name."

"To what?" I asked.

"Pardon?" Edna asked, licking granules of NutraSweet from the rim of her cup.

"He changed his name."

"I just said that," Edna said.

"To what?" I asked.

"Festus," she said. She found the doughnut, picked it up in the hand with the cigarette, and made a detour to drop the butt into the film can that served her as an ashtray. The can held a little Matterhorn of cigarette butts.

"Why Festus?" I asked.

"Are you going to buy me lunch?" Edna said, squinting suspiciously.

"I promised that I would."

"Well, I asked him why," she said, placated. "Who wouldn't? It was after Hephaestus," she said. "The blacksmith of the gods, remember? Another gimp. Lame, same like him, and his mother—that was Zeus' wife, Hera—tossed him out of Olympus because he was deformed. Poor baby," she said, "bet he had mother trouble, too. We never would have fired him, he was terrific at his job, except that manuscripts kept disappearing."

"Illuminated manuscripts," I said.

Edna took a bite off what remained of her doughnut. "Sure," she said, "well, bits and pieces anyway. Isn't that what we're talking about?"

"At the moment," I said, "we're talking about Hephaestus. Just yesterday, or maybe it was two days ago, Blinkins was reminding me about how Prometheus stole fire from Hephaestus' forge."

"Blinkins," Edna Vercini said, making a face. "There's a guy with rubber whips in his room if I ever saw one. But let's not get confused. Tiltin' got into illuminateds because the boy had a Byronic bent—no pun intended, but Byron had a clubfoot, too, you know. It was all that Romance stuff Byron loved, the *Song of Roland* and so forth, the what-do-you-callems, the troubadours or chanticleers. Dated from the same time as most of the great French illuminateds. Or, I don't know, maybe it didn't, although that was what he said. Maybe he'd made a list of great clubfoots through history. He was certainly off enough."

"Off how?"

"You don't remember him?"

"I met him twice, I think. He helped me research one section of a paper. To tell you the truth, I don't recall him at all."

"I always had the feeling," Edna said, looking for something to put into her mouth, "that he went to the men's room whenever he had something to say to me and rehearsed it for ten minutes. It always came out perfect. If I had a question, he thought for so long before he answered it that at first I figured he was hard of hearing and raised my voice and repeated it. Felt like an ass, too. He had a way of lifting a hand to shut you up while he formulated a reply. See?" she said, picking a cup at random and drinking from it. "'Formulated a reply.' Just thinking about him has me talking that way. It was like he was translating his answer from a different language. And he had no temper."

"Everyone has a temper."

"Not old Tiltin'. Take a day when everything went wrong, and I was mad enough to spit, and everybody was yelling at everybody else, and there was Festus, calm as a cucumber. He shut a file drawer on his finger once, and the whole place went quiet, waiting to see what would happen. What happened was that he opened the file drawer very slowly with his other hand and looked down at the finger he'd slammed, which was bleeding in a fashion to capture a lot of attention, and he said, 'Darn.' Then he went into the bathroom and bandaged it, and when he came out he said, 'Clumsy me.' I mean, it was enough to give you the creeps." She glanced down at my own bandaged finger.

"Did he have a girlfriend?"

"No. He thought the only thing anyone saw was that foot. Girls literally made him cringe. I'm hungry. Why are you asking about him?"

"He's been trying to get in touch with me," I said, not entirely untruthfully.

"He sure has," she said.

I sat up. "Edna," I said, "what are you talking about?"

"He phoned here, just two days ago, and left a message for you." She smiled at me and pulled open a drawer. From it she took a tiny pink origami swan.

As she painstakingly unfolded it into a telephone-message slip, I silently recited the days of the week twice, and then asked, "Why didn't you tell me that before?"

"I wanted lunch," she said simply. "Anyway, I was curious. Want to know what it says?"

"If you don't tell me," I said, treating her to a view of my teeth, "I'll rip your throat out."

"He said to tell you 'Congratulations, Sherlock.' And then he asked me to say 'I'm in the book.'"

"In the book," I said stupidly.

"The phone book," Edna said, with discreet pity. "Can we eat now?"

Hoxley, Festus 3921 Normal St.,#7 L.A. 555-2403

It was two-thirty. Edna, content on a Big Mac and three orders of fries, was back at her desk. I was in an oven of a phone booth, staring at the directory, feeling exhausted and excited at the same time. Since, as usual, I had nothing to write with, I tore out the page and headed for the underground garage where Alice was waiting for me.

Normal Street, another of Hoxley's little jokes, was a lower-middle class, or upper-lower class, enclave that stretched for two densely populated blocks just east of Virgil. Number 3921 was a

stucco apartment building, two stories high. I drove the street at
least a dozen times, making long spirals around the neighboring
blocks, looking for a gray Mazda. I wasn't expecting to see it, and
I didn't, although 3921 had no garages. He'd handed me the address on a platter, so he wasn't there anymore, and he had a reason for wanting his hidey-hole discovered. Something to do,
perhaps, with his rules.

Of course, it could have been a booby trap. As I'd learned,
he liked tricks.

The tiny, narrow yards on the block were littered with bicy-
cles and tricycles, and brown children rocketed up and down the
cracked sidewalk, playing Indianapolis 500 and Indiana Jones in
loud, musical Spanish. Dotted among them, like raisins in a pudding, were kids who might have been Vietnamese or Cambodians.
They seemed to get along fine. Very little kids usually do.

Unless one of them has a defect, such as a clubfoot.

As I walked the street, I tried to remember whether I'd ever
seen Wilton Hoxley standing up. It took me two passes to be sure
I hadn't. He'd always sat behind his desk, directing me politely
to the volumes I'd need for my asinine paper. "Faces of God,"
indeed. Now that I'd identified the context, now that I had his
name, for Christ's sake, I remembered him. What I remembered,
mostly, was how polite he was.

Then I stopped cold, dead center in front of 3921, something
I hadn't planned to do at all, frozen in my tracks by the unlocking
of a memory. I'd seen him not twice but three times, and the
second time I'd seen him, Eleanor had been with me. We'd been
dating only a few weeks, and we were almost literally inseparable.
And I remembered that he'd stood when she came in and given
her something that looked like a stiff little German bow, and that
he'd asked me, the third and last time, about her, and said something about how beautiful she was.

And I'd replied with some asinine remark, offhand and
falsely modest, to the effect that she was my girlfriend. Then he'd
told me that I was a lucky man, and I'd said, and I remembered
my exact words, "Well, that's what UCLA is for. There are thousands of them."

Standing there, in the middle of Normal Street, with Hoxley's apartment ten feet from me, I felt myself blush. What an
asshole I had been. And then I saw myself on the preceding evening, being an asshole again in Eleanor's house.

So booby-trap me, I thought, and went up the paved walkway.

The manager, a sign informed me, resided in Apartment 1. I lifted my hand to knock on the screen door, but a woman was already standing behind it, a stolid Mexican woman with a baby on one hip and the clearest, whitest eyes I'd seen in weeks.

"Mr. Hoxley," I said, feeling my own eyes scratch as I blinked, "is he in?"

"No," she said, "not here."

"He's an old friend," I said, thinking maybe I should just call the cops.

"You name?" the woman said unexpectedly.

"Um, Grist," I said, actually having to think about it. "Simeon Grist."

"Moment," she said, going away. A moment later, as promised, she opened the screen door and handed me a key. "Give back when you finish," she said.

I assured her that I would and climbed the stairs to the Incinerator's apartment, inserted the key, took a deep breath, and stepped into the Empire of the Sun.

As I pushed the door open, the lights came on. Enough pinspots to light a small musical hung from the ceiling, hooked up to some kind of rheostat that was activated, to use Schultz's word, by the movement of the door. When I opened it further, the lights brightened, and when I pulled it toward me, they dimmed. The spots picked out various items of interest on the walls, but the first thing I saw was the throne.

It stood on a platform with two steps leading up to it, making the whole assemblage more than seven feet high. What had once been a high-backed wooden armchair had been completely covered in gold and silver foil, with big red and yellow plastic jewels, ironic in their complete falsity, studded everywhere.

I was staring, openmouthed, when I realized that the light hadn't died when the door closed behind me. Another control somewhere, then, one that took charge when he surveyed his domain and opened the door all the way. With the door shut, no daylight whatsoever entered the apartment; the aluminum foil taped over the windows locked out the sun and ensured that the only light came from the system of tightly focused pinspots. The spots glowed on objects and pictures and bounced off the walls.

The walls had been covered entirely in ruby-red metallic gift-wrap foil. Pasted to the foil wherever the brightest spots fell were terrible things.

The Polaroids were the worst of all. Swaddled in rags and sprawled on pavements, the Incinerator's victims burned. Most of them had managed to sit up before the flash went off, and many of them had a flaming hand out and stretched toward the camera, a reflexive appeal for help that had been greeted by the laugh Mrs. Gottfried had described to me. There were thirteen of them. One of them, his mouth open so far that the flash had bounced off his uvula, was clearly Abraham Winston. Another was the lady who'd wanted the bath.

The awful Polaroids provided the only color in the collage, and they were arranged symmetrically, like the blacked-out squares in a crossword puzzle of agony. Everything else was reproduced in black-and-white, but the black-and-white was enough. A little Vietnamese girl, arms aflame, raced toward the camera of an Associated Press photographer. A burning monk tilted sideways, putting a hand—already largely bone—against the surface of the road on which he'd immolated himself. Photos of burn victims, clipped from medical texts, puffed at me like beached blowfish, their eyes receding from the world into pillows of swelling flesh. The men, women, and children who had fed the human bonfires of Hiroshima and Nagasaki obediently displayed their melted backs and arms with exquisite Japanese politeness.

It was a lot more than I could take, but it was almost harder to turn my back on it. When I did, I found myself looking at a bed and a desk. Well, okay, there was no bedroom. The bed was narrow and monastically uncomfortable, an iron frame and a thin mattress, and the desk was made from materials that reminded me of my own student days: a door over two sawhorses. This door, however, was made of metal. Stenciled onto it were the words FIRE DOOR. Over the makeshift desk sagged a shelf, bowed downward in the middle, crammed every which way with books.

All the books dealt with fire in one way or another. *Gods of the Sun* nestled between Franz Cumont's *The Mysteries of Mithra* and a popular history called *The Fire-Bombing of Dresden*. Next to that was a scientific text economically titled *Combustion*, and beside that was a biography of Lavoisier. Three books on Zoroaster comprised a subsection in themselves. There were at least fifty volumes in all, and they were all stolen library books.

Pasted to the wall between the books and the desk was the Incinerator's classical annex.

Paintings, etchings, and engravings of all periods detailed the unhappy career of Hephaestus. A historiated initial or a fragment from a miniature cut from UCLA's stock of illuminated manuscripts glowed here and there like a little jewel among images depicting the key moments—his being thrown from Olympus by his angry mother, Hera, revolted at her deformed offspring, the gathering of the gods to witness Hephaestus' cuckoldry as his perfect wife, Aphrodite, writhed with Apollo on her marriage bed, the two of them trapped by a net of Hephaestus' devising. An oddly masochistic reaction, I thought, making your cuckoldry public. Further along was Prometheus, fennel stalk in hand, creeping toward the forge as Hephaestus, wizened and tilting to one side, absently hammered at a piece of glowing iron.

There were others. Together they comprised an altar to an off-mix of self-loathing and pride. History presents us with a large and sometimes tragic gallery of clubfoots, just as it gives us a surprising number of overachieving epileptics. Wilton Hoxley had chosen to identify himself with the clubfoots, but he'd chosen the only one I knew of who had been a god.

Not looking for much of anything but not wanting to turn back to the collage on the opposite wall, I studied the little classical gallery again. Leading the pack were four images of Hephaestus' expulsion from heaven, all of them featuring the glowering face of Hera. Hera alone figured in three others.

"Mother trouble," Edna Vercini had said. Edna had never been a dope.

It wasn't until I had turned my attention to the desk that I registered that the images above it were of different sizes. I backed off and surveyed it again. The pictures had been clipped from whatever sources he had found them in and pasted to the wall in any which way, big against small, with the tiny scraps from the illuminated manuscripts employed as fillers to block the glow of the red metallic paper beneath the images. If there had been an organizational principle, it seemed to be that the pictures followed the chronology of the Hephaestus myth, but they'd been assembled with no regard to size.

I wondered why that troubled me, and then I turned around and answered my own question.

The first thing I'd thought of when I looked at the other collage, the collage of fire, had been a crossword puzzle. At the time, I'd dismissed it as my mind's way of distancing me from the content of the pictures, but from across the room I could see that the pictures were all the same size, exactly the same size. They formed a perfect square, about three feet by three feet. A square three feet by three feet covers nine square feet, and that's a lot of area to cover when your squares are approximately three inches by three inches, which is the size of a Polaroid that's had its bottom strip, the white strip that you grasp when you pull it from the camera, trimmed off.

Not wanting to do it, hating every step, I pulled myself back across the apartment to take a closer look at the other collage. I hadn't seen police photographs of all the victims, but I'd forced myself to look at enough of them. In some cases, as with poor Helena Troy, I'd also seen photos of them before they were burned.

As nearly as I could tell, the Polaroids were in chronological order.

That meant one of two things. Either he'd glued down the other images first, leaving the careful pattern of empty squares for the Polaroids and filling them in as he took them, or he'd created the whole thing before he vacated the apartment as part of the statement he was trying to make. One way or the other, though, the square was full. No three-inch-squares of ruby gift-wrap paper gleamed at me from anywhere within it. There were no odd images pasted beyond the perimeter of the square. The square, as ghastly as it was, was a finished work.

Outside, I heard children playing and laughing. Children have a higher fat content, relative to total body weight, than do average adults, Nature's way of storing food in the helpless in case they should be prematurely abandoned. It also ensures that they float. Of course, it also makes them more flammable.

I went back to the desk. Positioned carefully in its center was a volume of Doré's etchings for *The Divine Comedy*. I'd always wondered what was comic about an epic packed chock-full of usurers up to their necks in manure and nepotistic popes being fricasseed head-down. When I closed the book and looked around, I realized that Wilton Hoxley had apparently found the laughs; above the door of the hallway that probably led to his bathroom were the words, hand-stenciled and a foot high, ABANDON HOPE, ALL YE WHO ENTER HERE. Getting up, I put what little hope I had on hold, went down the short hallway, and opened the bathroom door.

There was no window, and the room was dark. The light from the hallway barely dented the gloom. The air was heavy with a mixture of odors that made me instinctively want to hold my breath. The light switch flipped up with a rewarding snap, but nothing happened. I wished again that I still smoked; at least then I'd have had a match. Since I didn't, I worked my way through the living room and into the minuscule kitchen, where I unscrewed the light bulb over the sink. Bulb in hand and feeling uncomfortably like a well-trained rat in a maze, I padded back to the bathroom.

There was an empty socket next to the bathroom mirror, and I wound the bulb into it. I'd left the light switch up, and I had to blink against the sudden glare.

Despite the dire warning, I'd seen worse bathrooms, my own, at times, among them. The toilet was stained and streaked and odorous, the tile was peeling away from the walls, the linoleum floor was as warped and rippling as the sea in a Hiroshige print. It wasn't until I slid aside the shower curtain that the Dante quote made sense.

The tub was full of rags and metal containers. Each was labeled. A square of white paper had been glued to the side of each, and on the labels, penned in the same metallic gold ink in which he'd written my letters, were the words GASOLINE, KEROSENE, BENZINE, DENATURED ALCOHOL. Fumes rolled out of the enclosure, heavy and ripe with fire. If I'd struck a match, I'd have been have been blown into memory.

After I closed the door and gave the keys back to the manager, I walked toward Alice, squinting into the bright summer sunlight of Normal Street and trying to figure out what the hell I was supposed to do.

15

Reverse Field

"He's finished with something," I said. "God knows what it is, but he's reached a point of completion."

The curtains in the suite in the Bel Air Hotel had been drawn, and the day had been locked outside. Annabelle Winston, draped in a white sheet, was a dim horizontal silhouette on a long table in the center of the room. A very tall woman dressed entirely in white compressed various of Annabelle's muscles and stretched others, and a very short woman dressed in more colors than a chemical bonfire sat on a footstool and pruned fingernails. Every time I heard her clippers snick together, the muscles in my back jumped and hunched.

"What's the Eighth Dwarf doing here?" Annabelle Winston demanded, without turning to face us. She'd turned away when she saw Schultz. Schultz wasted an amber grin on her hair. "And what gives you the idea he's finished?"

"For Christ's sake, shut up," I said. It got her attention. She even turned her head to face me.

"You don't want to make that a habit," she said. "Or is it our intention to get out of line?"

"You want your money back?"

"Can you get that, please?" She waved a hand at the phone.

Two gold bracelets rattled against a Vacheron-Constantine watch, making a sound that Scrooge McDuck could have heard six blocks away.

"Oh, sure," I said. I picked up the receiver and said, "Miss Winston will call you back. She's being landscaped." I hung up and pulled out the plug.

"Do I want the money back?" she said reflectively. "What would I do with it?"

"How would I know? Get your elbows pumiced."

"Well," she said, completely unruffled, "I think at this point that I'm entitled to know what I'm buying." She withdrew a hand from the manicurist's grasp, shifted beneath the sheet, and rested her chin on her hand. Deprived of a focal point, the manicurist gazed into the middle distance.

"At the moment, you're buying Dr. Norbert Schultz," I said. "Dr. Schultz. Miss Annabelle Winston."

"We've met," Annabelle Winston said, "and it hasn't been an impressive experience."

"Boy, oh boy," Schultz said, "I'm sorry about that."

"With all due respect," Annabelle Winston said, "what I'm asking is why you've brought him here. And why in the world I should pay for him."

"He's here," I said, "because I know who the Incinerator is and because I've been to his apartment—by his invitation—and because I don't know what to do about it. Dr. Schultz is my alternative to a real cop."

"And a real psychologist, too," Annabelle Winston said. "Two alternatives for the price of one genuine item." Then her eyes widened and she said "Cigarette" to the woman working on her back. "You *saw* him?" she demanded. "What do you mean, you saw him?"

"I didn't say I'd seen him," I said. "By which I mean I have seen him, but not recently."

Annabelle Winston held up a slender hand, ignoring the fact that the sheet had slipped from her shoulder, and a cigarette was placed between her fingers. She never took her eyes off me. The manicurist, glad to have something to do, grabbed a lighter, and Annabelle Winston inhaled. Schultz, following her movements as though from a great distance, took out a new pack of Dunhills and pried one loose. The two of them lit up almost simultaneously, from opposite ends of the room.

"I told you," Annabelle Winston said, looking away from me and seeing him exhale, but she didn't finish her sentence. Schultz gave her a broad holiday smile and pointed his cigarette at the one in her own hand.

"So get cancer, *Doctor,*" she said dismissively. "But my question still stands. Or, rather, questions. What do you mean, you've seen him but you haven't seen him? What do you mean, you know who he is?"

"Wait a minute," I said, feeling as though everything was moving too fast for me.

"Fine," Annabelle Winston said. "I'll get dressed." The manicurist and the masseuse were tipped and dismissed, and Annabelle Winston exited the room wrapped demurely in the sheet and reentered seconds later in the inevitable silk. Then the two of them, Schultz and Annabelle Winston, smoked furiously while I told them about Wilton Hoxley and explained my reasoning about the crossword puzzle in the Incinerator's apartment, and Schultz said, "Hmmm," several times in the best psychologist's manner. By the time I was finished, I had swallowed two of Annabelle's cigarettes in an effort to keep myself awake, and Schultz had seated himself uncomfortably on the corner of a fake Empire desk, his feet dangling. His feet, I saw with some dismay, were clad in a pair of white patent-leather loafers of the type affected by retired Beverly Hills gentlemen who may once have had something to do with show business.

"Did he change his name legally?" Schultz snapped authoritatively. It was a new tone from him, at least in Annabelle Winston's presence.

"That's an interesting question," I said, trying to blink the fatigue away, "and I don't know the answer to it."

"Why's it so interesting?" Annabelle Winston asked.

"Because he'd have to give a permanent address," Schultz said. "A name change takes a while."

"My father's name change took months," Annabelle Winston said.

"Months," Schultz said, working at not gloating. "In California, it can take *years*. Remember H. L. Mencken. The continent slopes down to the west, and everything that's loose eventually rolls to California. We're careful about name changes."

"Can you check it for me?" I asked Schultz.

"Without the cops knowing?"

"That depends," I said, "on what we come up with. And on what happens after we come up with it."

"Only the first name?" Schultz said, pulling out a pad. "He keep Hoxley, or did he change both of them?"

"He changed the first to Festus," I said again, "or maybe Hephaestus, I don't know. He kept Hoxley. He's Hoxley in the phone book."

"Hah," Schultz said.

"Why 'hah'?" Annabelle Winston asked Schultz, in spite of herself.

"Hephaestus. Blacksmith of the gods," Schultz said happily. "Keeper of the flame, et cetera. Not a name, I'd say, chosen at random."

"I'm still not exactly sure that I care what you'd say," Annabelle Winston said, presumably to make up for her lapse.

"Listen," I said. "Maybe I should try Esperanto. We need help. This guy is playing me like a fish, letting me out and then reeling me in again whenever he feels like it. He's a trickster. Dr. Schultz is a psychologist who specializes in people who murder for fun. I've got a promise of legal secrecy from him because I'm his patient. You're paying his hourly rate. Whatever you think about his nicotine addiction, he's on our side now."

I picked up another of Annabelle Winston's cigarettes and flicked her 24-karat Bic. "Since the police double-crossed me, I've played it Hoxley's way," I said. "I went on TV. I did my best to make him sound like the greatest genius since Giotto. I delivered a heartfelt message. In response, he booby-trapped my house. I've been playing by his rules, and all I've gotten is an eighty-octane mattress. So what am I supposed to do now?"

"Who's this girl you're protecting?" Annabelle Winston asked.

"What's that got to do with anything?"

Annabelle Winston shrugged an economical quarter-inch. "Just asking."

"Not relevant," I said. "Here's what's relevant. Once I figured out who he is, I went to a place he'd already guessed I'd go and found out he'd left a message for me. The message directed me to his apartment, where I found some stuff that seems to say he's finished."

"People like this don't just fold their tents and get a job selling shoes," Annabelle Winston said.

"The Zodiac quit," Schultz said. "Emil Kemper quit. They
fulfilled their mission, whatever it was, and just stopped. We
never would have caught Kemper if he hadn't phoned in a confes-
sion and waited in the phone booth until the police arrived."

"Mission?" I asked.

"In the classic sense of the word," Schultz said, billowing
smoke. "These people have a mission. God speaks to them.
Angels sit on their shoulders to help them pick out the next one.
When the score is even, whatever score, they quit." He was gaining confidence from the sound of his own voice. "Who knows
what the score is? One life for every slap they suffered as a kid.
One for every man their mother slept with while the kid listened
through the wall. One for every book in the Old Testament. You
mean, what's the math? We're talking about people who see patterns in the way leaves cluster on trees. He could be killing one
person for every stop sign he passed walking home from sixth
grade."

"But you don't believe that," I said.

Schultz licked his thumb and applied saliva to a tear in his
cigarette. "No," he said, "I don't. I think it has something to do
with his mother and father. Jesus, look at the Hephaestus bit."
He grasped the cigarette between thumb and forefinger, looking
like an imitation Russian in a B-movie of the forties, and puffed.
"Born lame, booted out of heaven by his own mother. Now that
he's killing both women and men," he said, "I think we were right
before. I think this is sexual, and sexual means Mommy." He gave
all of us the dubious benefit of the amber smile. "So why did he
guide you to the apartment?"

"Because he's playing with me," I said slowly, feeling the
atmosphere of the room gather around me and weigh me down.
"Because he knows he can jerk me around. I think the real question is what he wants me to do about it."

"You've got his name," Schultz said. "That means that DMV
could give us the plate on that Mazda."

"*You* can get it," I said. "Give it to the cops, I don't care. If
they get him, great, but they won't. I'm betting that he's finished
with the Mazda, too. Let me know if they find it, but I think he's
finished with it, just as he is with the apartment. Hell, put the

cops on the name change, too, if you think it'll help. Just keep them away from me. I've got to figure out whether to do what he wants me to do."

"Maybe he's not finished," Schultz said.

"Back off, Doctor," Annabelle Winston said. "You just heard Simeon say that the puzzle was complete."

"*That* puzzle," Schultz said. "*That* apartment. How do we know he doesn't have another puzzle, and another apartment? Maybe he's got another mission, too."

We all listened to the words hitting the carpet.

"And what does he want you to do?" Schultz said. "Put yourself in his place."

"I don't know. To make him famous, I guess."

Schultz nodded and lighted another Dunhill. "And what *doesn't* he want you to do?" Schultz asked around a cumulus cloud of smoke.

"I don't know that either." I closed my eyes so tightly that I could see little red dots, blood vessels rupturing in the retina. "To get closer, I guess. He figures he can control how close I get."

"Right," Schultz said. "And how do you get closer?"

I was all grit, a cement mixer filled with dry sand and gravel. "Mommy, I suppose," I said. "But that means he's going to come for me."

Annabelle Winston started to say something and thought better of it.

"Right," Schultz said again. "You get to Mommy, he's going to come for you. But he's only going to come for you if you're clear of the cops." He sighed. "No publicity on the apartment." He rubbed his face. "So what you do, you reverse field. Stop doing what he wants. Do what he doesn't want. I'll keep the cops away from you, and you go talk to Mommy, if you can find her. Are you ready for that?"

I nodded. It was easier than talking. I wasn't certain I could make my jaws work. I'd just discovered that it was possible to feel sad, weary, and panicked simultaneously.

"He's not bait," Annabelle Winston said.

"Oh, yes, he is," Schultz replied complacently. "And he knew that a long time ago, and so did you. We can't find the Incinerator's hole, so we have to bring him out of it. It's like killing a gopher."

I could hear Annabelle Winston swallow all the way across the room.

"And you know how to find her," Schultz said.

"Sure," I said, feeling like an emotional lottery. "Get me the address on the name change."

For two more days, I stayed away from home, ricocheting around Los Angeles and threatening the drivers and pedestrians of Los Angeles by driving with one, and sometimes two, eyes on the rearview mirror, twelve to sixteen hours a day. Schultz was as good as his word, or if he wasn't, I didn't find out about it. I slept, when I slept at all, in hotels with multiple stories and internal elevators, safe from outside eyes, dozing no more than two or three hours before checking out and hitting the freeways again. I did the whole internal loop: Ventura Freeway to Hollywood Freeway to San Bernardino Freeway, cutting through surface streets in the Chinese enclave of Monterey Park before picking up yet another freeway. As far as I could tell he wasn't behind me. But, of course, there was the dance card. I hadn't thought he was behind me then, either.

I'd never felt so disconnected in my life. No one I loved—or even particularly liked—was available. Eleanor was in a hotel somewhere, and even if she wanted to see me, I was afraid to see her. She might be with Burt, and Wilton Hoxley might be with me. Friends like Wyatt and Annie Wilmington were too dear to take a chance on hauling Hoxley along in my wake. Even worse, most of them had children. Little fatty children. One night I had a dream in which a child exploded in flame.

Hammond hated my guts. No one can hate you like an old friend.

From time to time, in various hotel rooms, I checked in with my answering machine before I collapsed, fully clothed, onto the bed. I slept lightly and badly, chased by dreams, and the hotel operator always awakened me after the requisite two or three hours, and I threw cold water into my face and hit the freeways again.

No one got burned. No lunatics in rubber trench coats stalked any of L.A.'s burgeoning skid rows.

There were, according to Billy Pinnace, who had been deputized by me to check my mailbox when he was absolutely sure no strangers were around, no letters.

Hermione had finally remembered her last name and been sent home to crawl the pubs, so another promise had been kept. The newspapers said that the heroine had traveled first class. The image of Norman signing the check had given me a brief moment of pleasure. Nothing more about Hermione.

Nothing in the papers about Mrs. Gottfried.

There was, in all, enough nothing to satisfy an atheist.

The police did, however, find the Mazda, gutted by fire about three blocks from Normal Street. He'd had the nerve to come back after the fire and hang a blond fright wig over the remnants of the rearview mirror. Well, I didn't have any doubts about his nerve.

I was stretched to the point of transparency, beginning to be grateful when I saw only double, when I called the answering machine from some hotel or another in the middle of the night and got Schultz's voice reciting an address.

"It's 13156 Via del Valle," he'd said before hanging up.

The hotel's electric clock, thoughtfully bolted to the table in case the weary traveler tried to pack it by mistake, said 5:20 A.M. The weary traveler slept for two rotten hours before performing his habitual ablutions—two handfuls of cold water, thrown directly into the eyes—and hitting the road.

Via del Valle, according to my Thomas map book, was a short, coiled rattlesnake of a street that had been brutally cut into one of the very small hills that comprised the exclusive San Fernando Valley enclave called Hidden Hills. Low ranch-style houses sat defiantly in the chaparral, daring the god of fire to drop by.

Number 13156 was the paragon of the street, a fact easily deduced from its position: It was the highest, the largest, the house most vulnerable to fire. There was a buzz-box at the bottom of the driveway with a button, a microphone, and a square numeric keypad on its face, and unless you knew the numerical code, an acceptable answer given to the buzz-box was the only way to prompt the electrical impulse that would open the iron gates. The gates wouldn't have slowed a fire down much. It was already 92 degrees.

"Yeah?" growled a male voice. He sounded as if he'd just gotten up, and since it was only nine o'clock and since it was that neighborhood, maybe he had.

"Wilton Hoxley," I said.

"Wilton? Punch up the goddamn code." The voice was like a cigar's garage.

"This isn't Wilton," I said. "I'm here to talk about Wilton."

"So talk," said the buzz-box.

"Face-to-face," I said.

"Eat it," said the buzz-box. It fell silent.

I pushed the button again. When it beeped in response, I said, "Listen, it's me. Or the cops."

"Well, shit," said the cigar's garage. "Goddamn Wilton, anyway. Come on up." The gates opened. "Drive in," the voice said.

I'd been trained into obedience, and I drove in.

16

Hera

Construction of some sort was going on behind the house, and I had to squeeze Alice around a knot of shirtless Hispanics gathered around a long silver catering truck. I parked beside a powder-blue Bentley. The front door was standing negligently open.

I found him in the living room with a phone shoved into one ear, wearing a white terry-cloth bathrobe at 9:00 A.M. with the insouciance of a man who plans to wear one all day. The phone cord was about forty feet long, and he paced the length of the room as he walked, talking a stream of mostly numbers into the mouthpiece. A cigar grew like a brown tusk out of the left corner of his mouth. "Sit," he said to me, pointing at the couch. "Fifteen minutes." He made a little gesture with his index finger over the dial of his gold Rolex to indicate a quarter of an hour, just in case the words hadn't found their way home. I sat on a fourteen-foot couch, covered in sky-blue satin ornamented with knotted little gold tufts. Kneeling in homage in front of it was a long veined marble coffee table on fat gilt legs, groaning beneath the weight of extravagant clusters of glass grapes. Marie Antoinette would have felt right at home.

"Yeah, yeah, yeah," he said. Then he said, "No, no, no." He flicked the ash from the cigar into a potted plant. There were

big crystal ashtrays everywhere. Talking numbers again, he paced
to the other end of the room, dodging furniture with a bull-
fighter's expertise, and deposited a fine tube of cigar ash the thick-
ness of a roll of nickels into the center of a crystal bowl filled with
potpourri. He had to reach across an ashtray to get to it. The ear
that didn't have the phone clapped to it was the hairiest I'd ever
seen; he looked like Bottom in the first moments of his transforma-
tion. I watched his broad white back recede and then focused on
an oil painting of a blond woman. Its subject gazed at the artist
with the remote assurance of the truly beautiful.

He hung up the phone and gave me a mistrustful stare. "So
who are you supposed to be?" he rasped.

"I don't know who I'm supposed to be. Who I am is an ac-
quaintance of your son's."

"He's not my son," he said. "I've done plenty, but I didn't
do that. And what about the cops? What's the little freak done
now?" The heavy lips formed a crescent moon with the cigar protruding from its center. The crescent's ends curved up, but it
wasn't a smile.

"Is that your wife?" I asked, indicating the portrait.

He made cigar-ash snow over a miniature orange tree,
weighing his answer. "Yeah," he finally said, coming clean despite
years of evident conditioning. "That's the little bride. That's the
expensive little bride."

"She's a very beautiful woman," I said.

"You'd be a very beautiful woman, too, you spent as much
time on it as she does," he said. "Weights, jogging, aquatic
aerobics, facials, Retin-A like it's ice cream, no ice cream, no
meat, hairdresser four times a week, manicures, pedicures, cosmetic dentistry, sheep's placenta injections, every year two
weeks in Switzerland for a complete blood change. You want
to see her about Junior?" He threw his cigar into the fireplace,
where it nestled among others like a convention of supernaturally large slugs.

"Right."

"Okay, okay. Another couple of minutes." He looked sourly
at the portrait and fished a fresh cigar out of the pocket of his
robe. "I figure I got left about ten percent of the woman I married," he said. He pulled the cigar from his mouth and gobbed a

gray oyster of sputum into a Boston fern. "Two years from now, she'll be completely new. It's like getting divorced and remarried. Only more expensive."

"Actually," I said, just to pass the time, "she's already completely new. The average molecule of human tissue has a half-life of two to three weeks."

"Yeah?" He glowered at me over the newly lighted cigar. "What's a half-life?"

"The amount of time it takes for half of all of any kinds of molecules—say, fat molecules, for example—to wear out and get replaced by other molecules just like them. And ninety-five percent of them have been replaced within a hundred days or so."

"You're shitting me."

The satin couch was comfortable, and I was tired, so I kept talking. "Well, some go faster and some go slower," I said. "Intestinal protein takes only about fourteen days. Bone, as you'd figure, lasts longer."

He held up a hand as hairy as a tarantula. "Wait a minute. It takes months for a face-lift to settle. You're telling me that the face she got nipped and tucked last month is gone by the time the lift is ready to take outdoors?"

"More or less."

"Fucking hell," he said. "*Alice!*"

He headed for the door next to the fireplace, but it opened before he got there, tugged inward by the lady herself. She wore a lavender leotard, yellow ankle-warmers, and a pink headband. Her face was filmed with sweat, but her eyes, the same pale sky blue as the Bentley, could have cooled the room. It was a very large room. "Yes, Eddie?" she said, as though she were talking to a tardy bellboy.

He stopped in midstride, and the phone began to ring. "This boyo's for you," he said in an entirely different tone, and picked up the phone gratefully.

"About Wilton," I said as the cold eyes fell on me.

"No news is good news," she said. "I suppose you have news."

"Yes," I said. "You might say I have news." I got up. Eddie was spouting numbers into the phone like a verbal ticker tape. He did not seem at all eager to look at his wife. She opened the door wider in invitation and said, "In here."

I followed her sculpted haunches down a long gray-carpeted hallway. She never glanced back. Despite a dark sweat mark, shaped more or less like sunny California, running down the center of her back, coolness seemed to flow from her. We turned right through a double sliding door into a windowless exercise room. Disco music pumped itself effervescently at us. The lack of windows was more than compensated for by what seemed to be an acre of mirrors that lined three of the walls. Other than the mirrors, all the fin-de-siècle decor had been banished. Maybe, when she was surrounded by mirrors, she was her own decor. She twisted a knob on the wall. The music stopped pushing the air around. "What about the little weirdo?" She still hadn't faced me.

"He *is* your son?"

"I'd deny it if I could. What's he done now?"

"What did he use to do?"

She waved an index finger at me. "That's not going to make it, sonny," she said. "I may not look busy to you, but I am. It would take months to tell you all the things Wilton used to do. And, to be frank, they're not months I would care to spend, even in your company. How old are you?"

"Thirty-seven," I said, surprised at the question.

"A good age," she said. "I remember it fondly."

"You don't look it now."

"If you're going to flatter me, you might as well sit. Wait," she said, holding up a hand. "Am I going to hate this?"

"Yes," I said. She held her gaze steady. "You sure as hell are."

"Then I need a shower," she said. "Look at yourself in the mirror for a few minutes. You're worth it. Get yourself a chair."

She pressed one of the mirrored panels, and it popped open and then closed behind her. I pulled up a chair and looked at myself. Nothing I saw particularly surprised me, except that I seemed to be bleeding to death through the eyeballs.

After a few minutes, my reflection slid away from me. "So what about Wilton?" she asked, coming through the mirrored panel in a fuchsia bathrobe.

"When was the last time you saw him?" I began.

"Honey," she said, sitting in a chair that was a twin to mine, "give and get. If you haven't figured out that's how it works, you're a late bloomer. What about Wilton?"

This was the moment I hadn't rehearsed. Up until now, I'd figured that I could put her off with generalities while I skillfully extracted precious information. Of course, I was exhausted, and that was before I'd met her.

"He's burning people," I said.

Nothing happened to her face. Nothing happened to her eyes. What she *did* do was look down at her lap and readjust the knot in her bathrobe. "I knew it," she said to the knot. "It's Wilton."

"You knew it."

"He was burning cats when he was ten," she said. She finished with the knot and looked back up at me. "You a cop?"

"If I were a cop," I said, "there'd be ten of me."

"It was his father," she said cryptically. "So what's your interest?" She and her reflection crossed their fine ankles in perfect unison. "Oh, Jesus," she said flatly. "You're that private detective, the one in the papers."

"So now you know. Your turn."

"My turn for what? Give and get, remember? What do I get out of this?"

"What do you want?"

"Anonymity," she said promptly.

"Can't do."

"Then get out of here." She stood.

"You get," I improvised, "the satisfaction of knowing that your son won't burn any more people."

"What do I care about that?" She was still standing. "At this point, what the hell do I care about that?"

"You're Mommy," I said, feeling like I was shouting into the wind. "He's still a few shy of being America's number-one mass murderer, but he's got a good shot at it. Is that a medal you'd like to win?"

She turned to regard herself in the mirror. She looked at her reflection as though it belonged to someone else.

"You're beautiful, too," I said. "That's a really terrible combination."

She was still looking deeply into her own eyes. I counted five before she turned away from the mirror and sat. "He's a genetic accident," she said.

"Explain to the *National Exposé*," I said, dredging up two words of print from Edna Vercini's desk. "They'll love the way you look."

She tightened her lips, and fine vertical lines appeared above them. Even Swiss blood exchanges couldn't vanquish those lines. "You know who he is," she said, biting and chewing the words. "Why do you need me?"

"Because I don't know *why* he is. Listen, Mrs. Lewis, I'm the bait. If I make a mistake, I'm the barbecue."

"May you make a lovely light," she said. Her eyes were as clear and white as the arctic circle.

"Or maybe *you're* the barbecue," I snapped, suddenly furious. "The best psychologist in these matters," I said, promoting Schultz, "thinks that all he's done so far is just an avoidance mechanism. What he really wants to burn is you."

"That's ridiculous," she said, but she'd already sat up straight.

"This house would go like a matchbox," I said.

"It was his father," she said again.

"You asked me what you were going to get. Well, maybe you're going to get to die of old age, as opposed to being Mommy flambé."

She gave the bathrobe another yank. The lines above her mouth were vertical rivulets. "He was here two weeks ago," she said. "He wanted money."

"Did you give it to him?"

"Eddie did. About five K."

"For what?" I asked. The answer popped into my mind. "Forget it. For a new car." Her eyes widened momentarily. "What do you mean, it's his father?"

"He was a fireman," Alice Lewis said. "How'd you know about the car?"

"Skip it. And?"

"And Wilton hated him."

I pulled my chair closer to her. It was easy; luckily for me, in my state, the chair didn't weigh much. "Why?"

"How do I know why? Because I lived there. Because Wilton, that's Daddy Wilton, not Son Wilton, didn't like the kid."

"Didn't like him?"

"And vice versa. Little Wilton hated the shit out of Big Wilton. Poured hot fat over his feet once."

"Where'd he get the hot fat?"

"Off the stove, where do you think?"

"What happened?"

"What do you mean, what happened? His father blistered the kid's hide and went to work with only one shoe on. He had socks on, you see, when the fat got poured. By the time we got the socks off, the right foot was bigger than a football." She shifted in her chair. "Wait, he didn't only tan little Wilton's hide. He sent him to school with only one shoe. Daddy has one shoe, Junior has one shoe."

"Which shoe?"

"Which one do you think?"

I closed my eyes and saw it. "He sent Wilton to school without the shoe on his clubfoot?"

"Kid had to learn," she said. I opened my eyes and found her watching me. "So it was rough. Little jerk," she said. "House always stunk of smoke. His daddy's smoke, smoke Daddy brought home from the fires where he made such a big hero of himself. It was a little house, just a one-bedroom stucco box stuck up on some dinky little lot in Reseda. The smoke filled the whole thing."

"And where's Wilton, Sr.?"

She looked over her shoulder as though she were checking for an escape route. "Dead," she said. "After my baby and I left him."

"When was that?"

"A year or so later. Wilton was burning cats by then, and Big Wilton appointed himself the Cats' Avenger. He was always saving something. So he saved cats."

"What do you mean?"

"Wilton was burning cats. Big Wilton burned Little Wilton."

"Nonsense," I said without thinking.

"Oh, but he did. Burned Wilton's fingers. Did it twice."

"What did you do about it?"

She shrugged. "What could I do? Eventually, I left."

"Did he use a cigarette?" We were sitting there in that calm room, talking about the deepest pits of the soul.

"What do you mean?" She used the lapel of her bathrobe to mop her neck.

"To burn Little Wilton's fingers."

"No," she said. She looked directly into my eyes. "He used matches."

"Wooden matches."

She stopped mopping. "You do seem to know a lot about this."

"Why wooden matches?" It seemed to be the twentieth time I'd asked the question.

"They were handy. We used them to light the stove. And don't say anything. Yes, the stove he took the fat from to pour it on his father's feet."

"He's using kitchen matches now," I said, just to see if I could get a reaction out of her.

"Makes sense," she said placidly.

"Are you saving your face up?" I asked. "Do you think it can only wrinkle so many times before they stick?"

"So I left him," she said, ignoring the nastiness. "And I met Eddie."

"Classy guy."

"I can still tell you to get out of here," she said. "This is a security community. One minute on the phone, and you'll be on your ass on the asphalt."

"How'd Wilton like Eddie?" I asked, remembering how fastidious Wilton had been.

"Hated his guts," she said. "Well, tough shit. Eddie killed himself to make friends with the kid. Bought him stuff, got him therapy—that was a laugh—took him places, took him to the track, for Christ's sake. Eddie never even took *me* to the track. But Eddie likes junk, you know? You saw the house. He likes to surround himself with expensive things and then shit all over them to show it doesn't mean anything. But his expensive things are junk. And Little Wilton, even when he was ten, Little Wilton could smell junk from around the corner. And Eddie doesn't talk right."

"Depends on who he's talking to."

She touched her index finger to the tip of her nose and pushed her head back slightly. "Not right for Little Wilton," she said. "You know, Eddie wasn't exactly the cavalier of my dreams, either. I'd always pictured someone who was a hero, like Big Wilton, shithead that he turned out to be, or a gentleman. Like you, even though you don't like me. You're obviously class. Listen to the way you talk. But Eddie's a good guy. He doesn't ask too many questions. He loves me, I guess, like he tried to love Wilton. I could have put up with Wilton not liking Eddie because, you know, maybe he was jealous or something. But what I absolutely could not forgive was that Wilton hated Eddie because Wilton was a snob."

"So you kicked him out."

"Honey, it was my kid or my husband. Being a woman is expensive. Wilton was too busy lighting fire to small animals and cutting out pictures from the Middle Ages and reading about clubfoots to write the checks. Anyway, he was eighteen—seventeen. It was time. We got him a nice apartment in Westwood, put him in that school, hoped he'd meet a couple of girls." She leaned forward and tapped my knee. "You know," she said, "he might have been all right if he'd ever gotten laid."

It took an effort not to pull my knee away. "Why the Middle Ages?"

"Who knows? It was the only thing he liked. Eddie took him to the Chivalry Faire the first year, and the kid went crazy. Put pictures of castles everywhere, played that awful music all the time. Eddie took him three times after that, every damn year. Fat lot of good it did."

"Did you go?"

"What's there? A bunch of weeds, some jerks sweating in their costumes, and a plywood slum pretending to be castles. Why should I go? The first time Eddie took him, Wilton didn't say a word to him. Just went limping around exploring while Eddie stood there and perspired. So we gave up. Sent him to college to get laid."

"I guess he didn't," I said.

She crossed her legs and let the free ankle swing. "We thought he was going to. He came home from time to time when he needed money and told us about this perfect girl he'd met, how she wanted to move in with him except that she wasn't that kind of girl, whatever that means. Except for the fact that she didn't put out, she was perfect, although if she had put out, she wouldn't have been perfect for Wilton. My God, we heard about her until I got sick of her name. How good she was, how beautiful. How she and he read poetry together and looked at pictures."

"But you never met her."

"I'm not sure *he* ever did. Nobody could have been that beautiful. This one wasn't even white."

The worm started to work its way up my back again. "You got sick of her name," I said. "What *was* her name?"

"Eleanor," Alice Lewis said. "Eleanor Chan. Chinese, can you imagine?"

"Yes," I said. "Yes, I can." My face was flaming. Whatever it had been, for Wilton it had been a grand passion, and I'd made it cheap with one thoughtless, unretractable remark. Even though I loved her.

"What happened to your first husband?" I asked, just to give myself some room. "Did he keep bothering you? Or Wilton?"

"He tried at first, but Eddie talked to some friends of his, and then he had an accident. He was—" She stopped. It was as though someone had pulled the plug from the wall.

"He was?" I prompted.

"He was laid up at home with two broken legs," she said in a monotone. "From the accident." Then she sat straight up and shook her head. "No way," she said.

"The house burned down," I said.

She turned back to the mirror, looking not at herself but over her shoulder at me. She breathed through her mouth once, then twice. "It wasn't Wilton," she said. A small galaxy of dimples appeared on her chin.

Despite the air-conditioning, my shirt was sticking to my chest, and I tugged it free. "Of course it wasn't," I said.

The dimples disappeared. "Go away," she said. She straightened imperiously. "Finished?" she asked, ready to get up and resume her real life, whatever she thought it was. "Things burn," she said.

"People, too." I wanted to see her chin dimple again. It didn't. "Do you know where he's living now?"

"I didn't know where he was living before. *Now* are you finished?" She swiveled to regard me directly. Annabelle Winston could have pulled it off, but Alice Hoxley Lewis wasn't big enough for it.

"No," I said. "You have to do one more thing for me."

She chewed on it for a second. "What is it?"

"Wilton's going to call and ask you if I've been here."

"He won't."

"I think he will."

"So don't worry. I won't tell him anything."

"You'll tell him I was here." Her jaw dropped in a reaction spontaneous enough to make her son snub her. "And you'll tell him," I said, fighting back a yawn, "that I'll be at home."

17

The Rabbi

Home was the only place to be, if he was supposed to find me.

It took hours to strip the sheets and scrub the mattress until the smell of gasoline had been banished into some parallel universe where Wilton Hoxley might conceivably get caught before he lit me up. When, at 1:00 A.M., I was finished, I went into the living room and pretended to sleep on the couch.

By the time the sun came up, I had dozed for perhaps forty minutes, the temperature was already in the 90s, and my arms felt heavier than my legs.

The clock said 7:00 A.M. The couch was sticky with sweat. I sponged myself off with a cold, wet towel, poured Bravo some water, and called Schultz.

He answered on the first ring despite the hour, sounding as though he'd been waiting all night. "Got her," I said. I barely recognized my own voice.

"Where are you? What's she like?"

"Like a freon cocktail. You were right, one hundred percent. She kicked him out. He burned his father. Her first husband."

"I *knew* I should have said it out loud," he said. "When I write it up, people will say it was second-guessing."

"If that's your biggest problem, relax. I'll tell everyone you told me days ago."

"That would be fudging," Dr. Norbert Schultz said fretfully.

"And we wouldn't want you to fudge. Not on something as important, something as *indispensable*, as writing this up. Think of the fame. You'll be a standard footnote."

"I'm an asshole," Schultz said promptly. I heard a match flare, not the most comforting sound at that moment. "Why are you at home?"

"How's he supposed to come for me," I asked Schultz, "if he doesn't know where I am?"

"Sheeez." Schultz blew smoke into the mouthpiece. "That's pushing it a little, don't you think?"

"I think nobody's been burned for three days." I swallowed. "Am I still right? Nobody last night?"

"Clean as a whistle. Except for a couple of houses." He listened to himself. "Was the father in a house?"

"Yes."

"Well, since then, houses haven't been his game, and we're in the goddamn fire season. We lose houses every night."

"Maybe houses are his new mission," I said.

"No," he said with certainty, sounding like the Schultz of old. "If he's got a new mission, it's something bigger than houses."

"I just thought I'd bring it up," I said, "because I'm in a house."

"You could be the exception," he admitted. "Do you want protection?"

"Oh, sure. Protect me from the west wind. This is a guy who could smell junk when he was twelve. He can smell cops the way you can smell an anxiety neurosis."

"Junk? Are we talking about dope?"

"No," I said, "we're talking about inferior interior decor. We're talking about glass grapes. I'll explain it all in time for your article. Unless, of course, you think it would be better for posterity if I were to explain it right now."

"Don't you know anybody," Schultz asked, sounding anxious, "who isn't a cop? Somebody who could keep an eye out?"

"Yeah," I said, thinking. "I do. When do you want me to call you next?"

"When something happens."

"After something happens, I may not be able to call."

"You'll be fine," Schultz said. Doctors are among the world's champion liars. "Call your friend, then call me every three hours. Here are the numbers for today."

"What is this, a onetime code?"

"I have office hours," he said, clearly affronted. "I have business at Parker Center today—nothing about you, don't worry. Do you want the numbers or don't you?"

I took them down and then called Billy Pinnace.

"Consciousness control," Billy said, answering the line his customers used. His parents, although they spent Billy's money, didn't want to talk to his clientele.

"How they growing, Billy?"

"High as an elephant's eye," he said. "No mail."

"I know. I'm home. Have you still got your rabbi?"

"My piece?" Billy said proudly. The rabbi was a semiautomatic from Israel. "I sleep with it under the mattress."

"Must make a lump."

"Other side of the bed, doofus."

"Lend it to me," I said.

"Hey," he said, sounding a lot less eager. "A guy and his piece, you know?"

"A man is only as tall," I said, "as he is in his stocking feet." Billy, who was financing a future at Harvard that would lead to a career either as a corporate lawyer or an international terrorist, was a fool for quotes.

"Where'd you read that?" Billy demanded.

"I'll tell you when you bring me the gun."

"Is it Zen?"

"Yeah," I said. "It's from *Now and Zen* by the French multiple murderer Maurice Chevalier. Every aspiring terrorist should read it, even though it's written in phonetics."

"You got a copy?"

"I sleep with it under the mattress. Trade you for the gun, one lump for another, and when you're finished with it, I'll give the gun back. What do you say?"

"A book for a gun?" Billy was a capitalist to his toenails.

"Ah, Billy," I said. "The revolution will be won with books, not bullets."

"Chairman Mao?" he guessed.

I was suddenly dizzy with fatigue, and my mouth refused to do anything more complicated than breathe. I could hear the sigh whistling in the earpiece of the phone.

"You in big trouble?" Billy asked.

"Billy," I said, "bring every bullet you own."

I was making coffee when the phone rang for the first time. I let it ring, concentrating on pouring. It didn't stop. On ring twelve or thirteen, I picked it up.

"Hello," I said.

Someone exhaled.

"I already said hello," I said, sipping. "Your move."

Nothing. But no hang-up, either.

"Hey, Wilton," I said. My pulse was trying to beat its way through the skin on my wrists. "How you doing?"

He might have cleared his throat. The sound in the earpiece was raspy enough.

"Mommy says hi," I said, watching my heart bump in the thin blue line leading down to the hand with the cup in it.

He hung up. The dial tone snored in my ear.

I was still sitting there, staring at the phone, twenty minutes later, when I heard someone climb the driveway. I was caught flat-footed; all I could do was pick up the heaviest thing in sight, my copy of Dreiser's *Sister Carrie*, hoist it two-handed over one shoulder, National League style, and stand behind the door opening into the kitchen. I'd already popped the door to make turning the knob unnecessary.

It flew open and hit me in the forehead, and I retaliated by bashing it with the book. *"Rat-a-tat-a-tat,"* Billy Pinnace said, throwing the barrel of the semi right and left in the approved Rambo manner. Then he looked at me and lowered it.

"You're reading Dreiser?" he asked, looking at the book. "You know, you're bleeding."

"You don't know," I said, wadding up a paper towel and pressing it to my eyebrow, "how grateful I am for that information. Your disquisition has enabled me to pursue that Hippocratic succor without which this injury might have dimmed, even truncated, my life. Is that thing loaded?"

"Are *you*?" Billy asked. As always, he looked like the kid you hope will ask your daughter to the prom.

"No. That's the way you talk when you're reading Dreiser."

"Lemme borrow it."

I checked the cut in the mirror over the sink. Still bleeding. "I pause," I said, "because there is in it such matter that, I fear, would not nourish the vigorous development of the young mind but might, rather, turn it in strange and dark directions."

"Hot shit," Billy said. "It's a swap." He handed me the gun, and I gave him *Sister Carrie*. Pound for pound, he got the better deal.

"How do you work it?" I asked.

"What do you mean? You point it and pull the trigger."

"Have you ever fired it?"

"At beer cans," Billy said grudgingly. Billy's father drank a lot of beer.

"How do you load it?"

"You should take care of that cut," Billy said, and the phone rang.

I took care of the cut by ignoring it. I swallowed some coffee and wiped the blood and perspiration from my face before I picked up the receiver.

"Hello," I said.

"Simeon," said a male voice.

"You got it right out of the box," I said. "What's happening, Wilton?"

"You're there," Wilton Hoxley said. Then he hung up.

"Billy," I said, the telephone still in my hand, "tell me how to work this thing and then get out of here."

The phone rang on the hour, every hour, thereafter. I answered it with the semi cradled between my knees, but it might as well have been a papoose for all the use I got out of it. Every time I picked up the phone, Wilton Hoxley hung up. Between the fourth and the fifth calls, I took a shower, the semi leaning against the shower stall, and when I was finished I made a butterfly bandage on the cut over my eye. Then I cleaned the house. Doing the everyday drudgery seemed to lessen the menace, but I cleaned with one hand, the other arm locked over the semi. Cleaning took a long time. Cleaning had always seemed to take a long time, which was perhaps one reason why I did it so seldom, but on this occasion it was like running through cooling lava. Still, by four o'clock I had finished the kitchen and was almost through with the living room, despite the periodic interruptions to phone Schultz and answer Wilton's mute queries. I'd thought a hundred times about kicking Alice into gear and drifting down the hill to the restful anonymity of some Holiday Inn, but I hadn't done it. For one thing, I had Billy's semi to shoot him with. For another, as long as Wilton was phoning regularly, I was in the classic double bind; he knew that I was there, and I knew that he wasn't. Wherever he was, even if it was at a phone booth just down the hill, I wanted to keep him there.

At four o'clock, the phone rang. The boy was punctual.

I was on my sixth pot of coffee by then, and my synapses had permanent caffeine bridges between them. "Woo-woo, Wilton," I said, "let me hear you respirate again."

"Respiration," he said calmly, "is a form of combustion."

I hoisted the coffee cup and said, "Interesting."

"It oxidizes the iron in your bloodstream," he said. "Rusts it, so to speak. Rusting is also a form of combustion, as I'm sure you know."

"I thought fire was supposed to be lethal," I said. Through the window, I heard a premature cricket chirp by way of announcing its presence to a hungry starling.

"Then you haven't understood me at all," Wilton Hoxley said. "You disappoint me. Well, life is just a succession of disappointments. What we mean, conventionally speaking, by growing up is just the process of adjusting to disappointment."

"I'm not all that disappointed," I said.

He laughed, a sound like a gate slipping its latch. "Is that so? Are you happy about where you are in your life?"

I wasn't. "I can handle it."

"Are you happy," he asked, "about whom Eleanor is sleeping with tonight?"

I tossed the coffee over my shoulder and onto my clean floor. "Are you happy about whom Mommy is sleeping with tonight?"

I could hear the friction of lips over gums. "There's no question that you're bright," he said. "You were always bright. Such a bright boy, such a golden boy."

"I had two feet," I said nastily. "And while we're at it, come and get me."

"Now you're trying to insult me," Wilton Hoxley said. "That makes me suspicious, even though we're old friends. Old friends should be able to talk. You know, it amazes me that you didn't realize that we were friends. After all, we had Eleanor in common."

"Eleanor was never common enough for you," I said, and closed my eyes.

"A little cheap," he said. "But then you're a nonentity, a footnote." Schultz's unwritten paper flashed before my eyes in its full unpublished glory. "You don't understand, do you? They're playing with you, just as I am. I can play with you until the cat comes home, and you won't figure it out, and Eleanor will still land in my lap. If I want her. Of course, I don't want her."

"You wanted her before," I said. "My, my, Wilton, the lies you told." He didn't say anything. "The lies you told to Mommy."

He hung up.

I was wetter than I'd been after my shower, but I barely felt it. I took my copy of Dreiser's *An American Tragedy* and put it on the back of the couch, trained Billy's semi at it, and blew it into satisfying smithereens. Feeling marginally more secure, I toted the gun into the kitchen and poured more coffee. Anything that could put commas into Dreiser could put a few well-placed full stops into Wilton Hoxley.

At five the phone rang again. I decided, for once, not to obey. It rang twenty-seven times before falling silent. I sat on the couch, hoping it wasn't a wrong number. I still wanted him on the other end of the phone. When it stopped, I called Schultz and gave him a progress report.

"Get out of there," he said.

"Skip it. He's getting crazy."

"Simeon," Schultz said. It might have been the first time he ever called me by my first name. "Simeon, speaking from a purely professional standpoint and evaluating him within the peripheries of any generally agreed clinical criteria, he's *already* crazy. He's been as loose as a bucket of moths for years."

"I think you should get off the line," I said. "He might be calling."

"He'll call at six," Schultz said. "Not before. You're going to stay in touch, right?"

"As long as the promise holds. I talk to you, and it ends there."

"*You're* the one who's crazy," Schultz said, hanging up.

It rang again precisely at six, and this time I picked it up.

"Why should I want Eleanor?" Wilton Hoxley said as though there'd been no interruption. "Eleanor, as beautiful as she is, is just a woman."

"Whoa, Wilton," I said. "Good for you. How come you never graduated?"

"And what's a woman?" he continued. "A vertical storage system, and a temporary storage system at that. Their insides gurgle like coal running downhill. Ever put your ear up against Eleanor's stomach? Gurgle, gurgle. Peristalsis at work. Women eat innocence, nice, photosynthetic plants that make sugar out of sunshine, and they eat dumb animals who think that people love them until they get their jugular veins cut as the first long step toward the table. Pigs are treated well, Simeon. You've obviously never spent any time around pigs."

"I'm rectifying that now."

"You can't insult me. You're not important enough. Pigs, as I was saying, are very intelligent, they learn to love the carnivore who tosses them their slops, they follow him around from place to place. To them, we're gods. To us, they're pork. The most beautiful woman in the world is just a mechanism for turning innocence into shit. The prima ballerina, dancing around on those torturous little shoes the French invented, looking lighter than air, is gurgling inside, turning some light-footed pig—have you ever seen how a pig walks on those tiny little hooves?—into shit. Sleeping Beauty, Odette the swan, they get offstage, the tutu comes down, and some poor dumb animal or some inoffending head of lettuce comes out, headed for the sewer. Women are a self-procreating system for turning the world into shit."

"Right," I said, gripping the semi with my knees, "and what do men live on?"

"Men," he said, with real scorn this time. "Skip it. We want women to be different, don't we? Don't you want Eleanor to be different? And they're not. That's the tragedy of the world, and the ancient gods knew it. Women are just like we are. Remember Pandora?"

"Vaguely."

"You persist in disappointing me. Pandora, say the Greeks, was the first woman. Another of Hephaestus' masterworks, created to torment mankind throughout eternity."

"Why would Hephaestus want to torment mankind?"

"Well, I'm really taken aback. I thought you were many things, but I never thought you were ignorant."

"So sue me," I said.

"You got the fennel, I believe, on several occasions."

"I can buy fennel in the supermarket. Not that I use a lot of it."

"I'm *sure*, Simeon, that you understood the fennel. Please say you understood the fennel. One can take only so much disillusionment in one dose."

"How do you know I'm not tracing this call?"

"Because you're alone. Because you wouldn't think it was *fair*. Because there's been no one at your house except that cretinous teenager who checked your mail and brought you that useless gun."

"It'll punch holes in you," I said, suddenly doubting that it would.

"You have to aim it at me first. And you won't get a chance. Pandora," he said.

"Listen, Wilton," I said, sweating buckets. "Stick Pandora in your ear. If she's too big, find someplace she'll fit." I hung up.

I wiped my forehead on the way to the refrigerator for a bottle of Singha. At the moment I reached for the phone to call Schultz, it rang.

"You're making me break the rules again," Wilton Hoxley said, and there was a nervous edge to his voice. "You already know how dangerous that is."

"You're scaring me to death," I said, hoping it sounded like a lie.

"If I'm not," he said, "something is seriously wrong with you. About Pandora."

"Oh, stuff Pandora."

"*Please* stop disappointing me. You said to my mother that you knew who I am, but not why I am. Is that more or less accurate?"

"More," I said, wiping my forehead with my sleeve and pulling the bandage away. The blood started immediately, and I held the cold bottle of Singha against the cut.

"Well, then, sit tight and listen. Have you got the gun with you?"

"I'm using it to keep my back straight."

"Get your shirts starched." Wilton Hoxley barked a laugh. "Listen, insect. After Prometheus took fire to earth in a stalk of fennel—"

"The fennel was painfully obvious," I said.

"Obvious? Please. Was that why you had to go see that old fart Blinkins?"

"Blinkins and I are old friends," I said, warding off a sudden desire to cross myself.

"Of course you are. We all love Blinkins. Do you like the Greeks?"

"As Greeks go." I was regretting the fact that I'd spurned Schultz's offer of protection.

"Then you'll like this," he said. "Pandora was Zeus' revenge against Prometheus' treachery. She was the first woman, remember? After Prometheus gave fire back to human beings—who were all apparently men at that point—"

"Sounds like a world you would have liked."

"You can't goad me," he said. "Listen. Prometheus had a stupid brother—"

"Epimetheus," I said.

"Bully for you. And Epimetheus was living, with a lot of other males, on the corrupt earth. Zeus commanded Hephaestus, who could do *anything* over the fire in his forge, to create Pandora. Then, just to cover his bets, he told Hephaestus' wife . . ." He faltered.

"Aphrodite," I said. "A beauty married to a clubfoot."

"Hera was Hephaestus' mother," he said. It was the first thing he hadn't meant to say.

"Chucked him out of heaven," I said.

"All the way to the glittering sea," Wilton Hoxley said. "But he got back—"

"Which is more than you've managed to do." The semi was still cold between my knees. My cut had stopped bleeding, so I drank some beer.

"You're boring me," Hoxley said flatly. "I'm way beyond baiting."

"What's next, Wilton? You got a new mission?"

"My mission at the moment is to explain to you about Pandora. Aphrodite made her irresistible, like a tailor cutting a coat for a dandy. And she went to earth, this *girl*, this ancestor of Eleanor's, and she attached herself, as she was meant to do, to stupid Epimetheus."

"And she brought her box with her."

"Oh, good, you *are* sentient. And the box contained all the evils that the gods could conceive to plague mankind, and she, with feminine curiosity, opened it. The only good thing in it, the spirit Hope, was trapped inside when Pandora, terrified by the things she had let loose upon the world, snapped the lid shut. Typical woman," he said. "Too little, too late, like all of them. And you think I still want Eleanor? Although I'll admit that it would be interesting to see her burn."

"What's next?" I asked out of sheer desperation.

"Oh, Simeon," Wilton Hoxley said, "out of all the people in the world, I would have thought you could have figured out what's next. You know my history. If you can't work it out, what's the use of faith in this world? I simply cannot tell you how disappointed I am. Why should Eleanor, why should *anybody*, trust you with her life when you're such a stumblefoot?"

"But wait," I said. He disconnected.

PART FOUR

INFERNO

I have slain my own dragon.
                    —Serial murderer Dennis Nilsen

18

Happiness Hills

This is what it said:

127.

The letters were black and even, set in type. They occupied maybe a square inch of paper that must once have been the upper right-hand corner of a left-facing page. There was nothing else.

The cheery canary-yellow envelope was tiny, the kind little kids get birthday cards in. It had arrived in the regular mail, and my name and address were in blue ballpoint in a normal, everyday handwriting, a small and precise handwriting but nothing as inhumanly rigid as the square, tightrope-straight gold calligraphy of the first notes.

I might have dismissed it, except for the return address on the envelope's back flap. It said: *From the forge of Hephaestus.*

"One twenty-seven," Schultz said over the phone. He lit up.

"*Page* one twenty-seven," I corrected him.

"Yeah," Schultz said. "Put it in the mailbox. We'll call the Topanga P.O. and tell them we'll be by to pick it up after they collect it. We'll analyze it six ways from Sunday." Then he started to cough.

"You really ought to quit," I said. "Your prognosis is terrible."

"Look who's talking," he said.

There's not a lot you can do to get ready for someone who's promised to burn you to death, but in the two days between my telephone conversation with Wilton Hoxley and the arrival of the three-number note, I'd done everything I could think of, mainly to keep moving. Sometimes even a futile gesture can be reassuring.

I'd started on Friday morning, the morning after the call.

"Six eight-gallon plastic buckets," said the checker at the Fernwood Market, ringing them up. "Twenty-four—can that be right, twenty-four?—cotton towels, two, um, sixteen-foot garden hoses, four of whatever *these* are called, at two-twenty-nine apiece." I didn't know what they were called either, but they were short lengths of metal tubing with spiral threads at both ends. She dropped them into the bag. "Two nozzles?"

"I've got two hoses," I explained.

"Piano wire?" she said, holding up a spool.

"It's a jazz piano. Always wants to get wired."

"And seven sets of wind chimes," she said, putting them onto the counter with an unmelodious clatter. "All those bells," she said. "Let's hope you're a sound sleeper."

"Let's hope I'm not," I said.

I coasted Alice into the Valley, where I bought an extralarge sweat suit. Last stop was a Thrifty Drug Store, all overbright white fluorescent lights and underpaid brown help. The help sold me three of those thin plastic raincoats that meteorological paranoids fold up and carry in their pockets. All the way home I hummed complacently.

But halfway up the driveway, toting my haul in two huge cardboard paper-towel cartons with Bravo Corrigan trotting along at my heels and offering moral support, I got mad. If I hadn't had to behave as though I were living under a mad scientist's microscope, I could have carried the things up a few at a time, like a normal suburban American, over the space of an hour or so; instead, I'd needed cartons so he couldn't see my surprises, pathetic as they were. I dumped the junk where I stood and clambered up to the phone to call Schultz's number of the moment.

"Where's he living, damn it?" I demanded.

"Nowhere." Schultz sounded hoarse, but there was no way to tell whether it was from nerves or nicotine. "He's underground."

"You're checking hotels?"

"And motels, and rooming houses. Literally every cop in this city has his picture. And it's just jerking off, Simeon, and you know it. It could take weeks."

"Has he bought a new Mazda?"

"*Nein*. We're plugged into the DMV. All Mazda sales are being filtered out and fed back to us. There's a lag of a couple of days from the sheer volume of the data, but so far—say, up to forty-eight hours ago—nothing."

I thought. "Maybe an RV. Something mobile. Does Mazda make an RV?"

"RVs," Schultz sighed. "Okay, we'll get the RV transfers, too. I don't think Mazda makes an RV, but he may not need a Mazda any more. That may have nothing to do with his new mission. He may be a new god by now."

"Something mobile," I said. It sounded right. "Something he could sleep in. It would solve all his problems. He could move around, plan whatever the hell the new mission is, not have to check in anywhere at night."

The line was silent for a moment. "An RV would be pretty big," Schultz said.

"So?"

"He saw the kid checking your mailbox. After he torched the Mazda."

"Whooee," I said.

"Can't be that many spots where you can park an RV," Schultz said. "Can there?"

"Check the RVs, okay?"

"Sure. Same forty-eight-hour lag, though."

"Norbert," I said. "You're a brick."

Before exploring Schultz's idea, I went out and lugged the cartons the rest of the way into the house. Bravo Corrigan had gone to sleep in the shade. The sun's heat sat on my shoulders like a fat, feverish kid. Thumb-sized bumblebees droned drunkenly through still air. A big one had decided to give up and rub its legs around in the dust. I stepped over it enviously, staggering along beneath the weight of the boxes.

The junk got dumped, like junk, in the center of the living room. I went into the bedroom to get my hawk-watching binoculars, a nice pair of lightweight Nikons that Eleanor had given me for my thirty-fifth birthday as a subtle way of contradicting my conviction that I was growing farsighted in my old age.

I closed the curtains to let the house cool, or at least stop heating up, for a few minutes. Then I moved methodically around the house, opening each curtain only a couple of inches and surveying the hills opposite.

The house perches very precariously on a ragged, triangular point of land that is almost the highest in the canyon. Rising behind it is a sheer cliff of decomposed granite that stretches twenty-five or twenty-six feet to the peak of the mountain. There is no way up to the peak except to leave the road and claw your way up through the rattlesnakes and chaparral, an unpleasant fifteen-minute hike highlighted by scratched arms and legs, branches in the eye, and worse. I'd done it, out of pigheaded curiosity, when I first rented the place. In front of the house and on both sides is nothing but air.

Half a mile through the air to the north is a tough-looking gang of scrub-covered granitic mounds, not quite mountains, that shoulder their way roughly northwest, toward the Pacific. They have not yet been developed, which makes them an endangered species. A raw interlocking system of dusty red firebreaks runs up and down them. To the south, three quarters of a mile away, is a long, high landslide-prone ridge, sharper than fur bristling on a mad dog's spine, which some optimistic realtor had named Happiness Hills Homes. The mountains in front and west of the house are almost five miles away, and beyond them the ocean wrinkles and smooths itself in the sun.

Seen through the binoculars, between four inches of open curtain, the firebreaks in the granite mounds to the north looked suicidally precipitous. Up the gentlest-sloping of them, though, ran an unsurfaced dirt road for heavy equipment that would easily accommodate traffic in two directions: a possible. The mountains in front of the house were just too damn far away for him to have seen anything, unless he had the Hubble Space Telescope and he'd managed to fix the mirrors.

Happiness Hills Homes looked pretty good. There was plenty of access, and five building lots had been gouged into the face of the rock. Some of them had even withstood the record rains of February and March. On three of them the unfinished Homes of Happiness Hills baked in the sun, all open beams and broken rectangles of sheetrock. The developer had been working on spec, and not a nail had been driven into the houses since two of the pads spilled down the hillside on a fifth consecutive day of rain. Another profitable tax write-off, another hillside ruined.

I hadn't bothered to look for Hoxley's spy-hole for two reasons. First, he was *supposed* to be looking at me so he could see there weren't any cops hanging around on the edges of things, and second, he could have been practically anywhere while he was driving the little Mazda. But now, if he was literally on the move, roaming the streets in a big, fat RV, he had a new set of requirements. And anyway, I thought, why not let him see me looking for him?

The problem, of course, was that I might find him.

Still, it felt good to be going on the offensive. I jumped lightly over the cartons in the living room, grabbed an apple from the refrigerator, and hiked down the driveway to Alice.

The southbound motorist on Old Topanga Canyon Boulevard, if he or she was stricken with an inexplicable compulsion to visit Happiness Hill Homes, would yield to the compulsion by turning left over an ugly raw concrete bridge that had been poured across Topanga Creek. He or she would then proceed almost vertically upward via a wide road, unpaved but liberally and repeatedly sprayed with oil. He or she would strike a substantial number of the large rocks that litter the road's surface, and he or she would watch his or her temperature gauge rise airily toward the red sector. By the time he or she reached the circle at the top, he or she would probably be swearing liberally. I stopped swearing when I got out of Alice, who was steaming like the teakettle in a British farce, and saw tire tracks in the dust around the periphery of the oiled circle.

A wind tugged at my shirt and threw dust in my face as it blew over the ridge, drawn out of the baking San Fernando Valley by the low atmospheric pressure over the ocean. A fire wind, a steady flow of dry air that can push flames in front of it for days. It dried the sweat on my forehead as I knelt and looked at the tracks. They were very wide, wider than any I'd ever seen on an RV. They could even have been from the wheels of a tractor. Maybe they were going to begin building again. Maybe I was wrong about Happiness Hills Homes.

The pads radiated off the circle like the petals of a daisy. Each of them was reached by a short path, probably an embryonic driveway, that cut through the waist-high brush. Lizards scuttled away from me as I took the path leading to the highest pad.

Pad number one was a fragment. Most of it had rumbled down into the canyon during the rainstorm, leaving a gaping red scar that stretched for a hundred feet or so below it. Granite boulders had rolled down onto what remained, probably during the same storm, creating a moonscape of jumble and clutter. I climbed out onto it nevertheless and found cigarette butts, tinsel from a fresh pack, and two used condoms.

Pad number two held one of the partially built houses, just a skeleton of timber with a few empty windows framed in place and some finished stonework around what was ultimately to have been the fireplace. A small rattler sunning on the warm stone of the hearth politely announced itself in plenty of time for me to stop and back away. Other than that, there was nothing at all of interest, unless you counted the splendid view of my house and mailbox, below and almost a mile away.

The rattler was the hero of the day. It was small, which meant that its brothers and sisters were likely to be frolicking in the neighborhood, the healthy rural children of Happiness Hills Homes. The small ones can be as venomous as the whoppers. Bearing that in mind, I negotiated the path to pad three much more slowly than I had to the other two, walking heavily and deliberately with my eyes on the ground. If I hadn't been looking at the ground, I wouldn't have seen the fishing line.

It ran, stretched taut, between the upright timbers of the frame, passing through screw-in eyelets about four inches above the ground. The line was transparent, but the sun was almost directly overhead, and a gleam scooted along it as I approached. The gleam was tiny, but, thanks to the rattler, it was enough.

He'd been thorough, just as he'd been at the Doopermart. The fishing line traversed the entire perimeter of the house, four inches above the concrete pad. After I'd stood there for about ten minutes, just looking, I stepped over the tripline and onto the pad. Moving very slowly, I traversed the pad. It was as clean as if it had been swept. I was pretty sure that it had been swept.

This house was Plan B. Unlike the one on lot two, a stairway ran down from the pad to reach a lower level. A tripwire, stretched across the stairway four inches above the fourth step down, was virtually invisible. A foot coming down on it would have done the job, whatever the job was. It took me quite a long time, standing absolutely still and cupping my hands around my eyes against the sun's glare, to determine that it was the only one. I stepped over it, going down, as though it were a foot thick.

When I reached the lower level, I stopped dead and took a long look around. I smelled oranges. What the architect evidently had in mind was a single, awkwardly long room with a glass wall looking out over the canyon, opening onto an outer deck from which one could enjoy the view. My house was in the center of the view.

There were no tripwires stretched over the skeleton of the deck. Dry weeds, thick and coated with dust, pressed up against the sides of the house. I took a loose two-by-four, lay down on my stomach on the deck, parted the weeds, and looked at dirt. I moved three or four feet and repeated the probe; more dirt. Not until I'd checked all three open sides of the deck did I climb down into the brush. The first thing I did when I got there was stamp my feet eight or ten times to let the snakes know I was around. That finished, I jumped up and down twice and waited. Nobody rattled at me.

Getting no closer to the edge of the house than a foot or two, I worked my way around to the west-facing side and started up the hill, moving sideways. I'd gone six feet when I spotted a line of filament running down from the tripwire surrounding the pad, and used the two-by-four to part the brush in front of it. The line ran into a little square silver device, bolted to the wooden frame of the house. Emerging from the center of the little silver device was a long fuse. The fuse traveled three or four inches before it entered the business end of yet another Fourth of July fire cone. The fire cone was pointed out, away from the house. Into the brush.

Something moved behind me.

I froze, trying to will myself into silent invisibility. Whoever it was waited, too.

All I could think of was to get under the house, get between the open timbers that led down into the foundation, get away from the brush. The brush would explode. I didn't want to burn, but I *certainly* didn't want to explode.

I sank slowly to a squatting position. The person behind me moved closer, accompanied by the sound of breaking brush. I had so much sweat in my eyes that the foundation timbers blurred and wavered.

Then he came fast, and I leaned forward and pushed off with all my strength, a human frog trying to get under the lily pad before the hawk hits. I landed on one shoulder and tumbled away, rolling uphill, toward the juncture of the concrete pad and the hillside.

Rolling, in other words, into a corner.

Transformed in seconds from a frog to a crab, I scuttled backward into my corner and watched the brush. I heard something rasping and realized it was my breath.

Then I saw his feet.

They were brown. They were covered with fur. He lowered his head, gazed lovingly at me, and drooled.

"Bravo," I said thickly. "God damn you, Bravo." He started to back away. "Good dog," I said very quickly. "Good Bravo. Stay, Bravo. Stay." I was working my way toward him on my hands and knees. "Stay, boy. If you don't stay, you'll be Barbecue Corrigan. You wouldn't like that, would you?" I emerged from my lair and twisted my fingers through the kerchief tied around his neck. He made a sound low in his throat, not really a growl, more like a canine "What's up?" but he didn't resist. United by a bond of love and cheap cotton, man and dog completed their surveillance.

I found three cones on that side of the house alone. When I got to the top, I brushed myself off, put Bravo into Alice and rolled up the windows for insurance, stepped over the tripwires again, and went downstairs. Anyone hitting one of those tripwires would have started a conflagration that could have burned half of Topanga Canyon. Wilton Hoxley was going in for mass immolation.

The smell of oranges came from one of the corners of the

lower room overlooking the canyon. In it I found a tidy litter of orange peels, melon rinds, peach pits, and seeds. The Incinerator, apparently, lived on fruit. When I finally turned to climb the stairs, something gleamed at me from the vertical portion of the fourth step from the top, the one with the fishing line over it. On a small square of brown paper, in gold ink, I read the words:

> *Hi!*
> *How do you like it?*

"I'm going to tell Finch to put a man up there," Schultz said.

"The hell you are. Why? I cut the lines and yanked the fireworks. He's not coming back. He booby-trapped it and went away." The phone was slick and wet in my hand.

"He reads the papers," Schultz said. "That thing doesn't go off, he's going to go up and check. He won't be able to keep himself from checking. Maybe you found it, maybe you disarmed it. There's nothing in the papers, he's going to be beside himself."

"Oh, for the love of God, Norbert. For this kind of thinking, they pay you eighty dollars an hour? He's not coming back. If it doesn't go off, then either it's intact or it's been discovered. If he thinks it's intact, he'll wait until someone trips over it and it makes the front page. If he thinks it's been discovered, he'll figure every cop in California is sitting in the sagebrush wearing asbestos and waiting for him."

"You're thinking *sane*," Schultz protested.

"I'm thinking, period."

"You can't think sane with this guy. Trust me on this."

"I've been trusting you. Have we caught him so far?"

"What's the note say? 'How do you like it?' Suppose you're keeping us from preventing his new mission?"

"This isn't his new mission. This is a prank."

"What makes you so sure?"

"Because he isn't around for the fun."

Schultz lit up and breathed smoke. "A lot of people could get killed if you're wrong," he said. "I can't keep this from Finch."

"Then I stop talking to you."

"Wait, wait. How you going to feel if you're wrong?"

"I'm not wrong."

"If you can say that right now, you're dumber than I thought you were. Let's say there's one chance in five thousand that you're wrong. Let's say that's the chance that comes up and he rerigs it and some kid sets it off and fifty people die in their houses. Remember how I felt when he burned the first woman?"

I used the time I needed for reflection to transfer the receiver to my other ear.

"You could be right about his mission," Schultz conceded. "That sounds good to me. He's going to want to be there. But if you're wrong about this, this prank or whatever it is, you're going to carry it with you until the day you die. There are little kids living up there."

Five thousand to one didn't sound good enough. "Only two cops," I said. "And they can't be uniforms."

"Fine," Schultz said. "I'll tell Finch."

"They have to go in on foot, over the fire roads. They can get dropped off about two miles away, at the top of Old Topanga Canyon, and pick up the fire road directly across the road from Deer Creek Ranch. You can get a map from the fire department. They should dress like hikers. I don't care if they're packing atomic cannons, they keep them in their backpacks until they're in position and they know no one is peeking. And they take every foot of the way like they're in enemy territory."

"Green Beret time."

"Eight- to ten-hour shifts," I said. "No endless line of over-sized Boy Scouts trekking heartily back and forth to Happiness Hills Homes."

"Yeah, yeah," Schultz said impatiently.

Since I had a lot to do, everybody called. I was threading the pipe gizmos into the faucets in the kitchen and bathroom when the phone rang the first time. It was my friend Annie Wilmington, the mother of my goddaughter, inviting me to an eighth birthday party for her son, Luke, on Sunday. I declined. I was screwing the garden hoses onto the pipe gizmos in the faucets when a lady from the *Los Angeles Times* called to suggest that what was missing from my life was a six-month trial subscription. I told her I wasn't sure I had six months to live. I was using the hoses to fill five of the six buckets with water when Stillman called to ask how the case was coming along. I told him it was coming along like a house afire and hung up on him. I was putting eighteen of the twenty-four towels into the buckets full of water when Annabelle Winston called.

"Are you all right?" she asked.

"Well," I said, "I've lost a little weight, but I've acquired a guard dog."

"I haven't wanted to bother you. I just wondered if you have anything to tell me. I want to go to Chicago for the weekend, but not if you think anything is likely to happen."

"I think that *exactly* anything is likely to happen."

"Should I stay?"

"Look, Miss Winston, I appreciate how patient you've—"

"I saw how stressed you were last time," she said, pouring it on just a bit. "I wouldn't add to the strain for the world, it's just that I'm not sure whether to leave or not. When you say you think anything might happen—"

"I mean that he might burn me, he might burn you, or he might burn half of southern California. I think he's on the move and that he's got something very big in mind. And I think it's going to happen soon."

"I'll stay," she said.

"Suit yourself," I said. "Now, if you'll excuse me, I've got to finish filling my moat."

I put each of the buckets, full of water and towels, dead center in a room. I fastened the garden nozzles onto the hoses and hauled them through the house to make sure there was no spot I couldn't hit. I filled the sixth bucket with water, dropped the remaining six towels into it, and toted it down to Alice. Bravo roused himself loyally and trotted down after me. When I got back to the top of the hill, I gave him a bowl of water and a full box of low-salt Triscuits, over which I poured bacon grease from some forgotten breakfast. He knocked it back as though it had been Chateaubriand.

Having purchased his territorial loyalty for one more night, I sat at the plywood breakfast counter and used a pair of needle-nose pliers to work the bells out of the wind chimes. I only pinched myself twice. The pliers doubled as wire cutters, so I took them outside as I strung the piano wire back and forth across the driveway and through the brush on the hillsides surrounding the house. Each wire or pair of wires ultimately passed through one of the many holes in the screen over my bedroom window, where I passed it under a bent nail driven into the wall and then tied it off through one of the metal rings that had held the bells in place in the wind chimes. The entire bouquet of bells dangled about twelve inches above where my nose would be when I was asleep. I was outside, tugging wires and listening to bells, when the phone rang again.

"Yeah?"

"Hello, Simeon," Eleanor said.

"Oh, Lord," I said, feeling as though I'd broken into a blush. "Let me get a beer."

I grabbed a bottle of Singha from the refrigerator and plopped down on the floor. "So hi," I said.

"How are you?"

"Everybody's asking. I'm not well done yet, and that's something."

"Have you got any protection?"

"Bravo Corrigan's here. I've put in an alarm system." I could hear a television in the background. "And you?"

"Getting tired of hotels."

"Call room service."

"I do," she said. "Continuously."

"How's good old Burt?"

"In New York."

"He's a New York type of guy. He should really move to New York. I bet he'd be happy as hell in New York."

"Well," Eleanor said. It was beginning to get dark.

I didn't want her to hang up. "Have you seen Hammond?"

"He's with me four hours a day. He's in terrible shape, Simeon. I think he's drunk all night long. He's got so much fluid under his eyes I'm surprised he can blink."

"Tough," I said. "He's a big boy. Time for him to stop feeling sorry for himself."

"She's going to take everything. She's got proof that he committed adultery."

"*Al?*" I asked in mock disbelief.

"Oh, stop it. He's your friend."

"I am now the One Musketeer," I said.

"Well," she said again. "He misses you."

I drank again. "He does?"

"I miss you, too."

"Eleanor," I said. "I'm sorry."

"Me, too," she said after a moment. "How did things get so complicated?"

"Maybe I'm not the best guy in the world. But I could get better." I felt like I was talking Tourist's English.

The television on her end of the line went *bang-bang*. "It would be good for you if you did," she said. "You can't run away from love forever."

"It's how I keep in shape," I said. "Stupid. Sorry, that was stupid."

"Well, it was certainly Simeon. Do you want me to come over?"

"No," I said quickly. "We're in Wilton's time zone here."

"Do you want to come here, then?"

There was nothing in the world I wanted more. "I'm afraid to leave."

"I'd think you'd be afraid to stay."

"That, too."

"And you think you can change," she said. "Well. When it's over, then. Promise?"

"I promise." I searched my brain for words that would prove I meant it.

"Please take care of yourself. For me, if not for you."

"I will." I drank half the bottle in a series of long, heart-clutchingly cold swallows.

"See you, then."

"See you." She hung up, and I finished the bottle and thought about the conversation we hadn't had.

When in doubt, Dreiser. Since I'd totaled *An American Tragedy*, I took a shovel to *The Titan* for an hour or two, then gave up once again and reread the first part of Trollope's richly venal *The Way We Live Now*. At about eleven I turned off the light and got into bed. Two minutes later, the phone rang. I pushed Bravo Corrigan off my feet, where he was already twitching his feet, chasing some dream cat, and went to answer it.

"Hello?" I said, hoping it was Eleanor again.

Silence.

"Oh, fuck you, Wilton," I said, slamming the phone down. I went back to bed. Ten minutes later, Bravo raised his head and growled. I picked up the flashlight I'd put on the table by the bed and pointed it out the bedroom window. Nothing. I lay down again.

All the bells went off.

19

Waiting for Wilton

All told, the bells went off three times that night. The third time, I went all the way to the kitchen, clutching Billy's rabbi, and old Bravo barreled out the door, and two seconds later a bunch of coyotes exploded past me and down the hill in a mad scrabble of claws on granite. There was no way to know about the first two times, so I went to bed and spent a couple of hours watching a big reddish fire moon sink itself below the hills, waiting for peal number four.

Another great night's sleep.

At ten in the morning, blinking and sneezing against the sunlight, I stumbled down the driveway and found the three-number note and sent it off to Schultz via the mailbox, in accordance with his instructions on the phone. My arms and legs behaved as though they'd never been introduced. I triggered one of my own wires carrying it back down. A bell in my bedroom rang derisively.

At eleven-thirty, Schultz called to tell me that the big Boy Scouts homesteading up in Happiness Hills had radioed in to say they hadn't seen anyone around my house all night. They'd been using infrared binoculars.

"The nightlife in your neighborhood," he said, "mostly has four legs."

"What about that piece of paper?" I said. My teeth felt as if I'd been eating sand all night.

"It's paper," he said. "We got it three minutes ago, okay?"

I said okay and brushed my teeth for the third time.

At noon precisely, the phone rang again.

"You really should watch your language," Wilton Hoxley said. Then he hung up. I sat on the floor and thought about shaving. I'd absolutely almost decided against it some fifteen minutes later, when the phone rang. It sounded as if it were getting a sore throat.

"I forgot to ask if you got it," Wilton Hoxley said.

"I got it. What does it mean?"

"Don't be silly. You're the detective. You got it, well, goody. One down, two to go." He hung up again, but this time I stayed on the line and heard a second disconnect, the coin-drop *click* a pay phone makes.

Scratching my chin seemed as good a way as any to pass the time. I'd run out of action the day before. After I'd scratched my chin really thoroughly, using no half-measures, I went into the bedroom and tried on my special survival outfit. It looked pretty silly.

Schultz phoned at one-fifteen to say that the bit of paper was eighty-pound coated Royal Roto stock, whatever that meant, and that it was clean of prints. The ink was carbon-based black, and the numbers were in a typeface called Bodoni, commonly used by IBM for its advertisements and manuals. Wilton was going high tech.

I hung up. There was literally nothing to do except wait for Wilton. Wilton came through at two on the dot.

"Do we have pencil in hand?" he asked.

"Do you want me to have a pencil in my hand, Wilton?"

"If you don't, you're going to miss something really, *really* important."

I picked up a pen; he'd never know. "Shoot," I said.

"*C!*" Wilton Hoxley shrieked into the phone.

I blinked. "See what?"

"See nothing, you appalling disappointment, *C* the letter itself. *C* as in castrato, as in castellated or crenellated, as in Alpha

Centauri, as in Charlie Company or Able Baker Charlie Thomas or Checkpoint Charlie, all that disgustingly banal hypermasculine stainless-steel jockstrap military fireman jargon, as in Charlie Chaplin, or, for Christ's sake, as in *clue*. This is a clue, Simeon the detective. *C-L-U-E*. Have you got it?"

"Sure," I said. I wrote *127* on a pad and put *C* under it, feeling like a life-form that had been promoted beyond its capacity by some evolutionary Peter Principle.

"*C?*" Schultz asked when I called him. "What the hell is that?"

I'd thrown the phone across the room, splashed cold water in my face for what felt like the thousandth time in a week, retrieved the phone, and called him.

"You're the psychologist," I said, adapting Hoxley's argument.

"One hundred twenty-seven *C?*" He covered the mouthpiece and said something. "Maybe a hotel room?"

"Have to be a pretty big hotel. What are we talking about? Room C on the hundred twenty-seventh floor? Room 127 on floor C? Who's helping you out, Willick?"

"An address," someone said in the background.

"I heard that," I told Schultz. "I thought of it, too. One twenty-seven North or South Something, apartment C. Not much help, though, is it? Who's with you?"

"Bunch of the guys," Schultz said defensively.

"Which guys, Norbert? Are you at a convention of the American Psychological Association, or are they cops? Listen, is Willick there or not?"

"*C* is the third letter of the alphabet," Schultz observed, ignoring the question. Someone in the room with him applauded. "Maybe it's cryptology. Maybe he means three, which would give us a four-digit number, 1273, which might mean December seventh at three A.M., which is nowhere, or maybe it's a word, maybe he means that all the numbers are letters, which would give us . . ."

"*ABGC,*" I said unhelpfully.

"Maybe it's a chord progression," Schultz said a little wildly. "Maybe a song title. Anybody here play piano?" I heard laughter.

"It *is* a chord progression," I said. "It's a particularly ugly chord progression. Do you really think he's playing 'Name That Awful Tune' with us?"

"No," Schultz said. "But I'm not sitting on my ass making smug comments, either."

"He said two out of three," I said. "Since you're sitting there wrecking your lungs with the boys in blue, why don't you get some computer time and let the computer play around with it as though it were code, which I don't think it is. I think he likes the idea of us chasing our tails until he gives us number three, and when he does that, I think it'll be showtime, and I think it'll be clear. Remember, Norbert, he *wants* me there."

"When did you start calling me Norbert?" Schultz asked crankily.

"I have so little time left in the world," I said, "that I can't stand on formality. I feel—if I may say this, Norbert—as though I've known you all my life."

"Oh, get outta here," Schultz said, hanging up.

It was a little too late to get a suntan and a little too early for a drink. So I made a sandwich and threw it away, and sat and patted Bravo until he got bored with it and went elsewhere to try to dig a tunnel through his head with his left rear foot.

The next call came at four. Not 3:59 or 4:01, but 4:00. I got it on the first ring.

There was a crackling sound, like fire licking at kindling. It began faintly and then sputtered and grew. Then it stopped.

"Cellophane," Wilton Hoxley said. "Old radio trick, courtesy of Orson Welles. Are you ready for your clue?"

"I'm sure glad you're having fun," I said.

"*Three*," Hoxley shouted. He crackled the cellophane some more.

"I'm waiting," I said.

"You're absolutely *trying* to vex me." He sounded genuinely upset. "I've remembered you for years, virtually carried your picture in my wallet, and you turn out to be dross. What in the world has happened to your intellect?"

My eyes were squeezed shut. Thinking of Schultz, I asked, "The number three or the word three?"

"Who *cares*?" Wilton Hoxley screeched. "Three, as in one, two, three, as in the perfect Trinity of Thomas Aquinas, as in Aristotle's three elements, earth, air, and fire, as in let's do a triple. Three."

"Got it," I said dutifully.

"Oh, no, you *don't*," Hoxley almost crowed. His adrenaline spigot was at full open. "At the risk of becoming a mathematical bore, I have to tell you that three is doubly important. Three is where it's going to happen, and three is the number of hours until it's going to happen. What time is it, smarty-pants?"

"Four."

"And what's three plus four?"

"Seven," I said. I was going to kill him if I got the chance.

"Well, just *look* at that, you've solved half of it. I'm sure you'll get the rest of it. I'll be so disappointed, of course I'm growing used to being disappointed by you, but I'll be so *very* disappointed if you're not there."

He hung up, and I heard the coin drop again. Yet another pay phone.

127.C.3. 127C3. 1-27-C3. 12-7C-3. I thought I recognized the pattern in which the numbers and letters were arranged, but I couldn't find the context. I wrote them out eight or ten times, rearranged them, reversed them, listed them vertically and horizontally. I was so tired that I was repeating patterns without noticing it, but it didn't matter; they were a mess in any order. I called Schultz but got a busy signal. Ten minutes later, I got another busy signal. Four twenty-eight.

I climbed out onto the deck and paced, staring at the mountains as they rippled through the heat and going through everything he'd said. Firemen and Alpha Centauri, Thomas Aquinas and Charlie Company. It was as though something were knocking on the inside of my skull, demanding to be let out.

At 4:43 I called Schultz again. Still busy. "Well, Jesus," I said to the phone, "I sure hope it's nothing important." I slammed it down and it rang.

"He got them," Schultz said. He sounded as though he'd just run a marathon.

"Got who?"

"Mommy and Daddy. He got them somehow."

"You mean he burned them?"

"No. They're gone. Not there. Missing."

"How do you know?"

"We had a couple of men there. At the entrance to the street."

"You shitheel," I said. "Privileged communication, my ass. On behalf of my client, I want a refund."

"After everything you told me, we were afraid he'd go after them."

"Well, you did a terrific job of preventing it," I said. "And you probably let him know I'm talking to the cops."

"So what?" Schultz said. "At this point, who cares? Did he give you the third clue?"

"Yes," I said.

"What was it?"

"Norbert, old friend," I said. "I don't think I'm talking to you any more."

The phone rang fifty-eight times before it stopped. I ignored it and concentrated on making a nice long chain out of safety pins. A minute after the phone quit, it started again. By then I was in the bedroom, putting on a pair of swimming trunks and a T-shirt. Then I unchained my safety pins, put them into a Ziploc bag, and rolled it up in the center of my poor little suit of armor, moving on automatic, thinking only about *127C3*. It was beginning to sound like a football pass pattern by the time the phone shut up. A mockingbird filled the silence in 6/8 time, and then the ringing resumed.

I picked it up. "I want information," I snapped before Schultz could speak.

"So dial four-one-one."

"Give it or good-bye. How'd he get them out?"

"We don't know."

"Tell me everything your idiots saw."

"They were there all night," Schultz said. "Nothing moved till eight, when Mommy came out in the Bentley. Alone. She came back, also alone, about eleven-fifty. Then the team changed. Total overlap, not a minute that no one was watching. Daddy never left the house. Couple of cars cruised the street, no one of Junior's description, looking at the houses for sale. Some business in and out of the other houses. The Lewises have some construction going on, but the workmen parked in the street and walked down to their cars. None of them was Wilton. We've been calling the house every couple of hours, just to get the busy signal or do the wrong number act. The phone was busy from twelve-twenty on, which felt too long. The guys rang the buzzer at two-thirty, got nothing, and went in. Place was a mess."

"What time did the workmen leave?"

"Two."

"All of them alone?"

"Like I said, they parked on the street."

"Swell," I said. "Obviously, somebody missed something. You've converted me. I now share my client's opinion of the LAPD."

Schultz ignored the rudeness. "What did he say?"

"He said three. He said three is where it would happen, and three hours from now is when it would happen."

"Three hours from *now?*" Schultz sounded panicked.

"Worse than that," I said. "Three hours from four o'clock."

"One-twenty-seven-*C*-three," Schultz said. "I thought you said it would be clear."

"*You* chew on it for a while," I said. "My jaws are sore."

After I'd gnawed my cheeks for twenty minutes, I dialed Schultz again.

"No other ways to get into that street," I said.

"You were there," he said, sounding frustrated. "It's a cul-de-sac."

"Maybe something runs real close behind it."

"It doesn't."

"God damn it, Schultz, check. They didn't go up the chimney."

"All right," he said a trifle sulkily. "Let me get a Thomas." The phone clattered to the table.

"Holy Mary, Mother of God," I said. That's all it took, a two-by-four between the eyes. I fidgeted from one foot to another, not knowing who could get to it more quickly, Schultz or I. Mine was just down at the foot of the driveway, in Alice's glove compartment.

Then I came to my senses, hung up the phone, jogged down to Alice, and opened the Thomas Brothers map book. The hell with Schultz; what I absolutely didn't need was thirty-seven squad cars, three or four swat teams, and a battery of heavy artillery. 'Bye-bye Wilton, at the first siren's squeal. Anyway, they hadn't been invited.

Page 127, Row C, Square 3, was a blank brown stretch surrounded by urban clutter. I finally located the legend. In print small enough to prove that I *was* getting farsighted, it said, *San Bernardino County Fairground.*

I left the Uzi up in the house; it didn't seem like the kind of hardware I'd be able to get into the fairgrounds.

Ten minutes later, I climbed out of Alice, leaving my suit of armor rolled up on the seat next to me, ran into the Fernwood Market, and tore open an *L.A. Times*. There it was on page 5 of the Calendar section, right out in the open for any fool to see, filling the San Bernardino County Fairgrounds with adventure and merriment for all.

The Chivalry Faire.

20

Knight in Armor

At quarter to seven, daylight saving time, the sun was still floating comfortably above the horizon, roasting everything within reach. I was rolling along unfamiliar surface streets in the tinder-dry hills of San Bernardino, trying to figure out where the hell I was.

The freeway had slowed and then stopped, jammed full of patient, happy weekenders on their way to a bracing dip into the fifteenth century, ready to encounter jugglers, jesters, troubadours, knights in armor, castles, and fair maidens. Maybe even a dragon.

When I hit the clog of traffic, I skated Alice along the freeway's shoulder to the first offramp, inviting and receiving stares of indignation from drivers who still believed in fair play. Once I coasted down the ramp and off the freeway grid, I was in terra incognita. I don't know much about San Bernardino, and I've tried for years to keep it that way.

The Thomas Brothers were no help. I knew I was somewhere in the two-dimensional cartographic fiction called C2, and I was pretty sure that I was heading toward C3, but that was only because C3 was east of C2, and the setting sun was grilling the back of my neck. Even stripped for preaction, in nothing but a T-shirt and swimming trunks, I felt like a four-minute egg.

The road, a two-lane unmarked tarmac, wound between sere, rolling hills that were stiff with weeds and thick with dust. A series of steps, a giant's stairway, had been cut into the skin of the hills to my right, the prelude to a bunch of new dream homes. There was so little anyone could want on the hillside that there was no fence: just the road's oily, uneven edge, a yard or so of tangled puncherweeds posing as shoulder, and then the spiky, overgrown weed garden of the hills.

Six forty-seven, and I needed altitude.

Alice grumbled to a stop at the foot of the new building development, and I sprinted up the dirt track that had been gouged for the earthmoving equipment. As I clambered past the pads onto which the houses would be dropped, I seemed to move in the center of a bubble. Outside the bubble were the heat, the dust, the larger sounds and smells of the day; inside were the rattle of wind in brush beside me, the scuff of my running shoes, and the rasp of my breathing. For a moment, I floated above myself and looked down, seeing my laboring body as a machine that existed simply to get my head to the top of that hill.

My knees began to buckle long before I made it. I was even more fatigued than I'd realized, worn down to nub ends and scraped nerves by Wilton Hoxley. I did the last third of the incline at a sorry trot, which was just as well because I ran right into a chest wound.

At the moment of impact, I thought I'd been shot. I bounced back, flung like a slingshot, and a bright spot of pain in my chest announced itself in crimson through my T-shirt. Both the red and the pain spread as I stood there stupidly, staring down and waiting for my lungs to collapse. When they didn't, when the sound of the shot didn't follow, when a second bullet failed to tear into me, I looked up and saw a barbed-wire fence.

A fence, by implication, has something on the other side of it. The thought formed altogether too slowly in my brain as I pressed at the torn skin on my chest and tried to stanch the bleeding. The hill crested some twenty feet beyond the fence. I left a piece of my shirt waving gaily on one of the barbs, but except for that and a scratched knee, I got through intact. I was almost to the top of the hill when I heard the music.

Polyphonal, rhythmic, anachronistic, something with drums and tambours and sackbuts, it floated on the breeze that blew hot on my face as I topped the hill and looked down on a miniature out of an illuminated manuscript brought to life, a fifteenth-century fairyland set down mistakenly in some obscure corner of the Gobi Desert.

Turrets rose gracefully against the nicotine-colored sky. Pennons snapped in the wind, arches arched, flying buttresses flew. I counted three crenellated pasteboard castles, stone-solid from here, several smaller structures, and a warlord's moated fortress. On a patch of green sward too healthy-looking at this time of year to be anything but Astroturf, mounted knights with lances gave each other the evil eye through upraised visors while their horses pawed the plastic. This had to be the place.

Revelers in costume pushed and shoved their way festively through the streets of a medieval town that huddled at the knees of the taller structures. People crowded against stages where jugglers made patterns of oranges in the air and mountebanks performed tumbling tricks and magicians did complicated things with geese and conical Merlin's hats. A sudden burst of flame, seen out of the corner of my eye, popped my goose bumps to attention in defiance of the heat. I focused to see a burly man on one of the stages, stripped to a pair of uncomfortable-looking leather bloomers, lift a torch to his mouth and spew an arc of fire five feet long.

The fire reminded me that I was underdressed. I clambered back through the fence and scuffed my way back down the hill to fetch my suit of armor.

The flat little automatic that I'd reclaimed from the cops was in the glove compartment, and I took it out and put it, plus two spare clips, on top of the car. The clip in place was full, and the bullets were illegal hollow-points that made an entrance wound the size of a tenpenny nail and an exit wound the size of a cantaloupe.

The bucket full of water and towels had been wedged on the floor between the backseat and the backrest of the front seat. I drew out one of the sopping towels and wrung it out over my head, soaking my shirt and shorts, and then twisted the excess water out of the others and went to work.

First, two wet towels, one on top of the other, wrapped tightly around my torso from armpits to crotch and fastened to each other and to the T-shirt with the heaviest of the safety pins. Then one towel, wound diagonally, around each of my arms and legs and pinned to my shirt and shorts. I had to leave open areas over my knees and elbows to give me bending room, and it took a little time to get it right. By that time I was as wrapped in white as Claude Rains in the middle reels of *The Invisible Man.*

I dipped the extralarge sweatpants into the bucket, gave them a squeeze, and climbed in. The towels didn't look all that bulky, given the size of the pants. The zippered sweatshirt, dripping wet, followed. Finally, I took one of the three plastic slickers from its little package, shook it out, and slipped into it. It had a sash instead of buttons, making it easier to get out of, and it reached almost all the way to my feet. If he sprayed me and threw a match, the fumes just above the surface of the plastic would ignite first, followed almost immediately by the plastic. I figured it would burn through in a couple of seconds, but at least it gave me one skin I could shed, and it would keep the gasoline from saturating cloth. I tucked the two spare slickers into the front of the wet sweatpants, tugged the drawstring on the pants tight to keep the spares in place, tied a simple one-tug bow in the sash on the coat I was wearing, slipped the flat automatic under the right wristband of the sweatshirt, and started up the hill. The two extra clips were in the shirt's single pocket, hard to get to through the coat. I hoped that would be my biggest problem.

It was 7:09, and I was late.

Halfway up the dirt track, I realized I had added at least twenty pounds to my weight and invented the world's first portable steam room. The slicker held the moisture in—which was one of the things it was supposed to do, prevent evaporation—and by the time I reached the fence, I was pouring sweat. The sun, which was finally on the verge of dropping behind a ridge of hills to the west, seared through the transparent plastic like a microwave through freezer wrap. When I'd thought this through, if my mental processes at the time could be so charitably described, I'd known I would be hot. I hadn't known I'd be exhausted.

The fence poked a few holes in my armor and tested the limits of my flexibility, but I barely noticed. It was 7:11, and the Incinerator was nothing if not punctual.

There must have been five thousand people enjoying themselves in the hollow below me. As I worked my way down the dry brush of the hill at an angle, I saw that most of them were in contemporary clothing; the medieval motley was apparently reserved for employees and nostalgic party animals. An edge of shadow was moving across the bottom of the large bowl that held the Chivalry Faire, and historically incorrect colored lights were blinking on here and there. With the night would come the Master of the Revels, in his cap and bells and black rubber trench coat.

But where was he? It was almost quarter after, and nothing seemed to be amiss. I didn't want to blunder into the crowd without having any idea where to find him, so I sat down next to a large, desiccated clump of sage and surveyed the scene.

The parking lot beyond the Faire, on the other side of the hollow, was already plunged into shadow. Between it and me were the main gates, through which people were still arriving, and the tall castles and ye quainte village. Studded here and there among the medieval set pieces, like walnuts in the crown jewels, were artifacts of the twentieth century: trailers that served as dressing rooms for the costumed help, Porta potties, ticket booth, a large catering truck, electrical generators. At the near periphery of the village was an area reserved for food booths, and on the far side was a concentration of carnival rides that had been gussied up with Arthurian trappings for the occasion. People squealed as they rode a small roller coaster painted to look like a dragon or whirled in cups that, for the moment, were supposed to be wine barrels. The largest of the rides was a haunted house bristling with cardboard turrets to turn it into a haunted castle, and the smallest was a six-foot pyramid made of rubber sheeting stretched over a padded metal frame, up which eight or ten very small children were trying to climb. As they bounced back down, their shrill squeals of laughter cut through the deeper noise of the crowd. Looking around, I suddenly saw children everywhere.

Above the Faire, the sloping hillsides that formed the hollow were packed with dry, explosive brush, the perfect fuel. My best guess was that Hoxley intended to crisp all five thousand revelers, children included.

A sharp smell overrode the acrid scent of the sage, and I recognized it as me. I tried to tell myself that it was just sweat, but any pack of dogs, smelling the fear on me, would have torn me to pieces, plastic and all.

Seven-eighteen.

Where was he?

Something was nagging at me, some detail I'd seen and had filed away in a part of my brain that had either shut down or gone to the end of the oxygen line so the areas needed to keep me alive could function without interference. I felt as I had when I'd seen Hoxley's face in my mind's eye on Caputo's show, and now, as then, I couldn't get whatever it was back again. The only thing to do was disregard it and trust some obscure little glop of gray matter to deal it faceup when it was needed.

I stood and stretched, yawning from sheer nerves. Originally, I'd planned to go in through the main entrance, figuring that Hoxley would be watching it from wherever he was, but when I'd blundered up against the fence I'd decided to improvise and see if I could see him before he saw me. Well, I *couldn't* see him, and the time had probably come to go back to Plan A. For all I knew, he was delaying the show, waiting for me.

Feeling broader than a billboard, I walked straight down the hillside, making no attempt to conceal myself. I was frantically fishing my memory, a dangerous diversion for someone walking downhill wrapped in twenty pounds of wet towels. What had I seen, and when had I seen it? From the top of the hill or sitting next to the sage? The thought nagged at me and distracted me, and I hoped that whatever Hoxley did to announce himself wouldn't be too subtle.

By now I was at the edge of the crowd, and folks were glancing at me in a way that informed me that I looked very odd indeed. In fact, people parted to let me through. Children pointed at me. I smiled reassuringly at a five-year-old girl, and she broke into tears. Weary, sweating, scared half out of my wits, I envied her the luxury.

The smell of food slapped me in the face. A guy in a leather apron was flipping unrecognizable pieces of mud that a sign identified as Joustburgers. Next to him, a fat man in a leather apron was carving thick slices off Ye Kinge's Jointe, which I thought was pretty rude. All around me people stopped chewing and making change to gawk at me. I waved harmlessly, like some ogre on a parade float, and grinned at everyone. I'd never smelled so much food in my life.

Food. I stopped dead. A man behind me bumped up against me and, as I turned around, gave me a startled glance, apologized profusely, and melted into the crowd. I barely saw him. I knew how Wilton had gotten Mommy and Daddy out.

I'd seen it from my first vantage point. It sat over to the right, behind the crooked turrets of the haunted castle, and I looked above the plywood roofs of the medieval town to find the right turret. One turret looks pretty much like another to me, but the haunted castle had a distinctively striking tackiness that made it easy to spot. The turrets seemed to be made out of papier-mâché and spray-painted, and one had a pronounced leftward tilt. Even by the relaxed standards of the Faire, it was an amateurish job.

A steeplechase, in the nineteenth century, was precisely that: a bunch of beefy so-called gentlemen on horseback, racing cross-country toward a church steeple several miles away, jumping, fording, or riding over anything in their path. I headed for that crooked turret with the same single-mindedness, bulling my way through people patiently waiting in line and shouldering through archways, and the crowd obediently let the lunatic in the wet jogging clothes and transparent plastic raincoat get by. Once past the turret, it would only be twenty or thirty yards to the catering truck, maybe the same catering truck that had been ministering to the workmen at the Lewises' house, the truck he'd taken them out in, and—I was willing to bet—the truck he'd been living in for the past few days.

But I didn't make it to the catering truck.

I'd barely hit the stretch of open ground between the medieval town and the rides when a burst of fireworks erupted from the turret of the haunted castle. Balls of fire hurtled into the darkening sky to explode into magnesium chrysanthemums, spiral whistlers shrilly corkscrewed themselves into space, and rockets sailed high above us and burst with a flat *whump*, like a slapstick hitting a wooden leg. The crowd around me erupted into applause and cheers.

A line waited in front of the haunted castle, but no one protested as I elbowed my way through it. My costume appeared to set urban-survival mechanisms on red alert. At the head of the line was a closed gate set into a rectangular metal frame, with a waist-high fence running from either side of the frame to the castle. On the other side of the fence was a narrow-gauge railroad track that connected the door on the left with the fake iron gate on the right.

"Anybody in there?" I asked the man in Bermuda shorts at

the front of the line, a triumph of will over gravity, his potbelly and four chins somehow held erect on legs that were thinner than his arms.

"Got me," he said, taking me in and stepping protectively in front of a woman who was probably his wife.

"How long have you been here?"

"Fifteen, twenty minutes."

"No one's gone in or out?"

His answer was drowned out by blare of trumpets, and the gates at the left of the castle opened. A rickety little chain of four cars rattled out on the tracks and stopped in front of the gate.

"About time," Spindle Legs said to his putative wife.

At the moment I smelled it, Wifey screamed. The second car wasn't empty. Its occupant was lying on his side, wrapped tightly in a heavy net. He was naked, but the woman wasn't screaming out of prudery.

He'd been roasted. The skin on his back was black and charred and creviced and fissured, like crackling on an overcooked suckling pig. His head was contorted backward against the pain, against the prison of the net, and on his fat, unburned throat, the tendons stretched taut as guitar strings. The fingers of his left hand splayed through the net, spread wide, as though he'd tried to grab coolness and wet and safety, and splash himself with it. The back of the hand was singed, its black hairs turned to ash above the porky crackling.

A brilliant rocket blossomed above us, bringing the obscene mess into bright, hard relief. There was something protruding from the center of Eddie Lewis's back, something that went straight through him. It was metallic and thin, and the end that came out through his spine was pointed. He'd been skewered on a sword or rapier of some kind, like a shish kebab.

Stuck onto the metal point that had insinuated its way between his charred vertebrae was a piece of cardboard. On it, in carefully squared letters that betrayed no hint of urgency, were the words IT'S ABOUT TIME.

People were in motion now, milling dangerously, the people up front trying to get back, the people behind jockeying for a better look. I let the automatic slip into my right hand, jumped the little fence, and moved, fast and bent low, to the right gate of the haunted castle.

It opened with a gentle push. It opened inward, and it opened almost soundlessly: no creaking Inner Sanctum hinges, no response of gibbering laughter. It was, altogether, too much to hope for.

Wilton Hoxley was not standing behind it.

The gate closed behind me, and I stopped counting my blessings. The haunted castle was darker inside than Charlemagne's tomb. I was standing on a track that moved upward at a gentle angle, and I could feel no walls on either side of me, even at full arm's length. As my fingers grasped for what wasn't there, I thought I heard someone sigh contentedly.

The sigh had been in front of me, not to the side. The railway was only about two feet wide, and I found that I could spread my feet until the inner edges of the rails touched the outside of my shoes, and that I could move relatively easily in that stance. And noisily. My wet sneakers squealed against the rails, and the plastic slicker hissed and crackled with every step.

I'd gone forward maybe six or eight feet when the whole place started to glow. At first I thought my eyes were getting used to the darkness, but the glow grew stronger until I found myself in a twisting corridor with walls of painted stone and electrical sconces set here and there to resemble torches. Their little pink filaments flickered faintly.

There were three open doorways ahead of me. The track went past two of them, and then turned left into the third, and the corridor I was in faded off beyond the turn to the left in a trick of painted perspective.

I had one comfort: Now that I could see, I didn't need the feel of the tracks to guide me. The first of the openings was to my right, and I put my back against the wall on that side of the corridor and edged slowly toward the doorway. When I reached the corner of the doorway, I counted three, pivoted on my right ankle, and whirled into the doorway, the gun extended in both hands. Ghosts attacked me.

When they flew at me, I shot both of them. They rushed me from the end of the tunnel, coming fast, weightless and fluttering, the ragged tatters of their robes barely brushing the ground. The bullets didn't even slow them. In less time than it took me to inhale they were brushing my face, and I listened to the echoing *spang* of the gunshots and smelled dusty muslin and felt wire stiffeners, and then the ghosts slid away from me as quickly as they'd come, back up into their waiting post at the end of the little tunnel.

I'd wasted two bullets. By firing, I'd told Hoxley I was armed, although I didn't figure that counted for much. On the other hand, I'd been made a fool of, which counted with me.

"That was pretty good," I said out loud. "What's next?"

What was next was the second opening, to the left this time. I approached it from the center of the tracks, not particularly eager to catch another face full of anything, and as I positioned myself in front of it, a light came on, and the medieval figure of Death, the image that has come down to us in the twentieth century as the Grim Reaper, black-hooded, with a scythe over its shoulder, and with a skull for a face, began to move toward me on some sort of rollers. It lifted its scythe.

"Too Ingmar Bergman for me," I said, and then about twelve things happened at once. The tracks shook, the doors behind me burst open, music erupted, cold air struck my neck, I tried to dodge, and the little train hit me on the back of the thighs. I tumbled backward into it, and the last thing I saw before it trundled me away was Death winking at me.

"Drive carefully," Death said.

21

Eddie's Ride

A second after the toy railroad landed me outside again, I was out of the car and running through dusk as though hell had opened behind me, toward the pair of doors I'd gone through the first time. Then I stopped and reversed field.

The doors to the left opened out, as quietly as the ones to the right had opened in. All I had to do was slip my fingers into the crack between the doors and tug. Maybe, just maybe, Wilton Hoxley's death's-head was still facing in the other direction.

Maybe he was expecting me to come back the way I'd come before. Maybe I could feel my way through the dark until I came up behind him, aimed, and pulled the trigger four or five times. Maybe the green cheese the moon is supposed to be made of can be bought at discount at Trader Joe's. Maybe, one of these days, it'll finally rain up.

The ragged sound like ripping paper that followed me into the blackness inside the castle was my own breathing. I put the automatic against my cheek and felt its reassuring cool as I willed my lungs to slow down. Water, my own water, was pouring down my sides, saturating the towels.

It was as dark as it had been before the lights went on. Once again my feet told me that I was going uphill. It made sense to whatever part of my brain was still trying to make sense: The train went up through the mild, programmed horrors of the Haunted Castle, and then it went down again. Simple amusement-park physics. Let the suckers get comfortable going uphill, scare the bejeezus out of them at the top, and then throw the whole phone book at them as the train accelerates—out of control?—downhill. Screw with their sense of gravity, the first thing a kid learns, so primal that we take it for granted.

At this point, there wasn't anything I was willing to take for granted.

Up and down, I thought. Very simple, dark or no dark. The rails went up, peaked, and went down again. Pseudo-ectoplasmic interruptions and living homicidal maniacs notwithstanding, I had a simple mental map.

I slid one dripping ankle uphill to find a tie. It had finally occurred to me that all sets of rails have ties between them. If I could measure the distance between the ties and hit them with every step, I could walk without the musical accompaniment of my sneakers squealing against the steel. All I had to do was walk along the right-hand edge of the ties, taking steps of exactly the right length and keeping my right hand extended, brushing the wall to follow the curves. Simple.

Except for the gun. If I wanted to follow the right-hand wall without making noise, I'd have to transfer the gun to my left hand. Skin is quieter than metal. I'd been born left-handed and trained to write with my right, and the training had stuck. I transferred the gun to my more or less useless left hand. It had fit into the right with a comfortingly familiar weight; in the left, it felt fat and cold and greasy.

Still, it was a gun. Did Hoxley have a gun? No way, I comforted myself, as I took the first steps. A gun would have been an affront against Ahura Mazda. The Fire was All. Fire was Beginning and End, and a gun would have been technological irritation.

The track and the walls began to bend to the right. I knew someone must have gone to call the police, but no sound from outside signaled the arrival of a SWAT team to quell the castle's resident lunatic. Listening as I climbed, I caught the sawtoothed sound of my breath again, and chewed down on my lip to silence it.

Then my right hand hit nothing. My fingers extended themselves without my permission, five little soldiers hopelessly assigned to the last patrol, and felt nothing whatsoever, just cool air against a perspiring palm. Another corridor, inhabited by mechanical spooks programmed to go *woo-woo* at the right moment to give the suckers their last fifty-cent thrill on the way out.

Stepping over the right-hand track, I backed into the corridor and stretched out my arms to feel its width. By extending my arms fully, I could just touch both of the corridor's walls. I couldn't hear anything at all, if I discounted muffled music that had to be coming from outside. Somewhere ahead of me, the Grim Reaper was waiting, counting down toward ignition with his squirt bottle and his kitchen matches. Some part of him was probably shrilling gleefully, but he was keeping still. He'd had practice. He'd made it through childhood and adolescence by keeping still, by not letting anyone hear the earsplitting screaming of his soul. He'd learned to muffle it in a pale ordinariness. Wilton Hoxley was an expert at stillness.

The walls of the corridor felt reassuringly solid. I stretched my arms out for support and sagged. I'd never needed a good sag quite so badly. Relaxing into my sag, I began, for the first time in four or five minutes, to think about where I was, rather than letting my mind bathe me in soothing, irrelevant data about where I'd rather be. The Crab Nebula, for example.

But I was here and Hoxley was ahead of me, waiting to shrill and squirt. My armor, so solid-seeming when I'd imagined it all those endless subjective years ago, felt as permeable as a wind sock. Then the walls on either side of my hands trembled, I heard a sound like a ratchet wrench, and then a bang. The trembling increased, and I stepped back and bit my tongue as the sound grew louder and a ghost's hand passed over my face. Air, just air. The little train had carried poor Eddie through his last ride again, a new and improved vision of hell: burn to death and then revisit the scenery.

The train was a probe sent to root me out, to push me noisily off the tracks. Hoxley was still in front of me, waiting. Whatever I meant to him, it was enough to keep him where he was, in the center of a web where he knew he might soon be discovered.

As the doors below me banged shut behind Eddie's ride, I lunged out of the corridor and up the incline, hugging the wall to my back and ignoring the ties, praying for the echo to linger. It boomed back and forth between the pasteboard walls long enough to cover the sound of my movement until another opening yawned behind me and I stepped backward into it, into the realm of some other ersatz ghost.

He'd sent the train to sound me out, or—maybe—to chase me out. Maybe he thought it had. Whatever buttons or levers controlled the train were obviously in front of me, where *he* was. Why go any farther? If he was ahead of me, he'd wait until he couldn't wait anymore, and then he'd move. If he came toward me, I could kill him. If he ran away from me, out through the right door, I could either chase him or go out the way I'd come in and shoot him in the face. With my left hand free, I swapped a gun into my right, and my fingers wrapped themselves gratefully around the automatic's handle. *End of the road*, I thought.

And feeling smug, I backed into the end of the road.

I had my left hand stretched protectively behind me and I dismissed the first wisp of cloth as more musty ectoplasm. It didn't even slow me. I brushed it aside and took two more backward steps and brushed it aside again. And felt a thigh under it.

"No," I said. And then flame bloomed behind me and I smelled gasoline and my shoulder was on fire, a yellow tongue seeking my face. My hair caught, and I lost it all, all the planning and calculation, and I swatted at my hair and dropped to my knees to get under the flame, shredding the plastic raincoat as I ripped it off me, and succeeded in tossing it a few feet, and kneeling with my spine curled tightly against the flame of death, I heard Wilton Hoxley say, above and behind me, "Simeon. What *terrible* clothes."

"Don't," I said, convulsing into an even smaller ball. The automatic clattered from my fingers, bounced once, hitting my knee, and then landed behind me.

"Don't what?" Hoxley said. He lit another match. "Ah, of course. Don't burn little Simeon. Well, I've heard *that* before. And what's this?" I heard the gun scrape the ground as he picked it up. "Well," he said, "this is an unfair advantage, is what it is. Is this how a couple of guys talk?" His hand touched my back. "Do you know that you're all wet?" He waited.

"I know," I said hopelessly, just biting air and spitting it out again.

"Well, this is something new," Wilton Hoxley said, sounding pleased. "Up until now, I've always felt that *I* was the one who was wet. All wet. The wet blanket. Wetback. To wet one's pants. Wet behind the ears. Not a very nice word, is it?" The match guttered and died, and my lungs collapsed, releasing enough air to inflate the Goodyear blimp.

"I guess not," I said over the torrent of air.

"And that's interesting, isn't it?" Hoxley said serenely. "I mean, in a purely linguistic sense. What's life, after all, except a little pocket of wet, a little envelope of wet that's trained itself to move around? 'Don't dehydrate,' life says to itself. 'If you dehydrate, you'll die.' Not fish, of course. Fish don't worry. But the terrestrials. What are they afraid of, hmmm? All these little dirt-dwelling bags of water, what are they afraid of? That the sun will dehydrate them? Or are they afraid—hold on a moment"—a match bloomed behind me—"of this?"

"Yes," I said instantly, cravenly. The gasoline fumes clogged my nose.

"And what's this?" he asked dispassionately, addressing some debating team from the moon. "A spark. A drop of the sun's sweat. Are you sweating, Simeon? I can think of only one phrase that addresses the issue." He touched the cold end of the match to my ear, and my reflexes yanked me away from it. "'No sweat,' kids say to each other, don't they? 'Dry up.' Do you think this is what they mean?"

"I don't know," I said, my lips so dry that they made popping sounds as they slid over my teeth.

"Did anyone ever tell you to dry up?"

"Oh, come on, Wilton."

He poked the match against my ear again. "Not my name," he chided. "You haven't earned the right to call me by my name. Did they ever tell you to dry up?"

"Sure," I said, "sure they did."

"I doubt it," he said. I heard him take a step back, and then a little puddling sound, and then a stream of something hit my neck, and the smell of more gasoline crowded into my skull. "Half a liter," he said conversationally as the stream trickled down the center of my back, "not much, considering the relative abundance of fossil fuels, but it should be enough. Do you know how often people told me to dry up? How many men and women told Wilton to dry up? Well, they'd all want to be wet now, wouldn't they?" I was waiting for the match, but even so it was impossible to miss the note of self-pity that threw his tone of triumph into a minor key, and I knew that I'd been playing the wrong card.

I forced myself back onto my knees and turned my head toward him. "They didn't say it often enough," I said. "Dry up, asshole."

There was a silence. Outside I heard the remote music of the carnival, a recording giving evidence of life on another planet, as I waited for the match. When the scraping sound came, it was his voice instead.

"A new tack." He sounded like he was being held together with baling wire.

"Oh," I said, driving my fingernails through my palms and trying for a tone of command, "just light the fucking match, you pathetic slug."

"You don't know who I am." His tone was almost plaintive.

"Listen up, Wilton," I said, counting down to my last moment, "who gives a shit?"

There was a booming sound, some bold soul hurling himself against the pair of doors that opened out.

And Hoxley laughed. "We never know, do we?" he said.

"*You* never know," I said, waiting for the match. "Most of us do."

"We never know," he said, "how important we are to others. The slightest thing we do or say, something we forget a minute later, can take root in the other person's soul. You clown. You never think about me?"

"About as often as I think about the United Arab Emirates."

He jostled me with his knee. "On your feet," he said. "Time to think about Wilton."

22

Mother's Hour

The back door to the Haunted Castle slammed shut behind us with a deceptively solid sound, and Hoxley located my sacroiliac with the barrel of the automatic and nudged. "Servants' entrance," he said, with a wobbly giggle that suddenly veered off in the direction of a sob. It was a new, and not particularly encouraging, giggle. He shoved the gun into me aggressively enough to make imaginary exit wounds bloom on either side of my navel like softballs hit into a screen. "Straight ahead," he said.

The gun, poised between where I thought my kidneys might be, shook more than his voice did. The portion of the fairgrounds behind the castle was untended and untransformed, a desiccated southern California field of brittle brown weeds. The pageantry, and the comfort of the crowd, were behind us.

"To the catering truck?"

"Don't get cute," he said, kicking a heavy shoe against my ankle and clipping my Achilles' tendon. I stumbled drunkenly. "This isn't the Age of Cute yet. We're still poised on the edge of the Age of Discovery."

"The thirteenth?" I guessed, knowing it was wrong, just wanting to keep him talking, to keep his foot slamming my ankle, if necessary, and his hands away from the trigger and the matches. In my own nostrils, I smelled like a trillion shares of Exxon stock.

"Late fifteenth," he corrected me pedantically. He came up beside me, one hand still trying to bore the gun barrel—*my* gun barrel—into my back and out through my navel, and I glanced over at his face, a sweating skull with the death's-head makeup dripping into vertical smears. He was limping along, perspiring profusely, the sweat carrying the greasepaint along with it in pewter-gray rivulets, and he didn't seem to be able to keep his eyes focused steadily in front of him. "America hasn't been discovered yet," he said, his voice rising in pitch, "and *stop looking at me.*" I did. "Isn't that nice, no America? No truncating the rhythms of life into patterns of convenience, no *convenience* stores, no *convenience* restaurants, no one-hour dry cleaning, or even wet cleaning, to return to an earlier theme. And yes, the catering truck, perspicacious of you, the late Mr. Moreno's catering truck. Poor Mr. Moreno. An enterprising gentleman. Catering trucks and a convenient concession license for the wonderland through which we now stroll, although Mr. Moreno didn't know about the concession license." He licked his lips with a pink tongue. "It's amazing, here in America, what you can do with a phone, a checkbook, and the number of someone else's business license. Mr. Moreno was even more of an entrepreneur than he knew. And newly arrived in the Land of the Free, too. Isn't immigration wonderful? One of the dynamics that drives America, I always say. Well, I don't *always* say it, of course. Wouldn't that be boring? On the other hand, he served microwaved burritos, Mr. Moreno did, and to his own countrymen."

We were most of the way to the catering truck by now, and although there were a few people in sight, here on the wrong side of the attractions, no one had even glanced at us. We were just Death and his good buddy Imminent Death hiking through the scraggle of weeds, and Death's little gun was hidden inside his long black sleeve. Whoever had banged on the door of the Haunted Castle hadn't followed us.

"So what happened to Mr. Moreno?"

"He got microwaved." The gun wiggled upward, seeking a soft space between my ribs, and found one. "And now shut up and walk." Hoxley fell back a step behind me, and I concentrated on doing what I was told.

"How's life in a catering truck?" I asked as we neared it.

"All the conveniences of home," Hoxley said from behind me. "Look at the light shining through the window. Here we are, the lonesome travelers cutting their way through the snowdrifts in a Book of Hours, heading for the homely candle."

"This isn't going to work," I said, with more bravado than I felt.

"Oh, please," Hoxley replied, pityingly. "I know that. This is my swan song. 'Nothing in his life became him like the leaving it.' Do you recognize the quote?"

"No," I said, without thinking.

"Well, it's a classic, and tough shit," Hoxley said. "I've long given up the idea that you might do anything but disappoint me. To the right, now, and watch the step."

We'd rounded the corner of the catering truck, and sure enough, there was a set of fold-down aluminum steps waiting for us to climb them. "Upsy-daisy," he said, wiggling the gun between my ribs.

"Wilton," I said. He poked me twice, hard. "Sorry," I said, "but what happens now?"

"The end of the comedy," he said. "Up the stairs."

"This is a comedy?" I was already at the door.

"Comedies, as you should know from your study of literature, don't have to be funny. They're just stories that end happily." He reached around me and fitted a key to the lock, the other hand pressing the gun into my back.

"But you said this was your swan song," I said as the door swung inward.

"In," Hoxley said, prodding me again.

"So what's so happy?" I said, stepping inside. "You're dead?" I heard him behind me, one foot heavier than the other. "That's a happy ending?"

"One can get bored," Hoxley said, pulling the door closed, "even with ecstasy. Hard to believe, but true. Hold still." An electric light went on, and I found myself looking at a world made entirely of aluminum.

The inside of the catering truck was a single dimly lighted metallic corridor: stoves and microwaves and cooking areas to the left, a counter across the wide door at the far end, across which food would normally have been served. A wooden block bolted to one wall held ladles and long wooden-handled forks and knives, the knives positioned sharp edge out and ready for business. The counter was littered with Hoxley's possessions, and the black trench coat was tossed into the corner behind the door. The straw-blond wig peeped out from the folds.

"Keep moving," he said. I heard him lick his lips, a small, dry popping sound that sounded like a snake's tongue looks. "Between the stoves," he said. "Then turn and sit on the counter, facing back. Don't look at me, hear?" I hesitated, and he shoved me again. "I said, *hear*?" His voice had taken on a tightwire shimmy, a quaver that threatened to broaden into an uncontrolled tremolo.

I said I heard and did as told, facing three quarters toward the rear of the truck. Opposite me was a line of tinted windows. Through them, in the exaggerated dusk, people drifted back and forth on business. Someone moaned in front of me, and in the darkness under the counter at the back of the truck I saw a large black plastic trash bag, two of them, actually, held together by a long spiral of fiber tape.

"You've met Mom," Hoxley said, extinguishing the kerosene lamp. He emitted a burst of sound that turned out to be a laugh.

He stepped to the left. "Okay, sit on the counter. *Don't look at me*. Just sit on the counter and be quiet."

I hoisted myself up onto the counter. Around me, like cosmetics on some grand and peculiar lady's vanity table, was an apparently random assortment of kitchen and bathroom objects: spoons, knives, heavy frying pans, soap, combs and brushes, deodorant, shaving cream and a razor, hair spray, toothpaste.

"You've made yourself comfortable," I said, sneaking a peek at him.

"It seemed like fun at first," Hoxley said without turning toward me, gazing instead at the tightly wrapped garbage bags, "like camping. And it was a nice way of getting *them* out. But, like everything else, it got boring."

"I wouldn't think you were the camping type."

"I'm not. And, because you're correct, you may look at me." I did, focusing on the sweat-smeared death's-head. His eyes were jumping like peas on a skillet.

"Imagine the Grim Reaper as a child," Hoxley was saying as though lecturing to a class, "way too skinny to be popular, not so much ugly as odd-looking, these terrible clothes"—he looked down and plucked at his robe—"probably hand-me-downs from his uncles, the Four Horsemen. Who's going to play with him? Too weird even for the Middle Ages."

I couldn't keep my eyes on his face, so I turned and gazed through the windows opposite me. Nothing seemed to be happening outside the truck.

"So what was he supposed to do with his youthful energy?" Hoxley mused. Then he coughed sharply. The muscles in my back leapt at the sound. "Auden says, 'Human beings are creatures who can never become something without pretending to be it first,' or something like that. I like to imagine the lonely little Reaper when he was still a black-robed tyke trying out his power, knocking on the doors of people's huts to give them the flu or strolling solo through the woods, obliterating ant colonies with a frown."

"You're the Grim Reaper now?" Outside, there was no sudden posse of Canadian Mounties riding to the rescue. No Hammond in his tight suit.

"This is makeup," he said, "remember?" I looked around to see him rub at his brow, the tight, hopeless gesture of someone with a migraine months old, and his hand spread the paint down the left side of his face, dragging his features down and sideways until he looked like a moon that had been ripped into fragments and reassembled itself amateurishly out of sheer will and gravity. The only things left in their correct places were his eyes, poisoned raisins in a botched Christmas pudding. "I'm the *Gay* Reaper," he said through the smear, "or, rather, given the corrupted state of the language at present, the Happy Reaper. And it's still boring, now that I've done it all. Well, *almost* all." He jerked his chin at me, an abrupt upward tic. "I've changed my mind, turn around. You've tried my patience enough in the past. You don't want to do it now."

"What about her?" I asked, facing out the window again and gesturing in what I hoped was the direction of his mother.

"I was thinking of cooking and eating her," Hoxley said, calming himself. "I've got all the equipment. How's that for religious symbolism? Enough to win your poor little psychologist, the one I saw on TV, a second Ph.D. But I'm afraid she'd be tough. She always was tough." He gave me the laugh again, sudden as a breaking violin string.

"Changing the subject," he said, "it always amazes me, a society as advanced as ours is supposed to be, playing host organism to psychologists. The most pernicious of social parasites. Paying money to priests and drug dealers I can understand, we have to have some fun, but psychologists? I could outsmart my psychologist when I was ten. He sat there getting off on my aggression at eighty dollars an hour, pretending to take a note or two whenever he remembered, and I made stuff up just to keep him breathing hard. I never burned any little animals, whatever *she* might have told you. For one thing, I hadn't thought of it, and for another they're not satisfying enough."

"Well, that's something," I said. "I figured every time you broke a shoelace, you set fire to a sow bug."

"That was later," he said, contradicting himself, "and it was just a phase, like acne. The things with exoskeletons explode, which is kind of cute, but they don't *feel* it. No nerves in an exoskeleton. With mammals, all the nerves are in the skin, and that goes first. Besides, most little animals don't have vocal cords. Vocal cords are essential."

He paused and looked down at the gun as though he'd forgotten he was holding it. "My head hurts," he said to the gun.

"Blow your brains out," I suggested.

He looked up at me quickly, and I glanced away. "Mr. Used-to-Be-Clever. Your paper was really good, you know."

"What paper?"

"'Faces of God.' I broke into Blinkins's office one night and read it. It infuriated me. I had spots in front of my eyes. I knew how little work you'd done. You broke appointments with me, yawned when I gave you facts and even pictures, wonderful pictures, probably cranked the whole thing out the weekend before it was due. And it was better than anything I could have written. Graceful, you know? All airy and light. If I'd written it, it would have taken me months, and there would have been quotes everywhere and footnotes speckled all over the pages like someone sneezed on them with his mouth full. You didn't even put a colon in the title. Didn't you know that all serious academic papers have colons in the title? I'd have probably named it 'The Faces of God: Representations of the Divine Visage in Post-Carolingian Northern Europe' or something like that. You just called it 'Faces of God' and said the hell with it."

"I barely remember it," I said.

"You don't have to tell me that." His voice was louder, and I could feel him looking at me. "I know that you were more important to me than I ever was to you."

"And why does that matter?"

"It doesn't," he said shortly. "Not any more."

"You haven't got much longer," I said, hoping it didn't sound wishful. "Sending Eddie out to meet me was like calling the cops yourself."

"We're *waiting* for the cops," he said. "Have you been shaving points off your IQ or something? Maybe people are right to avoid reunions, they're always a let-down. Here I've been thinking about you for years—not often, but from time to time—and bang, you surface in the newspaper, and *what* are you doing? You're a detective. Well, I think, could be he's remained interesting, although so few people do. Aging seems mainly to be a matter of getting duller. Do you think I've gotten duller?"

"Not at all."

"Well, you have. It's actually funny. You've gotten little and pinched and tiny, and I've gotten, well, enormously interesting, and *you're* the one who doesn't remember *me*. Don't you think that's funny?"

His mother moaned again. I heard Hoxley's feet scuff against the floor as he turned toward her, and I put both hands on the counter and swiveled toward him, ready to leap, and found myself looking into the end of the gun.

"Not yet," he said. Then he smiled, his teeth yellow in the smeared gray-and-white face. "We'll just ignore Mom for now. I'm sure she'd prefer that to the alternative." He looked around the truck. "It's sort of cozy, just the three of us. You never came over to my house when we were in school, did you? No, of course not. *I* never went over to my house when I was in school. Not with the little Hebe there. 'What a falling-off was this.' Another quote. The beast with two backs and so forth. Not much of a quoting man, are you? I should have known from your paper."

"I'm too dull," I said. "Quoting requires an original mind."

"The little greaseball," Hoxley said scornfully, not listening to me. "He was a bookie, did you know that? A real, honest-to-God Damon Runyon bookie. Took me to the track from time to time, you know, get to know the boy, make like a best pal." He shuddered from head to foot, and I became aware that the gun in his hand was shaking violently. "A *pal*. Me and that revolting gob of phlegm. Shame you never came around. What fun the three of us could have had, him spitting numbers at Lady Luck and you writing airy prose with your left hand and me figuring out how to burn a horse. I did, too, finally. Working my way up, I burned one for Eddie."

"Do horses have vocal cords?"

"Nay," he said, and released the shrill laugh from its cage again. "That's a pun, nay. Do you get it? Say you get it."

"I get it."

"Then explain it." His eyes twitched toward the windows. "Never mind. What time is it?"

"Past eight." I was watching the gun. It was jumping around in his hand like a live fish.

"Okay," he said. He pulled his eyes away from the windows and slid his tongue over his lips again, as if unsure what came next. "Here's the deal. I hate to cut this short, just as we're getting to know each other again, but fuck it. Get off the counter and turn around. Do it very slowly." He retreated a step to watch me.

I slid my fanny over the edge of the counter until my feet hit the floor and turned my back to him. "Hands behind you," he said. "Knot your fingers together. Good and tight now, hear?"

"I hear."

"I want your knuckles to turn white. You're doing fine. Now over there, under the counter next to Mom. First, get the stool."

A tall, four-legged wooden stool stood beneath the counter. I went slowly to it, not looking back at Hoxley, unknotted my fingers, and pulled it out.

"Put it behind you," he said. *"Don't turn around.* Just slide the stool around you until it's behind your back. Good. Now kneel down—try to do it gracefully—and put your hands back between the legs of the stool. You'll have to unlace your fingers, of course, and you have my permission to do so. Do it now."

As I knelt, my knee touched Mrs. Lewis through the plastic sack, and she started violently. Then she began to weep. Small air holes had been torn in the bag covering her head.

"Calm down, Mom," Hoxley said. "Everything's going to be fine. Simeon, I want one hand on either side of the leg of the stool. The leg farthest from you. Now put your fingers back together. Shake hands with yourself, my little man. Be your own best pal." I knotted my fingers together, the wood rough and thick between my wrists. My elbows were captive between the nearer legs. Hoxley opened a drawer behind me, a grinding metallic sound.

Mrs. Lewis went on crying, long, gulping sobs that seemed to tear her soul up by the roots and scatter its pieces into the air. She was quivering, the plastic bags rustling and shaking.

"Now I'm going to have to use both hands for a minute, Simeon," Hoxley said, "but don't revert to your youth and get clever, because by the time you pull your arms free, I'll have lots of time to pick up the gun and blow your head off. Clear?"

"Clear," I said. My voice sounded like a raven's croak.

"A little fiber," Hoxley was saying, "can do us all a world of good." Something thick was being wrapped around my wrists, pulling at the hair. "Of course, I think you're suppose to eat it." Whatever it was went over my fingers, and then I felt him reach around the leg of the stool and wrap it around my forearms. "When in doubt," he said, "wear it. There we are, fiber tape. Tensile strength, three thousand pounds per square inch. Stronger than affection, stronger than the ties that bind. Stronger than hate? Good question. And while we're at it, shut up, Mom. Did you know that the web of the common garden spider is the strongest fiber in nature?" He paused, and then knocked something against the stool.

"No," I said promptly.

"Well, it probably isn't. Anyway, this will have to do." He gave my hand a proprietorial pat, and I heard him stand up. "Fine," he said. "Like the turtle, you carry your home on your back. Now turn around, on your knees, so you can see me. I've really *lacked* an audience, did you know that? Here I am, the greatest act since Houdini, and all the people who've seen me in action had short attention spans. Distracted by the here and now, although I can't really blame them. The here and now was pretty diverting. Still, there have been times when I felt like a great painting hanging in a miser's basement. For whom, after all, does the Mona Lisa smile? *Turn around.*"

The stool made it impossible for me to shift my weight, and I almost fell as I turned. Only by throwing one knee in front of me could I stay upright.

"Good boy," Hoxley said as I faced him. He'd shed the black robe and stood in front of me in a white T-shirt and blossoming boxer shorts. His arms and legs were thin and white, filmed with reddish hair, and I felt my eyes being drawn down to the black shoes, the left one thick and heavy, with a brace that stretched partway up his calf.

"Ah-ah," he said in a warning tone.

"I knew you'd wear boxer shorts," I said. "And an undershirt. Even in this weather."

"That's marginally safer ground," he said. "But only marginally. You won't tell anybody, will you? No, you won't." He hobbled over to the black rubber trench coat and put it on, catching the wig in midair as it slipped from the coat's folds. Another coat, the third one Willick said he had bought, lay crumpled at the bottom of the pile. Turning to a polished aluminum surface above the sink, he adjusted the wig until it was perfect and then intentionally knocked it askew. "Jauntier this way," he said, studying his reflection. "I really should have thought of the makeup earlier." Satisfied, he spread his arms and pirouetted toward me, pivoting on the heavy shoe. "So. What do you think?"

"All dressed up," I said, "and no place to go."

"Wrong as usual," he said, sounding smug. "Listen, I really can't tell you what a pleasure this has been." He leaned over and picked up a long black cylinder that had been hidden by the coat, vaguely familiar-looking, with straps hanging down from it. "We all have to go sometime, of course," he said, slipping the straps over his shoulder so that the cylinder was cradled against his chest. It culminated at the top in a stretch of flex cord connected to a funnel. "But what a treat to see an old friend again just before Act Five."

The thing against his chest was a fire extinguisher.

"Cute, no?" Hoxley said. He took the funnel in his right hand and pointed it at me. "*Fwooooooo*," he said. I cringed. "Opposites attract, hey? Here I am, with Mom and my friend along for the epiphany. Except, looky here."

He backed to the far end of the catering truck and pulled out a box of wooden matches. Pulling the box open, he took one out and struck it. It broke, and he swore and struck another, holding it in front of the funnel.

"Prepare," he said, "to meet your maker." I was scrambling

backward until the stool struck the counter and its edge cracked me on the back of the head, and Hoxley turned a sort of faucet handle at the top of the cylinder and fire spewed out. I think I screamed.

"Wasn't that dramatic?" Hoxley asked happily, turning the faucet closed. "'Prepare to meet your maker.' Those nineteenth-century playwrights really knew their audience. Well, your maker is going to have to wait a few minutes. And why shouldn't he? The bugger invented time, didn't he?"

The smell of kerosene filled the truck. I felt my eyes slam shut, and I sagged against the rigidity of the stool.

"I'm sorry we won't have a chance to discuss time," Hoxley said, and I opened my eyes to see him turning knobs on the larger of the two stoves. "Is it a straight line or a circle? Does it only happen once. Is there some price, as Dylan said, that we can pay to get out of going through all this nonsense twice? Another quote, maybe more to your liking than the earlier ones." He twisted the last knob and limped to the door, opened it, and stood in it, a tall black silhouette with the face of death.

"There are children out there," I said in a voice higher than Shirley Temple's. The stove was hissing.

He shrugged. "Can't be helped. Everything gets boring. Well, this is new. Maybe I'll experience a last flicker of interest before it's over. I think I'd like that."

"Wilton," I said.

"Or maybe not," he continued, oblivious. "It's so hard to find something one truly enjoys these days." He gave the faucet handle an experimental twirl and then turned it off again. For a moment he stood silent, head down, as though listening to something. Then he looked up and straightened his shoulders. "'Bye, Simeon," he said. "And, hey. 'Bye, Mom."

The door closed behind him, and a moment later, flames erupted outside the windows.

23

Last Spark

The instant the door closed behind Hoxley, Mrs. Lewis began to scream.

I found my way to my feet, the stool pinning my arms behind me, and went to the window. A ridge of flame leapt and shimmered in the weeds about ten feet from the truck. It extended from one edge of my view to the other. For all I knew, it went all the way around.

Now that I was standing, I could smell the gas from the stove. Well, at least we weren't going to burn to death. When the flames reached the truck, we were going to be spread like peanut butter all over San Bernardino. A last favor for an old friend.

Mrs. Lewis continued to shriek as I backed to the stove and felt for the knobs. I found them, but with my fingers taped together, there was nothing I could do. I tried to brush up against the sides of the knobs and turn them that way, but they wouldn't move. The gas was sweet and foul and heavy in my throat.

"Be quiet," I said, and then I started to cough. I was too close to the stove to grab a safe breath, so I backed away from it until I hit the far wall of the truck. I took a lungful of air, held it, and went back to the stove, pushing against its edge, crowding against it, and then, with all my strength, shoved myself away from it and across the corridor into the wall behind me.

The seat of the stool smashed into the back of my head, and I went down like a tree. There was no way to catch myself with my arms immobilized, and my forehead cracked the floor. For a moment I may have gone out, because it seemed to me that Mrs. Lewis stopped crying.

Then a high wail split my ears, and I was back, lying on the truck's dirty floor with blood in my eyes. The corrupt smell of the propane invaded my nostrils as I fought to my feet again. Okay, change of plan.

Don't hit something high enough to drive the seat into your head, stupid. Hit something lower.

This time I pushed off from the wall and hurtled back into the edge of the stove. I collapsed immediately to my knees, my head ringing and the hand I'd slammed on the counter firing off high-voltage pain signals, maybe something broken there, but I'd heard one of the stool's legs crack.

I tried to breathe shallowly as I waited to gain the strength to rise again, and Mrs. Lewis suddenly said, "What are you doing?"

"Tell you later," I said. My voice was thinner than Kleenex. "Can you get out of that thing?"

"Of course not," she said, sounding like her old self. "If I could, do you think I'd be in it?"

"Right. Well, hang tight. Here we go again."

When I stood this time, I seemed to feel the trailer heaving beneath my feet. For a moment, I thought my knees would give way, and I narrowed my focus against panoramic death until I was seeing and feeling one thing only, the stool crumbling like matchwood the next time I hit the counter. When I'd reached the far wall, I wiped the blood from my forehead onto the cool glass of the window and watched the fire. It had advanced a foot or so, and the flames were higher, feeding frantically on the weeds.

"This is going to hurt me more than it does you," I said to Mrs. Lewis, and this time I threw myself back with such force that I stumbled even before I hit the counter, the leg of the stool striking the counter's edge *above* my hands this time, and even as I smashed onto the floor, watching bright points of light bounce around inside my skull, I felt the stool go to pieces behind me.

Well, not quite to pieces. The seat, as I saw when I could open my eyes, was next to me on the floor, but I still had at least two of the legs trapped between my back and my arms, and of course there was the one good old Wilton had taped directly to my wrists. But the important thing was that I could get them over toward one side now; the important thing was that I might be able to sit down.

First, though, I had to stand up. I counted to ten and tried, but I couldn't make my muscles work. I could tell them to do anything from the neck up, but below the Mason-Dixon Line they weren't listening. I flexed everything I could locate, including a hand that felt bigger than a boxing glove. The pain had shut down, shock coming to the rescue, and I was happily and comfortably congratulating shock on having the sense to intervene when I realized I had to get away from the hissing stove.

Like a sidewinder, I wiggled across the floor to the door and tried to breathe through the crack at its bottom. The air coming through it was hot.

"Are you all right?" Mrs. Lewis said.

"Practicing my polka," I said. "We'll be dancing in no time."

"Where's Eddie?" she asked. It shut me up. "He took Eddie," she said.

I managed to get to my knees without blacking out. I was wringing wet, and I'd left an oval pool of blood on the floor. I got one foot under me and then the other, and, leaning against the wall, pushed myself upright. My ears were ringing, and my eyes refused to focus. The truck's interior looked as it might have if I'd been seeing it through moving water.

Taking one slow step after another, I crossed to the counter. I had to sit on the counter.

It had been so easy the first time, the time Wilton had told me to do it. Put the hands on the counter behind me, give a little jump, and *allez-oop*. But now I couldn't use my hands, and I didn't have a little jump in me, not even a very little jump. Not a single decorous Easter-bunny hop. The counter was almost as high as the small of my back. It might as well have been as high as the walls of Troy.

"I can't get up there," I said to myself.

"Up where?" Mrs. Lewis said. Then she began to cry again. "Where's Eddie?"

I was getting sleepy. I thought about resting. I'd closed my eyes and let my head slump forward when I heard screams. They were outside, far from the truck, but they cut through the aluminum and through Mrs. Lewis's sobs, and they galvanized me. Wilton had gone to work.

The frog's legs twitched on the electrified plate again, only they were *my* legs this time, and I was sitting on the counter, my arms twisted impossibly to one side, the legs of the stool bisecting my back at an angle like misaligned bicycle spokes. The wooden block with the carving knives wedged into it was directly behind me, and I pushed my hands against it, feeling blades slicing through tape and into skin, feeling hot new wetness behind me, but sawing up and down anyway until the stool leg taped between my hands fell free with a clatter onto the countertop, and I could open my slick, wet fingers. Willing myself to be careful, I pushed the tape between my wrists against the blade at the edge of the block, angling veins and arteries away from the other one. I cut myself, deeply, and yanked upward involuntarily, and my wrists were loose.

They were a mess. They looked as though I'd loaned them to someone for suicide practice, but the cuts were clean, and the blood, while plentiful and disconcertingly red, wasn't alarming. I held my hands above my head for a moment, willing the blood to stop, and then realized I didn't have the time.

"We're going," I said to Mrs. Lewis. "Can you walk?"

No answer, just a kind of steady keening that put me in mind of an Irish wake. "Well," I said, sliding down from the counter, "you're going to have to." I pulled both of the knives from the block and glanced outside the windows. The fire was washing against the walls of the truck. "In fact," I said, "you're going to have to run."

First I snapped off the knobs on the gas stove. Then I went to her and sliced through the first spiral of fiber tape. "You're going to do what I say," I said, pausing. "Because if you don't, you're going to die. Do you understand me?"

She stopped crying.

"That's better," I said, sawing away. "Here's the plot. Wilton turned the gas on in the big stove and then set fire to the weeds outside." I'd started at her feet, and the plastic had parted to reveal slippers and a pale blue terry-cloth robe. She probably dressed for national holidays. "The second problem is how to run across the fire, but even in those slippers you can probably manage it. The first problem is how to open the door without blowing ourselves over the rainbow." I cut through the last length of tape, and she glared up at me, face shiny with sweat, blond hair matted against her face. Her eyes were puffy, but whatever despair had seized her, it had had the sense to retreat. "Can you stand up?" I asked.

"You look terrible," she said. It wasn't a particularly compassionate tone.

"I'm not going to look any better, either," I said, using a bloody sleeve to smear more blood across my face. "Not unless we work out a way to step outside while remaining physically intact." I heard my voice enunciate the fussily correct words from a distance, like listening to a practiced orator talking to me from the bottom of a well. I put out a hand to keep myself upright.

"Gas," she said, wrinkling her nose.

"Are you *listening* to me? I told you, Wilton—"

"Wilton," said the Ice Princess dismissively. "We need something to put over the door."

I looked at her for eight or nine of my remaining heartbeats. "Right," I said. "Something to put over the door."

With both knives in my right hand, moving more carefully than may or may not have been strictly necessary, I got myself to the door. It didn't seem to take more than a week. Wilton's rubber coat was heavier than I'd thought it would be, or maybe I was weaker than I'd realized, but I lifted it up, stretched it open, and drove a knife through its shoulder at the upper left-hand corner of the door. Then I repeated the action with the other shoulder, and there it hung, a more or less impermeable air curtain.

"Suppose it's locked?" she said at my side. I hadn't heard her move.

"Why would catering trucks lock from the inside?" I asked. "To keep the food from escaping?"

"Try it," she said.

I lifted the right edge of the coat and tried the handle. Locked.

"Smart guy," she said. "I always get smart guys."

I leaned against the counter. It was either that or fall down. "Well, lady," I said, "I'm the last one you're going to get."

"I doubt it," she said. "Excuse me." And she shouldered past me and slipped beneath the rubber coat. I stood there, watching the bulge of her back, and then I heard a sharp *snap*, and the coat flapped as the door banged open against the side of the truck, and she was gone.

Having let the little lady kick the door out, the smart guy had no choice but to follow. I eased the coat back an inch or two and looked out at the panorama of flame, and then she called, "*Left*, stupid," and I saw that Hoxley hadn't ringed the truck with fire; intentionally or not, he'd left a path for us, and it was still open.

But the flames were licking at the right-hand side of the door, and the coat was blowing away behind me, and it all seemed to add up to a good reason to run. I jumped off the steps and sprinted around the truck, heading back toward the Haunted Castle, and I was almost there before the truck blew behind me with a *whoosh* and then a sound like a train hitting a timpani, and the shock wave knocked me flat on my bleeding face into the weeds.

When I looked up, the hills in front of me were on fire.

The screaming was louder now, a kind of steady white noise, and people who, I realized, had been rushing by me, toward the truck and the parking lot, suddenly dropped to their knees or fell on their backs. Those who were still standing milled uncertainly, regarding the flames from the truck like the last chapter in their personal serial. A child let out a shrill sound like a steam whistle.

"Go on," I shouted, getting up. I pushed a man and woman in the direction of the truck. "You can get around it. Go to the parking lot. Get out of here. *Go!*"

In front of me, the turrets of the castle and the roofs of the town beyond it were black silhouettes against a slanting line of flame that climbed slowly upward, circling the natural hollow in which the Faire had been set. I scrubbed blood from my eyes and followed the blazing track up the slope as though it were the trail of a prey, and at the end of it *there he was*, spiraling upward and around the bowl like the Flaming Man in a nightmare, leaving footprints of fire wherever he stepped. And, for another precious heartbeat, everything froze.

Fire burns up.

Except for the trailer, he hadn't ignited anything between the people and the exit.

He was sparing them.

There were police now, pushing people in front of them, big men in blue uniforms, swearing and sweating as they shoved. One of them, like a cliché on a crude recruiting poster, held a little girl in his arms.

I pushed against the crowd, fighting my way upstream with fists and elbows, heading for the other side of the bowl. In the streets of the ersatz town, the reflections of fire danced the flame fandango on the walls. It was emptier here, and I could run. Most of the people were already behind me, sprinting for the relative safety of internal combustion, their magic carpet out of C3.

My ankles told me I was running uphill before my head knew it. I was too busy sucking air and following Wilton's stick-thin figure with my eyes to know what my body was up to. He'd gone more than halfway around the bowl now, slanting uphill all the way and moving laterally ahead of the flames. His track, I saw, would eventually lead him to the crest. It would have to; he couldn't double back without roasting in his own fire.

Shots.

They popped softly in the air like dud fireworks, and I saw men, just dark shapes, on top of the hill. As I labored upward, they fanned out, some ahead of Wilton and some behind him. A few of the men extended their arms and silly little spurts of flame, insignificant in the Kingdom of Conflagration, were followed by more pops.

Wilton stopped suddenly and sat down as though the hill had pushed a chair beneath his feet.

He was seventy-five yards above me now, and the men were a hundred yards above him. The funnel spouted fire over his head as he sat, a nimbus for the god of combustion, probably roasting gnats but not much else. I stumbled and fell, and he got up.

He was moving again, in the same direction as before, touching the fire to the ground at every step. Some of the police who had tried to get at him from behind found flames climbing the hill below them and retreated, either straight up or up and toward Wilton. I was running again, much closer to him now, making an impossible amount of noise, and when Wilton finally heard me, I was near enough to see the smeared death's-head of his face and the irregular line of his teeth. They were bared as though he were trying to chew his way through the air.

I stumbled to my right, trying to get in front of him. He was only a few yards away now and watching me, the funnel pointed back over his shoulder, spewing a spire of flame. I stopped dead, and he looked at me for a long moment, and then pointed the funnel directly at me.

And turned the little faucet handle off.

I was backing up by then, and I slammed into something heavy. Flailing, I lost my balance and turned in midair to gaze up into the clear blue eyes of Willick, who glanced down at me surprisedly as I hit the ground and then lifted his arm and pointed it at Wilton.

"*Stop*," I cried, and Willick looked startled just long enough for me to grab his ankles and yank his feet out from under him. The gun went off as he fell, and he rolled down the hill and away from us like a felled log, crashing the undergrowth as he went. I managed to pull myself to my hands and knees, and found Wilton staring down at me. Above the black coat his face was gray and almost featureless except for the holes that were his eyes. There was blood gleaming on the black rubber of his coat.

He raised the funnel and pointed it at me.

"*Simeon*," he said, "will you *never* cease to disappoint me?"

And then he backed uphill a few steps and sat heavily. Men crashed their way downhill above him as he twisted the funnel toward himself, turned the handle, and opened a box of wooden matches. He closed his eyes and struck one.

The first one lit.

24

Ashes by Now

The heat had broken. Cooler air from the sea flowed into the canyon, bringing morning fog with it. The fog would spread its marine damp over the fuel, turning it sodden and useless for the gods of fire. Zoroaster would be taking his seasonal holiday, probably in Miami with everybody else.

The house was both damper and emptier than I would have liked it to be. I had bandages on both hands and a jagged cut on my forehead, courtesy of the floor of the catering truck, that extended perversely several inches into my hairline. They'd had to shave a shape like a very large comma into my scalp, just above my left eye. In all, I looked like someone who arched his eyebrow so often that space had been carved to make room for it.

On the stereo, Rodney Crowell was stretching country music into new shapes while remaining within the same immemorial scraggly whiskered, whiskey-soaked, heartbroken mode.

"You're just like a wildfire," he sang, sounding like someone whose heart was tattooed on his sleeve;

"Spreading all over town.

"As much as you burn me, baby . . ."

I turned over on the couch, a fat book in my hands.

"I should be ashes by now."

Eleanor was in chilly New York with Burt, "exploring his space," as she'd said semiapologetically from an airport pay phone. When I'd suggested that his space was the nicest present he could give her, she'd hung up. She'd snorted unpleasantly first, though, and later called from New York to apologize for the snort. Small blessings are sometimes the only ones at hand.

Hoxley was dead. Burning rubber, it turned out, was the hardest fire of all to put out. Ashes by now, although he still stalked through my dreams. In my dreams, his eyes were on fire.

Eddie was moldering in the ground, or, alternatively, laying bets on the fastest seraphim in the sky. I had no idea which, and I didn't particularly care. I'd liked Eddie, but he was as dead as Wilton. Some things you can't fight. Schultz, almost preternaturally disconsolate, had resigned from the cops to go back into private practice.

My bank account was nearly full enough to compensate for my empty house. Annabelle Winston had been free with the zeroes. Zeroes, I soon discovered, are cold comfort, especially when you can't think of anything you want to buy.

I could think of lots of things I wanted. Problem was, none of them happened to be for sale.

"Ashes by now."

On the other hand, I was finally enjoying Dreiser. Billy Pinnace had whistled through *Sister Carrie*, stinging my vanity, and I'd taken another whack. Poor Carrie was making all the wrong choices, and I was sympathizing with her heartily, my sympathy perhaps oiled slightly by an indistinct number of Singha beers, when the phone rang.

The room was getting dark enough to make me turn on a light, so I had to get up anyway. I dropped the book to the floor, and Bravo Corrigan, still hanging around in the hope of a free lunch, thumped his tail. To him, the phone held out a vague promise of future fun.

First, I snapped on the light. Then I picked up the phone and said, "Yeah?"

"Ho," somebody said. Rodney Crowell's bassist whopped his strings.

I looked at *Sister Carrie*. Many wrong choices, safe on the page, beckoned to me.

"Ho, yourself," I said.

There was a silence, enlivened by the random electronic cackle.

"I've got this apartment," the voice said. "It's an okay apartment." There was another pause. "Um," the voice said.

I waited. Sister Carrie gave me a despairing wave.

"Do you know how to hook up a stereo?" the voice said.

"Yeah," I said to Al Hammond, "I think I can hook up a stereo."

I tripped over *Sister Carrie* on the way out.